FABLES, FOLKLORE & ANCIENT STORIES

KOREAN

FOLK & FAIRY TALES

FLAME TREE PUBLISHING
6 Melbray Mews, Fulham,
London SW6 3NS, United Kingdom
www.flametreepublishing.com

First published and copyright © 2025
Flame Tree Publishing Ltd

25 27 29 28 26
1 3 5 7 9 10 8 6 4 2

ISBN: 978-1-83562-565-1

All rights reserved. No part of this publication may be reproduced,
stored in a retrieval system, or transmitted in any form or by any means, electronic,
mechanical, photocopying, recording or otherwise, without the prior
written permission of the publisher.

Cover and pattern art was created by Flame Tree Studio, including a photograph of a
traditional Korean mask courtesy of Richard Fisher.
Inside decoration courtesy of Shutterstock.com/satori.artwork.

Judith John (Glossary) is a writer and editor specializing in literature and history.
A former secondary school English Language and Literature teacher, she has
subsequently worked as an editor on major educational projects, including *English A:
Literature* for the Pearson International Baccalaureate series. Judith's major research
interests include Romantic and Gothic literature, and Renaissance drama.

The stories in this book are selected and edited from the following original sources:
Korean Folk Tales: Imps, Ghosts and Fairies by Im Bang and Yi Ryuk;
translated by James S. Gale (London: J.M. Dent & Sons Ltd., New
York: E.P. Dutton & Co., 1913); *Korean Tales* by H.N. Allen (New York
& London: G.P. Putnam's Sons, 1889); *Korean Fairy Tales* by William
Elliot Griffis (New York: Thomas Y. Crowell Company, 1911/22); and
Fairy Tales from Far and Near by Katharine Pyle (Boston: Little, Brown, and
Company, 1922).

A copy of the CIP data for this book is available
from the British Library.

Designed and created in the UK | Printed and bound in China

COLLECTOR'S EDITIONS

FABLES, FOLKLORE & ANCIENT STORIES

KOREAN

FOLK & FAIRY TALES

Reading List & Glossary of Terms
with a New Introduction by
DR. PERRY MILLER

FLAME TREE PUBLISHING

CONTENTS

Series Foreword 10

**A New Introduction to Korean Folk &
Fairy Tales** 16
Korea: The Next Chapter 16
Korea's Story: A Complex Tapestry 17
'K-Lore' and the Tradition of Remaking
   the Old in Endlessly New Ways 17
'Authorship' and Translation of Oral Literatures 19
Literacy in Korea 19
A Meeting of Myths: Belief Syncretism in Folklore ... 20
Syncretism and Didacticism in the Folktales 21
Making Sense of Folktales in Modernity 22
Structuring Beliefs 23
Buddhism in Korean Folklore 24

Further Reading 25

CONTENTS

Love, Marriage & Family 27
Charan 28
The Plucky Maiden 39
The Boxed-Up Governor 44
Faithful Mo 49
Ta-Hong 51
Ching Yuh and Kyain Oo: The Trials of
   Two Heavenly Lovers 61
Chun Yang, the Faithful Dancing-Girl Wife 85
Pigling and Her Proud Sister 110

Powerful Spirits & Mystical Realms 117
The Story of Chang To-Ryong 118
Ten Thousand Devils 123
The Home of the Fairies 127
The Temple to the God of War 137
The King of Yom-Na (Hell) 140
Hong's Experiences in Hades 144
The Dutiful Daughter 149
The King of the Flowers 165
Cat-Kin and the Queen Mother 169
The Magic Peach 177
The Great Stone Fire Eater 186

The Magical & the Supernatural 194
The Soldier of Kang-Wha 194
The Man on the Road 196

The Geomancer 197
The Grateful Ghost 200
The Honest Witch 202
A Visit from the Shades 205
The Fearless Captain 208
Haunted Houses 210
The Magic Invasion of Seoul 213
The Mysterious Hoi Tree 215
Hong Kil Tong; or, the Adventures
 of an Abused Boy 216
East Light and the Bridge Of Fishes 233
The Sneezing Colossus 237

Tales of Animals & Mythical Creatures 242
The Old Woman Who Became a Goblin 245
The Man Who Lost His Legs 246
The Brave Magistrate 249
The Awful Little Goblin 250
Rabbit's Eyes: A Korean Fairy Tale 252
The Magic Rice Kettle 257
Hyung Bo And Nahl Bo; Or,
 The Swallow-King's Rewards 270
The Unmannerly Tiger 289
Tokgabi and His Pranks 292
Prince Sandalwood, the Father of Korea 296
A Bridegroom for Miss Mole 301
Old White Whiskers and Mr Bunny 305

CONTENTS

Old Timber Top 309
A Frog for a Husband 321
The King of the Sparrows 330
The Woodman and the Mountain Fairies 335

A Glossary of Myth & Folklore 344

KOREAN FOLK & FAIRY TALES

FABLES, FOLKLORE & ANCIENT STORIES

KOREAN

FOLK & FAIRY TALES

SERIES FOREWORD

Stretching back to the oral traditions of thousands of years ago, tales of heroes and disaster, creation and conquest have been told by many different civilizations in many different ways. Their impact sits deep within our culture even though the detail in the tales themselves are a loose mix of historical record, transformed narrative and the distortions of hundreds of storytellers.

Today the language of mythology lives with us: our mood is jovial, our countenance is saturnine, we are narcissistic and our modern life is hermetically sealed from others. The nuances of myths and legends form part of our daily routines and help us navigate the world around us, with its half truths and biased reported facts.

The nature of a myth is that its story is already known by most of those who hear it, or read it. Every generation brings a new emphasis, but the fundamentals remain the same: a desire to understand and describe the events and relationships of the world. Many of the great stories are archetypes that help us find our own place, equipping us with tools for self-understanding, both individually and as part of a broader culture.

For Western societies it is Greek mythology that speaks to us most clearly. It greatly influenced the mythological heritage of the ancient Roman civilization and is the lens through which we still see the Celts, the Norse and many of the other great peoples

SERIES FOREWORD

and religions. The Greeks themselves learned much from their neighbours, the Egyptians, an older culture that became weak with age and incestuous leadership.

It is important to understand that what we perceive now as mythology had its own origins in perceptions of the divine and the rituals of the sacred. The earliest civilizations, in the crucible of the Middle East, in the Sumer of the third millennium BCE, are the source to which many of the mythic archetypes can be traced. As humankind collected together in cities for the first time, developed writing and industrial scale agriculture, started to irrigate the rivers and attempted to control rather than be at the mercy of its environment, humanity began to write down its tentative explanations of natural events, of floods and plagues, of disease.

Early stories tell of Gods (or god-like animals in the case of tribal societies such as African, Native American or Aboriginal cultures) who are crafty and use their wits to survive, and it is reasonable to suggest that these were the first rulers of the gathering peoples of the earth, later elevated to god-like status with the distance of time. Such tales became more political as cities vied with each other for supremacy, creating new Gods, new hierarchies for their pantheons. The older Gods took on primordial roles and became the preserve of creation and destruction, leaving the new gods to deal with more current, everyday affairs. Empires rose and fell, with Babylon assuming the mantle from Sumeria in the 1800s BCE, then in turn to be swept away by the Assyrians of the 1200s BCE; then the Assyrians and the Egyptians were subjugated by the Greeks, the Greeks by the Romans and so on, leading to the spread and assimilation of common themes, ideas and stories throughout the world.

The survival of history is dependent on the telling of good tales, but each one must have the 'feeling' of truth, otherwise it will be ignored. Around the firesides, or embedded in a book or a computer, the myths and legends of the past are still the living materials of retold myth, not restricted to an exploration of origins. Now we have devices and global communications that give us unparalleled access to a diversity of traditions. We can find out about Native American, Indian, Chinese and tribal African mythology in a way that was denied to our ancestors, we can find connections, match the archaeology, religion and the mythologies of the world to build a comprehensive image of the human experience that is endlessly fascinating.

The stories in this book provide an introduction to the themes and concerns of the myths and legends of their respective cultures, with a short introduction to provide a linguistic, geographic and political context. This is where the myths have arrived today, but undoubtedly over the next millennia, they will transform again whilst retaining their essential truths and signs.

Jake Jackson
General Editor

FABLES, FOLKLORE & ANCIENT STORIES KOREAN FOLK & FAIRY TALES

FABLES, FOLKLORE & ANCIENT STORIES

INTRODUCTION
& FURTHER READING

A NEW INTRODUCTION TO KOREAN FOLK AND FAIRY TALES

KOREA: THE NEXT CHAPTER

The Republic of Korea (also 'South Korea' and hereafter referred to as 'Korea') is located at and below the 38th parallel across a mountainous peninsula in northeast Asia. Comprising the demi-peninsula as well as dozens of nearby islands, Korea ranks between Iceland and Hungary in terms of its land area. Belying the small form factor, however, this nation-state is a juggernaut in today's world economy.

As with other political and economic centres, its popular culture is well received by consumers and fans around the world. Today, 'Korea' may evoke associations with the 'K' culture industry, for instance with K-Pop, intricate skincare regimens and cosmetic tutorials, television dramas, flavour inventions, and other vibrant life practices. Encountering media in the flow of global culture, one may be further inspired to delve into Korea's traditions of expression and performance. The Hallyu (Korean Wave) has reinvigorated interest in Korean folklore, and a recent illustrated re-publication of James S. Gale's translation of 53 tales from Im Bang and Yi Ryuk (Tuttle, 2023) attests to the important role of folklore in defining Korean culture for a world readership.

INTRODUCTION

KOREA'S STORY: A COMPLEX TAPESTRY

As with other archaic civilizations, Korea's origins amalgamate anthropological probability and myth. The established consensus on Korea's foundations (retold in 'Prince Sandalwood, The Father of Korea') date the origin of this civilization (called 'Gojoseon' or 'Old Joseon') to 2333 BCE. Foundation Day (in Korean, literally, 'sky-opening day') is an actual holiday celebrated on 3 October. Early inhabitants of the peninsula were akin to the semi-nomadic peoples of present-day China and the Russian Federation, who practised hunter-gathering and held shamanic beliefs. Early traces of storytelling are found on the Bangudae cliff in the southeastern Youngnam province. Dating to the Neolithic era (10,000 BCE–4,000 BCE), these etchings feature marine animals, land animals, and human hunter-gatherers and fishers. In the more recent past, people of the Three Kingdoms (100s BCE–700s CE) and later consolidated nation-state eras regarded the cliff etchings with wonder and used them as the inspiration for song and poetry, as well as scenic natural artwork for major celebrations and picnics.

'K-LORE' AND THE TRADITION OF REMAKING THE OLD IN ENDLESSLY NEW WAYS

The featured collection of stories, excerpted from translations of nineteenth-century missionaries from the Anglo-American West, make an invaluable contribution to the collective imagination of shared pasts. Read in today's K-cultural context, this archive of folktales, myths, legends, unauthorized biographies, and ghost stories teem just below the sheen of contemporary culture. In the same way that a walk through a Seoul underground depot immerses today's subway rider in layers of contemporary history, the reader of stories of sneezing statues or mischievous goblins is in both ancient and modern times. The backpacker navigating Seoul with digital geolocation amidst the frenetic bustle of 11 million Seoulites will wander through luxury shopping districts and the palaces of Joseon next to twenty-storey highrise concrete apartment complexes with the names 'Palace' or 'Castle.' Folktales bridge the traditional and the modern, just as a walk down a typical London street would meet with self-checkout supermarkets within sight of eighteenth-century cemeteries.

The old and the new are endlessly entangled in architecture, space and imagination. Along these labyrinthine neighbourhood roads crisscrossing the redeveloped main thoroughfares, everyday life will oftentimes look, feel or even smell just as it did in the decades prior to the arrival of Hallyu or Korean football exploits in the World Cup. And one or two bullet-train stops outside of the megalopolis, the many regionally varied traditional Korean customs are as much a part of people's lifeworlds as are the advanced smartphones, talking rice cookers, or keyless entry systems. Also woven into these aspects of culture are the ways of life and migration stories of new Koreans, including those emigrating from North Korea (formally the Democratic People's Republic of North Korea) and many more, often from debtor nations who have a vital role in Korean family and industry without any legal recognition of their place in Korea.

INTRODUCTION

'AUTHORSHIP' AND TRANSLATION OF ORAL LITERATURES

Folklore, a crystallization of disparate and changing oral literatures, serves as a reminder of who we each are, as Koreans and non-Koreans, where we come from and what makes us different from tools or machines that can now generate an epic or an essay in fractions of a second. Folklore anchors the human imagination and psyche in societies that are unmoored by the demands for ever-accelerated tempo.

Over a century after the translators and compilers of this volume, James G. Gale (1863–1937), Horace N. Allen (1858–1932), William Elliot Griffiths (1843–1928) and Katharine Pyle (1863–1938), translated the stories of Yi Ryuk (1443–1498) and Im Bang (1640–1724) for an English-speaking readership intrigued by the obscure, autonomous 'Hermit Kingdom' with a reputation for hostility toward Western missionaries, Korea is no longer the fairy-tale world of mystery and oddity. Self-nicknamed the 'Miracle on the Han River' for its story of economic growth and development after the Korean War (1950–1953) and colonization by Japan (1910–1945), Korea is currently a hub of technoscientific learning.

LITERACY IN KOREA

Korea is today known for an intense industry of education, with not a small proportion of the nation's economy devoted to supplemental college preparatory curriculum. Many students do academic work from early morning till late night. There is fierce competition for what are perceived to be increasingly scarce white-collar jobs, and the college entrance examination, modelled after the civil service examination of Joseon, is an existential moment for Korean youth. Twenty-first century Korea is a knowledge economy with hierarchies of inclusion and exclusion that have increasing numbers of the next generation feeling disenchanted. In what may appear to be an atavistic moment of progressive vision, the monarch Sejong, Fourth King of Joseon, and his group of scholar-philologists developed a phonetic script for Korean. In no small part due to concerted efforts by aristocracy fighting to maintain their hegemony over the illiterate Korean masses, Hangul was not commonly used until the mid-nineteenth century. Until then, script literacies were exclusively the provenance of the elite intellectual class who had the time and resources to school their male children in classical literary Chinese. But before and throughout these revolutions in literacy and language for Joseon people, there was a rich tradition of folklore. People sang, chanted and told stories in a number of daily life situations. The pansori singer of tales could be found in marketplaces or in front of aristocratic patron audiences, singing and chanting one of 12 song cycles to the accompaniment of a drummer. Puppet theatres and masked dancers similarly used props, dolls, masks and movement to narrate well-known tropes, even satirical phrases. Today the Republic of Korea has one of the highest rates of literacy in the world, and their traditions of oral literature are a point of pride.

A MEETING OF MYTHS: BELIEF SYNCRETISM IN FOLKLORE

As scholars and practitioners of Korean culture have noted, Korean culture is syncretic. Throughout most of its history, it

INTRODUCTION

has not had any organized religion in the way that Christendom promulgated European sociocultural institutions and structures. Instead, there were four main belief systems that structured everyday life practices as well as formal rituals, including the arts and literature. These belief systems are indigenous shamanism, Buddhism, Neo-Confucianism (transmitted from Northern Song China through the late Goryeo and early Joseon eras in Korea) and, later, Christianity, which was first encountered in the 1590s and took hold as a culture of belief in the nineteenth century. While Christianity, neo-Confucianism, and Buddhism were most integrated into politics and administrative life, shamans were closest to the everyday Joseon person. Theirs was mostly a hereditary trade, one of the eight subaltern castes in highly class-divided Joseon. In sum, throughout most of the last two millennia, Koreans have had a syncretic belief system structuring their everyday lives, and other philosophical systems such as Daoism also percolated in the culture. The missionaries translating Korean folktales intended to create a portal into the Korean psyche that would be available to their readers, who were most likely a successive cohort of missionaries to Korea. Yet the stories themselves are varied and amenable to multiple interpretations.

SYNCRETISM AND DIDACTICISM IN THE FOLKTALES

While these adaptations of the folktales are from the period of Christian missionaries in Korea (1800s and 1900s) and the Japanese annexation/colonial era (1910–1945), it is important to note that readers today can find in these classical folktales thematic and symbolic elements that align with Korean Christian belief. Today, about 25 per cent of modern Koreans identify with Christianity or are members of a church. To illustrate, the ethos so formulaic in Korean stories (of 'reward virtue, punish vice') can be read as an indigenous folk reverence of the spiritual realm, a reflection of Buddhist karmic law, or even the Christian teaching of *agape* or care for one's neighbours. Indeed, the number of stories involving characters' encounters with or travels to Hell or Hades reflect not just the translators' investments in converging indigenous beliefs with Christian beliefs, but also people's abiding curiosity about the life and worlds beyond this one.

MAKING SENSE OF FOLKTALES IN MODERNITY

These stories, having been filtered through the Neo-Confucian lens of Yi Ryuk and Im Bang, then the Anglo-American Protestant lens of Gale, Allen, Griffiths and others, may not tell us much about who the original storytellers were or what they actually believed, so much as remind us about how we encounter the world and ourselves within it today. Yet there are also hints of the worldviews of Korean peoples from the ancient era. These stories show a reverence for the natural world, respect for animals, and a sense of wonder and awe about the natural and supernatural worlds. These attitudes are vastly different from today's technologized society, where nature is often a resource for industrial exploitation, and people's sense of wonder and fascination are captured, rather than cultivated, by the media saturating their fields of perception, and harnessed into consumerism. One critical takeaway from this story collection is the vital role of storying and storytelling in rapidly changing conditions of human existence.

INTRODUCTION

STRUCTURING BELIEFS

Confucianism may be one of several structuring beliefs for Korea. As the official state ideology of Joseon (1392–2020), it has had lasting effects on the organization of all institutions in Korea, from family or peer social ties to workplace dynamics, from sound conduct of friendships to the proper ceremonies for ancestor memorial rites. Just as the natural world existed in some type of order, relationships in human society should operate according to the principle of harmony. And this harmony was achieved and preserved through role designations and hierarchical relationships. Seniors (older in terms of number of years on the planet, or at an institution such as a school or workplace) were to be treated by juniors with deference, obedience and loyalty. In turn, seniors were implicitly responsible for the wellbeing of juniors. The five basic relationships prescribed by Confucianism include those between ruler and subject, parents and children, wife and husband, elder and younger siblings, and friends. Among the narratives translated by the missionaries, the five canonical pansori story-singing epics (the Obatang) are included. Each of these pansori narratives is structured with didactic elements (alongside burlesque, satire, comedy, and tragedy) that model these five relationships. These beliefs continue to be important today and present in everyday life habits, even amid major social transformations. One such major transformation occurred in youth-led social movements in the wake of the *Sewol* ferry disaster in 2014, which claimed the lives of hundreds of high-school children who had obeyed the ship's captain by staying in their cabins while the captain evacuated and was rescued. Named the 'Sewol' Generation, today's young adult generation have a participatory role in transforming social institutions that lead to corruption or endemic bullying. Thus, like other traditional beliefs, neo-Confucian mores realign with new progressivism, and it remains to be seen how the Sewol Generation will adapt their inherited folklore.

BUDDHISM IN KOREAN FOLKLORE

The Buddhist practice of showing kindness to and reverence for nature, for taking responsibility for the collective wellbeing of a community, and the Taoist non-action or reflective stance are all prevalent in Korean folklore. Oftentimes animals serve as agents of karma, bringing rewards for compassionate and virtuous conduct, or alternately retribution or justice for wrongs committed. From the folktales it is clear that ancient Korean peoples practised kindness to animals and nature as a standard of good human conduct. Buddhism is also thematized in folklore through the appearance of Buddhist monks in many narratives, usually to represent ethical authority, but sometimes (especially in satirical narratives such as the mask dance of the naughty monk) as a critique of corrupted political or religious authority. Reverence for the wonder and awe of nature is also evident in idiomatic expressions (not available to readers of the translated versions except through the creative translations afforded by Gale, Griffith and Allen).

A wonderfully unique aspect of oral literature is collective authorship and collective ownership. Folktales are the original creative and intellectual commons. The Flame Tree Myths and Legends series presents storying as a commonly shared inheritance from diverse, multiple pasts.

Dr. Perry D. Miller

FURTHER READING

Berg, Sebastian, *Korean Mythology: Folklore and Legends from the Korean Peninsula* (Creek Ridge Publishing, 2022)

Carpenter, Frances, *Tales of a Korean Grandmother: 32 Traditional Tales from Korea* (Tuttle Publishing 2011)

Damron, Julie, and Ryu EunSun, and EunSun You, *Korean Stories For Language Learners: Traditional Folktales in Korean and English* (Tuttle Publishing 2018)

Fenkl, Heinz Insu, *The Korean Myths: A Guide to the Gods, Heroes and Legends* (Thames and Hudson Ltd, 2024)

Hwang, Kyung Moon, *A History of Korea*, Bloomsbury Essential Histories, 3rd edition (New York: Bloomsbury Academic, 2022)

Xu, Stella, *Korean Ancient Origins* (Flame Tree Publishing, 2024)

Dr. Perry D. Miller teaches in the Department of East Asian Languages and Literatures at The Ohio State University. Miller received the Ph.D. in Comparative Culture and Literature Studies from Ohio State in 2016 and is currently completing a Doctor of Education through Indiana University. She researches affect, ecohumanities, and literacy through Korea-focused texts.

KOREAN FOLK & FAIRY TALES

LOVE, MARRIAGE & FAMILY

Unlike cultures of the West that valued romance-based marriage, the Korean counterpart was a formal union of two families. People did not choose their partners but instead were matched to each other through family negotiations and sometimes a go-between who would arrange the match. Love was considered secondary to family duty and obligation. Also, love was not shown in overt or public ways but rather integrated into acts of kindness, or was not exactly demonstrative. The concept of Jeong (emotion, or heart) is understood to be a form of love that supersedes but does not exclude romantic attachment.

Women of the Joseon era had far less freedom and agency than their foremothers of Goryeo, Silla, and the Three Kingdoms era, when women owned property, started and ended relationships of their own will, rode and fought on horseback, and were even (in two rare instances) political heads of state. The formulaic fairytale ending of marriage signalling a happy-ever-after is rare in Korean folktales, where the hunter and the weaver meet once a year along the Milky Way thanks to legions of magpies who form a bird-bridge; or where Shim Cheong's happy conclusion is not with her marrying the king of the realm, but instead being reunited with her visually impaired father who, with a cosmic blessing, has his eyesight miraculously restored.

CHARAN

Some think that love, strong, true, and self-sacrificing, is not to be found in the Orient; but the story of Charan, which comes down four hundred years and more, proves the contrary, for it still has the fresh, sweet flavour of a romance of yesterday; albeit the setting of the East provides an odd and interesting background.

In the days of King Sung-jong (AD 1488–1495) one of Korea's noted men became governor of Pyong-an Province. Now Pyong-an stands first of all the eight provinces in the attainments of erudition and polite society. Many of her *literati* are good musicians, and show ability in the affairs of State.

At the time of this story there was a famous dancing girl in Pyong-an whose name was Charan. She was very beautiful, and sang and danced to the delight of all beholders. Her ability, too, was specially marked, for she understood the classics and was acquainted with history. The brightest of all the *geisha* was she, famous and far-renowned.

The Governor's family consisted of a son, whose age was sixteen, and whose face was comely as a picture. Though so young, he was thoroughly grounded in Chinese, and was a gifted scholar. His judgment was excellent, and he had a fine appreciation of literary form, so that the moment he lifted his pen the written line took on admirable expression. His name became known as Keydong (The Gifted Lad). The Governor had no other children, neither son nor daughter, so his heart was wrapped up in this boy. On his birthday he had all the officials invited and other special guests, who came to drink his health. There were present also a company of dancing-girls and a large band of musicians. The Governor, during a lull in the banquet, called his son to him, and ordered the chief of the dancing-girls to choose one of the prettiest of their number, that he and she might dance together and delight the assembled guests. On hearing this, the company, with one accord, called for Charan, as the one suited by her talents, attainments and age to be a fitting partner for his son. They came out and danced like fairies, graceful as the wavings of the willow, light and airy as the swallow. All who saw them were charmed. The Governor, too, greatly pleased, called Charan to him, had her sit on the dais, treated her to a share in the banquet, gave her a present of silk, and commanded that from that day forth she be the special dancing maiden to attend upon his son.

From this birthday forth they became fast friends together. They thought the world of each other. More than all the delightful stories of history was their love – such as had never been seen.

The Governor's term of office was extended for six years more, and so they remained in the north country. Finally, at the time of return, he and his wife were in great anxiety over their son being separated from Charan. If they were to force them to separate, they feared he would die of a broken heart. If they took her with them, she not being his wife, they feared for his reputation. They could not possibly decide, so they concluded to refer the matter to the son himself. They called him and said, "Even parents cannot decide as to the love of their son for a maiden. What ought we to do? You love Charan so that it will be very hard for you to part, and yet to have a dancing-girl before you are married is not good form, and will interfere with your marriage prospects and promotion. However, the having of a second wife is a common custom in Korea, and one that the world recognizes. Do as you think best in the matter." The son replied, "There is no difficulty; when she is before my eyes, of course she is everything, but when the time comes for me to start for home she will be like a pair of worn shoes, set aside; so please do not be anxious."

The Governor and his wife were greatly delighted, and said he was a "superior man" indeed.

When the time came to part Charan cried bitterly, so that those standing by could not bear to look at her; but the son showed not the slightest sign of emotion. Those looking on were filled with wonder at his fortitude. Although he had already loved Charan for six years, he had never been separated from her for a single day, so he knew not what it meant to say Good-bye, nor did he know how it felt to be parted.

The Governor returned to Seoul to fill the office of Chief Justice, and the son came also. After this return thoughts of love for Charan possessed Keydong, though he never expressed them in word or manner. It was almost the time of the *Kam-see* Examination. The father, therefore, ordered his son to go with some of his friends to a neighbouring monastery to study and prepare. They went, and one night, after the day's work was over and all were asleep, the young man stole out into the courtyard. It was winter, with frost and snow and a cold, clear moon. The mountains were deep and the world was quiet, so that the slightest sound could be heard. The young man looked up at the moon and his thoughts were full of sorrow. He so wished to see Charan that he could no longer control himself, and fearing that he would lose his reason, he decided that very night to set out for far-distant Pyong-an. He had on a fur head-dress, a thick coat, a leather belt and a heavy pair of shoes. When he had gone less than ten *lee*, however, his feet were blistered, and he had to go into a neighbouring village and change his leather shoes for straw sandals, and his expensive head-cover for an ordinary servant's hat. He went thus on his way, begging as he went. He was often very hungry, and when night came, was very, very cold. He was a rich man's son and had always dressed in silk and eaten dainty fare, and had never in his life walked more than a few feet from his father's door. Now there lay before him a journey of hundreds of miles. He went stumbling along through the snow, making but poor progress. Hungry, and frozen nearly to death, he had never known such suffering before. His clothes were torn and his face became worn down and blackened till he looked like a goblin. Still on he went, little by little, day after day, till at last, when a whole month had gone by, he reached Pyong-an.

Straight to Charan's home he went, but Charan was not there, only her mother. She looked at him, but did not recognize him. He said he was the former Governor's son and that out of love for Charan he had walked five hundred *lee*. "Where is she?" he asked. The mother heard, but instead of being pleased was very angry. She said, "My daughter is now with the son of the new Governor, and I never see her at all; she never comes home, and she has been away for two or three months. Even though you have made this long journey there is no possible way to meet her."

She did not invite him in, so cold was her welcome. He thought to himself, "I came to see Charan, but she is not here. Her mother refuses me; I cannot go back, and I cannot stay. What shall I do?" While thus in this dilemma a plan occurred to him. There was a scribe in Pyong-an, who, during his father's term of office, had offended, and was sentenced to death. There were extenuating circumstances, however, and he, when he went to pay his morning salutations, had besought and secured his pardon. His father, out of regard for his son's petition, had forgiven the scribe. He thought, "I was the means of saving the man's life, he will take me in;" so he went straight from Charan's to the house of the scribe. But at first this writer did not recognize him. When he gave his name and told who he was, the scribe gave a great start, and fell at his feet making obeisance. He cleared out an inner room and made him comfortable, prepared dainty fare and treated him with all respect.

A little later he talked over with his host the possibility of his meeting Charan. The scribe said, "I am afraid that there is no way for you to meet her alone, but if you would like to see even her face, I think I can manage it. Will you consent?"

He asked as to the plan. It was this: It being now a time of snow, daily coolies were called to sweep it away from the inner court of the Governor's *yamen*, and just now the scribe was in charge of this particular work. Said he, "If you will join the sweepers, take a broom and go in; you will no doubt catch a glimpse of Charan as she is said to be in the Hill Kiosk. I know of no other plan."

Keydong consented. In the early morning he mixed with the company of sweepers and went with his broom into the inner enclosure, where the Hill Kiosk was, and so they worked at sweeping. Just then the Governor's son was sitting by the open window and Charan was by him, but not visible from the outside. The other workers, being all practised hands, swept well; Keydong alone handled his broom to no advantage, knowing not how to sweep. The Governor's son, watching the process, looked out and laughed, called Charan and invited her to see this sweeper. Charan stepped out into the open hall and the sweeper raised his eyes to see. She glanced at him but once, and but for a moment, then turned quickly, went into the room, and shut the door, not appearing again, to the disappointment of the sweeper, who came back in despair to the scribe's house.

Charan was first of all a wise and highly gifted woman. One look had told her who the sweeper was. She came back into the room and began to cry. The Governor's son looked in surprise and displeasure, and asked, "Why do you cry?" She did not reply at once, but after two or three insistent demands told the reason thus: "I am a low class woman; you are mistaken in thinking highly of me, or counting me of worth. Already I have not been home for two whole months and more. This is a special compliment and a high honour, and so there is not the slightest reason for any complaint on my part. But still, I think of my home, which is poor, and my mother. It is customary on the anniversary of my father's death to prepare food from the official quarters, and offer a sacrifice to his spirit, but here I am imprisoned and to-morrow is the sacrificial day. I fear that not a single act of devotion will be paid, I am disturbed over it, and that's why I cry."

The Governor's son was so taken in by this fair statement that he trusted her fully and without a question. Sympathetically he asked, "Why didn't you tell me before?" He prepared the food and told her to hurry home and carry out the ceremony. So Charan came like flaming fire back to her house, and said to her mother, "Keydong has come and I have seen him. Is he not here? Tell me where he is if you know." The mother said, "He came here, it is true, all the way on foot to see you, but I told him that you were in the *yamen* and that there was no possible way for you to meet, so he went away and where he is I know not."

Then Charan broke down and began to cry. "Oh, my mother, why had you the heart to do so cruelly?" she sobbed. "As far as I am concerned I can never break with him nor give him up. We were each sixteen when chosen to dance together, and while it may be said that men chose us, it is truer still to say that God hath chosen. We grew into each other's lives, and there was never such love as ours. Though he forgot and left me, I can never forget and can never give him up. The Governor, too, called me the beloved wife of his son, and did not once refer to my low station. He cherished me and gave me many gifts. 'Twas all like heaven and not like earth. To the city of Pyong-an gentry and officials gather as men crowd into a boat; I have seen so many, but for grace and ability no one was ever like Keydong. I must find him, and even though he casts me aside I never shall forget him. I have not kept myself even unto death as I should have, because I have been under the power and influence of the Governor. How could he ever have come so far for one so low and vile? He, a gentleman of the highest birth, for the sake of a wretched dancing-girl has endured all this hardship and come so far. Could you not have thought, mother, of these things and given him at least some kindly welcome? Could my heart be other than broken?" And a great flow of tears came from Charan's eyes. She thought and thought as to where he could possibly be. "I know of no place," said she, "unless it be at such and such a scribe's home." Quick as thought she flew thence, and there they met. They clasped each other and cried, not a word was spoken. Thus came they back to Charan's home side by side. When it was night Charan said, "When to-morrow

LOVE, MARRIAGE & FAMILY

comes we shall have to part. What shall we do?" They talked it over, and agreed to make their escape that night. So Charan got together her clothing, and her treasures and jewels, and made two bundles, and thus, he carrying his on his back and she hers on her head, away they went while the city slept. They followed the road that leads toward the mountains that lie between Yang-tok and Maing-san counties. There they found a country house, where they put up, and where the Governor's son became a sort of better-class servant. He did not know how to do anything well, but Charan understood weaving and sewing, and so they lived. After some time they got a little thatched hut by themselves in the village and lived there. Charan was a beautiful sewing-woman, and ceased not day and night to ply her needle, and sold her treasures and her jewels to make ends meet. Charan, too, knew how to make friends, and was praised and loved by all the village. Everybody felt sorry for the hard times that had befallen this mysterious young couple, and helped them so that the days passed peacefully and happily together.

To return in the story: On awaking in the morning in the temple where he and his friends had gone to study, they found Keydong missing. All was in a state of confusion as to what had become of the son of the Chief Justice. They hunted for him far and wide, but he was nowhere to be found, so word was sent to the parents accordingly. There was untold consternation in the home of the former governor. So great a loss, what could equal it? They searched the country about the temple, but no trace or shadow of him was to be found. Some said they thought he had been inveigled away and metamorphosed by the fox; others that he had been eaten by the tiger. The parents decided that he was dead and went into mourning for him, burning his clothing in a sacrificial fire.

In Pyong-an the Governor's son, when he found that he had lost Charan, had Charan's mother imprisoned and all the relatives, but after a month or so, when the search proved futile, he gave up the matter and let them go.

Charan, at last happy with her chosen one, said one day to him, "You, a son of the gentry, for the sake of a dancing-girl have given up parents and home to live in this hidden corner of the hills. It is a matter, too, that touches your filial piety, this leaving your father and mother in doubt as to whether you are alive or not. They ought to know. We cannot live here all our lives, neither can we return home; what do you think we ought to do?" Keydong made a hopeless reply. "I am in distress," said he, "and know not."

Charan said brightly, "I have a plan by which we can cover over the faults of the past, and win a new start for the future. By means of it, you can serve your parents and look the world in the face. Will you consent?"

"What do you propose?" asked he. Her reply was, "There is only one way, and that is by means of the Official Examination. I know of no other. You will understand what I mean, even though I do not tell you more."

He said, "Enough, your plan is just the thing to help us out. But how can I get hold of the books I need?"

Charan replied, "Don't be anxious about that, I'll get the books." From that day forth she sent through all the neighbourhood for books, to be secured at all costs; but there were few or none, it being a mountain village. One day there came by, all unexpectedly, a pack-peddler, who had in his bundle a book that he wished to sell. Some of the village people wanted to buy it for wall-paper. Charan, however, secured it first and showed it to Keydong. It was none other than a special work for Examinations, with all the exercises written out. It was written in small characters, and was a huge book containing several thousand exercises. Keydong was delighted, and said, "This is enough for all needed preparation." She bought it and gave it to him, and there he pegged away day after day. In the night he studied by candle-light, while she sat by his side and did silk-spinning. Thus they shared the light together. If he showed any remissness, Charan urged him on, and thus they worked for two years. To begin with, he, being a highly talented scholar, made steady advancement day by day. He was a beautiful writer and a master of the pen. His compositions, too, were without a peer, and every indication pointed to his winning the highest place in the *Kwago* (Examination).

At this time a proclamation was issued that there would be a special examination held before His Majesty the King, so Charan made ready the food required and all necessaries for him to go afoot to Seoul to try his hand.

At last here he was, within the Palace enclosure. His Majesty came out into the examination arena and posted up the subject. Keydong took his pen and wrote his finished composition. Under the inspiration of the moment his lines came forth like bubbling water. It was finished.

When the announcement was made as to the winner, the King ordered the sealed name of the writer to be opened. It was, and they found that Keydong was first. At that time his father was Prime Minister and waiting in attendance upon the King. The King called the Prime Minister, and said, "It looks to me as though the winner was your son, but he writes that his father is Chief Justice and not Prime Minister; what can that mean?"

He handed the composition paper to the father, and asked him to look and see. The Minister gazed at it in wonder, burst into tears, and said, "It is your servant's son. Three years ago he went with some friends to a monastery to study, but one night he disappeared, and though I searched far and wide I have had no word of him since. I concluded that he had been destroyed by some wild animal, so I had a funeral service held and the house went into mourning. I had no other children but this son only. He was greatly gifted and I lost him in this strange way. The memory has never left me, for it seems as though I had lost him but yesterday. Now that I look at this paper I see indeed that it is the writing of my son. When I lost him I was Chief Justice, and thus he records the office; but where he has been for these three years, and how he comes now to take part in the examination, I know not."

The King, hearing this, was greatly astonished, and at once before all the assembled ministers had him called. Thus he came in his scholar's dress into the presence of the King. All the officials wondered at this summoning of a candidate before the announcement of the result. The King asked him why he had left the monastery and where he had been for these three years. He bowed low, and said, "I have been a very wicked man, have left my parents, have broken all the laws of filial devotion, and deserve condign punishment." The King replied, saying, "There is no law of concealment before the King. I shall not condemn you even though you are guilty; tell me all." Then he told his story to the King. All the officials on each side bent their ears to hear. The King sighed, and said to the father, "Your son has repented and made amends for his fault. He has won first place and now stands as a member of the Court. We cannot condemn him for his love for this woman. Forgive him for all the past and give him a start for the future." His Majesty said further, "The woman Charan, who has shared your life in the lonely mountains, is no common woman. Her plans, too, for your restoration were the plans of a master hand. She is no dancing-girl, this Charan. Let no other be your lawful wife but she only; let her be raised to equal rank with her husband, and let her children and her children's children hold highest office in the realm." So was Keydong honoured with the winner's crown, and so the Prime Minister received his son back to life at the hands of the King. The winner's cap was placed upon his head, and the whole house was whirled into raptures of joy.

So the Minister sent forth a palanquin and servants to bring up Charan. In a great festival of joy she was proclaimed the wife of the Minister's son. Later he became one of Korea's first men of State, and they lived their happy life to a good old age. They had two sons, both graduates and men who held high office.

THE PLUCKY MAIDEN

Han Myong-hoi – We are told in the *Yol-ryok Keui-sul* that when Han was a boy he had for protector and friend a tiger, who used to accompany him as a dog does his master. One evening, when he started off into the hills, he heard the distant tramp of the great beast, who had got scent of his going, and had come rushing after him. When Han saw him he turned, and said, "Good old chap, you come all this distance to be my friend; I love you for it." The tiger prostrated himself and nodded with his head several times. He used to accompany Han all through the nights, but when the day dawned he would leave him. Han later fell into bad company, grew fond of drink, and was one of the boisterous companions of King Se-jo.

The Story

Han Myong-hoi was a renowned Minister of the Reign of Se-jo (AD 1455–1468). The King appreciated and enjoyed him greatly, and there was no one of the Court who could surpass him for influence and royal favour. Confident in his position, Han did as he pleased, wielding absolute power. At that time, like grass before the wind, the world bowed at his coming; no one dared utter a word of remonstrance.

When Han went as governor to Pyong-an Province he did all manner of lawless things. Any one daring to cross his wishes in the least was dealt with by torture and death. The whole Province feared him as they would a tiger.

On a certain day Governor Han, hearing that the Deputy Prefect of Son-chon had a very beautiful daughter, called the Deputy, and said, "I hear that you have a very beautiful daughter, whom I would like to make my concubine. When I am on my official rounds shortly, I shall expect to stop at your town and take her. So be ready for me."

The Deputy, alarmed, said, "How can your Excellency say that your servant's contemptible daughter is beautiful? Some one has reported her wrongly. But since you so command, how can I do but accede gladly?" So he bowed, said his farewell, and went home.

On his return his family noticed that his face was clouded with anxiety, and the daughter asked why it was. "Did the Governor call you, father?" asked she; "and why are you so anxious? Tell me, please." At first, fearing that she would be disturbed, he did not reply, but her repeated questions forced him, so that he said, "I am in trouble on your account," and then told of how the Governor wanted her for his concubine. "If I had refused I would have been killed, so I yielded; but a gentleman's daughter being made a concubine is a disgrace unheard of."

The daughter made light of it and laughed. "Why did you not think it out better than that, father? Why should a grown man lose his life for the sake of a girl? Let the daughter go. By losing one daughter and saving your life, you surely do better than saving your daughter and losing your life. One can easily see where the greater advantage lies. A daughter does not count; give her over, that's all. Don't for a moment think otherwise, just put away your distress and anxiety. We women, every one of us, are under the ban, and such things are decreed by Fate. I shall accept without any opposition, so please have no anxiety. It is settled now, and you, father, must yield and follow. If you do so all will be well."

The father sighed, and said in reply, "Since you seem so willing, my mind is somewhat relieved." But from this time on the whole house was in distress. The girl alone seemed perfectly unmoved, not showing the slightest sign of fear. She laughed as usual, her light and happy laugh, and her actions seemed wonderfully free.

In a little the Governor reached Son-chon on his rounds. He then called the Deputy, and said, "Make ready your daughter for to-morrow and all the things needed." The Deputy came home and made preparation for the so-called wedding. The daughter said, "This is not a real wedding; it is only the taking of a concubine, but still, make everything ready in the way of refreshments and ceremony as for a real marriage." So the father did as she requested.

On the day following the Governor came to the house of the Deputy. He was not dressed in his official robes, but came simply in the dress and hat of a commoner. When he went into the inner quarters he met the daughter; she stood straight before him. Her two hands were lifted in ceremonial form, but instead of holding a fan to hide her face she held a sword before her. She was very pretty. He gave a great start of surprise, and asked the meaning of the knife that she held. She ordered her nurse to reply, who said, "Even though I am an obscure countrywoman, I do not forget that I am born of the gentry; and though your Excellency is a high Minister of State, still to take me by force is an unheard-of dishonour. If you take me as your real and true wife I'll serve you with all my heart, but if you are determined to take me as a concubine I shall die now by this sword. For that reason I hold it. My life rests on one word from your Excellency. Speak it, please, before I decide."

The Governor, though a man who observed no ceremony and never brooked a question, when he saw how beautiful and how determined this maiden was, fell a victim to her at once, and said, "If you so decide, then, of course, I'll make you my real wife."

Her answer was, "If you truly mean it, then please withdraw and write out the certificate; send the gifts; provide the goose; dress in the proper way; come, and let us go through the required ceremony; drink the pledge-glass, and wed."

The Governor did as she suggested, carried out the forms to the letter, and they were married.

LOVE, MARRIAGE & FAMILY

She was not only a very pretty woman, but upright and true of soul – a rare person indeed. The Governor took her home, loved her and held her dear. He had, however, a real wife before and concubines, but he set them all aside and fixed his affections on this one only. She remonstrated with him over his wrongs and unrighteous acts, and he listened and made improvement. The world took note of it, and praised her as a true and wonderful woman. She counted herself the real wife, but the first wife treated her as a concubine, and all the relatives said likewise that she could never be considered a real wife. At that time King Se-jo frequently, in the dress of a commoner, used to visit Han's house. Han entertained him royally with refreshments, which his wife used to bring and offer before him. He called her his "little sister." On a certain day King Se-jo, as he was accustomed, came to the house, and while he was drinking he suddenly saw the woman fall on her face before him. The King in surprise inquired as to what she could possibly mean by such an act. She then told all the story of her being taken by force and brought to Seoul. She wept while she said, "Though I am from a far-distant part of the country I am of the gentry by ancestry, and my husband took me with all the required ceremonies of a wife, so that I ought not to be counted a concubine. But there is no law in this land by which a second real wife may be taken after a first real wife exists, so they call me a concubine, a matter of deepest disgrace. Please, your Majesty, take pity on me and decide my case."

The King laughed, and said, "This is a simple matter to settle; why should my little sister make so great an affair of it, and bow before me? I will decide your case at once. Come." He then wrote out with his own hand a document making her a real wife, and her children eligible for the highest office. He wrote it, signed it, stamped it and gave it to her.

From that time on she was known as a real wife, in rank and standing equal to the first one. No further word was ever slightingly spoken, and her children shared in the affairs of State.

THE BOXED-UP GOVERNOR

A **certain literary** official was at one time Governor of the city of Kyong-ju. Whenever he visited the Mayor of the place, it was his custom, on seeing dancing-girls, to tap them on the head with his pipe, and say, "These girls are devils, ogres, goblins. How can you tolerate them in presence?"

Naturally, those who heard this disliked him, and the Mayor himself detested his behaviour and manners. He sent a secret message to the dancing-girls, saying, "If any of you, by any means whatever, can deceive this governor, and put him to shame, I'll reward you richly." Among them there was one girl, a mere child, who said she could.

The Governor resided in the quarter of the city where the Confucian Temple was, and he had but one servant with him, a young lad. The dancing-girl who had decided to ensnare him, in the dress of a common woman of the town, used frequently to go by the main gateway of the Temple, and in going would call the Governor's boy to her. Sometimes she showed her profile and sometimes she showed her whole form, as she stood in the gateway. The boy would go out to her and she would speak to him for a moment or two and then go. She came sometimes once a day, sometimes twice, and this she kept up for a long time. The Governor at last inquired of the boy as to who this woman was that came so frequently to call him.

"She is my sister," said the boy. "Her husband went away on a peddling round a year or so ago, and has not yet returned; consequently she has no one else to help her, so she frequently calls and confers with me."

One evening, when the boy had gone to eat his meal and the Governor was alone, the woman came to the main gateway, and called for the boy.

His Excellency answered for him, and invited her in. When she came, she blushed, and appeared very diffident, standing modestly aside.

The Governor said, "My boy is absent just now, but I want a smoke; go and get a light for my pipe, will you, please."

She brought the light, and then he said, "Sit down too, and smoke a little, won't you?"

She replied, "How could I dare do such a thing?"

He said, "There is no one else here now; never mind."

There being no help for it, she did as he bade her, and smoked a little. He felt his heart suddenly inclined in her favour, and he said, "I have seen many beautiful women, but I surely think that you are the prettiest of them all. Once seeing you, I have quite forgotten how to eat or sleep. Could you not come to me to live here? I am quite alone and no one will know it."

She pretended to be greatly scandalized. "Your Excellency is a noble, and I am a low-class woman; how can you think of such a thing? Do you mean it as a joke?"

He replied, "I mean it truly, no joke at all." He swore an oath, saying, "Really I mean it, every word."

She then said, "Since you speak so, I am really very grateful, and shall come."

Said he, "Meeting you thus is wonderful indeed."

She went on to say, "There is another matter, however, that I wish to call to your attention. I understand that where your Excellency is now staying is a very sacred place, and that according to ancient law men were forbidden to have women here. Is that true?"

The Governor clapped her shoulder, and said, "Well, really now, how is it that you know of this? You are right. What shall we do about it?"

She made answer, "If you'll depend on me, I'll arrange a plan. My home is near by, and I am also alone, so if you come quietly at night to me, we can meet and no one will know. I shall send a felt hat by the boy, and you can wear that for disguise. With this commoner's felt hat on no one will know you."

The Governor was greatly delighted, and said, "How is it that you can plan so wonderfully? I shall do as you suggest. Now you be sure to be on hand." He repeated this two or three times.

The woman went and entered the house indicated. When evening came she sent the hat by the boy. The Governor arrived as agreed, and she received him, lit the lamp, and brought him refreshments and drink. They talked and drank together, and he called her to come to him. The woman hesitated for a moment, when suddenly there was a call heard from the outside, and a great disturbance took place. She bent her head to listen and then gave a cry of alarm, saying, "That's the voice of my husband, who has come. I was unfortunate, and so had this miserable wretch apportioned to my lot. He is the most despicable among mortals. For murder and arson he has no equal. Three years ago he left me and I took another husband, and we've had nothing to do with each other since. I can't imagine why he should come now. He is evidently very drunk, too, from the sound of his voice. Your Excellency has really fallen into a terrible plight. What shall I do?"

The woman went out then and answered, saying, "Who comes thus at midnight to make such a disturbance?"

The voice replied, "Don't you know my voice? Why don't you open the door?"

She answered, "Are you not *Chol-lo* (Brass Tiger), and have we not separated for good, years ago? Why have you come?"

The voice from without answered back, "Your leaving me and taking another man has always been a matter of deepest resentment on my part; I have something special to say to you," and he pounded the door open and came thundering in.

The woman rushed back into the room, saying, "Your Excellency must escape in some way or other."

In such a little thatched hut there was no place possible for concealment but an empty rice-box only. "Please get into this," said she, and she lifted the lid and hurried him in. The Governor, in his haste and déshabille, was bundled into the box. He then heard, from within, this fellow come into the room and quarrel with his wife. She said, "We have been separated three years already; what reason have you to come now and make such a disturbance?"

Said he, "You cast me off and took another man, therefore I have come for the clothes that I left, and the other things that belong to me."

Then she threw out his belongings to him, but he said, pointing to the box, "That's mine."

She replied, "That's not yours; I bought that myself with two rolls of silk goods."

"But," said he, "one of those rolls I gave you, and I'm not going to let you have it."

"Even though you did give it, do you mean to say that for one roll of silk you will carry away this box? I'll not consent to it." Thus they quarrelled, and contradicted each other.

"If you don't give me the box," said he, "I'll enter a suit against you at the Mayor's."

A little later the day dawned, and so he had the box carried off to the Mayor's office to have the case decided by law, while the woman followed.

When they entered the court, already the Mayor was seated in the judgment-place, and here they presented their case concerning the box.

The Mayor, after hearing, decided thus: "Since you each have a half-share in its purchase, there is nothing for me to do but to divide it between you. Bring a saw," said he.

The servants brought the saw and began on the box, when suddenly from the inner regions came forth a cry, "Save me; oh, save me!"

The Mayor, in pretended astonishment, said, "Why, there's a man's voice from the inside," and ordered that it should be opened. The servants managed to find the key, and at last the lid came back, and from the inner quarters there came forth a half-dressed man.

On seeing him the whole place was put into convulsions of laughter, for it was none other than the Governor.

"How is it that your Excellency finds yourself in this box in this unaccountable way?" asked the Mayor. "Please come out."

The Governor, huddling himself together as well as he could, climbed on to the open verandah. He held his head down and nearly died for shame.

The Mayor, splitting his sides with laughter, ordered clothes to be brought, and the first thing that came was a woman's green dress-coat. The Governor hastily turned it inside out, slipped it on, and made a dash for his quarters in the Confucian Temple. That day he left the place never to return, and even to the present time in Kyong-ju they laugh and tell the story of the Boxed-up Governor.

FAITHFUL MO

Prince Ha had a slave who was a landed proprieter and lived in Yang-ju county. He had a daughter, fairest of the fair, whom he called Mo (Nobody), beautiful beyond expression. An Yun was a noted scholar, a man of distinction in letters. He saw Mo, fell in love with her and took her for his wife. Prince Ha heard of this and was furiously angry. Said he, "How is it that you, a slave, dare to marry with a man of the aristocracy?" He had her arrested and brought home, intending to marry her to one of his bondsmen. Mo learned of this with tears and sorrow, but knew not what to do. At last she made her escape over the wall and went back to An. An was delighted beyond expression to see her; but, in view of the old prince, he knew not what to do. Together they took an oath to die rather than to be parted.

Later Prince Ha, on learning of this, sent his underlings to arrest her again and carry her off. After this all trace of her was lost till Mo was discovered one day in a room hanging by the neck dead.

Months of sorrow passed over An till once, under cover of the night, he was returning from the Confucian Temple to his house over the ridge of Camel Mountain. It was early autumn and the wooded tops were shimmering in the moonlight. All the world had sunk softly to rest and no passers were on the way. An was just then musing longingly of Mo, and in heartbroken accents repeating love verses to her memory, when suddenly a soft footfall was heard as though coming from among the pines. He took careful notice and there was Mo. An knew that she was long dead, and so must have known that it was her spirit, but because he was so buried in thought of her, doubting nothing, he ran to her and caught her by the hand, saying, "How did you come here?" but she disappeared. An gave a great cry and broke into tears. On account of this he fell ill. He ate, but his grief was so great he could not swallow, and a little later he died of a broken heart.

Kim Champan, who was of the same age as I, and my special friend, was also a cousin of An, and he frequently spoke of this. Yu Hyo-jang, also, An's nephew by marriage, told the story many times. Said he, "Faithful unto death was she. For even a woman of the *literati*, who has been born and brought up at the gates of ceremonial form, it is a difficult matter enough to die, but for a slave, the lowest of the low, who knew not the first thing of Ceremony, Righteousness, Truth or Devotion, what about her? To the end, out of love for her husband, she held fast to her purity and yielded up her life without a blemish. Even of the faithful among the ancients was there ever a better than Mo?"

LOVE, MARRIAGE & FAMILY

TA-HONG

Sim Heui-su studied as a young man at the feet of No Su-sin, who was sent as an exile to a distant island in the sea. Thither he followed his master and worked at the Sacred Books. He matriculated in 1570 and graduated in 1572. In 1589 he remonstrated with King Son-jo over the disorders of his reign, and was the means of quelling a great national disturbance; but he made a *faux pas* one day when he said laughingly to a friend –

> "These sea-gull waves ride so high,
> Who can tame them?"

Those who heard caught at this, and it became a source of unpopularity, as it indicated an unfavourable opinion of the Court.

In 1592, when the King made his escape to Eui-ju, before the invading Japanese army, he was the State's Chief Secretary, and after the return of the King he became Chief Justice. He resigned office, but the King refused to accept his resignation, saying, "I cannot do without you." He became chief of the *literati* and Special Adviser. Afterwards he became Minister of the Right, then of the Left, at which time he wrote out ten suggestions for His Majesty to follow. He saw the wrongs done around the King, and resigned office again and again, but was constantly recalled.

In 1608 Im Suk-yong, a young candidate writing for his matriculation, wrote an essay exposing the wrongs of the Court. Sim heard of this, and took the young man under his protection. The King, reading the essay, was furiously angry, and ordered the degradation of Im, but Sim said, "He is with me; I am behind what he wrote and approve; degrade me and not him," and so the King withdrew his displeasure. He was faithful of the faithful.

When he was old he went and lived in Tun-san in a little tumble-down hut, like the poorest of the *literati*. He called himself "Water-thunder Muddy-man," a name derived from the Book of Changes.

He died in 1622 at the age of seventy-four, and is recorded as one of Korea's great patriots.

The Story

Minister Sim Heui-su was, when young, handsome as polished marble, and white as the snow, rarely and beautifully formed. When eight years of age he was already an adept at the character, and a wonder in the eyes of his people. The boy's nickname was Soondong (the godlike one). From the passing of his first examination, step by step he advanced, till at last he became First Minister of the land. When old he was honoured as the most renowned of all ministers. At seventy he still held office, and one day, when occupied with the affairs of State, he suddenly said to those about him, "To-day is my last on earth, and my farewell wishes to you all are that you may prosper and do bravely and well."

His associates replied in wonder, "Your Excellency is still strong and hearty, and able for many years of work; why do you speak so?"

Sim laughingly made answer, "Our span of life is fixed. Why should I not know? We cannot pass the predestined limit. Please feel no regret. Use all your efforts to serve His Majesty the King, and make grateful acknowledgment of his many favours."

Thus he exhorted them, and took his departure. Every one wondered over this strange announcement. From that day on he returned no more, it being said that he was ailing.

There was at that time attached to the War Office a young secretary directly under Sim. Hearing that his master was ill, the young man went to pay his respects and to make inquiry. Sim called him into his private room, where all was quiet. Said he, "I am about to die, and this is a long farewell, so take good care of yourself, and do your part honourably."

The young man looked, and in Sim's eyes were tears. He said, "Your Excellency is still vigorous, and even though you are slightly ailing, there is surely no cause for anxiety. I am at a loss to understand your tears, and what you mean by saying that you are about to die. I would like to ask the reason."

Sim smiled and said, "I have never told any person, but since you ask and there is no longer cause for concealment, I shall tell you the whole story. When I was young certain things happened in my life that may make you smile.

"At about sixteen years of age I was said to be a handsome boy and fair to see. Once in Seoul, when a banquet was in progress and many dancing-girls and other representatives of good cheer were called, I went too, with a half-dozen comrades, to see. There was among the dancing-girls a young woman whose face was very beautiful. She was not like an earthly person, but like some angelic being. Inquiring as to her name, some of those seated near said it was Ta-hong (Flower-bud).

"When all was over and the guests had separated, I went home, but I thought of Ta-hong's pretty face, and recalled her repeatedly, over and over; seemingly I could not forget her. Ten days or so later I was returning from my teacher's house along the main street, carrying my books under my arm, when I suddenly met a pretty girl, who was beautifully dressed and riding a handsome horse. She alighted just in front of me, and to my surprise, taking my hand, said, 'Are you not Sim Heui-su?'

"In my astonishment I looked at her and saw that it was Ta-hong. I said, 'Yes, but how do you know me?' I was not married then, nor had I my hair done up, and as there were many people in the street looking on I was very much ashamed. Flower-bud, with a look of gladness in her face, said to her pony-boy, 'I have something to see to just now; you return and say to the master that I shall be present at the banquet to-morrow.' Then we went aside into a neighbouring house and sat down. She said, 'Did you not on such and such a day go to such and such a Minister's house and look on at the gathering?' I answered, 'Yes, I did.' 'I saw you,' said she, 'and to me your face was like a god's. I asked those present who you were, and they said your family name was Sim and your given-name Heui-su, and that your character and gifts were very superior. From that day on I longed to meet you, but as there was no possibility of this I could only think of you. Our meeting thus is surely of God's appointment.'

"I replied laughingly, 'I, too, felt just the same towards you.'

"Then Ta-hong said, 'We cannot meet here; let's go to my aunt's home in the next ward, where it's quiet, and talk there.' We went to the aunt's home. It was neat and clean and somewhat isolated, and apparently the aunt loved Flower-bud with all the devotion of a mother. From that day forth we plighted our troth together. Flower-bud had never had a lover; I was her first and only choice. She said, however, 'This plan of ours cannot be consummated to-day; let us separate for the present and make plans for our union in the future.' I asked her how we could do so, and she replied, 'I have sworn my soul to you, and it is decided for ever, but you have your parents to think of, and you have not yet had a wife chosen, so there will be no chance of their advising you to have a second wife as my social standing would require for me. As I reflect upon your ability and chances for promotion, I see you already a Minister of State. Let us separate just now, and I'll keep myself for you till the time when you win the first place at the Examination and have your three days of public rejoicing. Then we'll meet once more. Let us make a compact never to be broken. So then, until you have won your honours, do not think of me, please. Do not be anxious, either, lest I should be taken from you, for I have a plan by which to hide myself away in safety. Know that on the day when you win your honours we shall meet again.'

"On this we clasped hands and spoke our farewells as though we parted easily. Where she was going I did not ask, but simply came home with a distressed and burdened heart, feeling that I had lost everything. On my return I found that my parents, who had missed me, were in a terrible state of consternation, but so delighted were they at my safe return that they scarcely asked where I had been. I did not tell them either, but gave another excuse.

"At first I could not desist from thoughts of Ta-hong. After a long time only was I able to regain my composure. From that time forth with all my might I went at my lessons. Day and night I pegged away, not for the sake of the Examination, but for the sake of once more meeting her.

"In two years or so my parents appointed my marriage. I did not dare to refuse, had to accept, but had no heart in it, and no joy in their choice.

"My gift for study was very marked, and by diligence I grew to be superior to all my competitors. It was five years after my farewell to Ta-hong that I won my honours. I was still but a youngster, and all the world rejoiced in my success. But my joy was in the secret understanding that the time had come for me to meet Ta-hong. On the first day of my graduation honours I expected to meet her, but did not. The second day passed, but I saw nothing of her, and the third day was passing and no word had reached me. My heart was so disturbed that I found not the slightest joy in the honours of the occasion. Evening was falling, when my father said to me, 'I have a friend of my younger days, who now lives in Chang-eui ward, and you must go and call on him this evening before the three days are over,' and so, there being no help for it, I went to pay my call. As I was returning the sun had gone down and it was dark, and just as I was passing a high gateway, I heard the *Sillai* call. It was the home of an old Minister, a man whom I did not know, but he being a high noble there was nothing for me to do but to dismount and enter. Here I found the master himself, an old gentleman, who put me through my humble exercises, and then ordered me gently to come up and sit beside him. He talked to me very kindly, and entertained me with all sorts of refreshments. Then he lifted his glass and inquired, 'Would you like to meet a very beautiful person?' I did not know what he meant, and so asked, 'What beautiful person?' The old man said, 'The most beautiful in the world to you. She has long been a member of my household.' Then he ordered a servant to call her. When she came it was my lost Ta-hong. I was startled, delighted, surprised, and speechless almost. 'How do you come here?' I gasped.

"She laughed and said, 'Is this not within the three days of your public celebration, and according to the agreement by which we parted?'

"The old man said, 'She is a wonderful woman. Her thoughts are high and noble, and her history is quite unique. I will tell it to you. I am an old man of eighty, and my wife and I have had no children, but on a certain day this young girl came to us saying, "May I have the place of slave with you, to wait on you and do your bidding?"

"'In surprise I asked the reason for this strange request, and she said, "I am not running away from any master, so do not mistrust me."

"'Still, I did not wish to take her in, and told her so, but she begged so persuasively that I yielded and let her stay, appointed her work to do, and watched her behaviour. She became a slave of her own accord, and simply lived to please us, preparing our meals during the day, and caring for our rooms for the night; responding to calls; ever ready to do our bidding; faithful beyond compare. We feeble old folks, often ill, found her a source of comfort and cheer unheard of, making life perfect peace and joy. Her needle, too, was exceedingly skilful, and according to the seasons she prepared all that we needed. Naturally we loved and pitied her more than I can say. My wife thought more of her than ever mother did of a daughter. During the day she was always at hand, and at night she slept by her side. At one time I asked her quietly concerning her past history. She said she was originally the child of a free-man, but that her parents had died when she was very young, and, having no place to go to, an old woman of the village had taken her in and brought her up. "Being so young," said she, "I was safe from harm. At last I met a young master with whom I plighted a hundred years of troth, a beautiful boy, none was ever like him. I determined to meet him again, but only after he had won his honours in the arena. If I had remained at the home of the old mother I could not have kept myself safe, and preserved my honour; I would have been helpless; so I came here for safety and to serve you. It is a plan by which to hide myself for a year or so, and then when he wins I shall ask your leave to go."

"'I then asked who the person was with whom she had made this contract, and she told me your name. I am so old that I no longer think of taking wives and concubines, but she called herself my concubine so as to be safe, and thus the years have passed. We watched the Examination reports, but till this time your name was absent. Through it all she expressed not a single word of anxiety, but kept up heart saying that before long your name would appear. So confident was she that not a shadow of disappointment was in her face. This time on looking over the list I found your name, and told her. She heard it without any special manifestation of joy, saying she knew it would come. She also said, "When we parted I promised to meet him before the three days of public celebration were over, and now I must make good my promise." So she climbed to the upper pavilion to watch the public way. But this ward being somewhat remote she did not see you going by on the first day, nor on the second. This morning she went again, saying, "He will surely pass to-day"; and so it came about. She said, "He is coming; call him in."

"'I am an old man and have read much history, and have heard of many famous women. There are many examples of devotion that move the heart, but I never saw so faithful a life nor one so devoted to another. God taking note of this has brought all her purposes to pass. And now, not to let this moment of joy go by, you must stay with me to-night.'

"When I met Ta-hong I was most happy, especially as I heard of her years of faithfulness. As to the invitation I declined it, saying I could not think, even though we had so agreed, of taking away one who waited in attendance upon His Excellency. But the old man laughed, saying, 'She is not mine. I simply let her be called my concubine in name lest my nephews or some younger members of the clan should steal her away. She is first of all a faithful woman: I have not known her like before.'

"The old man then had the horse sent back and the servants, also a letter to my parents saying that I would stay the night. He ordered the servants to prepare a room, to put in beautiful screens and embroidered matting, to hang up lights and to decorate as for a bridegroom. Thus he celebrated our meeting.

"Next morning I bade good-bye, and went and told my parents all about my meeting with Ta-hong and what had happened. They gave consent that I should have her, and she was brought and made a member of our family, really my only wife.

"Her life and behaviour being beyond that of the ordinary, in serving those above her and in helping those below, she fulfilled all the requirements of the ancient code. Her work, too, was faithfully done, and her gifts in the way of music and chess were most exceptional. I loved her as I never can tell.

"A little later I went as magistrate to Keumsan county in Chulla Province, and Ta-hong went with me. We were there for two years. She declined our too frequent happy times together, saying that it interfered with efficiency and duty. One day, all unexpectedly, she came to me and requested that we should have a little quiet time, with no others present, as she had something special to tell me. I asked her what it was, and she said to me, 'I am going to die, for my span of life is finished; so let us be glad once more and forget all the sorrows of the world.' I wondered when I heard this. I could not think it true, and asked her how she could tell beforehand that she was going to die. She said, 'I know, there is no mistake about it.'

"In four or five days she fell ill, but not seriously, and yet a day or two later she died. She said to me when dying, 'Our life is ordered, God decides it all. While I lived I gave myself to you, and you most kindly responded in return. I have no regrets. As I die I ask only that my body be buried where it may rest by the side of my master when he passes away, so that when we meet in the regions beyond I shall be with you once again.' When she had so said she died.

"Her face was beautiful, not like the face of the dead, but like the face of the living. I was plunged into deepest grief, prepared her body with my own hands for burial. Our custom is that when a second wife dies she is not buried with the family, but I made some excuse and had her interred in our family site in the county of Ko-yang. I did so to carry out her wishes. When I came as far as Keum-chang on my sad journey, I wrote a verse –

> 'O beautiful Bud, of the beautiful Flower,
> We bear thy form on the willow bier;
> Whither has gone thy sweet perfumed soul?
> The rains fall on us
> To tell us of thy tears and of thy faithful way.'

"I wrote this as a love tribute to my faithful Ta-hong. After her death, whenever anything serious was to happen in my home, she always came to tell me beforehand, and never was there a mistake in her announcements. For several years it has continued thus, till a few days ago she appeared in a dream saying, 'Master, the time of your departure has come, and we are to meet again. I am now making ready for your glad reception.'

"For this reason I have bidden all my associates farewell. Last night she came once more and said to me, 'To-morrow is your day.' We wept together in the dream as we met and talked. In the morning, when I awoke, marks of tears were still upon my cheeks. This is not because I fear to die, but because I have seen my Ta-hong. Now that you have asked me I have told you all. Tell it to no one." So Sim died, as was foretold, on the day following. Strange, indeed!

CHING YUH AND KYAIN OO: THE TRIALS OF TWO HEAVENLY LOVERS

Prelude

Ching Yuh and Kyain Oo were stars attendant upon the Sun. They fell madly in love with each other, and, obtaining the royal permission, they were married. It was to them a most happy union, and having reached the consummation of their joys they lived only for one another, and sought only each other's company. They were continually in each other's embrace, and as the honey-moon bade fair to continue during the rest of their lives, rendering them unfit for the discharge of their duties, their master decided to punish them. He therefore banished them, one to the farthest edge of the eastern heavens, the other to the extreme opposite side of the great river that divides the heavenly plains (the Milky Way).

They were sent so far away that it required full six months to make the journey, or a whole year to go and come. As they must be at their post at the annual inspection, they therefore could only hope to journey back and forth for the scant comfort of spending one short night in each other's company. Even should they violate their orders and risk punishment by returning sooner, they could only see each other from either bank of the broad river, which they could only hope to cross at the season when the great bridge is completed by the crows, who carry the materials for its construction upon their heads, as any one may know, who cares to notice, how bald and worn are the heads of the crows during the seventh moon.

Naturally this fond couple are always heart-broken and discouraged at being so soon compelled to part after such a brief but long-deferred meeting, and 'tis not strange that their grief should manifest itself in weeping tears so copious that the whole earth beneath is deluged with rains.

This sad meeting occurs on the night of the seventh day of the seventh moon, unless prevented by some untoward circumstance, in which case the usual rainy season is withheld, and the parched earth then unites in lamentation with the fond lovers, whose increased trials so sadden their hearts that even the fountain of tears refuses to flow for their relief.

I

You Tah Jung was a very wise official, and a remarkably good man. He could ill endure the corrupt practices of many of his associate officials, and becoming dissatisfied with life at court, he sought and obtained permission to retire from official life and go to the country. His marriage had fortunately been a happy one, hence he was the more content with the somewhat solitary life he now began to lead. His wife was peculiarly gifted, and they were in perfect sympathy with each other, so that they longed not for the society of others. They had one desire, however, that was ever before them and that could not be laid aside. They had no children; not even a daughter had been granted them.

As You Tah Jung superintended the cultivation of his estate, he felt that he would be wholly happy and content were it not for the lack of offspring. He gave himself up to the fascinating pastime of fishing, and took great delight in spending the most of his time in the fields listening to the birds and absorbing wisdom, with peace and contentment, from nature. As spring brought the mating and budding season, however, he again got to brooding over his unfortunate condition. For as he was the last of an illustrious family, the line seemed like to cease with his childless life. He knew of the displeasure his ancestors would experience, and that he would be unable to face them in paradise; while he would leave no one to bow before his grave and make offerings to his spirit. Again he bemoaned their condition with his poor wife, who begged him to avail himself of his prerogative and remove their reproach by marrying another wife. This he stoutly refused to do, as he would not risk ruining his now pleasant home by bringing another wife and the usual discord into it.

Instead of estranging them, their misfortune seemed but to bind this pair the closer together. They were very devout people, and they prayed to heaven continually for a son. One night the wife fell asleep while praying, and dreamed a remarkable dream. She fancied that she saw a commotion in the vicinity of the North Star, and presently a most beautiful boy came down to her, riding upon a wonderful fan made of white feathers. The boy came direct to her and made a low obeisance, upon which she asked him who he was and where he came from. He said: "I am the attendant of the great North Star, and because of a mistake I fell into he banished me to earth for a term of years, telling me to come to you and bring this fan, which will eventually be the means of saving your life and my own."

In the intensity of her joy she awoke, and found to her infinite sorrow that the beautiful vision was but a dream. She cherished it in her mind, however, and was transported with joy when a beautiful boy came to them with the succeeding spring-tide. The beauty of the child was the comment of the neighborhood, and every one loved him. As he grew older it was noticed that the graces of his mind were even more remarkable than those of his person.

The next ten years were simply one unending period of blissful contentment in the happy country home. They called the boy Pang Noo (his family name being You, made him You Pang Noo). His mother taught him his early lessons herself, but by the expiration of his first ten years he had grown far beyond her powers, and his brilliant mind even taxed his intelligent father in his attempts to keep pace with him.

About this time they learned of a wonderful teacher, a Mr. Nam Juh Oon, whose ability was of great repute. It was decided that the boy should be sent to this man to school, and great was the agitation and sorrow at home at thought of the separation. He was made ready, however, and with the benediction of father and caresses of mother, he started for his new teacher, bearing with him a wonderful feather fan which his father had given him, and which had descended from his great-grandfather.

This he was to guard with especial care, as, since his mother's remarkable dream, preceding his birth, it was believed that this old family relic, which bore such a likeness to the fan of the dream, was to prove a talisman to him, and by it evil was to be warded off, and good brought down upon him.

II

Strange as it may seem, events very similar in nature to those just narrated were taking place in a neighboring district, where lived another exemplary man named Cho Sung Noo. He was a man of great rank, but was not in active service at present, simply because of ill-health induced by constant brooding over his ill-fortune; for, like You Tah Jung, he was the last of an illustrious family, and had no offspring. He was so happily married, furthermore, that he had never taken a second wife, and would not do so.

About the time of the events just related concerning the You family, the wife of Cho, who had never neglected bowing to heaven and requesting a child, dreamed. She had gone to a hill-side apart from the house, and sitting in the moonlight on a clean plat of ground, free from the litter of the domestic animals, she was gazing into the heavens, hoping to witness the meeting of *Ching Yuh* and *Kyain Oo*, and feeling sad at the thought of their fabled tribulations. While thus engaged she fell asleep, and while sleeping dreamed that the four winds were bearing to her a beautiful litter, supported upon five rich, soft clouds. In the chair reclined a beautiful little girl, far lovelier than any being she had ever dreamed of before, and the like of which is never seen in real life. The chair itself was made of gold and jade. As the procession drew nearer the dreamer exclaimed: "Who are you, my beautiful child?"

"Oh," replied the child, "I am glad you think me beautiful, for then, may be, you will let me stay with you."

"I think I should like to have you very much, but you haven't yet answered my question."

"Well," she said, "I was an attendant upon the Queen of Heaven, but I have been very bad, though I meant no wrong, and I am banished to earth for a season; won't you let me live with you, please?"

"I shall be delighted, my child, for we have no children. But what did you do that the stars should banish you from their midst?"

"Well, I will tell you," she answered. "You see, when the annual union of Ching Yuh and Kyain Oo takes place, I hear them mourning because they can only see each other once a year, while mortal pairs have each other's company constantly. They never consider that while mortals have but eighty years of life at most, their lives are without limit, and they, therefore, have each other to a greater extent than do the mortals, whom they selfishly envy. In a spirit of mischief I determined to teach this unhappy couple a lesson; consequently, on the last seventh moon, seventh day, when the bridge was about completed and ready for the eager pair to cross heaven's river to each others' embrace, I drove the crows away, and ruined their bridge before they could reach each other. I did it for mischief, 'tis true, and did not count on the drought that would occur, but for my misconduct and the consequent suffering entailed on mortals, I am banished, and I trust you will take and care for me, kind lady."

When she had finished speaking, the winds began to blow around as though in preparation for departure with the chair, minus its occupant. Then the woman awoke and found it but a dream, though the winds were, indeed, blowing about her so as to cause her to feel quite chilly. The dream left a pleasant impression, and when, to their intense joy, a daughter was really born to them, the fond parents could scarcely be blamed for associating her somewhat with the vision of the ravishing dream.

The child was a marvel of beauty, and her development was rapid and perfect. The neighbors were so charmed with her, that some of them seemed to think she was really supernatural, and she was popularly known as the "divine maiden," before her first ten years were finished.

It was about the time of her tenth birthday that little Uhn Hah had the interesting encounter upon which her whole future was to hinge.

It happened in this way: One day she was riding along on her nurses' back, on her way to visit her grandmother. Coming to a nice shady spot they sat down by the road-side to rest. While they were sitting there, along came Pang Noo on his way to school. As Uhn Hah was still but a girl she was not veiled, and the lad was confronted with her matchless beauty, which seemed to intoxicate him. He could not pass by, neither could he find words to utter, but at last he bethought him of an expedient. Seeing some oranges in her lap, he stepped up and spoke politely to the nurse, saying, "I am You Pang Noo, a lad on my way to school, and I am very thirsty, won't you ask your little girl to let me have one of her oranges?" Uhn Hah was likewise smitten with the charms of the beautiful lad, and in her confusion she gave him two oranges. Pang Noo gallantly said, "I wish to give you something in return for your kindness, and if you will allow me I will write your name on this fan and present it to you."

Having obtained the name and permission, he wrote: "No girl was ever possessed of such incomparable graces as the beautiful Uhn Hah. I now betroth myself to her, and vow never to marry other so long as I live." He handed her the fan, and feasting his eyes on her beauty, they separated. The fan being closed, no one read the characters, and Uhn Hah carefully put it away for safe keeping without examining it sufficiently close to discover the written sentiment.

III

Pang Noo went to school and worked steadily for three years. He learned amazingly fast, and did far more in three years than the brightest pupils usually do in ten. His noted teacher soon found that the boy could even lead him, and it became evident that further stay at the school was unnecessary. The boy also was very anxious to go and see his parents. At last he bade his teacher good-by, to the sorrow of both, for their companionship had been very pleasant and profitable, and they had more than the usual attachment of teacher and pupil for each other. Pang Noo and his attendant journeyed leisurely to their home, where they were received with the greatest delight. His mother had not seen her son during his schooling, and even her fond pride was hardly prepared for the great improvement the boy had made, both in body and mind, since last she saw him. The father eventually asked to see the ancestral fan he had given him, and the boy had to confess that he had it not, giving as an excuse that he had lost it on the road. His father could not conceal his anger, and for some time their pleasure was marred by this unfortunate circumstance. Such a youth and an only son could not long remain unforgiven, however, and soon all was forgotten, and he enjoyed the fullest love of his parents and admiration of his friends as he quietly pursued his studies and recreation.

In this way he came down to his sixteenth year, the pride of the neighborhood. His quiet was remarked, but no one knew the secret cause, and how much of his apparent studious attention was devoted to the charming little maiden image that was framed in his mental vision. About this time a very great official from the neighborhood called upon his father, and after the usual formalities, announced that he had heard of the remarkable son You Tah Jung was the father of, and he had come to consult upon the advisability of uniting their families, as he himself had been blessed with a daughter who was beautiful and accomplished. You Tah Jung was delighted at the prospect of making such a fine alliance for his son, and gave his immediate consent, but to his dismay, his son objected so strenuously and withal so honorably that the proposition had to be declined as graciously as the rather awkward circumstances would allow. Both men being sensible, however, they but admired the boy the more, for the clever rascal had begged his father to postpone all matrimonial matters, as far as he was concerned, till he had been able to make a name for himself, and had secured rank, that he might merit such attention.

Pang Noo was soon to have an opportunity to distinguish himself. A great *quaga* (civil-service examination) was to be held at the capital, and Pang Noo announced his intention of entering the lists and competing for civil rank. His father was glad, and in due time started him off in proper style. The examination was held in a great enclosure at the rear of the palace, where the King and his counsellors sat in a pavilion upon a raised stage of masonry. The hundreds of men and youths from all parts of the country were seated upon the ground under large umbrellas. Pang Noo was given a subject, and soon finished his essay, after which he folded it up carefully and tossed the manuscript over a wall into an enclosure, where it was received and delivered to the board of examiners. These gentlemen, as well as His Majesty, were at once struck with the rare merit of the production, and made instant inquiry concerning the writer. Of course he was successful, and a herald soon announced that Pang, the son of You Tah Jung had taken the highest honors. He was summoned before the King, who was pleased with the young man's brightness and wisdom. In addition to his own rank, his father was made governor of a province, and made haste to come to court and thank his sovereign for the double honor, and to congratulate his son.

Pang was given permission to go and bow at the tomb of his ancestors, in grateful acknowledgment for Heaven's blessings. Having done which, he went to pay his respects to his mother, who fairly worshipped her son now, if she had not done so before. During his absence the King had authorized the board of appointments to give him the high rank of *Ussa*, for, though he was young, His Majesty thought one so wise and quick, well fitted to travel in disguise and spy out the acts of evil officials, learn the condition of the people, and bring the corrupt and usurous to punishment. Pang Noo was amazed at his success, yet the position just suited him, for, aside from a desire to better the condition of his fellow-men, he felt that in this position he would be apt to learn the whereabouts of his lady-love, whose beautiful vision was ever before him. Donning a suitable disguise, therefore, he set out upon the business at hand with a light heart.

IV

Uhn Hah during all this time had been progressing in a quiet way as a girl should, but she also was quite the wonder of her neighborhood. All this time she had had many, if not constant, dreams of the handsome youth she had met by the roadside. She had lived over the incident time and again, and many a time did she take down and gaze upon the beautiful fan, which, however, opened and closed in such a manner that, ordinarily, the characters were concealed. At last, however, she discovered them, and great was her surprise and delight at the message. She dwelt on it much, and finally concluded it was a heaven arranged union, and as the lad had pledged his faith to her, she vowed she would be his, or never marry at all. This thought she nourished, longing to see Pang Noo, and wondering how she should ever find him, till she began to regard herself as really the wife of her lover.

About this time one of His Majesty's greatest generals, who had a reputation for bravery and cruelty as well, came to stop at his country holding near by, and hearing of the remarkable girl, daughter of the retired, but very honorable, brother official, he made a call at the house of Mr. Cho, and explained that he was willing to betroth his son to Cho's daughter. The matter was considered at length, and Cho gave his willing consent. Upon the departure of the General, the father went to acquaint his daughter with her good fortune. Upon hearing it, she seemed struck dumb, and then began to weep and moan, as though some great calamity had befallen her. She could say nothing, nor bear to hear any more said of the matter. She could neither eat nor sleep, and the roses fled from her tear-bedewed cheeks. Her parents were dismayed, but wisely abstained from troubling her.

Her mother, however, betimes lovingly coaxed her daughter to confide in her, but it was long before the girl could bring herself to disclose a secret so peculiar and apparently so unwomanly. The mother prevailed at last, and the whole story of the early infatuation eventually came forth. "He has pledged himself to me," she said, "he recognized me at sight as his heaven-sent bride, and I have pledged myself to him. I cannot marry another, and, should I never find him on earth, this fan shall be my husband till death liberates my spirit to join his in the skies." She enumerated his great charms of manner and person, and begged her mother not to press this other marriage upon her, but rather let her die, insisting, however, that should she die her mother must tell Pang Noo how true she had been to him.

The father was in a great dilemma. "Why did you not tell this to your mother before? Here the General has done me the honor to ask that our families be united, and I have consented. Now I must decline, and his anger will be so great that he will ruin me at the Capitol. And then, after all, this is but an absurd piece of childish foolishness. Your fine young man, had he half the graces you give him, would have been betrothed long before this."

"No! No!" she exclaimed, "he has pledged himself, and I know he is even now coming to me. He will not marry another, nor can I. Would you ask one woman to marry two men? Yet that is what you ask in this, for I am already the wife of Pang Noo in my heart. Kill me, if you will, but spare me this, I beg and entreat," and she writhed about on her cot, crying till the mat was saturated with her tears.

The parents loved her too well to withstand her pleadings, and resigning themselves to the inevitable persecution that must result, they dispatched a letter to the General declining his kind offer, in as unobjectionable a manner as possible. It had the result that was feared. The General, in a towering rage, sent soldiers to arrest Mr. Cho, but before he could go further, a messenger arrived from Seoul with despatches summoning him to the Capitol immediately, as a rebellion had broken out on the borders. Before leaving, however, he instructed the local magistrate to imprison the man and not release him till he consented to the marriage. It chanced that the magistrate was an honest man and knew the General to be a very cruel, relentless warrior. He therefore listened to Cho's story, and believed the strange case. Furthermore, his love for the girl softened his heart, and he bade them to collect what they could and go to another province to live. Cho did so, with deep gratitude to the magistrate, while the latter wrote to the General that the prisoner had avoided arrest and fled to unknown parts, taking his family with him.

V

Poor Pang Noo did his inspection work with a heavy heart as time wore on, and the personal object of his search was not attained. In the course of his travels he finally came to his uncle, the magistrate who had dismissed the Cho family. The uncle welcomed his popular nephew right warmly, but questioned him much as to the cause of his poor health and haggard looks, which so ill-became a man of his youth and prospects. At last the kind old man secured the secret with its whole story, and then it was his turn to be sad, for had he not just sent away the very person the Ussa so much desired to see?

When Pang learned this his malady increased, and he declared he could do no more active service till this matter was cleared up. Consequently he sent a despatch to court begging to be released, as he was in such poor health he could not properly discharge his arduous duties longer. His request was granted, and he journeyed to Seoul, hoping to find some trace of her who more and more seemed to absorb his every thought and ambition.

VI

In the meantime the banished family, heart-sick and travel-worn, had settled temporarily in a distant hamlet, where the worn and discouraged parents were taken sick. Uhn Hah did all she could for them, but in spite of care and attention, in spite of prayers and tears, they passed on to join their ancestors. The poor girl beat her breast and tore her hair in an agony of despair. Alone in a strange country, with no money and no one to shield and support her, it seemed that she too must, perforce, give up. But her old nurse urged her to cheer up, and suggested their donning male attire, in which disguise they could safely journey to another place unmolested.

The idea seemed a good one, and it was adopted. They allowed their hair to fall down the back in a long braid, after the fashion of the unmarried men, and, putting on men's clothes, they had no trouble in passing unnoticed along the roads. After having gone but a short distance they found themselves near the capital of the province – the home of the Governor. While sitting under some trees by the roadside the Governor's procession passed by. The couple arose respectfully, but the Governor (it was Pang Noo's father), espying the peculiar feather fan, ordered one of the runners to seize the women and bring them along. It was done; and when they were arrived at the official yamen, he questioned the supposed man as to where he had secured that peculiar fan. "It is a family relic," replied Uhn Hah, to the intense amazement of the Governor, who pronounced the statement false, as the fan was a peculiar feature in his own family, and must be one that had descended from his own ancestors and been found or stolen by the present possessor.

However, the Governor offered to pay a good round sum for the fan. But Uhn Hah declared she would die rather than part with it, and the two women in disguise were locked up in prison. A man of clever speech was sent to interview them, and he offered them a considerable sum for the fan, which the servant urged Uhn Hah to take, as they were sadly in want. After the man had departed in disgust, however, the girl upbraided her old nurse roundly for forsaking her in her time of trial. "My parents are dead," she said. "All I have to represent my husband is this fan that I carry in my bosom. Would you rob me of this? Never speak so again if you wish to retain my love"; and, weeping, she fell into the servant's arms, where, exhausted and overwrought nature asserting itself, sleep closed her eyes.

While sleeping she dreamed of a wonderful palace on high, where she saw a company of women, who pointed her to the blood-red reeds that lined the river bank below, explaining that their tears had turned to blood during their long search for their lovers, and dropping on the reeds they were dyed blood-red. One of them prophesied, however, that Uhn Hah was to be given superhuman strength and powers, and that she would soon succeed in finding her lover, who was now a high official, and so true to her that he was sick because he could not find her. She awakened far more refreshed by the dream than by the nap, and was soon delighted by being dismissed. The Governor's steward took pity on the handsome "boy," and gave him a parting gift of wine and food to carry with them, as well as some cash to help them on, and, bidding him good-by, the women announced their intention of travelling to a distant province.

VII

Meanwhile Pang Noo had reached home, and was weary both in body and mind. The King offered him service at court, but he asked to be excused, and seemed to wish to hide himself and avoid meeting people. His father marvelled much at this, and again urged the young man to marry; but this seemed only to aggravate his complaint. His uncle happened to come to his father's gubernatorial seat on a business errand, and in pity for the young man, explained the cause of the trouble to the father. He saw it all, and recalled the strange beauty of the lad who had risked his life for the possession of the fan, and as the uncle told the story of her excellent parentage, and the trouble and death that resulted from the refusal to marry, he saw through the whole strange train of circumstances, and marvelled that heaven should have selected such an exemplary maiden for his son. And then, as he realized how nearly he had come to punishing her severely, for her persistent refusal to surrender the fan, and that, whereas, he might have retained her and united her to his son, he had sent her away unattended to wander alone; he heaped blame upon the son in no stinted manner for his lack of confidence in not telling his father his troubles. The attendants were carefully questioned concerning the conduct of the strange couple while in custody at the governor's yamen, and as to the probable direction they took in departure. The steward alone could give information. He was well rewarded for having shown them kindness, but his information cast a gloom upon the trio, for he said they had started for the district where civil war was in progress.

"You unnatural son," groaned the father. "What have you done? You secretly pledge yourself to this noble girl, and then, by your foolish silence, twice allow her to escape, while you came near being the cause of her death at the very hands of your father; and even now by your foolishness she is journeying to certain death. Oh, my son! we have not seen the last of this rash conduct; this noble woman's blood will be upon our hands, and you will bring your poor father to ruin and shame. Up! Stop your lovesick idling, and do something. Ask His Majesty, with my consent, for military duty; go to the seat of war, and there find your wife or your honor."

The father's advice was just what was needed; the son could not, of necessity, disobey, nor did he wish to; but arming himself with the courage of a desperate resolve to save his sweetheart, whom he fancied already in danger from the rebels, he hurried to Seoul, and surprising his sovereign by his strange and ardent desire for military service, easily secured the favor, for the general in command was the same who had wished to marry his son to Uhn Hah; he was also an enemy to Pang Noo's father, and would like to see the only son of his enemy killed.

With apparently strange haste the expedition was started off, and no time was lost on the long, hard march. Arriving near the seat of war, the road led by a mountain, where the black weather-worn stone was as bare as a wall, sloping down to the road. Fearing lest he was going to his death, the young commander had some characters cut high on the face of the rock, which read:

"Standing at the gate of war, I, You Pang Noo, humbly bow to Heaven's decree. Is it victory, or is it death? Heaven alone knows the issue. My only remaining desire is to behold the face of my lady Cho Gah." He put this inscription in this conspicuous place, with the hope that if she were in the district she would see it, and not only know he was true to her, but also that she might be able to ascertain his whereabouts and come to him. He met the rebels, and fought with a will, bringing victory to the royal arms. But soon their provisions gave out, and, though daily despatches arrived, no rations were sent in answer to their constant demands. The soldiers sickened and died. Many more, driven mad by hardship and starvation, buried their troubles deep in the silent river, which their loyal spears had stained crimson with their enemies blood.

You Pang Noo was about to retire against orders, when the rebels, emboldened by the weak condition of their adversaries, came in force, conquered and slew the remnant, and would have slain the commander but for the counsel of two of their number, who urged that he be imprisoned and held for ransom.

VIII

Again fate had interfered to further separate the lovers, for, instead of continuing her journey, Uhn Hah had received news that induced her to start for Seoul. While resting, on

LOVE, MARRIAGE & FAMILY

one occasion, they had some conversation with a passer-by. He was from the capital, and stated that he had gone there from a place near Uhn Hah's childhood home as an attendant of the *Ussa* You Pang Noo, who had taken sick at his uncle's, the magistrate, and had gone to Seoul, where he was excused from *ussa* duty and offered service at court. He knew not of the recent changes, but told his eager listener all he knew of Pang Noo's family.

The weary, foot-sore girl and her companion turned their faces toward the capital, hoping at last to be rewarded by finding the object of their search. That evening darkness overtook them before they had found shelter, and spying a light through the trees, they sought it out, and found a little hut occupied by an old man. He was reading a book, but laid it aside as they answered his invitation to enter, given in response to their knock. The usual salutations were exchanged, but instead of asking who the visitors were, where they lived, etc., etc., the old man called her by her true name, Cho Nang Jah. "I am not a Nang Jah" (a female appellation), she exclaimed; "I am a man!"

"Oh! I know you, laughed the old man; "you are Cho Nang Jah in very truth, and you are seeking your future husband in this disguise. But you are perfectly safe here."

"Ask me no questions," said he, as she was about to utter some surprised inquiries. "I have been waiting for you and expecting you. You are soon to do great things, for which I will prepare you. Never mind your hunger, but devour this pill; it will give you superhuman strength and courage." He gave her a pill of great size, which she ate, and then fell asleep on the floor. The old man went away, and soon the tired servant slept also. When they awoke it was bright morning, and the birds were singing in the trees above them, which were their only shelter, for the hut of the previous evening had disappeared entirely, as had also the old man. Concluding that the old man must be some heaven-sent messenger, she devoutly bowed herself in grateful acknowledgment of the gracious manifestation.

Journeying on, they soon came to a wayside inn kept by an old farmer, and here they procured food. While they were eating, a blind man was prophesying for the people. When he came to Uhn Hah he said: "This is a woman in disguise; she is seeking for her husband, who is fighting the rebels, and searching for her. He is now nearly dead; but he will not die, for she will rescue him." On hearing this she was delighted and sad at the same time, and explaining some of her history to the master of the house, he took her in with the women and treated her kindly. She was very anxious to be about her work, however, since heaven had apparently so clearly pointed it out to her, and, bidding the simple but kind friends good-by, she started for the seat of war, where she arrived after a long, tedious, but uneventful tramp.

Almost the first thing she saw was the inscription on the rocks left by the very one she sought, and she cried bitterly at the thought that maybe she was too late. The servant cheered her up, however, by reciting the blind man's prophecy, and they went on their way till they came to a miserable little inn, where they secured lodging. After being there some time, Uhn Hah noticed that the innkeeper's wife was very sad, and continually in tears. She therefore questioned her as to the cause of her grief. "I am mourning over the fate of the poor starved soldiers, killed by the neglect of some one at Seoul, and for the brave young officer, You Pang Noo, whom the rebels have carried away captive." At this Uhn Hah fainted away, and the nurse made such explanation as she could. Restoratives were applied, and she slowly recovered, when, on further questioning, it was found that the inn-people were slaves of You Pang Noo, and had followed him thus far. It was also learned that the absence of stores was generally believed to be due to the corrupt general-in-chief, who not only hated his gallant young officer, but was unwilling to let him achieve glory, so long as he could prevent it.

After consultation, and learning further of the matter, Uhn Hah wrote a letter explaining the condition of affairs, and dispatched it to Pang Noo's father by the innkeeper. The Governor was not at his country place, and the messenger had to go to Seoul, where, to his horror, he found that his old master was in prison, sent there by the influence of the corrupt General, his enemy, because his son had been accused of being a traitor, giving over the royal troops to the rebels, and escaping with them himself. The innkeeper, however, secured access to the prison, and delivered the letter to the unfortunate parent. Of course, nothing could be done, and again he blamed his son for his stupid secrecy in concealing his troubles from his father, and thus bringing ruin upon the family and injury to the young lady. However, he wrote a letter to the good uncle, relating the facts, and requesting him to find the girl, place her in his home, and care for her as tenderly as possible. He could do nothing more. The innkeeper delivered this letter to the uncle, and was then instructed to carry a litter and attendants to his home and bring back the young lady, attired in suitable garments. He did so as speedily as possible, though the journey was a long and tedious one.

Once installed in a comfortable home poor Uhn Hah became more and more lonely. She seemed to have nothing now to hope for, and the stagnation of idleness was more than she could endure. She fancied her lover in prison, and suffering, while she was in the midst of comfort and luxury. She could not endure the thought, and prevailed upon her benefactor to convey to His Majesty a petition praying that she be given a body of soldiers and be allowed to go and punish the rebels, reclaim the territory, and liberate her husband. The King marvelled much at such a request, coming from one of her retiring, seclusive sex, and upon the advice of the wicked General, who was still in command, the petition was not granted. Still she persisted, and found other ways of reaching the throne, till the King, out of curiosity to see such a brave and loyal woman, bade her come before him.

When she entered the royal presence her beauty and dignity of carriage at once won attention and respectful admiration, so that her request was about to be granted, when the General suggested, as a last resort, that she first give some evidence of her strength and prowess before the national military reputation be entrusted to her keeping. It seemed a wise thought, and the King asked her what she could do to show that she was warranted in heading such a perilous expedition. She breathed a prayer to her departed parents for help, and remembering the strange promise of the old man who gave her the pill, she felt that she could do almost any thing, and seizing a large weather-worn stone that stood in an ornamental rock basin in the court, she threw it over the enclosing wall as easily as two men would have lifted it from the ground. Then, taking the General's sword, she began slowly to manipulate it, increasing gradually, as though in keeping with hidden music, till the movement became so rapid that the sword seemed like one continuous ring of burning steel – now in the air, now about her own person, and, again, menacingly near the wicked General, who cowered in abject terror before the remarkable sight. His Majesty was completely captivated, and himself gave the orders for her expedition, raising her to relative rank, and giving her the choicest battalion of troops. In her own peculiarly dignified way she expressed her gratitude, and, bowing to the ground, went forth to execute her sovereign's commands, and attain her heart's desire.

Again donning male attire, she completed her preparations, and departed with eager delight to accomplish her mission. The troops having obtained an inkling of the strange character and almost supernatural power of their handsome, dashing leader, were filled with courage and eager for the fray. But to the dismay of all, they had no sooner arrived at the rebel infested country than severe rains began to fall, making it impossible to accomplish any thing. This was explained, however, by the spirits of the departed soldiers, who appeared to the officers in dreams, and announced that as they had been sacrificed by the cruel General, who had intentionally withheld their rations, they would allow no success to the royal arms till their death was avenged by his death. This was dispatched to court, and believed by His Majesty, who had heard similar reports, oft repeated. He therefore confined the General in prison, and sent his son (the one who wished to marry Uhn Hah) to the front to be executed.

He was slain and his blood scattered to the winds. A feast was prepared for the spirits of the departed soldiers, and this sacrifice having been made, the storm ceased, the sun shone, and the royal troops met and completely vanquished the rebels, restoring peace to the troubled districts, but not obtaining the real object of the leaders' search. After much questioning, among the captives, a man was found who knew all about You Pang Noo, and where he was secreted. Upon the promise of pardon, he conducted a party who rescued the captive and brought him before their commander. Of course for a time the lovers could not recognize each other after the years that had elapsed since their first chance meeting.

You Pang Noo was given command and Uhn Hah modestly retired, adopted her proper dress, and was borne back to Seoul in a litter. The whole country rang with their praises. You Pang Noo was appointed governor of a province, and the father was reinstated in office, while the General who had caused the trouble was ignominiously put to death, and his whole family and his estates were confiscated.

As Cho Uhn Hah had no parents, His Majesty determined that she should have royal patronage, and decreed that their wedding should take place in the great hall where the members of the royal family are united in marriage. This was done with all the pomp and circumstance of a royal wedding, and no official stood so high in the estimation of the King, as the valiant, true-hearted You, while the virtues of his spouse were the subject of songs and ballads, and she was extolled as the model for the women of the country.

LOVE, MARRIAGE & FAMILY

CHUN YANG, THE FAITHFUL DANCING-GIRL WIFE

In the city of **Nam Won**, in Chull Lah Do (the southern province of Korea), lived the Prefect Ye Tung Uhi. He was the happy father of a son of some sixteen years of age. Being an only child the boy was naturally much petted. He was not an ordinary young man, however, for in addition to a handsome, manly face and stalwart figure, he possessed a bright, quick mind, and was naturally clever. A more dutiful son could not be found. He occupied a house in the rear of his father's quarters, and devoted himself to his books, going regularly each evening to make his obeisance to his father, and express his wish that pleasant, refreshing sleep might come to him; then, in the morning, before breakfasting, he was wont to go and enquire how the new day had found his father.

The Prefect was but recently appointed to rule over the Nam Won district when the events about to be recorded occurred. The winter months had been spent mostly indoors, but as the mild spring weather approached and the buds began to open to the singing of the joyful birds, Ye Toh Ryung, or Toh Ryung, the son, felt that he must get out and enjoy nature. Like an animal that has buried itself in a hole in the earth, he came forth rejoicing; the bright yellow birds welcomed him from the willow trees, the soft breezes fanned his cheeks, and the freshness of the air exhilarated him. He called his *pang san* (valet) and asked him concerning the neighboring views. The servant was a native of the district, and knew the place well; he enumerated the various places especially prized for their scenery, but concluded with: "But of all rare views, 'Kang Hal Loo' is the rarest. Officers from the eight provinces come to enjoy the scenery, and the temple is covered with verses they have left in praise of the place." "Very well, then, we will go there," said Toh Ryung "Go you and clean up the place for my reception."

The servant hurried off to order the temple swept and spread with clean mats, while his young master sauntered along almost intoxicated by the freshness and new life of every thing around him. Arrived at the place, after a long, tedious ascent of the mountain side, he flung himself upon a huge bolster-like cushion, and with half-closed eyes, drank in the beauty of the scene along with the balmy, perfume-laden spring zephyrs. He called his servant, and congratulated him upon his taste, declaring that were the gods in search of a fine view, they could not find a place that would surpass this; to which the man answered:

"That is true; so true, in fact, that it is well known that the spirits do frequent this place for its beauty."

As he said this, Toh Ryung had raised himself, and was leaning on one arm, gazing out toward one side, when, as though it were one of the spirits just mentioned, the vision of a beautiful girl shot up into the air and soon fell back out of sight in the shrubbery of an adjoining court-yard. He could just get a confused picture of an angelic face, surrounded by hair like the black thunder-cloud, a neck of ravishing beauty, and a dazzle of bright silks, – when the whole had vanished. He was dumb with amazement, for he felt sure he must have seen one of the spirits said to frequent the place; but before he could speak, the vision arose again, and he then had time to see that it was but a beautiful girl swinging in her dooryard. He did not move, he scarcely breathed, but sat with bulging eyes absorbing the prettiest view he had ever seen. He noted the handsome, laughing face, the silken black hair, held back in a coil by a huge coral pin; he saw the jewels sparkling on the gay robes, the dainty white hands and full round arms, from which the breezes blew back the sleeves; and as she flew higher in her wild sport, oh, joy! two little shoeless feet encased in white stockings, shot up among the peach blossoms, causing them to fall in showers all about her. In the midst of the sport her hairpin loosened and fell, allowing her raven locks to float about her shoulders; but, alas! the costly ornament fell on a rock and broke, for Toh Ryung could hear the sharp click where he sat. This ended the sport, and the little maid disappeared, all unconscious of the agitation she had caused in a young man's breast by her harmless spring exercise.

After some silence, the young man asked his servant if he had seen any thing, for even yet he feared his mind had been wandering close to the dreamland. After some joking, the servant confessed to having seen the girl swinging, whereupon his master demanded her name. "She is Uhl Mahs' daughter, a *gee sang* (public dancing girl) of this city; her name is Chun Yang Ye" – fragrant spring. "*I yah!* superb; I can see her then, and have her sing and dance for me," exclaimed Toh Ryung. "Go and call her at once, you slave."

The man ran, over good road and bad alike, up hill and down, panting as he went; for while the back of the women's quarters of the adjoining compound was near at hand, the entrance had to be reached by a long circuit. Arriving out of breath, he pounded at the gate, calling the girl by name.

"Who is that calls me?" she enquired when the noise had attracted her attention.

"Oh, never mind who," answered the exhausted man, "it is great business; open the door."

"Who are you, and what do you want?"

"I am nobody, and I want nothing; but Ye Toh Ryung is the Governor's son, and he wants to see the Fragrant Spring."

"Who told Ye Toh Ryung my name?"

"Never mind who told him; if you did not want him to know you, then why did you swing so publicly? The great man's son came here to rest and see the beautiful views; he saw you swinging, and can see nothing since. You must go, but you need not fear. He is a gentleman, and will treat you nicely; if your dancing pleases him as did your swinging, he may present you with rich gifts, for he is his father's only son."

Regretting in her proud spirit that fates had placed her in a profession where she was expected to entertain the nobility whether it suited her or not, the girl combed and arranged her hair, tightened her sash, smoothed her disordered clothes, and prepared to look as any vain woman would wish who was about to be presented to the handsomest and most gifted young nobleman of the province. She followed the servant slowly till they reached Toh Ryung's stopping place. She waited while the servant announced her arrival, for a gee sang must not enter a nobleman's presence unbidden. Toh Ryung was too excited to invite her in, however, and his servant had to prompt him, when, laughing at his own agitation, he pleasantly bade her enter and sit down.

"What is your name?" asked he.

"My name is Chun Yang Ye," she said, with a voice that resembled silver jingling in a pouch.

"How old are you?"

"My age is just twice eight years."

"Ah ha!" laughed the now composed boy, "how fortunate; you are twice eight, and I am four fours. We are of the same age. Your name, Fragrant Spring, is the same as your face – very beautiful. Your cheeks are like the petals of the *mah hah* that ushers in the soft spring. Your eyes are like those of the eagle sitting on the ancient tree, but soft and gentle as the moonlight," ran on the enraptured youth. "When is your birthday?"

"My birthday occurs at midnight on the eighth day of the fourth moon," modestly replied the flattered girl, who was quickly succumbing to the charms of the ardent and handsome young fellow, whose heart she could see was already her own.

"Is it possible?" exclaimed he; "that is the date of the lantern festival, and it is also my own birthday, only I was born at eleven instead of twelve. I am sorry I was not born at twelve now. But it doesn't matter. Surely the gods had some motive in sending us into the world at the same time, and thus bringing us together at our sixteenth spring-tide. Heaven must have intended us to be man and wife"; and he bade her sit still as she started as though to take her departure. Then he began to plead with her, pacing the room in his excitement, till his attendant likened the sound to the combat of ancient warriors. "This chance meeting of ours has a meaning," he argued. "Often when the buds were bursting, or when the forest trees were turning to fire and blood, have I played and supped with pretty gee sang, watched them dance, and wrote them verses, but never before have I lost my heart; never before have I seen any one so incomparably beautiful. You are no common mortal. You were destined to be my wife; you must be mine, you must marry me."

She wrinkled her fair brow and thought, for she was no silly, foolish thing, and while her heart was almost, if not quite won by this tempestuous lover, yet she saw where his blind love would not let him see. "You know," she said, "the son of a nobleman may not marry a gee sang without the consent of his parents. I know I am a gee sang by name, the fates have so ordained, but, nevertheless, I am an honorable woman, always have been, and expect to remain so."

"Certainly," he answered, "we cannot celebrate the 'six customs ceremony' (parental arrangements, exchange of letters, contracts, exchange of presents, preliminary visits, ceremony proper), but we can be privately married just the same."

"No, it cannot be. Your father would not consent, and should we be privately married, and your father be ordered to duty at some other place, you would not dare take me with you. Then you would marry the daughter of some nobleman, and I would be forgotten. It must not, cannot be," and she arose to depart. "Stay, stay," he begged. "You do me an injustice. I will never forsake you, or marry another. I swear it. And a *yang ban* (noble) has but one mouth, he cannot speak two ways. Even should we leave this place I will take you with me, or return soon to you. You must not refuse me."

"But suppose you change your mind or forget your promises; words fly out of the mouth and are soon lost, ink and paper are more lasting; give me your promises in writing," she says.

Instantly the young man took up paper and brush; having rubbed the ink well, he wrote: "A memorandum. Desiring to enjoy the spring scenery, I came to Kang Hal Loo. There I saw for the first time my heaven-sent bride. Meeting for the first time, I pledge myself for one hundred years; to be her faithful husband. Should I change, show this paper to the magistrate." Folding up the manuscript with care he handed it to her. While putting it into her pocket she said: "Speech has no legs, yet it can travel many thousands of miles. Suppose this matter should reach your father's ears, what would you do?"

"Never fear; my father was once young, who knows but I may be following the example of his early days. I have contracted with you, and we now are married, even my father cannot change it. Should he discover our alliance and disown me, I will still be yours, and together we shall live and die."

She arose to go, and pointing with her jade-like hand to a clump of bamboos, said: "There is my house; as I cannot come to you, you must come to me and make my mother's house your home, as much as your duty to your parents will allow."

As the sun began to burn red above the mountains' peaks, they bade each other a fond adieu, and each departed for home accompanied by their respective attendants.

Ye Toh Ryung went to his room, which now seemed a prison-like place instead of the pleasant study he had found it. He took up a book, but reading was no satisfaction, every word seemed to transform itself into Chun or Yang. Every thought was of the little maid of the spring fragrance. He changed his books, but it was no use, he could not even keep them right side up, not to mention using them properly. Instead of singing off his lessons as usual, he kept singing, *Chun Yang Ye poh go sip so* (I want to see the spring fragrance), till his father, hearing the confused sounds, sent to ascertain what was the matter with his son. The boy was singing, "As the parched earth cries for rain after the seven years' drought, so my heart pants for my Chun Yang Ye, whose face to me is like the rays of the sun upon the earth after a nine years' rain." He paid no heed to the servants, and soon his father sent his private secretary, demanding what it was the boy desired so much that he should keep singing. "I want to see, I want to see." Toh Ryung answered that he was reading an uninteresting book, and looking for another. Though he remained more quiet after this, he still was all impatience to be off to his sweetheart-wife, and calling his attendant, he sent him out to see how near the sun was to setting. Enjoying the sport, the man returned, saying the sun was now high over head.

"Begone," said he, "can any one hold back the sun; it had reached the mountain tops before I came home."

At last the servant brought his dinner, for which he had no appetite. He could ill abide the long delay between the dinner hour and the regular time for his father's retiring. The time did come, however, and when the lights were extinguished and his father had gone to sleep, he took his trusty servant, and, scaling the back wall, they hurried to the house of Chun Yang Ye.

As they approached they heard someone playing the harp, and singing of the "dull pace of the hours when one's lover is away." Being admitted, they met the mother, who, with some distrust, received Toh Ryung's assurances and sent him to her daughter's apartments.

The house pleased him; it was neat and well-appointed. The public room, facing the court, was lighted by a blue lantern, which in the mellow light resembled a pleasure barge drifting on the spring flood. Banners of poetry hung upon the walls. Upon the door leading to Chun Yang's little parlor hung a banner inscribed with verses to her ancestors and descendants, praying that "a century be short to span her life and happiness, and that her children's children be blessed with prosperity for a thousand years." Through the open windows could be seen moonlight glimpses of the little garden of the swinging girl. There was a miniature lake almost filled with lotus plants, where two sleepy swans floated with heads beneath their wings, while the occasional gleam of a gold or silver scale showed that the water was inhabited. A summer-house on the water's edge was almost covered with fragrant spring blossoms, the whole being enclosed in a little grove of bamboo and willows, that shut out the view of outsiders.

While gazing at this restful sight, Chun Yang Ye herself came out, and all was lost in the lustre of her greater beauty. She asked him into her little parlor, where was a profusion of choice carved cabinets and ornaments of jade and metal, while richly embroidered mats covered the highly-polished floor. She was so delighted that she took both his hands in her pretty, white, soft ones, and gazing longingly into each other's eyes, she led him into another room, where, on a low table, a most elegant lunch was spread. They sat down on the floor and surveyed the loaded table. There were fruits preserved in sugar, candied nuts arranged in many dainty, nested boxes; sweet pickles and confections, pears that had grown in the warmth of a summer now dead, and grapes that had been saved from decay by the same sun that had called them forth. Quaint old bottles with long, twisted necks, contained choice medicated wines, to be drunk from the little crackled cups, such as the ancients used.

Pouring out a cup, she sang to him: "This is the elixir of youth; drinking this, may you never grow old; though ten thousand years pass over your head, may you stand like the mountain that never changes." He drank half of the cup's contents, and praised her sweet voice, asking for another song. She sang: "Let us drain the cup while we may. In the grave who will be our cup-bearer. While we are young let us play. When old, mirth gives place to care. The flowers can bloom but a few days at best, and must then die, that the seed may be born. The moon is no sooner full than it begins to wane, that the young moon may rise."

The sentiments suited him, the wine exhilarated him, and his spirits rose. He drained his cup, and called for more wine and song; but she restrained him. They ate the dainty food, and more wine and song followed. She talked of the sweet contract they had made, and anon they pledged themselves anew. Not content with promises for this short life, they went into the future, and he yielded readily to her request, that when death should at last o'ertake them, she would enter a flower, while he would become a butterfly, coming and resting on her bosom, and feasting off her fragrant sweetness.

The father did not know of his son's recent alliance, though the young man honestly went and removed Chun Yang's name from the list of the district gee sang, kept in his father's office; for, now that she was a married woman, she need no longer go out with the dancing-girls. Every morning, as before, the dutiful son presented himself before his father, with respectful inquiries after his health, and his rest the preceding night. But, nevertheless, each night the young man's apartments were deserted, while he spent the time in the house of his wife.

Thus the months rolled on with amazing speed. The lovers were in paradise. The father enjoyed his work, and labored hard for the betterment of the condition of his subjects. Never before had so large a tribute been sent by this district. Yet the people were not burdened as much as when far less of their products reached the government granaries. The honest integrity of the officer reached the King in many reports, and when a vacancy occurred at the head of the Treasury Department, he was raised to be Ho Joh Pansa (Secretary of Finance). Delighted, the father sent for his son and told him the news, but, to his amazement, the young man had naught to say, in fact he seemed as one struck

LOVE, MARRIAGE & FAMILY

dumb, as well he might. Within himself there was a great tumult; his heart beat so violently as to seem perceptible, and at times it arose and filled his throat, cutting off any speech he might wish to utter. Surprised at the conduct of his son, the father bade him go and inform his mother, that she might order the packing to commence.

He went; but soon found a chance to fly to Chun Yang, who, at first, was much concerned for his health, as his looks denoted a serious illness. When he had made her understand, however, despair seized her, and they gazed at each other in mute dismay and utter helplessness. At last she seemed to awaken from her stupor, and, in an agony of despair, she beat her breast, and moaned: "Oh, how can we separate. We must die, we cannot live apart"; and tears coming to her relief, she cried: "If we say good-by, it will be forever; we can never meet again. Oh, I feared it; we have been too happy – too happy. The one who made this order is a murderer; it must be my death. If you go to Seoul and leave me, I must die. I am but a poor weak woman, and I cannot live without you."

He took her, and laying her head on his breast, tried to soothe her. "Don't cry so bitterly," he begged; "my heart is almost broken now. I cannot bear it. I wish it could always be spring-time; but this is only like the cruel winter that, lingering in the mountain, sometimes sweeps down the valley, drives out the spring, and kills the blossoms. We will not give up and die, though. We have contracted for one hundred years, and this will be but a bitter separation that will make our speedy reunion more blissful."

"Oh," she says, "but how can I live here alone, with you in Seoul? Just think of the long, tedious summer days, the long and lonely winter nights. I must see no one. I cannot know of you, for who will tell me, and how am I to endure it?"

"Had not my father been given this great honor, we would perhaps not have been parted; as it is I must go, there is no help for it, but you must believe me when I promise I will come again. Here, take this crystal mirror as a pledge that I will keep my word"; and he gave her his pocket-mirror of rock crystal.

"Promise me when you will return," said she; and then, without awaiting an answer, she sang: "When the sear and withered trunk begins to bloom, and the dead bird sings in the branches, then my lover will come to me. When the river flows over the eastern mountains, then may I see him glide along in his ship to me." He chided her for her lack of faith, and assured her again it was as hard for one as the other. After a time she became more reconciled, and taking off her jade ring, gave it to him for a keepsake, saying: "My love, like this ring, knows no end. You must go, alas! but my love will go with you, and may it protect you when crossing wild mountains and distant rivers, and bring you again safely to me. If you go to Seoul, you must not trifle, but take your books, study hard, and enter the examinations, then, perhaps, you may obtain rank and come to me. I will stand with my hand shading my eyes, ever watching for your return."

Promising to cherish her speech, with her image in his breast, they made their final adieu, and tore apart.

The long journey seemed like a funeral to the lover. Everywhere her image rose before him. He could think of nothing else; but by the time he arrived at the capital he had made up his mind as to his future course, and from that day forth his parents wondered at his stern, determined manner. He shut himself up in his room with his books. He would neither go out, or form acquaintances among the young noblemen of the gay city. Thus he spent months in hard study, taking no note of passing events.

LOVE, MARRIAGE & FAMILY

In the meantime a new magistrate came to Nam Won. He was a hard-faced, hard-hearted politician. He associated with the dissolute, and devoted himself to riotous living, instead of caring for the welfare of the people. He had not been long in the place till he had heard so much of the matchless beauty of Chun Yang Ye that he determined to see, and if, as reported, marry her. Accordingly he called the clerk of the yamen, and asked concerning "the beautiful gee sang Chun Yang Ye." The clerk answered that such a name had appeared on the records of the dancing girls, but that it had been removed, as she had contracted a marriage with the son of the previous magistrate, and was now a lady of position and respectability.

"You lying rascal!" yelled the enraged officer, who could ill brook any interference with plans he had formed. "A nobleman's son cannot really marry a dancing girl; leave my presence at once, and summon this remarkable 'lady' to appear before me." The clerk could only do as he was bidden, and, summoning the yamen runners, he sent to the house of Chun Yang Ye to acquaint her with the official order.

The runners, being natives of the locality, were loath to do as commanded, and when the fair young woman gave them "wine money" they willingly agreed to report her "too sick to attend the court." Upon doing so, however, the wrath of their master came down upon them. They were well beaten, and then commanded to go with a chair and bring the woman, sick or well, while if they disobeyed him a second time they would be put to death.

Of course they went, but after they had explained to Chun Yang Ye their treatment, her beauty and concern for their safety so affected them, that they offered to go back without her, and face their doom. She would not hear to their being sacrificed for her sake, and prepared to accompany them. She disordered her hair, soiled her fair face, and clad herself in dingy, ill-fitting gowns, which, however, seemed only to cause her natural beauty the more to shine forth. She wept bitterly on entering the yamen, which fired the anger of the official. He ordered her to stop her crying or be beaten, and then as he looked at her disordered and tear-stained face, that resembled choice jade spattered with mud, he found that her beauty was not overstated.

"What does your conduct mean?" said he. "Why have you not presented yourself at this office with the other gee sang?"

"Because, though born a gee sang, I am by marriage a lady, and not subject to the rules of my former profession," she answered.

"Hush!" roared the Prefect. "No more of this nonsense. Present yourself here with the other gee sang, or pay the penalty."

"Never" she bravely cried. "A thousand deaths first. You have no right to exact such a thing of me. You are the King's servant, and should see that the laws are executed, rather than violated."

The man was fairly beside himself with wrath at this, and ordered her chained and thrown into prison at once. The people all wept with her, which but increased her oppressor's anger, and calling the jailer he ordered him to treat her with especial rigor, and be extra vigilant lest some sympathizers should assist her to escape. The jailer promised, but nevertheless he made things as easy for her as was possible under the circumstances. Her mother came and moaned over her daughter's condition, declaring that she was foolish in clinging to her faithless husband, who had brought all this trouble upon them. The neighbors, however, upbraided the old woman for her words, and assured the daughter that she had done just right, and would yet be rewarded. They brought presents of food, and endeavored to make her condition slightly less miserable by their attentions.

She passed the night in bowing before Heaven and calling on the gods and her husband to release her, and in the morning when her mother came, she answered the latter's inquiries as to whether she was alive or not, in a feeble voice which alarmed her parent.

"I am still alive, but surely dying. I can never see my Toh Ryung again; but when I am dead you must take my body to Seoul and bury it near the road over which he travels the most, that even in death I may be near him, though separated in life." Again the mother scolded her for her devotion and for making the contract that binds her strongly to such a man. She could stand it no longer, and begged her mother that she would go away and come to see her no more if she had no pleasanter speech than such to make. "I followed the dictates of my heart and my mind. I did what was right. Can I foretell the future? Because the sun shines to-day are we assured that to-morrow it will shine? The deed is done. I do not regret it; leave me to my grief, but do not add to it by your unkindness."

Thus the days lengthened into months, but she seemed like one dead, and took no thought of time or its flight. She was really ill, and would have died but for the kindness of the jailer. At last one night she dreamed that she was in her own room, dressing, and using the little mirror Toh Ryung had given her, when, without apparent cause, it suddenly broke in halves. She awoke, startled, and felt sure that death was now to liberate her from her sorrows, for what other meaning could the strange occurrence have than that her body was thus to be broken. Although anxious to die and be free, she could not bear the thought of leaving this world without a last look at her loved husband whose hands alone could close her eyes when her spirit had departed. Pondering much upon the dream, she called the jailer and asked him to summon a blind man, as she wished her fortune told. The jailer did so. It was no trouble, for almost as she spoke they heard one picking his way along the street with his long stick, and uttering his peculiar call. He came in and sat down, when they soon discovered that they were friends, for before the man became blind he had been in comfortable circumstances, and had known her father intimately. She therefore asked him to be to her as a kind father, and faithfully tell her when and how death would come to her. He said: "When the blossoms fade and fall they do not die, their life simply enters the seed to bloom again. Death to you would but liberate your spirit to shine again in a fairer body."

She thanked him for his kind generalities, but was impatient, and telling her dream, she begged a careful interpretation of it. He promptly answered, that to be an ill omen a mirror in breaking must make a noise. And on further questioning, he found that in her dream a bird had flown into the room just as the mirror was breaking.

"I see," said he. "The bird was bearer of good news, and the breaking of the mirror, which Toh Ryung gave you, indicates that the news concerned him; let us see." Thereupon he arranged a bunch of sticks, shook them well, while uttering his chant, and threw them upon the floor. Then he soon answered that the news was good. "Your husband has done well. He has passed his examinations, been promoted, and will soon come to you."

She was too happy to believe it, thinking the old man had made it up to please his old friend's distressed child. Yet she cherished the dream and the interpretation in her breast, finding in it solace to her weary, troubled heart.

In the meantime Ye Toh Ryung had continued his studious work day and night, to the anxiety of his parents. Just as he began to feel well prepared for the contest he awaited, a royal proclamation announced, that owing to the fact that peace reigned throughout the whole country, that the closing year had been one of prosperity, and no national calamity had befallen the country, His Gracious Majesty had ordered a grand *guaga*, or competitive examination, to be held. As soon as it became known, literary pilgrims began to pour in from all parts of the country, bent on improving their condition.

The day of the examination found a vast host seated on the grass in front of the pavilion where His Majesty and his officers were. Ye Toh Ryung was given as a subject for his composition, "A lad playing in the shade of a pine tree is questioned by an aged wayfarer."

The young man long rubbed his ink-stick on the stone, thinking very intently meanwhile, but when he began to write in the beautiful characters for which he was noted he seemed inspired, and the composition rolled forth as though he had committed it from the ancient classics. He made the boy express such sentiments of reverence to age as would have charmed the ancients, and the wisdom he put into the conversation was worthy of a king. The matter came so freely that his task was soon finished; in fact many were still wrinkling their brows in preliminary thought, while he was carefully folding up his paper, concealing his name so that the author should not be recognized till the paper had been judged on its merits. He tossed his composition into the pen, and it was at once inspected, being the first one, and remarkably quickly done. When His Majesty heard it read, and saw the perfect characters, he was astonished. Such excellence in writing, composition, and sentiment was unparalleled, and before any other papers were received it was known that none could excel this one. The writer's name was ascertained, and the King was delighted to learn that 'twas the son of his favorite officer. The young man was sent for, and received the congratulations of his King. The latter gave him the usual three glasses of wine, which he drank with modesty. He was then given a wreath of flowers from the King's own hands; the court hat was presented to him, with lateral wings, denoting the rapidity – as the flight of a bird – with which he must execute his Sovereign's commands. Richly embroidered breast-plates were given him, to be worn over the front and back of his court robes. He then went forth, riding on a gayly caparisoned horse, preceded by a band of palace musicians and attendants. Everywhere he was greeted with the cheers of the populace, as for three days he devoted his time to this public display. This duty having been fulfilled, he devotedly went to the graves of his ancestors, and prostrated himself with offerings before them, bemoaning the fact that they could not be present to rejoice in his success. He then presented himself before his King, humbly thanking him for his gracious condescension in bestowing such great honors upon one so utterly unworthy.

His Sovereign was pleased, and told the young man to strive to imitate the example of his honest father. He then asked him what position he wished. Ye Toh Ryung answered that he wished no other position than one that would enable him to be of service to his King. "The year has been one of great prosperity," said he. "The plentiful harvest will tempt corrupt men to oppress the people to their own advantage. I would like, therefore, should it meet with Your Majesty's approval, to undertake the arduous duties of *Ussa*" – government inspector.

He said this as he knew he would then be free to go in search of his wife, while he could also do much good at the same time. The King was delighted, and had his appointment – a private one naturally – made at once, giving him the peculiar seal of the office.

The new Ussa disguised himself as a beggar, putting on straw sandals, a broken hat, underneath which his hair, uncombed and without the encircling band to hold it in place, streamed out in all directions. He wore no white strip in the neck of his shabby gown, and with dirty face he certainly presented a beggarly appearance. Presenting himself at the stables outside of the city, where horses and attendants are provided for the ussas, he soon arranged matters by showing his seal, and with proper attendants started on his journey towards his former home in the southern province.

Arriving at his destination, he remained outside in a miserable hamlet while his servants went into the city to investigate the people and learn the news.

It was spring-time again. The buds were bursting, the birds were singing, and in the warm valley a band of farmers were plowing with lazy bulls, and singing, meanwhile, a grateful song in praise of their just King, their peaceful, prosperous country, and their full stomachs. As the Ussa came along in his disguise he began to jest with them, but they did not like him, and were rude in their jokes at his expense; when an old man, evidently the father, cautioned them to be careful. "Don't you see," said he, "this man's speech is only half made up of our common talk; he is playing a part. I think he must be a gentleman in disguise." The Ussa drew the old man into conversation, asking about various local events, and finally questioning him concerning the character of the Prefect. "Is he just or oppressive, drunken or sober? Does he devote himself to his duties, or give himself up to riotous living?" "Our Magistrate we know little of. His heart is as hard and unbending as the dead heart of the ancient oak. He cares not for the people; the people care not for him but to avoid him. He extorts rice and money unjustly, and spends his ill-gotten gains in riotous living. He has imprisoned and beaten the fair Chun Yang Ye because she repulsed him, and she now lies near to death in the prison, because she married and is true to the poor dog of a son of our former just magistrate."

Ye Toh Ryung was stung by these unjust remarks, filled with the deepest anxiety for his wife, and the bitterest resentment toward the brute of an official, whom, he promised himself, soon to bring to justice. As he moved away, too full of emotion for further conversation, he heard the farmers singing, "Why are some men born to riches, others born to toil, some to marry and live in peace, others too poor to possess a hut."

He walked away meditating. He had placed himself down on the people's level, and began to feel with them. Thus meditating he crossed a valley, through which a cheery mountain brook rushed merrily along. Near its banks, in front of a poor hut, sat an aged man twisting twine. Accosting him, the old man paid no attention; he repeated his salutation, when the old man, surveying him from head to foot, said: "In the government service age does not count for much, there rank is every thing; an aged man may have to bow to a younger, who is his superior officer. 'Tis not so in the country, however; here age alone is respected. Then why am I addressed thus by such a miserable looking stripling?" The young man asked his elder's pardon, and then requested him to answer a question. "I hear," says he, "that the new Magistrate is about to marry the gee sang, Chun Yang Ye; is it true?"

"Don't mention her name," said the old man, angrily. "You are not worthy to speak of her. She is dying in prison, because of her loyal devotion to the brute beast who married and deserted her."

Ye Toh Ryung could hear no more. He hurried from the place, and finding his attendants, announced his intention of going at once into the city, lest the officials should hear of his presence and prepare for him. Entering the city, he went direct to Chun Yang Ye's house. It presented little of the former pleasant appearance. Most of the rich furniture had been sold to buy comforts for the imprisoned girl. The mother, seeing him come, and supposing him to be a beggar, almost shrieked at him to get away. "Are you such a stranger, that you don't know the news? My only child is imprisoned, my husband long since dead, my property almost gone, and you come to me for alms. Begone, and learn the news of the town."

"Look! Don't you know me? I am Ye Toh Ryung, your son-in-law," he said.

"Ye Toh Ryung, and a beggar! Oh, it cannot be. Our only hope is in you, and now you are worse than helpless. My poor girl will die."

"What is the matter with her?" said he, pretending.

The woman related the history of the past months in full, not sparing the man in the least, giving him such a rating as only a woman can. He then asked to be taken to the prison, and she accompanied him with a strange feeling of gratification in her heart that after all she was right, and her daughter's confidence was ill-placed. Arriving at the prison, the mother expressed her feelings by calling to her daughter: "Here is your wonderful husband. You have been so anxious to simply see Ye Toh Ryung before you die; here he is; look at the beggar, and see what your devotion amounts to! Curse him and send him away."

The Ussa called to her, and she recognized the voice. "I surely must be dreaming again," she said, as she tried to arise; but she had the huge neck-encircling board upon her shoulders that marked the latest of her tormentor's acts of oppression, and could not get up. Stung by the pain and the calmness of her lover's voice, she sarcastically asked: "Why have you not come to me? Have you been so busy in official life? Have the rivers been so deep and rapid that you dared not cross them? Did you go so far away that it has required all this time to retrace your steps?" And then, regretting her harsh words, she said: "I cannot tell my rapture. I had expected to have to go to Heaven to meet you, and now you are here. Get them to unbind my feet, and remove this yoke from my neck, that I may come to you."

He came to the little window through which food is passed, and looked upon her. As she saw his face and garb, she moaned: "Oh, what have we done to be so afflicted? You cannot help me now; we must die. Heaven has deserted us."

"Yes," he answered; "granting I am poor, yet should we not be happy in our reunion. I have come as I promised, and we will yet be happy. Do yourself no injury, but trust to me."

She called her mother, who sneeringly inquired of what service she could be, now that the longed-for husband had returned in answer to her prayers. She paid no attention to these cruel words, but told her mother of certain jewels she had concealed in a case in her room. "Sell these," she said, "and buy some food and raiment for my husband; take him home and care for him well. Have him sleep on my couch, and do not reproach him for what he cannot help."

He went with the old woman, but soon left to confer with his attendants, who informed him that the next day was the birthday of the Magistrate, and that great preparations were being made for the celebration that would commence early. A great feast, when wine would flow like water, was to take place in the morning. The gee sang from the whole district were to perform for the assembled guests; bands of music were practising for the occasion, and the whole bade fair to be a great, riotous debauch, which would afford the Ussa just the opportunity the consummation of his plans awaited.

Early the next morning the disguised Ussa presented himself at the yamen gate, where the servants jeered at him, telling him: "This is no beggars' feast," and driving him away. He hung around the street, however, listening to the music inside, and finally he made another attempt, which was more successful than the first, for the servants, thinking him crazy, tried to restrain him, when, in the melée, he made a passage and rushed through the inner gate into the court off the reception hall. The annoyed host, red with wine, ordered him at once ejected and the gate men whipped. His order was promptly obeyed, but Ye did not leave the place. He found a break in the outside wall, through which he climbed, and again presented himself before the feasters. While the Prefect was too blind with rage to be able to speak, the stranger said: "I am a beggar, give me food and drink that I, too, may enjoy myself." The guests laughed at the man's presumption, and thinking him crazy, they urged their host to humor him for their entertainment. To which he finally consented, and, sending him some food and wine, bade him stay in a corner and eat.

To the surprise of all, the fellow seemed still discontented, for he claimed that, as the other guests each had a fair gee sang to sing a wine song while they drank, he should be treated likewise. This amused the guests immensely, and they got the master to send one. The girl went with a poor grace, however, saying: "One would think from the looks of you that your poor throat would open to the wine without a song to oil it," and sang him a song that wished him speedy death instead of long life.

After submitting to their taunts for some time, he said, "I thank you for your food and wine and the graciousness of my reception, in return for which I will amuse you by writing you some verses"; and, taking pencil and paper, he wrote: "The oil that enriches the food of the official is but the life blood of the down-trodden people, whose tears are of no more merit in the eyes of the oppressor than the drippings of a burning candle."

When this was read, a troubled look passed over all; the guests shook their heads and assured their host that it meant ill to him. And each began to make excuses, saying that one and another engagement of importance called them hence. The host laughed and bade them be seated, while he ordered attendants to take the intruder and cast him into prison for his impudence. They came to do so, but the Ussa took out his official seal, giving the preconcerted signal meanwhile, which summoned his ready followers. At sight of the King's seal terror blanched the faces of each of the half-drunken men. The wicked host tried to crawl under the house and escape, but he was at once caught and bound with chains. One of the guests in fleeing through an attic-way caught his topknot of hair in a rat-hole, and stood for some time yelling for mercy, supposing that his captors had him. It was as though an earthquake had shaken the house; all was the wildest confusion.

The Ussa put on decent clothes and gave his orders in a calm manner. He sent the Magistrate to the capital at once, and began to look further into the affairs of the office. Soon, however, he sent a chair for Chun Yang Ye, delegating his own servants, and commanding them not to explain what had happened. She supposed that the Magistrate, full of wine, had sent for her, intending to kill her, and she begged the amused servants to call her Toh Ryung to come and stay with her. They assured her that he could not come, as already he too was at the yamen, and she feared that harm had befallen him on her account.

They removed her shackles and bore her to the yamen, where the Ussa addressed her in a changed voice, commanding her to look up and answer her charges. She refused to look up or speak, feeling that the sooner death came the better. Failing in this way, he then asked her in his own voice to just glance at him. Surprised she looked up, and her dazed eyes saw her lover standing there in his proper guise, and with a delighted cry she tried to run to him, but fainted in the attempt, and was borne in his arms to a room. Just then the old woman, coming along with food, which she had brought as a last service to her daughter, heard the good news from the excited throng outside, and dashing away her dishes and their contents, she tore around for joy, crying: "What a delightful birthday surprise for a cruel magistrate!"

All the people rejoiced with the daughter, but no one seemed to think the old mother deserved such good fortune. The Ussa's conduct was approved at court. A new magistrate was appointed. The marriage was publicly solemnized at Seoul, and the Ussa was raised to a high position, in which he was just to the people, who loved him for his virtues, while the country rang with the praises of his faithful wife, who became the mother of many children.

PIGLING AND HER PROUD SISTER

Pear Blossom had been the name of a little Korean maid who was suddenly left motherless. When her father, Kang Wa, who was a magistrate high in office, married again, he took for his wife a proud widow whose daughter, born to Kang Wa, was named Violet. Mother and daughter hated housework and made Pear Blossom clean the rice, cook the food and attend to the fire in the kitchen. They were hateful in their treatment of Pear Blossom, and, besides never speaking a kind word, called her Pigling, or Little Pig, which made the girl weep often.

It did no good to complain to her father, for he was always busy. He smoked his yard-long pipe and played checkers hour by hour, apparently caring more about having his great white coat properly starched and lustred than for his daughter to be happy. His linen had to be beaten with a laundry club until it glistened like hoar frost, and, except his wide-brimmed black horsehair hat, he looked immaculately white when he went out of the house to the Government office.

Poor Pigling had to perform this task of washing, starching and glossing, in addition to the kitchen work and the rat-tat-tat of her laundry stick was often heard in the outer room till after midnight, when her heartless stepsister and mother had long been asleep.

There was to be a great festival in the city and for many days preparations were made in the house to get the father ready in his best robe and hat, and the women in their finery, to go out and see the king and the royal procession.

Poor Pigling wanted very much to have a look at the pageant, but the cruel stepmother, setting before her a huge straw bag of unhulled rice and a big cracked water jar, told her she must husk all the rice, and, drawing water from the well, fill the crock to the brim before she dared to go out on the street.

What a task to hull with her fingers three bushels of rice and fill up a leaky vessel! Pigling wept bitterly. How could it ever be done?

While she was brooding thus and opening the straw bag to begin spreading the rice out on mats, she heard a whir and a rush of wings and down came a flock of pigeons. They first lighted on her head and shoulders, and then hopping to the floor began diligently, with beak and claw, and in a few minutes the rice lay in a heap, clean, white, and glistening, while with their pink toes they pulled away the hulls and put these in a separate pile.

Then, after a great chattering and cooing, the flock was off and away.

Pigling was so amazed at this wonderful work of the birds that she scarcely knew how to be thankful enough. But, alas, there was still the cracked crock to be filled. Just as she took hold of the bucket to begin there crawled out of the fire hole a sooty black imp, named Tokgabi.

"Don't cry," he squeaked out. "I'll mend the broken part and fill the big jar for you." Forthwith, he stopped up the crack with clay, and pouring a dozen buckets of water from the well into the crock, it was filled to brimming and the water spilled over on all sides. Then Tokgabi the imp bowed and crawled into the flues again, before the astonished girl could thank her helper.

So Pigling had time to dress in her plain but clean clothes that were snow-white. She went off and saw the royal banners and the king's grand procession of thousands of loyal men.

The next time, the stepmother and her favorite daughter planned a picnic on the mountain. So the refreshments were prepared and Pigling had to work hard in starching the dresses to be worn – jackets, long skirts, belts, sashes, and what not, until she nearly dropped with fatigue. Yet instead of thanking and cheering her, the cruel stepmother told Pigling she must not go out until she had hoed all the weeds out of the garden and pulled up all the grass between the stones of the walk.

Again the poor girl's face was wet with tears. She was left at home alone, while the others went off in fine clothes, with plenty to eat and drink, for a day of merrymaking.

While weeping thus, a huge black cow came along and out of its great liquid eyes seemed to beam compassion upon the kitchen slave. Then, in ten mouthfuls, the animal ate up the weeds, and, between its hoof and lips, soon made an end of the grass in the stone pathway.

With her tears dried Pigling followed this wonderful brute out over the meadows into the woods, where she found the most delicious fruit her eyes ever rested upon. She tasted and enjoyed, feasting to the full and then returned home.

When the jealous stepsister heard of the astonishing doings of the black cow, she determined to enjoy a feast in the forest also. So on the next gala-day she stayed home and let the kitchen drudge go to see the royal parade. Pigling could not understand why she was excused, even for a few hours, from the pots and kettles, but she was still more surprised by the gift from her stepmother of a rope of cash to spend for dainties. Gratefully thanking the woman, she put on her best clothes and was soon on the main street of the city enjoying the gay sights and looking at the happy people. There were tight rope dancing, music with drum and flute by bands of strolling players, tricks by conjurers and mountebanks, with mimicking and castanets, posturing by the singing girls and fun of all sorts. Boys peddling honey candy, barley sugar and sweetmeats were out by the dozen. At the eating-house, Pigling had a good dinner of fried fish, boiled rice with red peppers, turnips, dried persimmons, roasted chestnuts and candied orange, and felt as happy as a queen.

The selfish stepsister had stayed home, not to relieve Pigling of work, but to see the wonderful cow. So, when the black animal appeared and found its friend gone and with nothing to do, it went off into the forest.

The stepsister at once followed in the tracks of the cow but the animal took it into its head to go very fast, and into unpleasant places. Soon the girl found herself in a swamp, wet, miry and full of brambles. Still hoping for wonderful fruit, she kept on until she was tired out and the cow was no longer to be seen. Then, muddy and bedraggled, she tried to go back, but the thorny bushes tore her clothes, spoiled her hands and so scratched her face that when at last, nearly dead, she got home, she was in rags and her beauty was gone.

But Pigling, rosy and round, looked so lovely that a young man from the south, of good family and at that time visiting the capital, was struck with her beauty. And as he wanted a wife, he immediately sought to find out where she lived. Then he secured a go-between who visited both families and made all the arrangements for the betrothal and marriage.

Grand was the wedding. The groom, Su-wen, was dressed in white and black silk robes, with a rich horsehair cap and headdress denoting his rank as a Yang-ban, or gentleman. On his breast, crossed by a silver-studded girdle, was a golden square embroidered with flying cranes rising above the waves – the symbols of civil office. He was tall, handsome, richly cultured, and quite famous as a writer of verses, besides being well read in the classics.

Charming, indeed, looked Pear Blossom as she was now called again, in her robe of brocade, and long undersleeves which extended from her inner dress of snow-white silk. Dainty were her red kid shoes curved upward at the toes. With a baldric of open-worked silver, a high-waisted long skirt, with several linings of her inner silk robes showing prettily at the neck, and the silver bridal ring on her finger, she looked as lovely as a princess.

Besides her bridal dower, her father asked Pear Blossom what she preferred as a special present. When she told him, he laughed heartily. Nevertheless he fulfilled her wishes and to this day, in the boudoir of Pear Blossom, now Mrs. Su-wen, there stands an earthen figure of a black cow moulded and baked from the clay of her home province, while the pigeons like to hover about a pear tree that bursts into bloom every spring time and sheds on the ground a snowy shower of fragrant petals.

POWERFUL SPIRITS & MYSTICAL REALMS

Magical and mystical elements of belief are found in much of the pre-Goryeo oral literature. These beliefs reflect the influence of shamanism (musok) on Korean people's sensemaking. While many sects of Buddhism maintain a belief in reincarnation (after but also within one's actual lifetime), Korean folklore is full of ghost stories. Ghosts reflect a disorder in the cosmological order, for instance when someone has met with foul play, or a young woman has died without having children.

Similar to how the animists believed that all things in nature contained spirits or spiritual power (e.g. mountaintops, wells – even outhouses could contain a ghost), people could shapeshift, taking on animal forms and then changing back into human figures. In addition, people believed that dreams could portend the future, from day-to-day life situations (e.g. coming into a sum of money, or having an argument with a friend). Even in today's techno-scientifically advanced Korea, people still affirm the power of dreams and everyday portents. Professional fortune-tellers and astrologers practice their craft, for example in sidewalk offices and also via social media. At the elite level, politicians and industrial leaders have been known to consult with professional shamans, though not without some controversy.

THE STORY OF CHANG TO-RYONG

Taoism has been one of the great religions of Korea. Its main thought is expressed in the phrase *su-sim yon-song*, "to correct the mind and reform the nature"; while Buddhism's is *myong-sim kyon-song*, "to enlighten the heart and see the soul."

The desire of all Taoists is "eternal life," *chang-saing pul-sa*; that of the Buddhists, to rid oneself of fleshly being. In the Taoist world of the genii, there are three great divisions: the upper genii, who live with God; the midway genii, who have to do with the world of angels and spirits; and the lower genii, who rule in sacred places on the earth, among the hills, just as we find in the story of Chang To-ryong.

* * *

In the days of King Chung-jong (AD 1507–1526) there lived a beggar in Seoul, whose face was extremely ugly and always dirty. He was forty years of age or so, but still wore his hair down his back like an unmarried boy. He carried a bag over his shoulder, and went about the streets begging. During the day he went from one part of the city to the other, visiting each section, and when night came on he would huddle up beside some one's gate and go to sleep. He was frequently seen in Chong-no (Bell Street) in company with the servants and underlings of the rich. They were great friends, he and they, joking and bantering as they met. He used to say that his name was Chang, and so they called him Chang To-ryong, To-ryong meaning an unmarried boy, son of the gentry. At that time the magician Chon U-chi, who was far-famed for his pride and arrogance, whenever he met Chang, in passing along the street, would dismount and prostrate himself most humbly. Not only did he bow, but he seemed to regard Chang with the greatest of fear, so that he dared not look him in the face. Chang, sometimes, without even inclining his head, would say, "Well, how goes it with you, eh?" Chon, with his hands in his sleeves, most respectfully would reply, "Very well, sir, thank you, very well." He had fear written on all his features when he faced Chang.

Sometimes, too, when Chon would bow, Chang would refuse to notice him at all, and go by without a word. Those who saw it were astonished, and asked Chon the reason. Chon said in reply, "There are only three spirit-men at present in Cho-sen, of whom the greatest is Chang To-ryong; the second is Cheung Puk-chang; and the third is Yun Se-pyong. People of the world do not know it, but I do. Such being the case, should I not bow before him and show him reverence?"

Those who heard this explanation, knowing that Chon himself was a strange being, paid no attention to it.

At that time in Seoul there was a certain literary undergraduate in office whose house joined hard on the street. This man used to see Chang frequently going about begging, and one day he called him and asked who he was, and why he begged. Chang made answer, "I was originally of a cultured family of Chulla Province, but my parents died of typhus fever, and I had no brothers or relations left to share my lot. I alone remained of all my clan, and having no home of my own I have gone about begging, and have at last reached Seoul. As I am not skilled in any handicraft, and do not know Chinese letters, what else can I do?" The undergraduate, hearing that he was a scholar, felt very sorry for him, gave him food and drink, and refreshed him.

From this time on, whenever there was any special celebration at his home, he used to call Chang in and have him share it.

On a certain day when the master was on his way to office, he saw a dead body being carried on a stretcher off toward the Water Gate. Looking at it closely from the horse on which he rode, he recognized it as the corpse of Chang To-ryong. He felt so sad that he turned back to his house and cried over it, saying, "There are lots of miserable people on earth, but who ever saw one as miserable as poor Chang? As I reckon the time over on my fingers, he has been begging in Bell Street for fifteen years, and now he passes out of the city a dead body."

Twenty years and more afterwards the master had to make a journey through South Chulla Province. As he was passing Chi-i Mountain, he lost his way and got into a maze among the hills. The day began to wane, and he could neither return nor go forward. He saw a narrow footpath, such as woodmen take, and turned into it to see if it led to any habitation. As he went along there were rocks and deep ravines. Little by little, as he advanced farther, the scene changed and seemed to become strangely transfigured. The farther he went the more wonderful it became. After he had gone some miles he discovered himself to be in another world entirely, no longer a world of earth and dust. He saw some one coming toward him dressed in ethereal green, mounted and carrying a shade, with servants accompanying. He seemed to sweep toward him with swiftness and without effort. He thought to himself, "Here is some high lord or other coming to meet me, but," he added, "how among these deeps and solitudes could a gentleman come riding so?" He led his horse aside and tried to withdraw into one of the groves by the side of the way, but before he could think to turn the man had reached him. The mysterious stranger lifted his two hands in salutation and inquired respectfully as to how he had been all this time. The master was speechless, and so astonished that he could make no reply. But the stranger smilingly said, "My house is quite near here; come with me and rest."

He turned, and leading the way seemed to glide and not to walk, while the master followed. At last they reached the place indicated. He suddenly saw before him great palace halls filling whole squares of space. Beautiful buildings they were, richly ornamented. Before the door attendants in official robes awaited them. They bowed to the master and led him into the hall. After passing a number of gorgeous, palace-like rooms, he arrived at a special one and ascended to the upper storey, where he met a very wonderful person. He was dressed in shining garments, and the servants that waited on him were exceedingly fair. There were, too, children about, so exquisitely beautiful that it seemed none other than a celestial palace. The master, alarmed at finding himself in such a place, hurried forward and made a low obeisance, not daring to lift his eyes. But the host smiled upon him, raised his hands and asked, "Do you not know me? Look now." Lifting his eyes, he then saw that it was the same person who had come riding out to meet him, but he could not tell who he was. "I see you," said he, "but as to who you are I cannot tell."

The kingly host then said, "I am Chang To-ryong. Do you not know me?" Then as the master looked more closely at him he could see the same features. The outlines of the face were there, but all the imperfections had gone, and only beauty remained. So wonderful was it that he was quite overcome.

A great feast was prepared, and the honoured guest was entertained. Such food, too, was placed before him as was never seen on earth. Angelic beings played on beautiful instruments and danced as no mortal eye ever looked upon. Their faces, too, were like pearls and precious stones.

Chang To-ryong said to his guest, "There are four famous mountains in Korea in which the genii reside. This hill is one. In days gone by, for a fault of mine, I was exiled to earth, and in the time of my exile you treated me with marked kindness, a favour that I have never forgotten. When you saw my dead body your pity went out to me; this, too, I remember. I was not dead then, it was simply that my days of exile were ended and I was returning home. I knew that you were passing this hill, and I desired to meet you and to thank you for all your kindness. Your treatment of me in another world is sufficient to bring about our meeting in this one." And so they met and feasted in joy and great delight.

When night came he was escorted to a special pavilion, where he was to sleep. The windows were made of jade and precious stones, and soft lights came streaming through them, so that there was no night. "My body was so rested and my soul so refreshed," said he, "that I felt no need of sleep."

When the day dawned a new feast was spread, and then farewells were spoken. Chang said, "This is not a place for you to stay long in; you must go. The ways differ of we genii and you men of the world. It will be difficult for us ever to meet again. Take good care of yourself and go in peace." He then called a servant to accompany him and show the way. The master made a low bow and withdrew. When he had gone but a short distance he suddenly found himself in the old world with its dusty accompaniments. The path by which he came out was not the way by which he had entered. In order to mark the entrance he planted a stake, and then the servant withdrew and disappeared.

The year following the master went again and tried to find the citadel of the genii, but there were only mountain peaks and impassable ravines, and where it was he never could discover.

As the years went by the master seemed to grow younger in spirit, and at last at the age of ninety he passed away without suffering. "When Chang was here on earth and I saw him for fifteen years," said the master, "I remember but one peculiarity about him, namely, that his face never grew older nor did his dirty clothing ever wear out. He never changed his garb, and yet it never varied in appearance in all the fifteen years. This alone would have marked him as a strange being, but our fleshly eyes did not recognize it."

TEN THOUSAND DEVILS

Han Chun-kyom was the son of a provincial secretary. He matriculated in the year 1579 and graduated in 1586. He received the last wishes of King Son-jo, and sat by his side taking notes for seven hours. From 1608 to 1623 he was *generalissimo* of the army, and later was raised to the rank of Prince.

* * *

A certain Prince Han of Choong-chong Province had a distant relative who was an uncouth countryman living in extreme poverty. This relative came to visit him from time to time. Han pitied his cold and hungry condition, gave him clothes to wear and shared his food, urging him to stay and to prolong his visit often into several months. He felt sorry for him, but disliked his uncouthness and stupidity.

On one of these visits the poor relation suddenly announced his intention to return home, although the New Year's season was just at hand. Han urged him to remain, saying, "It would be better for you to be comfortably housed at my home, eating cake and soup and enjoying quiet sleep rather than riding through wind and weather at this season of the year."

He said at first that he would have to go, until his host so insistently urged on him to stay that at last he yielded and gave consent. At New Year's Eve he remarked to Prince Han, "I am possessor of a peculiar kind of magic, by which I have under my control all manner of evil genii, and New Year is the season at which I call them up, run over their names, and inspect them. If I did not do so I should lose control altogether, and there would follow no end of trouble among mortals. It is a matter of no small moment, and that is why I wished to go. Since, however, you have detained me, I shall have to call them up in your Excellency's house and look them over. I hope you will not object."

Han was greatly astonished and alarmed, but gave his consent. The poor relation went on to say further, "This is an extremely important matter, and I would like to have for it your central guest hall."

Han consented to this also, so that night they washed the floors and scoured them clean. The relation also sat himself with all dignity facing the south, while Prince Han took up his station on the outside prepared to spy. Soon he saw a startling variety of demons crushing in at the door, horrible in appearance and awesome of manner. They lined up one after another, and still another, and another, till they filled the entire court, each bowing as he came before the master, who, at this point, drew

POWERFUL SPIRITS & MYSTICAL REALMS

out a book, opened it before him, and began calling off the names. Demon guards who stood by the threshold repeated the call and checked off the names just as they do in a government yamen. From the second watch it went on till the fifth of the morning. Han remarked, "It was indeed no lie when he told me 'ten thousand devils.'"

One late-comer arrived after the marking was over, and still another came climbing over the wall. The man ordered them to be arrested, and inquiry made of them under the paddle. The late arrival said, "I really have had a hard time of it of late to live, and so was obliged, in order to find anything, to inject smallpox into the home of a scholar who lives in Yong-nam. It is a long way off, and so I have arrived too late for the roll-call, a serious fault indeed, I confess."

The one who climbed the wall, said, "I, too, have known want and hunger, and so had to insert a little typhus into the family of a gentleman who lives in Kyong-keui, but hearing that roll-call was due I came helter-skelter, fearing lest I should arrive too late, and so climbed the wall, which was indeed a sin."

The man then, in a loud voice, rated them soundly, saying, "These devils have disobeyed my orders, caused disease and sinned grievously. Worse than everything, they have climbed the wall of a high official's house." He ordered a hundred blows to be given them with the paddle, the cangue to be put on, and to have them locked fast in prison. Then, calling the others to him, he said, "Do not spread disease! Do you understand?" Three times he ordered it and five times he repeated it. Then they were all dismissed. The crowd of devils lined off before him, taking their departure and crushing out through the gate with no end of noise and confusion. After a long time they had all disappeared.

Prince Han, looking on during this time, saw the man now seated alone in the hall. It was quiet, and all had vanished. The cocks crew and morning came. Han was astonished above measure, and asked as to the law that governed such work as this. The poor relation said in reply, "When I was young I studied in a monastery in the mountains. In that monastery was an old priest who had a most peculiar countenance. A man feeble and ready to die, he seemed. All the priests made sport of him and treated him with contempt. I alone had pity on his age, and often gave him of my food and always treated him kindly. One evening, when the moon was bright, the old priest said to me, 'There is a cave behind this monastery from which a beautiful view may be had; will you not come with me and share it?'

"I went with him, and when we crossed the ridge of the hills into the stillness of the night he drew a book from his breast and gave it to me, saying, 'I, who am old and ready to die, have here a great secret, which I have long wished to pass on to some one worthy. I have travelled over the wide length of Korea, and have never found the man till now I meet you, and my heart is satisfied, so please receive it.'

"I opened the book and found it a catalogue list of devils, with magic writing interspersed, and an explanation of the laws that govern the spirit world. The old priest wrote out one magic recipe, and having set fire to it countless devils at once assembled, at which I was greatly alarmed. He then sat with me and called over the names one after the other, and said to the devils, 'I am an old man now, am going away, and so am about to put you under the care of this young man; obey him and all will be well.'

"I already had the book, and so called them to me, read out the new orders, and dismissed them.

"The old priest and I returned to the Temple and went to sleep. I awoke early next morning and went to call on him, but he was gone. Thus I came into possession of the magic art, and have possessed it for a score of years and more. What the world knows nothing of I have thus made known to your Excellency."

Han was astonished beyond measure, and asked, "May I not also come into possession of this wonderful gift?"

The man replied, "Your Excellency has great ability, and can do wonderful things; but the possessor of this craft must be one poor and despised, and of no account. For you, a minister, it would never do."

The next day he left suddenly, and returned no more. Han sent a servant with a message to him. The servant, with great difficulty, at last found him alone among a thousand mountain peaks, living in a little straw hut no bigger than a cockle shell. No neighbours were there, nor any one beside. He called him, but he refused to come. He sent another messenger to invite him, but he had moved away and no trace of him was left.

Prince Han's children had heard this story from himself, and I, the writer, received it from them.

THE HOME OF THE FAIRIES

In the days of King In-jo (1623–1649) there was a student of Confucius who lived in Ka-pyong. He was still a young man and unmarried. His education had not been extensive, for he had read only a little in the way of history and literature. For some reason or other he left his home and went into Kang-won Province. Travelling on horseback, and with a servant, he reached a mountain, where he was overtaken by rain that wet him through. Mysteriously, from some unknown cause, his servant suddenly died, and the man, in fear and distress, drew the body to the side of the hill, where he left it and went on his way weeping. When he had gone but a short distance, the horse he rode fell under him and died also. Such was his plight: his servant dead, his horse dead, rain falling fast, and the road an unknown one. He did not know what to do or where to go, and reduced thus to walking, he broke down and cried. At this point there met him an old man with very wonderful eyes, and hair as white as snow. He asked the young man why he wept, and the reply was that his servant was dead, his horse was dead, that it was raining, and that he did not know the way. The patriarch, on hearing this, took pity on him, and lifting his staff, pointed, saying, "There is a house yonder, just beyond those pines, follow that stream and it will bring you to where there are people."

The young man looked as directed, and a *li* or so beyond he saw a clump of trees. He bowed, thanked the stranger, and started on his way. When he had gone a few paces he looked back, but the friend had disappeared. Greatly wondering, he went on toward the place indicated, and as he drew near he saw a grove of pines, huge trees they were, a whole forest of them. Bamboos appeared, too, in countless numbers, with a wide stream of water flowing by. Underneath the water there seemed to be a marble flooring like a great pavement, white and pure. As he went along he saw that the water was all of an even depth, such as one could cross easily. A mile or so farther on he saw a beautifully decorated house. The pillars and entrance approaches were perfect in form. He continued his way, wet as he was, carrying his thorn staff, and entered the gate and sat down to rest. It was paved, too, with marble, and smooth as polished glass. There were no chinks or creases in it, all was of one perfect surface. In the room was a marble table, and on it a copy of the Book of Changes; there was also a brazier of jade just in front. Incense was burning in it, and the fragrance filled the room. Beside these, nothing else was visible. The rain had ceased and all was quiet and clear, with no wind nor anything to disturb. The world of confusion seemed to have receded from him.

While he sat there, looking in astonishment, he suddenly heard the sound of footfalls from the rear of the building. Startled by it, he turned to see, when an old man appeared. He looked as though he might equal the turtle or the crane as to age, and was very dignified. He wore a green dress and carried a jade staff of nine sections. The appearance of the old man was such as to stun any inhabitant of the earth. He recognized him as the master of the place, and so he went forward and made a low obeisance.

The old man received him kindly, and said, "I am the master and have long waited for you." He took him by the hand and led him away. As they went along, the hills grew more and more enchanting, while the soft breezes and the light touched him with mystifying favour. Suddenly, as he looked the man was gone, so he went on by himself, and arrived soon at another palace built likewise of precious stones. It was a great hall, stretching on into the distance as far as the eye could see.

The young man had seen the Royal Palace frequently when in Seoul attending examinations, but compared with this, the Royal Palace was as a mud hut thatched with straw.

As he reached the gate a man in ceremonial robes received him and led him in. He passed two or three pavilions, and at last reached a special one and went up to the upper storey. There, reclining at a table, he saw the ancient sage whom he had met before. Again he bowed.

This young man, brought up poorly in the country, was never accustomed to seeing or dealing with the great. In fear, he did not dare to lift his eyes. The ancient master, however, again welcomed him and asked him to be seated, saying, "This is not the dusty world that you are accustomed to, but the abode of the genii. I knew you were coming, and so was waiting to receive you." He turned and called, saying, "Bring something for the guest to eat."

In a little a servant brought a richly laden table. It was such fare as was never seen on earth, and there was abundance of it. The young man, hungry as he was, ate heartily of these strange viands. Then the dishes were carried away and the old man said, "I have a daughter who has arrived at a marriageable age, and I have been trying to find a son-in-law, but as yet have not succeeded. Your coming accords with this need. Live here, then, and become my son-in-law." The young man, not knowing what to think, bowed and was silent. Then the host turned and gave an order, saying, "Call in the children."

Two boys about twelve or thirteen years of age came running in and sat down beside him. Their faces were so beautifully white they seemed like jewels. The master pointed to them and said to the guest, "These are my sons," and to the sons he said, "This young man is he whom I have chosen for my son-in-law; when should we have the wedding? Choose you a lucky day and let me know."

The two boys reckoned over the days on their fingers, and then together said, "The day after to-morrow is a lucky day."

The old man, turning to the stranger, said, "That decides as to the wedding, and now you must wait in the guest-chamber till the time arrives." He then gave a command to call So and So. In a little an official of the genii came forward, dressed in light and airy garments. His appearance and expression were very beautiful, a man, he seemed, of glad and happy mien.

The master said, "Show this young man the way to his apartments and treat him well till the time of the wedding."

The official then led the way, and the young man bowed as he left the room. When he had passed outside the gate, a red sedan chair was in waiting for him. He was asked to mount. Eight bearers bore him smoothly along. A mile or so distant they reached another palace, equally wonderful, with no speck or flaw of any kind to mar its beauty. In graceful groves of flowers and trees he descended to enter his pavilion. Beautiful garments were taken from jewelled boxes, and a perfumed bath was given him and a change made. Thus he laid aside his weather-beaten clothes and donned the vestments of the genii. The official remained as company for him till the appointed time.

When that day arrived other beautiful robes were brought, and again he bathed and changed. When he was dressed, he mounted the palanquin and rode to the Palace of the master, twenty or more officials accompanying. On arrival, a guide directed them to the special Palace Beautiful. Here he saw preparations for the wedding, and here he made his bow. This finished he moved as directed, further in. The tinkling sound of jade bells and the breath of sweet perfumes filled the air. Thus he made his entry into the inner quarters.

Many beautiful women were in waiting, all gorgeously apparelled, like the women of the gods. Among these he imagined that he would meet the master's daughter. In a little, accompanied by a host of others, she came, shining in jewels and beautiful clothing so that she lighted up the Palace. He took his stand before her, though her face was hidden from him by a fan of pearls. When he saw her at last, so beautiful was she that his eyes were dazzled. The other women, compared with her, were as the magpie to the phœnix. So bewildered was he that he dared not look up. The friend accompanying assisted him to bow and to go through the necessary forms. The ceremony was much the same as that observed among men. When it was over the young man went back to his bridegroom's chamber. There the embroidered curtains, the golden screens, the silken clothing, the jewelled floor, were such as no men of earth ever see.

On the second day his mother-in-law called him to her. Her age would be about thirty, and her face was like a freshly-blown lotus flower. Here a great feast was spread, with many guests invited. The accompaniments thereof in the way of music were sweeter than mortals ever dreamed of. When the feast was over, the women caught up their skirts, and, lifting their sleeves, danced together and sang in sweet accord. The sound of their singing caused even the clouds to stop and listen. When the day was over, and all had well dined, the feast broke up.

A young man, brought up in a country hut, had all of a sudden met the chief of the genii, and had become a sharer in his glory and the accompaniments of his life. His mind was dazed and his thoughts overcame him. Doubts were mixed with fears. He knew not what to do.

A sharer in the joys of the fairies he had actually become, and a year or so passed in such delight as no words can ever describe.

One day his wife said to him, "Would you like to enter into the inner enclosure and see as the fairies see?"

He replied, "Gladly would I."

She then led him into a special park where there were lovely walks, surrounded by green hills. As they advanced there were charming views, with springs of water and sparkling cascades. The scene grew gradually more entrancing, with jewelled flowers and scintillating spray, lovely birds and animals disporting themselves. A man once entering here would never again think of earth as a place to return to.

After seeing this he ascended the highest peak of all, which was like a tower of many stories. Before him lay a wide stretch of sea, with islands of the blessed standing out of the water, and long stretches of pleasant land in view. His wife showed them all to him, pointing out this and that. They seemed filled with golden palaces and surrounded with a halo of light. They were peopled with happy souls, some riding on cranes, some on the phœnix, some on the unicorn; some were sitting on the clouds, some sailing by on the wind, some walking on the air, some gliding gently up the streams, some descending from above, some ascending, some moving west, some north, some gathering in groups. Flutes and harps sounded sweetly. So many and so startling were the things seen that he could never tell the tale of them. After the day had passed they returned.

Thus was their joy unbroken, and when two years had gone by she bore him two sons.

Time moved on, when one day, unexpectedly, as he was seated with his wife, he began to cry and tears soiled his face. She asked in amazement for the cause of it. "I was thinking," said he, "of how a plain countryman living in poverty had thus become the son-in-law of the king of the genii. But in my home is my poor old mother, whom I have not seen for these years; I would so like to see her that my tears flow."

The wife laughed, and said, "Would you really like to see her? Then go, but do not cry." She told her father that her husband would like to go and see his mother. The master called him and gave his permission. The son thought, of course, that he would call many servants and send him in state, but not so. His wife gave him one little bundle and that was all, so he said good-bye to his father-in-law, whose parting word was, "Go now and see your mother, and in a little I shall call for you again."

He sent with him one servant, and so he passed out through the main gateway. There he saw a poor thin horse with a worn rag of a saddle on his back. He looked carefully and found that they were the dead horse and the dead servant, whom he had lost, restored to him. He gave a start, and asked, "How did you come here?"

The servant answered, "I was coming with you on the road when some one caught me away and brought me here. I did not know the reason, but I have been here for a long time."

The man, in great fear, fastened on his bundle and started on his journey. The genie servant brought up the rear, but after a short distance the world of wonder had become transformed into the old weary world again. Here it was with its fogs, and thorn, and precipice. He looked off toward the world of the genii, and it was but a dream. So overcome was he by his feelings that he broke down and cried.

The genie servant said to him when he saw him weeping, "You have been for several years in the abode of the immortals, but you have not yet attained thereto, for you have not yet forgotten the seven things of earth: anger, sorrow, fear, ambition, hate and selfishness. If you once get rid of these there will be no tears for you." On hearing this he stopped his crying, wiped his cheeks, and asked pardon.

When he had gone a mile farther he found himself on the main road. The servant said to him, "You know the way from this point on, so I shall go back," and thus at last the young man reached his home.

He found there an exorcising ceremony in progress. Witches and spirit worshippers had been called and were saying their prayers. The family, seeing the young man come home thus, were all aghast. "It is his ghost," said they. However, they saw in a little that it was really he himself. The mother asked why he had not come home in all that time. She being a very violent woman in disposition, he did not dare to tell her the truth, so he made up something else. The day of his return was the anniversary of his supposed death, and so they had called the witches for a prayer ceremony. Here he opened the bundle that his wife had given him and found four suits of clothes, one for each season.

In about a year after his return home the mother, seeing him alone, made application for the daughter of one of the village *literati*. The man, being timid by nature and afraid of offending his mother, did not dare to refuse, and was therefore married; but there was no joy in it, and the two never looked at each other.

The young man had a friend whom he had known intimately from childhood. After his return the friend came to see him frequently, and they used to spend the nights talking together. In their talks the friend inquired why in all these years he had never come home. The young man then told him what had befallen him in the land of the genii, and how he had been there and had been married. The friend looked at him in wonder, for he seemed just as he had remembered him except in the matter of clothing. This he found on examination was of very strange material, neither grass cloth, silk nor cotton, but different from them all, and yet warm and comfortable. When spring came the spring clothes sufficed, when summer came those for summer, and for autumn and winter each special suit. They were never washed, and yet never became soiled; they never wore out, and always looked fresh and new. The friend was greatly astonished.

Some three years passed when one day there came once more a servant from the master of the genii, bringing his two sons. There were also letters, saying, "Next year the place where you dwell will be destroyed and all the people will become 'fish and meat' for the enemy, therefore follow this messenger and come, all of you."

He told his friend of this and showed him his two sons. The friend, when he saw these children that looked like silk and jade, confessed the matter to the mother also. She, too, gladly agreed, and so they sold out and had a great feast for all the people of the town, and then bade farewell. This was the year 1635. They left and were never heard of again.

The year following was the Manchu invasion, when the village where the young man had lived was all destroyed. To this day young and old in Ka-pyong tell this story.

THE TEMPLE TO THE GOD OF WAR

Yi Hang-bok. – When he was a child a blind fortune-teller came and cast his future, saying, "This boy will be very great indeed."

At seven years of age his father gave him for subject to write a verse on "The Harp and the Sword," and he wrote –

> *"The Sword pertains to the Hand of the Warrior*
> *And the Harp to the Music of the Ancients."*

At eight he took the subject of the "Willow before the Door," and wrote –

> *"The east wind brushes the brow of the cliff*
> *And the willow on the edge nods fresh and green."*

On seeing a picture of a great banquet among the fierce Turks of Central Asia, he wrote thus –

> *"The hunt is off in the wild dark hills,*
> *And the moon is cold and gray,*
> *While the tramping feet of a thousand horse*
> *Ring on the frosty way.*
> *In the tents of the Turk the music thrills*
> *And the wine-cups chink for joy,*
> *'Mid the noise of the dancer's savage tread*
> *And the lilt of the wild hautboy."*

At twelve years of age he was proud, we are told, and haughty. He dressed well, and was envied by the poorer lads of the place, and once he took off his coat and gave it to a boy who looked with envy on him. He gave his shoes as well, and came back barefoot. His mother, wishing to know his mind in the matter, pretended to reprimand him, but he replied, saying, "Mother, when others wanted it so, how could I refuse giving?" His mother pondered these things in her heart.

When he was fifteen he was strong and well-built, and liked vigorous exercise, so that he was a noted wrestler and skilful at shuttlecock. His mother, however, frowned upon these things, saying that they were not dignified, so that he gave them up and confined his attention to literary studies, graduating at twenty-five years of age.

In 1592, during the Japanese War, when the King escaped to Eui-ju, Yi Hang-bok went with him in his flight, and there he met the Chinese (Ming) representative, who said in surprise to his Majesty, "Do you mean to tell me that you have men in Cho-sen like Yi Hang-bok?" Yang Ho, the general of the rescuing forces, also continually referred to him for advice and counsel. He lived to see the troubles in the reign of the wicked Kwang-hai, and at last went into exile to Puk-chong. When he crossed the Iron Pass near Wonsan, he wrote –

"From the giddy height of the Iron Peak,
I call on the passing cloud,
To take up a lonely exile's tears
In the folds of its feathery shroud,
And drop them as rain on the Palace Gates,
On the King, and his shameless crowd."

The Story

During the Japanese War in the reign of Son-jo, the Mings sent a great army that came east, drove out the enemy and restored peace. At that time the general of the Mings informed his Korean Majesty that the victory was due to the help of Kwan, the God of War. "This being the case," said he, "you ought not to continue without temples in which to express your gratitude to him." So they built him houses of worship and offered him sacrifice. The Temples built were one to the south and one to the east of the city. In examining sites for these they could not agree on the one to the south. Some wanted it nearer the wall and some farther away. At that time an official, called Yi Hang-bok, was in charge of the conference. On a certain day when Yi was at home a military officer called and wished to see him. Ordering him in he found him a great strapping fellow, splendidly built. His request was that Yi should send out all his retainers till he talked to him privately. They were sent out, and then the stranger gave his message. After he had finished, he said good-bye and left.

Yi had at that time an old friend stopping with him. The friend went out with the servants when they were asked to leave, and now he came back again. When he came in he noticed that the face of the master had a very peculiar expression, and he asked him the reason of it. Yi made no reply at first, but later told his friend that a very extraordinary thing had happened. The military man who had come and called was none other than a messenger of the God of War. His coming, too, was on account of their not yet having decided in regard to the site for the Temple. "He came," said Yi, "to show me where it ought to be. He urged that it was not a matter for time only, but for the eternities to come. If we do not get it right the God of War will find no peace. I told him in reply that I would do my best. Was this not strange?"

The friend who heard this was greatly exercised, but Yi warned him not to repeat it to any one. Yi used all his efforts, and at last the building was placed on the approved site, where it now stands.

THE KING OF YOM-NA (HELL)

Pak Chom was one of the Royal Censors, and died in the Japanese War of 1592.

The Story

In Yon-nan County, Whang-hai Province, there was a certain literary graduate whose name I have forgotten. He fell ill one day and remained in his room, leaning helplessly against his arm-rest. Suddenly several spirit soldiers appeared to him, saying, "The Governor of the lower hell has ordered your arrest," so they bound him with a chain about his neck, and led him away. They journeyed for many hundreds of miles, and at last reached a place that had a very high wall. The spirits then took him within the walls and went on for a long distance.

There was within this enclosure a great structure whose height reached to heaven. They arrived at the gate, and the spirits who had him in hand led him in, and when they entered the inner courtyard they laid him down on his face.

Glancing up he saw what looked like a king seated on a throne; grouped about him on each side were attendant officers. There were also scores of secretaries and soldiers going and coming on pressing errands. The King's appearance was most terrible, and his commands such as to fill one with awe. The graduate felt the perspiration break out on his back, and he dared not look up. In a little a secretary came forward, stood in front of the raised dais to transmit commands, and the King asked, "Where do you come from? What is your name? How old are you? What do you do for a living? Tell me the truth now, and no dissembling."

The scholar, frightened to death, replied, "My clan name is So-and-so, and my given name is So-and-so. I am so old, and I have lived for several generations at Yon-nan, Whanghai Province. I am stupid and ill-equipped by nature, so have not done anything special. I have heard all my life that if you say your beads with love and pity in your heart you will escape hell, and so have given my time to calling on the Buddha, and dispensing alms."

The secretary, hearing this, went at once and reported it to the King. After some time he came back with a message, saying, "Come up closer to the steps, for you are not the person intended. It happens that you bear the same name and you have thus been wrongly arrested. You may go now."

The scholar joined his hands and made a deep bow. Again the secretary transmitted a message from the King, saying, "My house, when on earth, was in such a place in such and such a ward of Seoul. When you go back I want to send a message by you. My coming here is long, and the outer coat I wear is worn to shreds. Ask my people to send me a new outer coat. If you do so I shall be greatly obliged, so see that you do not forget."

The scholar said, "Your Majesty's message given me thus direct I shall pass on without fail, but the ways of the two worlds, the dark world and the light, are so different that when I give the message the hearers will say I am talking nonsense. True, I'll give it just as you have commanded, but what about it if they refuse to listen? I ought to have some evidence as proof to help me out."

The King made answer, "Your words are true, very true. This will help you: When I was on earth," said he, "one of my head buttons that I wore had a broken edge, and I hid it in the third volume of the Book of History. I alone know of it, no one else in the world. If you give this as a proof they will listen."

The scholar replied, "That will be satisfactory, but again, how shall I do in case they make the new coat?"

The reply was, "Prepare a sacrifice, offer the coat by fire, and it will reach me."

He then bade good-bye, and the King sent with him two soldier guards. He asked the soldiers, as they came out, who the one seated on the throne was. "He is the King of Hades," said they; "his surname is Pak and his given name is Oo."

They arrived at the bank of a river, and the two soldiers pushed him into the water. He awoke with a start, and found that he had been dead for three days.

When he recovered from his sickness he came up to Seoul, searched out the house indicated, and made careful inquiry as to the name, finding that it was no other than Pak Oo. Pak Oo had two sons, who at that time had graduated and were holding office. The graduate wanted to see the sons of this King of Hades, but the gatekeeper would not let him in. Therefore he stood before the red gate waiting helplessly till the sun went down. Then came out from the inner quarters of the house an old servant, to whom he earnestly made petition that he might see the master. On being thus requested, the servant returned and reported it to the master, who, a little later, ordered him in. On entering, he saw two gentlemen who seemed to be chiefs. They had him sit down, and then questioned him as to who he was and what he had to say.

He replied, "I am a student living in Yon-nan County, Whang-hai Province. On such and such a day I died and went into the other world, where your honorable father gave me such and such a commission."

The two listened for a little and then, without waiting to hear all that he had to say, grew very angry and began to scold him, saying, "How dare such a scarecrow as you come into our house and say such things as these? This is stuff and nonsense that you talk. Pitch him out," they shouted to the servants.

He, however, called back saying, "I have a proof; listen. If it fails, why then, pitch me out."

One of the two said, "What possible proof can you have?" Then the scholar told with great exactness and care the story of the head button.

The two, in astonishment over this, had the book taken down and examined, and sure enough in Vol. III of the Book of History was the button referred to. Not a single particular had failed. It proved to be a button that they had missed after the death of their father, and that they had searched for in vain.

Accepting the message now as true, they all entered upon a period of mourning.

The women of the family also called in the scholar and asked him specially of what he had seen. So they made the outer coat, chose a day, and offered it by fire before the ancestral altar. Three days after the sacrifice the scholar dreamed, and the family of Pak dreamed too, that the King of Hades had come and given to each one of them his thanks for the coat. They long kept the scholar at their home, treating him with great respect, and became his firm friends for ever after.

Pak Oo was a great-grandson of Minister Pak Chom. While he held office he was honest and just and was highly honoured by the people. When he was Mayor of Hai-ju there arose a dispute between him and the Governor, which proved also that Pak was the honest man.

When I was at Hai-ju, Choi Yu-chom, a graduate, told me this story.

* * *

Note. – The head button is the insignia of rank, and is consequently a valuable heirloom in a Korean home.

HONG'S EXPERIENCES IN HADES

Hong Nai-pom was a military graduate who was born in the year AD 1561, and lived in the city of Pyeng-yang. He passed his examination in the year 1603, and in the year 1637 attained to the Third Degree. He was 82 in the year 1643, and his son Sonn memorialized the King asking that his father be given rank appropriate to his age. At that time a certain Han Hong-kil was chief of the Royal Secretaries, and he refused to pass on the request to his Majesty; but in the year 1644, when the Crown Prince was returning from his exile in China, he came by way of Pyeng-yang. Sonn took advantage of this to present the same request to the Crown Prince. His Highness received it, and had it brought to the notice of the King. In consequence, Hong received the rank of Second Degree.

On receiving it he said, "This year I shall die," and a little later he died.

In the year 1594, Hong fell ill of typhus fever, and after ten days of suffering, died. They prepared his body for burial, and placed it in a coffin. Then the friends and relatives left, and his wife remained alone in charge. Of a sudden the body turned itself and fell with a thud to the ground. The woman, frightened, fainted away, and the other members of the family came rushing to her help. From this time on the body resumed its functions, and Hong lived.

Said he, "In my dream I went to a certain region, a place of great fear where many persons were standing around, and awful ogres, some of them wearing bulls' heads, and some with faces of wild beasts. They crowded about and jumped and pounced toward me in all directions. A scribe robed in black sat on a platform and addressed me, saying, 'There are three religions on earth, Confucianism, Buddhism and Taoism. According to Buddhism, you know that heaven and hell are places that decide between man's good and evil deeds. You have ever been a blasphemer of the Buddha, and a denier of a future life, acting always as though you knew everything, blustering and storming. You are now to be sent to hell, and ten thousand kalpas[1] will not see you out of it.'

"Then two or three constables carrying spears came and took me off. I screamed, 'You are wrong, I am innocently condemned.' Just at that moment a certain Buddha, with a face of shining gold, came smiling toward me, and said, 'There is truly a mistake somewhere; this man must attain to the age of eighty-three and become an officer of the Second Degree ere he dies.' Then addressing me he asked, 'How is it that you have come here? The order was that a certain Hong of Chon-ju be arrested and brought, not you; but now that you have come, look about the place before you go, and tell the world afterwards of what you have seen.'

"The guards, on hearing this, took me in hand and brought me first to a prison-house, where a sign was posted up, marked, 'Stirrers up of Strife.' I saw in this prison a great brazier-shaped pit, built of stones and filled with fire. Flames arose and forked tongues. The stirrers up of strife were taken and made to sit close before it. I then saw one infernal guard take a long rod of iron, heat it red-hot, and put out the eyes of the guilty ones. I saw also that the offenders were hung up like dried fish. The guides who accompanied me, said, 'While these were on earth they did not love their brethren, but looked at others as enemies. They scoffed at the laws of God and sought only selfish gain, so they are punished.'

"The next hell was marked, 'Liars.' In that hell I saw an iron pillar of several yards in height, and great stones placed before it. The offenders were called up, and made to kneel before the pillar. Then I saw an executioner take a knife and drive a hole through the tongues of the offenders, pass an iron chain through each, and hang them to the pillar so that they dangled by their tongues several feet from the ground. A stone was then taken and tied to each culprit's feet. The stones thus bearing down, and the chains being fast to the pillar, their tongues were pulled out a foot or more, and their eyes rolled in their sockets.

Their agonies were appalling. The guides again said, 'These offenders when on earth used their tongues skilfully to tell lies and to separate friend from friend, and so they are punished.'

"The next hell had inscribed on it, 'Deceivers.' I saw in it many scores of people. There were ogres that cut the flesh from their bodies, and fed it to starving demons. These ate and ate, and the flesh was cut and cut till only the bones remained. When the winds of hell blew, flesh returned to them; then metal snakes and copper dogs crowded in to bite them and suck their blood. Their screams of pain made the earth to tremble. The guides said to me, 'When these offenders were on earth they held high office, and while they pretended to be true and good they received bribes in secret and were doers of all evil. As Ministers of State they ate the fat of the land and sucked the blood of the people, and yet advertised themselves as benefactors and were highly applauded. While in reality they lived as thieves, they pretended to be holy, as Confucius and Mencius are holy. They were deceivers of the world, and robbers, and so are punished thus.'

"The guides then said, 'It is not necessary that you see all the hells.' They said to one another, 'Let's take him yonder and show him;' so they went some distance to the south-east. There was a great house with a sign painted thus, 'The Home of the Blessed.' As I looked, there were beautiful haloes encircling it, and clouds of glory. There were hundreds of priests in cassock and surplice. Some carried fresh-blown lotus flowers; some were seated like the Buddha; some were reading prayers.

"The guides said, 'These when on earth kept the faith, and with undivided hearts served the Buddha, and so have escaped the Eight Sorrows and the Ten Punishments, and are now in the home of the happy, which is called heaven.' When we had seen all these things we returned.

"The golden-faced Buddha said to me, 'Not many on earth believe in the Buddha, and few know of heaven and hell. What do you think of it?'

"I bowed low and thanked him.

"Then the black-coated scribe said, 'I am sending this man away; see him safely off.' The spirit soldiers took me with them, and while on the way I awakened with a start, and found that I had been dead for four days."

Hong's mind was filled with pride on this account, and he frequently boasted of it. His age and Second Degree of rank came about just as the Buddha had predicted.

His experience, alas! was used as a means to deceive people, for the Superior Man does not talk of these strange and wonderful things.

Yi Tan, a Chinaman of the Song Kingdom, used to say, "If there is no heaven, there is no heaven, but if there is one, the Superior Man alone can attain to it. If there is no hell, there is no hell, but if there is one the bad man must inherit it."

If we examine Hong's story, while it looks like a yarn to deceive the world, it really is a story to arouse one to right action. I, Im Bang, have recorded it like Toi-chi, saying, "Don't find fault with the story, but learn its lesson."

* * *

Note. – *Kalpa* means a Buddhistic age.

THE DUTIFUL DAUGHTER

There once lived in Korea a rich merchant and his wife who had no children, though they greatly desired them and prayed every day that a child might be granted them.

They had been married sixteen years and were no longer young, when the wife had a wonderful dream.

In her dream she walked in a garden full of beauteous fruits and flowers and singing birds, and as she walked, suddenly a star fell from heaven into her bosom.

As soon as the wife awoke, she told this dream to her husband. "I feel assured," said she, "that this dream can mean only one thing, and that is that heaven is about to send us a child, and that this child will be as a star for beauty and wonder and grace."

The merchant could hardly believe that this good fortune was really to be theirs; but it was indeed as the wife had said, and in due time a daughter was born to the couple, and this child was so beautiful that she was the wonder of all who saw her.

The husband and wife, who had hoped for a son, were greatly disappointed that the long-wished-for child was only a daughter, but their disappointment was soon forgotten in the joy and pride they felt in her beauty and wit and goodness.

Unhappily, while Sim Ching (for so the girl was named) was still a child, her mother died, and her father's grief over the loss of his wife was so great that he became completely blind. He was now obliged to leave the most of his business affairs in the hands of his servants, and these servants were so dishonest and so idle that they either wasted or stole all his money. At last he became so poor that he could scarcely provide enough food to keep himself and his daughter alive.

One day the merchant in his unhappiness wandered away from home, and being blind and so unable to tell where he was going, he fell into a deep pit out of which he was unable to climb.

He feared he would die there, but presently, hearing footsteps on the road above, he called out loudly for help.

The footsteps he heard were those of a greedy and dishonest priest who lived near by. Every day he passed by this way on his walks to and from the temple.

Hearing the voice from the pit, the priest went to the edge of it and looking down into it, saw the blind man there below.

"Who are you?" asked the priest, "and how have you fallen into this pit?"

"I am a poor blind man, who was once a rich merchant," replied the man in the pit. "I lost at once both my sight and my wealth, and because I cannot see I fell into this pit from which I am not able to climb. For the sake of mercy reach down your hand and draw me out."

"Not so," replied the priest. "That would be a foolish thing for me to do. Instead of drawing you out, I might myself be pulled in. But if you will promise to give me a hundred and fifty bags of rice that I may offer them up in the temple, I will go and get a rope, and throw the end of it down to you, and by that means I may be able to pull you out without danger to either of us."

The priest asked for the rice for the temple not because he really wished to make an offering of it, for indeed he meant to keep it for himself, but he thought, "If this man was once rich, no doubt he must still know some wealthy people, and if he goes to them and asks for rice to offer up in the temple they will be more likely to give it to him than if he told them it was for me."

POWERFUL SPIRITS & MYSTICAL REALMS

When the poor man heard that the priest demanded his promise of a hundred and fifty bags of rice before he would help him, he cried aloud with grief and wonder.

"How is it possible I should promise you such a thing as that?" he cried. "None but a very rich man could make such a gift to the temple, and I am so poor that I cannot even provide food enough for myself and my daughter."

"Your daughter!" cried the priest. "You have then a daughter?"

"Yes; and she is so beautiful that no one in the whole land can compare with her for fairness, and she is as good as she is beautiful, and as witty as she is good."

"Now listen!" said the priest. "If you will swear to give me the bags of rice, not only will I pull you out of the pit, but I foresee that because of this gift your daughter will be raised to the highest place in the land, and you yourself will receive great wealth and honor, and your sight will return to you."

This the priest said, not because he really foresaw anything of the kind, but because he wished to tempt the blind man into making him the promise of the rice.

The poor man still declared that he had no means of making such an offering, but the priest urged and begged and threatened, until at last the blind man gave his promise.

The priest then ran and got a rope, and soon pulled the blind merchant out of the pit.

"Now remember!" said he. "Exactly a month from now I will send my servants for the rice, and you must in some way have it ready, whether you beg or borrow or steal it, and if you do not, you shall receive a good beating for breaking your bargain with me, and be thrown into a prison that is worse than any pit."

KOREAN FOLK & FAIRY TALES

The priest then went on to the temple, while the blind man returned home, very sad and sorrowful.

As soon as he entered the door, his daughter saw by his look that something unfortunate had happened and begged him to tell her what it was.

At first he would not say because he feared to frighten her, but she asked him so many questions that at last he was obliged to tell her the whole story.

Sim Ching was indeed terrified when she heard what her father had promised the priest.

"Alas! Alas!" she cried. "How can we possibly get the rice ready for him? You know it is only by the kindness of the neighbors that we have the handful that I have cooked for our dinner to-day."

The poor man began to weep. "What you say is true," he cried. "Better that I should have died in the pit than be thrown into prison as will surely happen to me if I cannot give the priest the hundred and fifty bags that I promised him."

The blind man now set out to beg, telling every one his sad story and asking them to help him to collect the rice, but the people of the village were themselves poor and had no more than enough food for their own families.

Time slipped by, until at last the day arrived when the priest's servants were to come to demand the rice, and the blind man had not yet been able to get together even one bagful of rice, let alone a hundred and fifty.

He and his daughter sat together very sorrowful, and now and then the blind man bemoaned himself as he thought of how he was to be beaten and thrown into prison, for he had now learned enough about the priest to know that he could expect no mercy from one as cruel and greedy as he.

POWERFUL SPIRITS & MYSTICAL REALMS

Now there lived in another city, not far away, a very rich merchant who owned many ships that traded in foreign lands. This merchant had become so proud of his wealth and his power that he called himself the Prince of the Sea, and so it was that he obliged others to address him. This greatly offended a powerful Water Spirit who lived under the sea over which the ships of the merchant sailed. And now, in order to punish the merchant, the Water Spirit sent storms down upon the ships. Many were destroyed, and others were driven on to reefs, or back to the ports they sailed from. So many misfortunes overtook the vessels that sailors became afraid to sail on them, and the merchant began to fear he would be ruined.

In his trouble he sent for a number of wise men and magicians and asked them why he was now so unlucky, and what he could do to bring back good fortune.

The wise men and magicians studied their books and consulted together for a long time, and then they came to the merchant and said, "We have found why you are so unlucky. Your pride has offended a powerful Water Spirit, and it is he who is wrecking your ships or driving them back into port. There is only one way in which to turn aside his anger. If a young and beautiful maiden can be found who will willingly offer herself as a sacrifice to him, then he will be satisfied and will punish you no further. Otherwise he will certainly destroy every vessel you send out, and so in the end you will be ruined."

When the merchant heard this, he was in despair. "Now indeed there is no hope for me," he cried, "for I am very sure there is not, in the whole of Korea, a maiden who would be willing to be sacrificed to this Water Spirit, however great the reward I might offer. For indeed of what use would any reward be to her, if in order to gain it she must be drowned in the sea."

However, his head steward, who had charge of his affairs, begged him at least to send out a proclamation and to offer a reward to the family of any maiden who would consent to the sacrifice. "It may be that such a one will be found," said he; – "some one who values the fortunes of her parents even above her own life."

The merchant finally agreed to the wishes of his steward, and messengers were sent forth to read the proclamation aloud in every city, town and village in the country. They went this way and that, East, West, North and South, and finally one of them came to the place where the blind man and his daughter lived. The day the messenger came to the village was the very day when the servants of the wicked priest were to come and demand the hundred and fifty bags of rice from the blind man.

The merchant's messenger took his stand not far from the blind man's house, and from there he read aloud the proclamation as to the sacrifice and the reward that would be paid to the parents of any maiden who would be willing to be thrown to the Water Spirit.

The people of the village gathered about him in a great crowd to listen, but after they had heard what he said, they began to make a great noise, with cries and laughter.

"Some parents there may be," they cried, "who would be wicked enough to sacrifice their daughters for the sake of the reward, but what girl would ever go willingly to such a fate; and the messenger himself tells us that unless the maiden went willingly, the sacrifice would be useless."

POWERFUL SPIRITS & MYSTICAL REALMS

Sim Ching heard the noise outside, the voice of the messenger, and the laughter of the crowd, and as she was of a very curious nature, she went to the door to hear what was going on.

The man was already turning away, and Sim Ching asked a woman who was standing near what the man had been saying. The woman told her, laughing as she spoke. "How could any one suppose that any maiden would consent to be thrown to this monster in order that her family might have the reward!" cried the woman.

But Sim Ching ran after the man and caught him by the sleeve.

"Wait!" cried she. "Do not go until you have told me something. You say your master will richly reward the family of any maiden who will willingly give herself to this Water Spirit. Would he give as much as a hundred and fifty bags of rice to such a family?"

"That and more," replied the messenger. "My master is very rich, and the reward will be generous."

"Then I will go with you and be the sacrifice," said Sim Ching. "Permit me only to go and bid farewell to my father, and then I will be ready."

The messenger was rejoiced that he had been able to secure the maiden for his master and gladly consented to wait until she had spoken with her father.

But when Sim Ching went back into the house and told her father what she intended to do he was in despair. He wept aloud and rent his clothes. "Never, never will I consent to such a sacrifice," cried he.

But his daughter comforted him. "Do you forget," said she, "what the priest promised you? Did he not tell you that if you offered up this rice to the temple, all would be well with us, and that I would be raised to the highest place in the kingdom? Let us have faith and believe that the gods of the temple can save me at the last even though I be thrown into the sea."

As her father listened to her, he grew quieter, and at last gave his consent for her to go.

The neighbors who had heard what she meant to do gathered about to bid her farewell and could not but weep for pity, even while they praised her for her dutifulness toward her father.

Sim Ching at once set out with the messenger, who was in haste to bring her before his master. Indeed he feared that if she thought too long of what she had consented to do, she might repent of her bargain.

When he reached the merchant's house and told him he had found a maiden for the sacrifice, his master could scarcely believe him. "Does she understand what is required of her, and is she willing?" he asked.

The messenger assured him that she understood perfectly and was rejoiced at the thought of securing the reward for her father.

Sim Ching was now brought before the merchant, and when he saw her beauty and youth, and her modest, gentle air, he was filled with pity for her. He would even have commanded that she should be taken back again to her father, but to this Sim Ching would not consent.

"No," said she. "I have come here to do a certain thing. I have promised, and I do not wish to break my word. All I ask is to be assured that the bags of rice will certainly be sent to my father, and that at once."

"Let it then be as you desire," said the merchant. "And be assured that my part of the bargain shall be kept as faithfully as yours." He then ordered that one hundred and fifty bags of rice should be loaded on as many mules and sent to the blind man at once, that Sim Ching might herself have the comfort of seeing them set forth.

This was done, and after the train of mules had departed, Sim Ching was taken to a chamber where magnificent robes and veils and jewels had been laid ready for her. Her attendants dressed her and hung the jewels on her neck and arms, and when all was done, she was so beautiful that even the attendants wept to think she must be sacrificed.

A barge had been made ready and hung about with garlands, and in it sat musicians to make sweet music while the rowers rowed to where the sacrifice was to be made.

And now Sim Ching would have been afraid, but she fixed her thoughts upon her father and on how he would now be saved from the cruelty of the priest, and then she became quite happy and was no longer frightened.

When the barge came to the place under which the Water Spirit lived, Sim Ching leaned over the side of the boat and looked down into the water. It was very deep and green, and it seemed to her that beneath she could see shining walls and towers, as though of some great castle, and that the spirits of the water were beckoning to her to come. Lower and lower she leaned, until, as though drawn by some power beneath, she sank over the side of the vessel and down and down through the water until she was lost to the sight of those above her.

Then the rowers took the barge back to the shore and told the merchant the sacrifice had been accepted.

The merchant was glad that now again his ships might sail in safety; but at the same time he felt pity for Sim Ching, believing she had been drowned.

But such was not the case. After she had sunk down and down through the waters for what seemed to her a long distance, she came to the land where the Water Spirit is king. All about her were things strange and beautiful. There were water weeds so tall they were like trees waving high above her, and through them, like birds, darted the shining fishes. There were water flowers of colors she had never seen before, and shining shells, and before her rose a castle made of mother of pearl and studded with precious stones that shone and glittered like stars in the light that came down through the water.

While she was looking at it, the doors of the castle swung open, and a train of attendants came out to meet her. These attendants were all dressed in green, and many of them would have been very handsome except that they themselves were green. Their faces, their hands, their hair, and eyes, – everything about them was green.

They spoke to Sim Ching in a strange language, but soon she understood them and knew they had come to bring her before their King who was waiting for her.

Sim Ching felt no doubt but that this King was the Water Spirit himself, and she was very much frightened, but still she did not hesitate, but went with them willingly, for it was for this purpose she had come hither.

The attendants led her through one room after another, until they came to the place where the Water Spirit sat upon a crystal throne, and he, too, was green, but his crown was of gold, and his garments were set all over with pearls and precious stones.

The King looked at Sim Ching kindly and bade her have no fear. "I intend you no harm," said he, "and indeed I wished for no sacrifice. My only wish was to punish the rich merchant for his pride, and so it was that I set him a task that I thought impossible for him to perform. But because of your dutifulness and your love for your father, he has been able to make the sacrifice. Now you must stay here patiently for a year and teach the sea-maidens the ways of the world above, and at the end of that time you shall return to the earth, and receive the happiness you deserve."

Sim Ching listened to him wondering, and when he had made an end of speaking, she gladly agreed to serve for a time in the palace and to teach the sea-people all she knew. So for a twelvemonth Sim Ching stayed there and was very happy, for though the ways and manners of the sea-people were strange to her, they themselves were kind and gentle, so that she soon lost all fear of them.

At the end of the twelve months, the King sent for Sim Ching, and when she had come before him, he said, "Sim Ching, for a year you have served us both faithfully and well, and now the time has come for you to return to the upper world. But in that world there are many dangers, and you have no one to protect you. I have, therefore, caused a great flower to be prepared for you. When you enter into this flower, the leaves will fold about you and hide you, so that none may suspect you are within it. The leaves will afford you food and drink as well as shelter. In this way you can live protected and in safety until fate sends you a husband to love and guard you."

After speaking thus, the Water Spirit led Sim Ching into another room and there showed her the flower that he had caused to be prepared for her. This flower was very large and of a beautiful rose color, and the leaves were of some rich, thick substance that had a most delicious smell and was good to eat.

The juice of the leaves also afforded a delicious drink. Sim Ching, as she examined it, knew not how to express her wonder and admiration.

The King bade her step into the flower. She did so, and at once the leaves closed about her, so that she was completely hidden, and at the same time the most delightful music breathed softly from the flower. It now floated softly up and up, through the roof of the palace, and through the waters above, until it reached the surface of the sea. There it rested, rocking gently with the motion of the waves.

Now it so happened that the place where the flower floated on the sea was not far from the palace of the young King of that country. The morning it arose through the waters, the King was looking from a window across the sea toward a pleasure island where he sometimes went. Suddenly, between himself and the island, he saw something glittering in the sunlight out upon the waters.

He could not make out what the object was, and he ordered that some of the castle servants should row out to it, see what it was, and if possible bring it back with them. This was done and when the rowers returned, they brought the flower with them and carried it in to where the young King was awaiting them.

When the King saw the flower, he was filled with wonder and admiration. Never before had he seen such a blossom. He examined it on all sides and exclaimed over its size and beauty.

"It must be some magic," said he, "that has created such a flower. A room shall be built for it, and there I will keep it, and if indeed, it has been made by magic, as I suspect, it may be that in time some fruit will come from it that will be even more beautiful than the flower itself."

The room that was now prepared for the flower was so magnificent that no other apartment in the palace could compare with it. The walls were of gold, overlaid with paintings and hung with silken embroidered hangings. The floors were set with precious stones. There were fountains, and couches heaped with soft cushions, and from the ceiling hung seven alabaster lamps that were kept burning both night and day.

When the room was finished, the King caused the flower to be carefully carried into it and placed in the center upon a raised dais covered with embroidered velvet. After this no one was allowed to enter the room except himself, and he carried the key of it hung on a jeweled chain about his neck. Every day he spent long hours with the flower admiring its beauty, enjoying its delicious perfume, and listening to the delicate music that sometimes breathed out from among its leaves.

All the while Sim Ching lay hidden in the center of the flower without the King's once suspecting it. All day the leaves were closed about her, and only at night did they open to allow her to come forth.

The first time they unfolded, she was very much surprised to find herself in a room of a palace, instead of out upon the sea as she had supposed. Wondering, she looked about her, and then she stepped from the flower and began, timidly, to examine the apartment to which she had been brought. The beauty of it delighted her. She rested among the soft cushions, and bathed in the fountains, and dressed her hair. But toward morning she reëntered the flower, and the leaves closed about her so that she was again hidden from view.

For some time life went on in this manner. All day Sim Ching slept in the flower, and only at night did she come forth, and as the King only visited the room in the daytime he never saw her, nor even guessed that a living maiden was inclosed by the leaves of the flower he admired so greatly.

But it so happened that one night the King could not sleep, and he took a fancy to visit the flower and see it by the light of the lamps. He therefore made his way along the corridors, and fitting the key into the lock, he turned it without having made a sound.

What was his surprise, when he opened the door, to see a maiden of surpassing beauty sitting beside a fountain and amusing herself by catching the water in her hands.

When Sim Ching saw the King, she gave a cry, and would have run back into the flower to hide, but the King called to her gently, bidding her stay.

"I will not harm you," said he. "Do but tell me who you are and how you have come here. It must be you are some spirit or fairy, for no human being could be as beautiful as you."

"I am no spirit, nor am I a fairy," answered Sim Ching, "but only the daughter of a poor blind beggar, and as to how I came here I know not. I was placed inside that flower by a Water Spirit, but who has brought the flower here, or why, I cannot tell."

The King then told her of how he had seen the flower floating on the sea, and how he had had it brought to the palace, and had ordered this room to be built for it, and after he had made an end of speaking, Sim Ching told him her history from the time her father had become blind and fallen into the pit, to the hour when the Water Spirit had bade her enter the flower and the leaves had closed about her.

The young King listened and wondered. "Yours is indeed a strange story," said he, "and this mischievous priest shall be sought out and punished as he deserves. And yet it may be his promises shall all come true, and you shall indeed be exalted to the highest place in the kingdom."

He then told Sim Ching he loved her and desired nothing in the world so much as to make her his wife.

To this Sim Ching joyfully consented for the young King was so handsome and gracious, and spoke so well and wisely, that she could not but love him with all her heart, even as he loved her.

All night they sat and talked together, and in the morning he opened the door of the chamber and led her forth, and called the courtiers and nobles together, and told them she was to be his bride.

Then there was great rejoicing, and every one who saw Sim Ching wondered at her beauty and loved her for her gentle and gracious manner.

Soon after she and the King were married, and they loved each other so dearly that Sim Ching would have been perfectly happy except for the thought of her old father and his griefs and sorrows.

Immediately after she was married, she sent messengers to the village where she had lived, bidding them find her father and bring him to her, but the old man had disappeared, and no one knew what had become of him.

Then the Queen had a great feast prepared and sent word throughout the length and breadth of the Kingdom that all who were both poor and blind were bidden to the palace to eat of it. All would be welcome, and none should be turned away.

Then from far and near the blind and poor came flocking to the palace, scores and hundreds of them. The tables for the feast were laid in a great hall, and the young King and Queen sat on raised thrones at one end of it. All who came to the feast were obliged to pass before this throne before they might take their places at the table, and as each one passed, the Queen looked at him eagerly, hoping to recognize her father, but none of all the multitude was the one she sought. At last every one was seated; the attendants were about to close the doors, when another beggar, the last of all, came stumbling into the hall. He was so feeble and so old that he could scarcely make his way to the throne, but no sooner did the Queen see him than she knew him as her father.

Then she gave a great cry, and came down from the throne, and threw her arms about him, and wept over him.

"It is I, oh, my father! It is thy daughter, Sim Ching," she wept.

Then her father knew her voice and cried aloud with joy. "Oh, my daughter, I had thought thee dead," he cried, "and now thou art alive and I can feel thy arms about me."

As he spoke the tears of joy ran down his cheeks, and these tears washed away the mists of sorrow that had clouded his eyes and he found he could see again.

Then there was great rejoicing, and the King called the old man father and made him welcome, and in due time he who had been blind and now could see was raised to great wealth and honor, and so the words of the priest, that he had spoken without believing, came true.

But as for the priest himself, the King had him sought for, and when he was found, he was thrown into prison and punished as he deserved for his greed and cruelty.

THE KING OF THE FLOWERS

Korea is the land of beautiful scenery and lovely flowers. Snow white and ruby red are their chief colors. In the spring time when the ice has melted and the rivers have poured their floods into the sea, the whole country blushes with the pink bloom of azaleas. The glens are white with lilies of the valley. The breezes as they sweep the land come laden with perfume.

The girls mark the season of the year and the time of the month by the blossoms even more than by the almanac, for they keep in mind the calendar of the flowers. Daughters that are especially beloved of their parents are named from the blossoms, and the Korean house-father, when affectionate, speaks of his wife as the plum tree. An old song says: The homesick husband, long away from his dear ones, inquires of a fellow townsman newly arrived:

> "'Have you seen my native land?
> Come tell me all you know;
> Did just before the old home door
> The plum tree blossoms show?'"

And the stranger answers promptly:

> "'They were in bloom, though pale, 'tis true,
> And sad, from waiting long for you.'"

This is like the Scotsman who calls his wife his "bonnie briar bush," for in the Land of Morning Glow, they have a language of flowers. Each plant and blossom has a meaning and either delightful or disagreeable associations. It is a compliment to speak of a girl as a pear blossom, for the pear is one of the most glorious of trees and its blooms are lovely to behold. It would hardly do, however, to call her a cinnamon rose, for this flower has evil associations. The gee-sang, as the Koreans pronounce the name of the gei-sha, as the Japanese call the dancing girls, are associated with the cinnamon rose, for did not the sages tell this story?

Twelve centuries ago lived the renowned scholar Sul Chong, the greatest of all the learned men of Korea. His head was as full of knowledge as a persimmon is of pulp, and his ideas were as numerous as the seeds in a pomegranate. He taught his countrymen all that was in the books of China, and in the temple of Confucius his portrait hangs to this day. He lived in the kingdom of Silla, in the days of its glory, when ships from Japan and China sailed into its seaports and the Arabs from Bagdad brought their pretty wares to exchange for gold, ginseng, camphor, porcelain, cinnamon, ginger and tiger skins, to take to their renowned Caliph and his turbaned nobles at court, of whom we read in the "Arabian Nights."

When the King of Silla, Sin Mun, was living in luxury and filling his palace with too many pretty dancing girls, who distracted his mind from attending properly to the affairs of state, Sul Chong warned his master against the increasing influence of these women by telling him the following story:

Once upon a time, in spring, the Peony, king of the flowers, blossomed so gorgeously that it became the admiration of all the lovers of beauty in the whole country. Hundreds of people made long journeys to the capital of Silla to see the bright blossoms. In the king's gardens, on very tall stalks, the many branches were heavily laden with large red flowers. These were indeed lovely to behold, but the king of the whole garden was a single peony, grown on one stem, so that all the strength and nourishment of the plant were concentrated in that unique royal bloom. All saluted this flower as king.

When all the other flowers heard of their king's glory, they came to pay their respects at the floral court, of which the Peony was sovereign. All the trees sent their choicest blooms as envoys. In one glorious procession of perfume and color the Peach, Plum, Pear, Apple, and Persimmon trooped in, each making its obeisance to the monarch of all flowers. All these tree blossoms prided themselves on their being so useful to man as harbingers of the delicious fruits to come.

Then, among the bright throng appeared sprightly young virgin flowers, the Tea-Rose, in pearl-tinted frock; the Azalea, in pink; the Lily, in white; the Strawberry Blossom; and a score of other pretty creatures of the garden. Last of all appeared the Cinnamon Rose. She tripped nimbly along in a green skirt and red jacket, with haughty air and breath of spice.

One after the other they were presented to King Peony, and gracefully made their salute. But of them all, the king seemed most to favor Miss Cinnamon Flower. He let the others pass out from the Court, but lingered long with the spicy visitor, spending much time in her society, as if smitten with her charms. By and by he invited Miss Cinnamon Rose to come and live in the palace, and leaving his ministers to carry on the government, he spent all his time in her society. She was installed in a place near His Majesty and seemed always to have his ear and attention, even when the king's prime minister had to wait long for an audience, or even a word. Miss Cinnamon Rose seemed to be the real ruler instead of the king himself.

But one day there came to the palace the flower called Old Man. He looked exactly like an aged beggar dressed in sackcloth and leaning on a staff. Respectfully bowing, he asked if he might share the hospitality of the king's palace. He was welcomed and fed, partaking of the royal bounty. When at last he was given audience of King Peony, and was invited to speak, he said:

"Out along the road, Your Majesty, I heard of your rich feast and good things to eat. Now I hear that you need medicine. Although you dress in Chinese silk and none are equal to you in the magnificence of your robes and the splendor of your Court, yet you are much like me in your wants, and you need a common knife string, as well as I. Is it not so?"

"You are quite right, Old Man," replied the king. "Yet I like this Cinnamon Rose and want her with me. I cannot do without her."

"Yes, Your Majesty. Yet, is it not true that if you keep company with the wise and prudent, your reign will be long, powerful and glorious? But if you consort with the foolish your house will fall? Did not three dynasties of the emperors of Great China fall because of the beautiful women who tempted their Majesties to forget their duties? If it were so with the ancients, how much more so is it now?"

The king blushed, even to a deep crimson. He confessed his faults and reformed his life.

It is said the lesson was not lost on the real human king. He dismissed his harem, sent away the dancing girls and ruled wisely till the day of his death.

CAT-KIN AND THE QUEEN MOTHER

Korea is called the Land of the Plum Blossom, but in winter the rivers freeze over. Then the men cut through the ice which is often several feet thick, to catch with their fishing lines and hooks the fish that swim in the water beneath. Yet they are very glad to welcome any sign of the coming spring, and they watch eagerly for the pussy willows to show themselves.

Now there was a farmer who lived in Nai-po, which is the grain garden of the Korean peninsula, who wanted a little daughter, though other parents cared more for sons.

One day farmer Pak, for that was his name, discovered a pussy willow which seemed to him, after the long winter, like a light shining in a dark place. He plucked it and carried proudly home this branch full of fuzzy little buds. This was a sign of his happiness at the return of spring. He was tired of ice and snow and now he knew that soon the gloomy hills would burst into a glory of bright colors from the blooming flowers, and look like an army with flags.

That same day his prayers were answered and a little girl was born into his home. Giving the pussy willow to his wife, he said: "We shall name our baby Cat-kin, that is Little Puss."

Cat-kin never saw a cradle, for the Korean mothers carry their babies on their backs. She was soon out of infancy, and then it was not long before she was standing up and toddling about and playing with her doggie and pet bull. These little pets on four legs usually take the place of kittens in a country home in Korea, for the cats are wild and do not allow children to fondle them.

Long before she was a dozen years old, Cat-kin became very fond of fairy stories, of which Korea has a great many, besides thousands of tales of wonderful people and animals and what happened to them. She often looked up towards the high hills and distant mountains, where she thought the fairies, dragons, ogres and tigers lived. Here also dwelt the sen-nin or mountain spirits, wise and good, of whom the old people talked and the soldiers painted on their banners when they went to war.

When about eight years old, Cat-kin wanted very much to walk up towards the north star, which her father showed her shining in the heavens. He had once traveled up into one of the Northern provinces, where during the daytime he could see afar off the great snow-white mass of the Ever White Mountain rising up to meet the azure sky. There, at the top he had heard, lay the Dragon Prince's Pool, out of which flowed the two rivers that made Korea an island. One was named the Tumen and the other the Yalu, after the beautiful green and blue sheen on the feathers of a drake's back, so richly colored were its shining waters. When her father told of his travels, Cat-kin also longed to go north to get to the very top and touch the sky.

But this she knew she could not do, even if she had had long legs and were as strong as a man, for the tigers were very numerous and always roaming about. These yellow and black striped brutes were man-eaters. They loved nothing better for a good dinner than a young girl.

So as she did not know any way of getting to the top of the Ever White Mountain and of seeing the deep blue waters of the Pool, except by riding on the back of a dragon, which she sometimes dreamed of, she kept waiting and waiting for one of these flying creatures to come, yet it never came.

Cat-kin was bound to have the fairies visit her, if possible. So one day, sitting under a persimmon tree and reading a story, she held the book in one hand, while she struck the ground several times, saying earnestly:

"Earth-spirit, earth-spirit, come to me; come up and see me."

All of a sudden the air seemed heavy with sweet perfume, and a silver mist like a cloud spread over her house and garden. Then a bright dazzling light flooded everything and there stood before her a glistening chariot, made of blue jade with golden wheels. It was drawn by milk-white horses and on a seat of shining silver sat the Western Heavenly Queen Mother herself.

Attendant upon the Mother Queen were thousands of the most beautiful maidens, who were all dressed in resplendent robes. They wore amber ornaments, and silver girdles, and necklaces of precious stones and silken robes with many tassels. Their feet were shod with gold embroidered velvet slippers, and on their heads were caps of gold studded with glittering gems. Cat-kin could hardly count the rich ornaments, necklaces, breast chains and the jade wands, like sceptres, which they held in their hands. These were shaped like lotus flowers. The faces of all these maidens were rosy, their eyes sparkled, and all had small hands and feet.

In a voice of great sweetness that sounded like music the Heavenly Queen Mother looked at Cat-kin and spoke to her, saying:

"Come forward, little maid, fear not. I shall take you with me to my palace, in the Island of Gems and give you all you want, besides showering blessings on your people, if you will come."

Cat-kin did not feel at all timid or frightened, but came boldly forward and knelt at the base of the chariot.

The Mother Queen first touched her with her milk-white jade wand, that was carved like a lotus bud, and made the little girl rise.

In a moment more, a silver chariot, with wheels made of turquoise and drawn by two young milk-white dragons, wheeled up close to her, and the attendant lady in golden robes bade her step in.

The dragons were fierce, powerful, fire-breathing creatures, with wide spreading wings, and their bodies and tails together were of the length of whales, while their eyes darted fire. Yet Cat-kin was not at all afraid, and thought it was great fun. Then up through and far above the clouds the host of bright beings flew. They followed the Queen Mother's chariot until, far away, they poised in mid-sky. Cat-kin was then told to look over the side of the chariot to the earth and ocean, miles and miles below. She was asked if she could recognize her father's cottage, but she could not. The whole village looked only like a grey mass of thatched roofs, and she could pick out only the temple.

There, spread out, was the great sea, as blue as a sapphire, and in places deep green, like an emerald, but she could see no ships nor any coast or shores, nor any ranges of mountains, nor signs of the land of Korea. Nothing but ripples and waves were visible. Yet in the center of the azure sea was an island. The trees were emeralds and the roofs of the houses were of gold, and the windows diamonds. These were so full of light that no lamps were necessary.

Beautiful beings, all maidens, as lovely in garb and face as those who filled the train of the Queen Mother, walked or played, or sang in the gardens. Or swam and sported in the sapphire waves, or rowed and sailed about in boats that seemed as if made of marble, they were so white.

At a signal from the Queen the singing ceased. Then there rose up wave upon wave of sweetest melody from the players on instruments who were in the gardens below.

Cat-kin thought she heard at intervals the chorus, sounding out the words, rising upward like pulses, through the air, "Welcome lovely mortal! Our Queen invites and we greet thee! Manifold be her gifts to thee and thine! Come, thou honored among all Korean maidens! Come to us and join our band and we shall love thee as one of ourselves."

In the wink of a falcon's eye – so short a time it seemed – the Mother Queen and her host descended.

As the chariots touched the island, a bevy of radiant maidens came forward, some to attend the Queen Mother and some to lead Cat-kin into her own room in the palace. There the most gorgeous robes were put on her, beside a cap begemmed with glittering, precious stones of various colors, and a pair of gold-embroidered velvet slippers.

Cat-kin was surprised when one of the shining maidens set a royal tiara adorned with five gems upon her brow.

"For me?" she asked in surprise.

"Yes for you, whom the Heavenly Mother Queen would honor."

"And what do these five gems, jade, crystal, malachite, amber and agate signify?" asked Cat-kin.

"Ah, that is not for us to tell you, but the Queen Mother ordered these. Tomorrow she will explain to you the secret of each gem."

Cat-kin walked about freely, enjoying the lovely sights and sounds. She also ate with keen appetite and to her full of the delicacies set on the table before her. Yet never once did she feel sleepy, nor see any beds, nor hear anyone talk of retiring. She wondered what they meant when they said "tomorrow"; for she could see no sun or moon or twilight. However, she did not think long about such things, and by and by forgot all about them.

When the entire court and all the hosts of the Queen Mother's attendants had assembled, Her Majesty's chamberlain read the proclamation, which declared that the Queen looked with great favor upon the Korean people, and had decided to bestow great gifts upon them. For this purpose, she had selected and brought to her palace the Korean maid named Cat-kin, to endow them through this, their daughter, with five precious traits of disposition and character. In token of gracious thought and tender love, Her Majesty would now present and explain the meaning of the five precious gems. These were jade, crystal, malachite, amber, and agate.

Cat-kin kneeled down before the Queen, who placed in Cat-kin's hands the shining gems, while an attendant fairy took them from her opened palm and placed each one of them on vermilion velvet, edged with gold. Then five maidens stood by, each with a gem laid on a cushion.

After the ceremony of presentation was over, the Queen made a speech, which told the Korean maiden's fortune and her future.

Cat-kin would be sent back over the clouds and ocean to the King's palace in the capital of her home land, and there be made a princess. Many nobles and king's sons from other countries, hearing of her beauty and her wonderful visit to the Island of Gems would come to pay her court as suitors. Many would ask for her hand, to be wedded to her; but she was to marry none but the king's son, a prince of her own people.

"Take these gems, fair maiden, and bestow their virtues and what they mean upon your people," said the Queen. "A thousand years from now – as men count time – we together will visit Korea again."

Then both the Queen and Cat-kin, stepping into the silver chariot, drawn by the fire-breathing dragons, plunged on and mounted up into space. First they sailed above the clouds and then dipped downwards, steering to Korea and over the mountains, bearing their precious charge to the capital. They reached the ground in a cloud and the wheels of the chariot stood still before the palace gate.

Yet before any mortal eyes could see their full forms, the Queen Mother and the dragons had disappeared, and Cat-kin stood alone, a resplendent maiden of dazzling appearance and in the robes given by the Heavenly Queen Mother, which all recognized at once as coming from the Island of Gems.

A throng of court ladies and palace attendants and a long line of nobles and princes were already waiting for the maiden, who they knew came gift-laden from the Queen Mother, of whom all had heard from childhood. The five gems were laid, each in a covered casket of perfumed wood, encrusted with gold on top and inlaid with mother-of-pearl.

Escorted into the throne room by a bevy of princesses, the Heavenly Mother's gifts in the five caskets were reverently placed on silken fans, spread out on a table having on its top the five cushions of crimson velvet.

Then, by lot and word of the diviners, the choice of a first drawing was awarded to a prince of fair face and mien. The other four nobles, one by one and in turn, approached and each was allowed to choose one of the caskets, all of which looked alike, and none was to be opened until the possessor was in his own home.

Now these were the gifts for body and mind, of which the polished gems were the tokens. According as each prince chose and received, so with the trait, which each gem signified, would his children and posterity be endowed. In the course of centuries, these would become the national features, of twenty millions of Koreans.

One by one the caskets were opened by each prince, and therein he discovered what was a trait in the character of the Korean people. These were:

Procrastination – Putting off until tomorrow, or some other time, what ought to be done today, and keeping back not only one person but the whole nation.

Hospitality – Always glad to see friends, to entertain people, even strangers, and to take care of relations, even to the making of one's self poor – a habit carried too far as the years and centuries rolled on.

Inexactness – The habit of not usually thinking clearly, counting correctly, or stating facts precisely, and when telling a story of "blowing a conch;" that is, of exaggerating.

Love of family – How the mothers and fathers in Korea do love their children, their kinsfolk and their relatives!

Sense of humor – A Korean can always see the funny side of things. He loves to joke and he bears his troubles well, because he likes to smile. As for the girls, they laugh as easily as the rain falls, or the flowers bloom.

And what the Queen Mother predicted came true. Just as five fingers make up the hand, so the average people among the Koreans are known by the five traits, for better or for worse.

THE MAGIC PEACH

Out on the ocean, so far away that no ship ever sailed there, is an island on which stood the seven storied palace of the royal lady, Su Wang Moo. In our language, this title means Western Queen Mother. She is always ready to help good mortals with her gifts and favors.

On this island thousands of genii wait to obey the commands of the Queen Mother. She has also chariots of silver and gold drawn by dragons, by which she sends her messages everywhere.

The genii and most of the shining maidens stay at home to fulfill the Queen's commands. In addition to these servants, she has hundreds of azure pigeons, which she often despatches to far-off places. In their bills, or under their wings, they carry some gift or promise to make people happy.

In the mind of many a Korean maiden there rises the dream, or there wells up the hope, that some day the Western Queen Mother will send to her pretty clothes of silk, with necklaces of jewels, a handsome youth to wed her, and a silver ring for the marriage ceremony.

Then she pictures to herself how splendidly she will be arrayed and how fine she will look in the costume of a bride; how her long black hair will be done up very high, with flowers and rosettes over the crown of her head, and ermine-edged slippers will be put on her feet. She wonders how she will feel when she drinks the cups of sacramental wine that make her a wife, after which she will go with her husband and bow to the memorial tablets of his ancestors.

She goes all over in her mind the happy times she will have in her husband's home. What she hopes for most, after all these things, is to have a kind mother-in-law. Then she will be a queen in her own little kingdom, with plenty of rice and kimchi, and cakes and goodies.

So it is that many Korean maidens go out under the blue sky to look up at the stars, or on moonlight nights scan the heavens to see if the birds are coming. Hoping to greet the azure pigeons, they put on their best clothes and watch. Many are their dreams.

Oh! how many lads also dream of the genii and of the riding on the dragon's back, to cross the mountain ranges and the great oceans, and to visit strange, far-off countries; or, they think of the pink coat which they will wear. The pink coat shows that the lad is engaged to be married and will, when grown up, be a husband to the little girl who may be in her cradle days; for in Korea children and even babies in arms are engaged to be married to other children.

Then the boy pictures the day when the long braid of hair, which he now has to wear down his back, shall be tucked up into a topknot, like a man's. No matter how old a bachelor may be, he must wear this boy's braid of hair. He must not speak, or talk with his elders, without first asking permission. He must be "seen and not heard" in company, and every one treats him as a child. So the boy also waits for the azure pigeons to come, for to be engaged to be married even when quite young, or to have a wife when older, means a great deal.

Then the young husband will wear a wide brimmed hat after school and go up to the city, with his fellow villagers, to try at the literary examinations. They will all march together, under a banner tufted at the top with pheasant feathers. If he passes successfully, he will be welcomed home with a parade and band of music. By and by, he will become a magistrate and have a

POWERFUL SPIRITS & MYSTICAL REALMS

string of amber beads over his ear, and wear on his breast a square of gold-embroidered velvet. Servants will carry him in a palanquin and his men will carry wooden paddles to punish folks who break the laws. Then he can strut about, in starched white flowing clothes, with the common people all afraid of him. No wonder that the boy waits for the coming of the blue pigeon!

Now in the gardens of the Queen's Palace, on the Island of Gems, there grow wonderful fruits of a rich, ripe color, brilliant with light and sheen. These, when served at the banquets and eaten, have the power of making the guest live very long, even for thousands of years.

Especially powerful is the celestial peach of longevity, which is served on little golden tables, its juice makes an old person's body new, so that one who eats the peach will live hundreds of years.

Sometimes the Queen sends one of these fruits to her favorites on the earth. Yet no one can ever get any of these peaches, unless the Queen herself gives them, and the peach trees are always jealously guarded by genii and dragons. None, even of the Queen's servants, or her waiting maids, or any of the genii, or dragons, can bestow the peach of longevity on mortals.

* * *

Now it happened that the Queen, hearing of the virtues of a certain king's son, despatched one of her lovely maidens, in one of her ten thousand dragon chariots, inviting him to visit Her Majesty, in the Island of Gems. She sent a message also to the prince's parents, telling them that their son would return before the end of the moon, which was then in its first quarter.

His anxious mother, who had a bride already picked out for her son to wed, warned him against looking too long at the lovely princesses, or pretty maids in the Queen's Palace of Gems. In truth she had her lurking suspicions. She feared for her darling son, that, beneath their rosy faces and moon-like eyes, they were really sirens, possibly even sea monsters in female form, and might eat him up.

She also urged him to be very careful as to etiquette. He must be especially decorous, because the code of behavior and manners might not be the same as those among polite people upon the earth. Moreover, he must notice and hear everything and, when he came back home, tell her all about it.

On the other hand, the Queen of the Island of Gems warned the lovely maiden, a princess whom she sent, to beware lest the prince might fall in love with her, either on the way, or when at the island. If he tried to persuade her to marry him and to stay on the earth and not come back to the Island of Gems, and to her duties to the Queen, the palace maid would be disgraced and die early.

Although the Queen laughed when she said it, and quoted the proverb, "Don't trust a pigeon to carry grain," she was really very serious, and the maiden knew that it would not do to thwart the royal wishes.

So this discreet princess made a firm resolve to be very careful. She decided that when she met the prince she would be very cold in her bearing. When delivering the Queen's invitation, she would appear to think it only a matter of business, though very important. She would not stay more than an hour in the prince's mansion.

When the dragon chariot was returning homeward she would be silent. She would hold no conversation, nor speak a word, nor let the prince sit beside her, but she would keep in the front seat nearest the dragon, while he should ride on the great creature's back.

So it was a very quiet journey which the prince made, while the chariot sped over the clouds, with the earth and oceans lying far beneath. Part of the time he sat on the dragon's back, as if in a saddle, but after a while he climbed back into the chariot again, and all the time he was so thrilled with the speed and the grandeur of it all that, to tell the truth, he forgot all about the lovely princess who had brought the Queen's message, until he found himself at the Queen's Palace of Gems and was invited to step out of the chariot.

Soon he was seated with others, similarly honored, at the table which was loaded down with dishes of gold and silver which were heaped with the choicest viands. The guests, all in fine clothes like the prince, were waited on by shining maidens of exquisite beauty and robed in golden garments gemmed with glittering jewels of the most precious workmanship.

Upon one of these lovely creatures, a maiden who seemed to be about sixteen, not far away from where he sat, the prince cast his eyes. She was kneeling on the floor ready to do his bidding. He was so filled with admiration at her loveliness that he could hardly pay any attention to the talk at the table. Despite his mother's warning, he made several mistakes in propriety.

Yet his appetite was very good after his long journey and he ate heartily of the delicious fare. Towards the end of the feast, feeling in a jolly mood, he picked up one of the peaches. Then he pared and sliced it, greatly enjoying its juicy nectar. Every morsel of the pulp, as he put it in his mouth, made him feel as if he were gaining a century of vigor. He knew he was lengthening his life and increasing his power to enjoy the pleasures of which he had always been very fond.

Indeed the prince was far less of a scholar and student than he ought to have been. Often at home when his teachers were all present and ready to begin the tasks of the day, the lad was still out at play. His older sister used to say laughingly of her brother, "He never let his studies interfere with his education."

Yet every moment this maiden kneeling near him seemed to grow more charming in both face and form, dress and adornment, ease and grace of motion. Indeed she seemed the very embodiment of all loveliness, and the prince could not keep his eyes off her. He did not know that this was the effect of eating the peach of longevity, for the maiden was really no prettier at the end of the banquet than she had been at the beginning. The change was in him, not in her.

So intoxicated was the prince, that he so far forgot himself and what his mother had told him not to do, that he picked out one of the finest-looking of the peaches from its golden basket on the table and tossed it over to the pretty maiden.

On her part the maid of honor had herself been so wrapped up in admiration of the young and princely guest, that when he motioned that he was about to toss a peach to her she broke the rule of the Palace of Gems. She threw out her hands and caught the peach deftly, as if playing ball.

The palace ladies were all horrified. They had been taught that, except to perform the duties of waiting and serving, they were to pay no attention to anything the guests might say or do. When heated with wine the guests might be only making sport of the attendants. They were to decline any personal attentions and continue in their duty of serving. But instead of averting her gaze, or bowing low with her face to the ground, or having her eyes downcast, the maid, actually threw out her hands, caught the peach and, to the horror of all who saw her, bit into it and swallowed the morsel.

What it was that happened the very next moment even the fairies could not tell or exactly remember; for a golden mist seemed to fall in the banquet hall, enveloping everything.

* * *

It happens that just here in the story a great gap occurs. At such a pause the Korean story-teller, who sits in his booth in one of the back streets of Seoul, would stop and send his boy to take up a collection from the crowd. Nor would he go on, until all had been invited to give and the coins rattled in the gourd shell.

When he began again some said it was the same story continued. Others were sure it was a new story, but that the palace maid and the prince were the same who had been in the banquet hall of the Western Queen Mother, in the Island of Gems and that the peach had never lost, since it never could lose its virtues, because given by the Queen. But such as it was, this is the way the story ran on:

* * *

More than a thousand years afterwards it was known that in the high mountains of the Ever White range lived a holy man, a hermit, who was honored, almost worshiped by the people in that region. In the summer time hundreds of pilgrims visited his hut to hear wise words about how to live and do good, and then to receive the hermit's blessing. Even the wild beasts appeared to be tame in his presence. At any rate, they never tried to bite or devour one another, or hurt the old man or to destroy his humble shelter. The tigers, the leopards and the bears seemed to forget they had claws, or teeth; while their little cubs played peacefully with each other.

The dress of this hermit was of the ancient style of a thousand years before, of the time of the ancient dynasty of Ko.

One day while out on one of his walks this old, white-bearded hermit met a woman of fair countenance, who seemed to be quite young, for her face was unwrinkled and rosy. It appeared that she had travelled far, yet she walked with the springing step of a maiden who was still in her teens. Her dress betokened that of ages gone, for it was of the sort and fashion which are revealed in the cave pictures painted on the walls of the dolmens, or the colossal stone chambers, in which kings and mighty men were buried, ten or fifteen centuries ago, which are very many in Korea.

The hermit and maid met in the path under the tall pine tree and exchanged greetings, the lady bowing very low. Then, as she looked up in his eyes, her face became radiant with joy as if she recognized a dear friend.

The sage inquired who she was, and whether she were the wandering lady, of whom rumor spoke of having been seen during centuries, over all the nine provinces of Korea, by people who were great grandfathers, as well as by the children of that day.

Then she told her story.

She was the same palace maid, who, in the Western Queen Mother's palace on the Island of Gems had waited upon him, once a gay prince and now the holy hermit. Then again she bowed low.

For catching and eating the peach which the princely guest had tossed to her, and thus breaking the rules of the palace, the Queen had ordered her banishment for a thousand years.

But during all this time she had been seeking the prince who tossed her the peach of longevity; for she knew that neither she nor he could die, till the thousand years had passed. Yet none of the men she met, however handsome, learned or wealthy, reached her ideal of the youth she had seen so long ago. Not finding him, she went back to the Island of Gems, traveling on a dragon's back, and humbly begged the Queen to extend her term of life, until she should meet the one she loved so dearly, even if she found him only after hundreds of years more of wandering and of hope deferred.

The Mother Queen listened to her petition and was gracious and extended the maiden's life. So on the earth she kept up her wanderings. Now, having met the holy hermit she was happy, for she felt sure that she had found the same prince, venerable in appearance though he was, for she could see his soul.

The hermit listened with delight to the lady's story of her life in the palace and of her wanderings, during a thousand years in search of one she loved; and, especially, that she had been willing to have the Mother Queen order her future.

As for the hermit, his long white beard which swept his breast fell off, his bald head was in a moment covered with luxuriant black hair, and he became young again in her presence, with springing step and bright eyes. He could not be more rosy in countenance, for the pure life he had led had kept his skin pink. They spent many hours together, in talking long and joyfully over their experiences in the Island of Gems.

Then both agreed that now, since they had met again, they would bow gladly to the Queen's decision concerning them both, and do whatever Her Majesty ordered.

But already by a flying dragon that was famous for gathering up news from all parts of the universe, the Queen had been told of the meeting of the lovers in the mountain path, and of their pious resolve to commit their future to Her Majesty in the Island of Gems.

Suddenly the pair of lovers heard near the mountain top a sound of sweet music, as of some fairy playing on a lute, and at every second the sounds seemed to come lower and nearer. Soon a great white cloud of sweet smelling odors, like incense, enveloped them. What was their surprise to see a golden chariot drawn by two dragons, whose eyes were like emeralds, come up close to where they stood. Both of them, prince-hermit and maid were then taken up into the chariot and borne swiftly over cloud, and mountain and sea, to the Island of Gems. There the Queen ordered them to be married, and, after a splendid wedding, they lived happily ever after.

THE GREAT STONE FIRE EATER

Ages ago, there lived a great Fire Spirit inside of a mountain to the southwest of Seoul, the capital of Korea. He was always hungry and his food was anything that would burn. He devoured trees, forests, dry grass, wood, and whatever he could get hold of. When those were not within his reach, he

POWERFUL SPIRITS & MYSTICAL REALMS

ate stones and rocks. He enjoyed the flames, but threw the hard stuff out of his mouth in the form of lava.

This Fire Monster spent most of his time in a huge volcano some distance away, but in sight of the capital. The city people used to watch the smoke coming out of the crater by day and issuing in red fire, between sunset and sunrise, until all the heavens seemed in flames. Then, they said, the Fire Spirit was lighting up his palace. On cloudy nights the inside of the volcano glowed like a furnace. The moulten mass inside the crater was reflected on the clouds, so that one could almost see into the monster's belly.

But nothing tasted so good to the Fire Eater as things which men built, such as houses, stables, fences, and general property. An especial titbit, that he longed to swallow, was the royal palace.

Looking out of its crater one day, he saw the king's palace all silver bright and brand new, rising in the City of Seoul. Thereupon he chuckled, and said to himself, for he was very happy:

"There's a feast for me! I'll just walk out of my mountain home and eat up that dainty morsel. I wonder how the king will like it."

But the Fire Spirit was in no hurry. He felt sure of his meal. So he waited until his friend, the South Wind, was prepared to join him.

"Let me know when you're ready," said the Fire Spirit to the South Wind, "and we'll have a splendid blaze. We'll go up at night and enjoy a lively dance before they can get a drop of water on us. Don't let the rain-clouds know anything about our picnic."

The South Wind promised easily, for she was always glad to have a frolic.

So when the sun went down and it was dark, the Fire Spirit climbed out of his rocky home in the volcano and strode toward Seoul. The South Wind pranced and capered with him until the streets of the capital were so gusty that no one with a wide-brimmed hat dared go outdoors, lest, in a lively puff, he might lose his head-gear. As for the men in mourning, who wear straw hats a yardstick wide and as big and deep as washtubs, they locked themselves up at home and played checkers. By the time all the palace guards were asleep the Fire Spirit was ready. He said to the South Wind:

"Blow, blow, your biggest blast, as I begin to touch the roofs of the smaller houses. This will whet my appetite for the palace, and then together we'll eat them all up."

Not till they heard a mighty roar and crackling did the people in Seoul push back their paper windows to find out what was the matter. Oh, what a blaze! It seemed to mount to heaven with red tongues that licked the stars. Those who could see in the direction of the palace supposed the sun had risen, but soon the crash of falling roofs and mighty columns of smoke and flame, with clouds of sparks, told the terrible story. By the time the sun did rise, there was nothing but a level waste of ashes, where the large buildings had been. Even the smoke had been driven away by the wind.

When the king and his people in the palace enclosure, who had saved their lives by running fast, thought over their loss, they began to plan how to stop the Fire Monster, when he should take it into his head to saunter forth on another walk and gobble up the king's dwelling.

A council of wise men was called to decide upon the question. Many long heads were bowed in hard thought over the matter. All the firemen, stone-cutters, fortune-tellers, dragon tamers, geomancers and people skilled in preventing conflagrations were invited to give their advice about the best way to fight the hungry Fire Demon.

After weeks spent in pondering the problem they all agreed that a dragon from China should be brought over to Korea. If kept in a swamp and fed well, he would surely prevent the Fire Imp from rambling too near Seoul. Besides, the dragon knew how to amuse and persuade the South Wind not to join in the mischief.

So, at tremendous cost and trouble, one of China's biggest dragons, capable of making rain and of spouting tons of water on its enemies, was shipped over and kept in a swamp. It was honored with a royal decoration, allowed to wear a string of amber beads over its ear, given a horsehair hat, a nobleman's girdle and fed all the turnips it desired to eat. In every way it was treated as the king's favorite.

But it was all in vain. Money and favor were alike wasted. The petted dragon made it rain too often, so that the land was soaked. Then when told not to do this, it grew sulky and neglected its duty. Finally it became fat and lazy and one night fell asleep when it ought to have been on guard, for the winds were out on a dance.

Seeing his jailer thus caught napping, the Fire Imp leaped out of its volcano prison, rode quickly on the South Wind to Seoul and in a few hours had again swallowed the royal palace. There was nothing seen next day except ashes, which the Fire Monster cared no more for than we for nutshells when the kernels are eaten up.

With big tears in their eyes, the king and his wise men met together again to decide on a new scheme to keep off the Fire Imp. They were ready to drown him, or to see him get eaten up, because he had twice swallowed up the palace. They sent the Chinese dragon home and this time, besides the fortune-tellers and the stone-cutters, the well-diggers were invited also. For many days the wise men studied maps, talked of geography, looked at mountains, valleys, and the volcano, and studied air currents. Finally one man, famous for his deep learning about wood and water, forests and rivers, spoke thus:

"It is evident that the fire has always come from the southwest and up this valley," pointing to a map.

"True, true," shouted all the wise men.

"Well, right in his path let us dig a big pond, a regular artificial lake and very deep, into which the Fire Monster will tumble. This will put him out and he can get no further."

"Agreed, agreed," shouted the wise men in chorus. "Why did we not think of this before?"

All the skilful diggers of wells and ditches were summoned to the capital. With shovel and spade they worked for weeks. Then they let in water from the river until the pond was full.

So everybody in Seoul went to bed thinking that the king's palace was now safe surely.

But the Fire Imp, seeing the dragon gone and his opportunity come, climbed out of his volcano and moved out for another meal. This time, the South Wind was busy elsewhere and could not go with him. So he went alone, but coming to the pond, tumbled and wet himself so badly that he was chilled and nearly put out when he got to the palace, which was only half burned. So he went home growling and hungry.

Again the wise men were called and the first thing they did was to thank the boss well-digger, who had made the pond. The king summoned him into his presence to confer rank upon him and his children. He was presented with four rolls of silk, forty pounds of white ginseng, a tiger-skin robe, sixty dried chestnuts and forty-four strings of copper cash. Loaded with such Korean wealth and honors, the man fell on his hands and knees and thanked His Majesty profusely.

Then they called the master stone-cutter or chief of the guild and asked him if he could chisel out the figure of a beast that could eat flames and be ugly enough to scare away the Fire Imp.

The master had long hoped that he would be invited to rear this bit of sculpture, but hitherto the king and Court had feared it might cost too much.

So the order was given, and out of the heart of the mountains, a mighty block of white granite was loosed and brought to Seoul on rollers, pushed, pulled, and hoisted by thousands of laborers. Then, hidden behind canvas, to keep the matter secret, lest the Fire Imp should find it out, the workmen toiled. Hammers and chisels clinked, until on a certain day the Great Stone Flame Eater was ready to take his permanent seat in front of the palace gate, as guardian of the royal buildings and treasures.

The Fire Imp laughed when the South Wind told him of what the Koreans in the capital were doing, even though she warned him of the danger of his being eaten up.

"I shall walk out and see for myself anyhow," said the Fire Imp.

One night he crept out quietly and moved toward the city. He was nearly drowned in the pond, but plucking up courage, he went on until he was near the king's dwelling. Hearing the Fire Imp coming, the Great Flame Eater turned his head and licked his chops in anticipation of swallowing the Fire Imp whole, as a toad does a fly.

But one sight of the hideous stony monster was enough for the Fire Imp. There, before him, on a high pedestal was something never before seen in heaven or on earth. It had enormous fire-proof scales like a salamander, with curly hair like asbestos and its mouth was full of big fangs. It was altogether hideous enough to give even a Volcano Spirit a chill.

"Just think of those jaws snapping on me," said the Fire Imp to himself, as he looked at them and the fangs. "I do believe that creature is half alligator and half water-tortoise. I had better go home. No dinner this time!"

So by his freezing glance alone, the Great Flame Eater frightened away the Fire Imp, so that he never came again and the royal palace was not once burned. To-day the ugly brute still keeps watch. You have only to look at him to enjoy this story.

FABLES, FOLKLORE & ANCIENT STORIES

THE MAGICAL & THE SUPERNATURAL

Korean folktales blend reality, superstition and fascinating encounters with the supernatural. This acknowledgment of the magical and supernatural realms is found in the earliest stories, folktales and myths, with Bear and Tiger each talking and planning to become human. Magic has always been a part of the Korean imagination.

Taoist sages (translated as 'wizards') were keepers of mystical knowledge, and were rumoured to have the power of teleportation, flying from mountaintop to mountaintop, or traversing all of Korea in a few short strides. They were keepers of arcane wisdoms on healing medicines and restoring order to the cosmos.

THE SOLDIER OF KANG-WHA

The East says that the air is full of invisible constituents that, once taken in hand and controlled, will take on various forms of life. The man of Kang-wha had acquired the art of calling together the elements necessary for the butterfly. This, too, comes from Taoism, and is called *son-sul*, Taoist magic

The Story

There was a soldier once of Kang-wha who was the chief man of his village; a low-class man, he was, apparently, without any gifts. One day his wife, overcome by a fit of jealousy, sat sewing in her inner room. It was midwinter, and he was obliged to be at home; so, with intent to cheer her up and take her mind off the blues, he said to her, "Would you like to see me make some butterflies?"

His wife, more angry than ever at this, rated him for his impudence, and paid no further attention.

The soldier then took her workbasket and from it selected bits of silk of various colours, tucked them into his palm, closed his hand upon them, and repeated a prayer, after which he threw the handful into the air. Immediately beautiful butterflies filled the room, dazzling the eyes and shining in all the colours of the silk itself.

The wife, mystified by the wonder of it, forgot her anger. The soldier a little later opened his hand, held it up, and they all flew into it. He closed it tight and then again opened his hand, and they were pieces of silk only. His wife alone saw this; it was unknown to others. No such strange magic was ever heard of before.

In 1637, when Kang-wha fell before the Manchus, all the people of the place fled crying for their lives, while the soldier remained undisturbed at his home, eating his meals with his wife and family just as usual. He laughed at the neighbours hurrying by. Said he, "The barbarians will not touch this town; why do you run so?" Thus it turned out that, while the whole island was devastated, the soldier's village escaped.

THE MAN ON THE ROAD

In the Manchu War of 1636, the people of Seoul rushed off in crowds to make their escape. One party of them came suddenly upon a great force of the enemy, armed and mounted. The hills and valleys seemed full of them, and there was no possible way of escape. What to do they knew not. In the midst of their perplexity they suddenly saw some one sitting peacefully in the main roadway just in front, underneath a pine tree, quite unconcerned. He had dismounted from his horse, which a servant held, standing close by. A screen of several yards of cotton cloth was hanging up just before him, as if to shield him from the dust of the passing army.

The people who were making their escape came up to this stranger, and said imploringly, "We are all doomed to die. What shall we do?"

The mysterious stranger said, "Why should you die? and why are you so frightened? Sit down by me and see the barbarians go by."

The people, perceiving his mind so composed and his appearance devoid of fear, and they having no way of escape, did as he bade them and sat down.

The cavalry of the enemy moved by in great numbers, killing every one they met, not a single person escaping; but when they reached the place where the magician sat, they went by without, apparently, seeing anything. Thus they continued till the evening, when all had passed by. The stranger and the people with him sat the day through without any harm overtaking them, even though they were in the midst of the enemy's camp, as it were.

At last awaking to the fact that he was possessor of some wonderful magic, they all with one accord came and bowed before him, asking his name and his place of residence. He made no answer, however, but mounted his beautiful horse and rode swiftly away, no one being able to overtake him.

The day following the party fell in with a man who had been captured but had made his escape. They asked if he had seen anything special the day before. He said, "When I followed the barbarian army, passing such and such a point" – indicating the place where the magician had sat with the people – "we skirted great walls and precipitous rocks, against which no one could move, and so we passed by."

Thus were the few yards of cotton cloth metamorphosed before the eyes of the passers-by.

THE GEOMANCER

Yi Eui-sin was a specialist in Geomancy. His craft came into being evidently as a by-product of Taoism, but has had mixed in it elements of ancient Chinese philosophy. The Positive and the Negative, the Two Primary Principles in Nature, play a great part; also the Five Elements, Metal, Wood, Water, Fire and Earth. In the selection of a site, that for a house is called a "male" choice, while the grave is denominated the "female" choice.

Millions of money have been expended in Korea on the geomancer and his associates in the hope of finding lucky homes for the living and auspicious resting-places for the dead, the Korean idea being that, in some mysterious way, all our fortune is associated with Mother Earth.

The Story

There was a geomancer once, Yi Eui-sin, who in seeking out a special mountain vein, started with the Dragon Ridge in North Ham-kyong Province, and traced it as far as Pine Mountain in Yang-ju County, where it stopped in a beautifully rounded end, forming a perfect site for burial. After wandering all day in the hills, Yi's hungry spirit cried out for food. He saw beneath the hill a small house, to which he went, and rapping at the door asked for something to eat. A mourner, recently bereaved, came out in a respectful and kindly way, and gave him a dish of white gruel. Yi, after he had eaten, asked what time the friend had become a mourner, and if he had already passed the funeral. The owner answered, "I am just now entering upon full mourning, but we have not yet arranged for the funeral." He spoke in a sad and disheartened way.

Yi felt sorry for him, and asked the reason. "I wonder if it's because you are poor that you have not yet made the necessary arrangements, or perhaps you have not yet found a suitable site! I am an expert in reading the hills, and I'll tell you of a site; would you care to see it?"

The mourner thanked him most gratefully, and said, "I'll be delighted to know of it."

Yi then showed him the end of the great vein that he had just discovered, also the spot for the grave and how to place its compass points. "After possessing this site," said he, "you will be greatly enriched, but in ten years you will have cause to arrange for another site. When that comes to pass please call me, won't you? In calling for me just ask for Yi So-pang, who lives in West School Ward, Seoul."

The mourner did as directed, and as the geomancer had foretold, all his affairs prospered. He built a large tiled house, and ornamented the grave with great stones as a prosperous and high-minded country gentleman should do.

After ten years a guest called one day, and saluting him asked, "Is that grave yonder, beyond the stream, yours?" The master answered, "It is mine." Then the stranger said, "That is a famous site, but ten years have passed since you have come into possession of it, and the luck is gone; why do you not make a change? If you wait too long you will rue it and may meet with great disaster."

The owner, hearing this, thought of Yi the geomancer, and what he had said years before. Remembering that, he asked the stranger to remain as his guest while he went next day to Seoul to look up Yi in West School Ward. He found him, and told him why he had come.

Yi said, "I already knew of this." So the two journeyed together to the inquirer's home. When there, they went with the guest up the hill. Yi asked of the guest, "Why did you tell the master to change the site?"

The guest replied, "This hill is a Kneeling Pheasant formation. If the pheasant kneels too long it cannot endure it, so that within a limited time it must fly. Ten years is the time; that's why I spoke."

Yi laughed and said, "Your idea is only a partial view, you have thought of only one thing, there are other conditions that enter." Then he showed the peak to the rear, and said, "Yonder is Dog Hill," and then one below, "which," said he, "is Falcon Hill," and then the stream in front, "which," said he, "is Cat River. This is the whole group, the dog behind, the falcon just above, and the cat in front, how then can the pheasant fly? It dares not."

The guest replied, "Teacher, surely your eyes are enlightened, and see further than those of ordinary men."

From that day forth the Yis of Pine Hill became a great and noted family..

THE GRATEFUL GHOST

It is often told that in the days of the Koryo Dynasty (AD 918–1392), when an examination was to be held, a certain scholar came from a far-distant part of the country to take part. Once on his journey the day was drawing to a close, and he found himself among the mountains. Suddenly he heard a sneezing from among the creepers and bushes by the roadside, but could see no one. Thinking it strange, he dismounted from his horse, went into the brake and listened. He heard it again, and it seemed to come from the roots of the creeper close beside him, so he ordered his servant to dig round it and see. He dug and found a dead man's skull. It was full of earth, and the roots of the creeper had passed through the nostrils. The sneezing was caused by the annoyance felt by the spirit from having the nose so discommoded.

The candidate felt sorry, washed the skull in clean water, wrapped it in paper and reburied it in its former place on the hill-side. He also brought a table of food and offered sacrifice, and said a prayer.

That night, in a dream, a scholar came to him, an old man with white hair, who bowed, thanked him, and said, "On account of sin committed in a former life, I died out of season before I had fulfilled my days. My posterity, too, were all destroyed, my body crumbled back into the dust, my skull alone remaining, and that is what you found below the creeper. On account of the root passing through it the annoyance was great, and I could not help but sneeze. By good luck you and your kind heart, blessed of Heaven, took pity on me, buried me in a clean place and gave me food. Your kindness is greater than the mountains, and like the blessing that first brought me into life. Though my soul is by no means perfect, yet I long for some way by which to requite your favour, and so I have exercised my powers in your behalf. Your present journey is for the purpose of trying the official Examination, so I shall tell you beforehand what the form is to be, and the subject. It is to be of character groups of fives, in couplets; the rhyme sound is 'pong,' and the subject 'Peaks and Spires of the Summer Clouds.' I have already composed one for you, which, if you care to use it, will undoubtedly win you the first place. It is this –

> 'The white sun rode high up in the heavens,
> And the floating clouds formed a lofty peak;
> The priest who saw them asked if there was a temple there,
> And the crane lamented the fact that no pines were visible;
> But the lightnings from the cloud were the
> flashings of the woodman's axe,
> And the muffled thunders were the bell calls of the holy temple.
> Will any say that the hills do not move?
> On the sunset breezes they sailed away.'"

After thus stating it, he bowed and took his departure.

The man, in wonder, awakened from his dream, came up to Seoul; and behold, the subject was as foretold by the spirit. He wrote what had been given him, and became first in the honours of the occasion.

THE HONEST WITCH

Song Sang-in matriculated in 1601. He was a just man, and feared by the dishonest element of the Court. In 1605 he graduated and became a provincial governor. He nearly lost his life in the disturbances of the reign of King Kwang-hai, and was exiled to Quelpart for a period of ten years, but in the spring of 1623 he was recalled.

The Story

There was a Korean once, called Song Sang-in, whose mind was upright and whose spirit was true. He hated witches with all his might, and regarded them as deceivers of the people. "By their so-called prayers," said he, "they devour the people's goods. There is no limit to the foolishness and extravagance that accompanies them. This doctrine of theirs is all nonsense. Would that I could rid the earth of them and wipe out their names for ever."

Some time later Song was appointed magistrate of Nam Won County in Chulla Province. On his arrival he issued the following order: "If any witch is found in this county, let her be beaten to death." The whole place was so thoroughly spied upon that all the witches made their escape to other prefectures. The magistrate thought, "Now we are rid of them, and that ends the matter for this county at any rate."

On a certain day he went out for a walk, and rested for a time at *Kwang-han* Pavilion. As he looked out from his coign of vantage, he saw a woman approaching on horseback with a witch's drum on her head. He looked intently to make sure, and to his astonishment he saw that she was indeed a *mutang* (witch). He sent a *yamen*-runner to have her arrested, and when she was brought before him he asked, "Are you a *mutang*?"

She replied, "Yes, I am."

"Then," said he, "you did not know of the official order issued?"

"Oh yes, I heard of it," was her reply.

He then asked, "Are you not afraid to die, that you stay here in this county?"

The *mutang* bowed, and made answer, "I have a matter of complaint to lay before your Excellency to be put right; please take note of it and grant my request. It is this: There are true *mutangs* and false *mutangs*. False *mutangs* ought to be killed, but you would not kill an honest *mutang*, would you? Your orders pertain to false *mutangs*; I do not understand them as pertaining to those who are true. I am an honest *mutang*; I knew you would not kill me, so I remained here in peace."

The magistrate asked, "How do you know that there are honest *mutangs*?"

The woman replied, "Let's put the matter to the test and see. If I am not proven honest, let me die."

"Very well," said the magistrate; "but can you really make good, and do you truly know how to call back departed spirits?"

The *mutang* answered, "I can."

The magistrate suddenly thought of an intimate friend who had been dead for some time, and he said to her, "I had a friend of such and such rank in Seoul; can you call his spirit back to me?"

The *mutang* replied, "Let me do so; but first you must prepare food, with wine, and serve it properly."

The magistrate thought for a moment, and then said to himself, "It is a serious matter to take a person's life; let me find out first if she is true or not, and then decide." So he had the food brought.

The *mutang* said also, "I want a suit of your clothes, too, please." This was brought, and she spread her mat in the courtyard, placed the food in order, donned the dress, and so made all preliminary arrangements. She then lifted her eyes toward heaven and uttered the strange magic sounds by which spirits are called, meanwhile shaking a tinkling bell. In a little she turned and said, "I've come." Then she began telling the sad story of his sickness and death and their separation. She reminded the magistrate of how they had played together, and of things that had happened when they were at school at their lessons; of the difficulties they had met in the examinations; of experiences that had come to them during their terms of office. She told secrets that they had confided to each other as intimate friends, and many matters most definitely that only they two knew. Not a single mistake did she make, but told the truth in every detail.

The magistrate, when he heard these things, began to cry, saying, "The soul of my friend is really present; I can no longer doubt or deny it." Then he ordered the choicest fare possible to be prepared as a sacrifice to his friend. In a little the friend bade him farewell and took his departure.

The magistrate said, "Alas! I thought *mutangs* were a brood of liars, but now I know that there are true *mutangs* as well as false." He gave her rich rewards, sent her away in safety, recalled his order against witches, and refrained from any matters pertaining to them for ever after.

A VISIT FROM THE SHADES

Choi Yu-won. – (The story of meeting his mother's ghost is reported to be of this man.)

Choi Yu-won matriculated in 1579 and graduated in 1602, becoming Chief Justice and having conferred on him the rank of prince. When he was a boy his great-aunt once gave him cloth for a suit of clothes, but he refused to accept of it, and from this his aunt prophesied that he would yet become a famous man. He studied in the home of the great teacher Yul-gok, and Yul-gok also foretold that the day would come when he would be an honour to Korea.

Yu-won once met Chang Han-kang and inquired of him concerning *Pyon-wha Keui-jil* (a law by which the weak became strong, the wicked good, and the stupid wise). He also asked that if one be truly transformed will the soul change as well as the body, or the body only? Chang replied, "Both are changed, for how could the body change without the soul?" Yu-won asked Yul-gok concerning this also, and Yul-gok replied that Chang's words were true.

In 1607 Choi Yu-won memorialized the King, calling attention to a letter received from Japan in answer to a communication sent by his Majesty, which had on its address the name of the

Prime Minister, written a space lower than good form required. The Korean envoy had not protested, as duty would require of him, and yet the King had advanced him in rank. The various officials commended him for his courage.

In 1612, while he was Chief Justice, King Kwang-hai tried to degrade the Queen Dowager, who was not his own mother, he being born of a concubine, but Yu-won besought him with tears not to do so illegal and unnatural a thing. Still the King overrode all opposition, and did according to his unfilial will. In it all Choi Yu-won was proven a good man and a just. He used to say to his companions, even as a youth, "Death is dreadful, but still, better death for righteousness' sake and honour than life in disgrace." Another saying of his runs, "All one's study is for the development of character; if it ends not in that it is in vain."

Korea's ancient belief was that the blood of a faithful son served as an elixir of life to the dying, so that when his mother was at the point of death Yu-won with a knife cut flesh from his thigh till the blood flowed, and with this he prepared his magic dose.

The Story

There was a minister in olden days who once, when he was Palace Secretary, was getting ready for office in the morning. He had on his ceremonial dress. It was rather early, and as he leaned on his arm-rest for a moment, sleep overcame him. He dreamt, and in the dream he thought he was mounted and on his journey. He was crossing the bridge at the entrance to East Palace Street, when suddenly he saw his mother coming towards him on foot. He at once dismounted, bowed, and said, "Why do you come thus, mother, not in a chair, but on foot?"

She replied, "I have already left the world, and things are not where I am as they are where you are, and so I walk."

The secretary asked, "Where are you going, please?"

She replied, "We have a servant living at Yong-san, and they are having a witches' prayer service there just now, so I am going to partake of the sacrifice."

"But," said the secretary, "we have sacrificial days, many of them, at our own home, those of the four seasons, also on the first and fifteenth of each month. Why do you go to a servant's house and not to mine?"

The mother replied, "Your sacrifices are of no interest to me, I like the prayers of the witches. If there is no medium we spirits find no satisfaction. I am in a hurry," said she, "and cannot wait longer," so she spoke her farewell and was gone.

The secretary awoke with a start, but felt that he had actually seen what had come to pass.

He then called a servant and told him to go at once to So-and-So's house in Yong-san, and tell a certain servant to come that night without fail. "Go quickly," said the secretary, "so that you can be back before I enter the Palace." Then he sat down to meditate over it.

In a little the servant had gone and come again. It was not yet broad daylight, and because it was cold the servant did not enter straight, but went first into the kitchen to warm his hands before the fire. There was a fellow-servant there who asked him, "Have you had something to drink?"

He replied, "They are having a big witch business on at Yong-san, and while the *mutang* (witch) was performing, she said that the spirit that possessed her was the mother of the master here. On my appearance she called out my name and said, 'This is a servant from our house.' Then she called me and gave me a big glass of spirit. She added further, 'On my way here I met my son going into the Palace.'"

The secretary, overhearing this talk from the room where he was waiting, broke down and began to cry. He called in the servant and made fuller inquiry, and more than ever he felt assured that his mother's spirit had really gone that morning to share in the *koot* (witches' sacrificial ceremony). He then called the *mutang*, and in behalf of the spirit of his mother made her a great offering. Ever afterwards he sacrificed to her four times a year at each returning season.

THE FEARLESS CAPTAIN

There was formerly a soldier, Yee Man-ji of Yong-nam, a strong and muscular fellow, and brave as a lion. He had green eyes and a terrible countenance. Frequently he said, "Fear! What is fear?" On a certain day when he was in his house a sudden storm of rain came on, when there were flashes of lightning and heavy claps of thunder. At one of them a great ball of fire came tumbling into his home and went rolling over the verandah, through the rooms, into the kitchen and out into the yard, and again into the servants' quarters. Several times it went and came bouncing about. Its blazing light and the accompanying noise made it a thing of terror.

Yee sat in the outer verandah, wholly undisturbed. He thought to himself, "I have done no wrong, therefore why need I fear the lightning?" A moment later a flash struck the large elm tree in front of the house and smashed it to pieces. The rain then ceased and the thunder likewise.

Yee turned to see how it fared with his family, and found them all fallen senseless. With the greatest of difficulty he had them restored to life. During that year they all fell ill and died, and Yee came to Seoul and became a Captain of the Right Guard. Shortly after he went to North Ham-kyong Province. There he took a second wife and settled down. All his predecessors had died of goblin influences, and the fact that calamity had overtaken them while in the official quarters had caused them to use one of the village houses instead.

Yee, however, determined to live down all fear and go back to the old quarters, which he extensively repaired.

One night his wife was in the inner room while he was alone in the public office with a light burning before him. In the second watch or thereabout, a strange-looking object came out of the inner quarters. It looked like the stump of a tree wrapped in black sackcloth. There was no outline or definite shape to it, and it came jumping along and sat itself immediately before Yee Man-ji. Also two other objects came following in its wake, shaped just like the first one. The three then sat in a row before Yee, coming little by little closer and closer to him. Yee moved away till he had backed up against the wall and could go no farther. Then he said, "Who are you, anyhow; what kind of devil, pray, that you dare to push towards me so in my office? If you have any complaint or matter to set right, say so, and I'll see to it."

The middle devil said in reply, "I'm hungry, I'm hungry, I'm hungry."

Yee answered, "Hungry, are you? Very well, now just move back and I'll have food prepared for you in abundance." He then repeated a magic formula that he had learned, and snapped his fingers. The three devils seemed to be afraid of this. Then Man-ji suddenly closed his fist and struck a blow at the first devil. It dodged, however, most deftly and he missed, but hit the floor a sounding blow that cut his hand.

Then they all shouted, "We'll go, we'll go, since you treat guests thus." At once they bundled out of the room and disappeared.

On the following day he had oxen killed and a sacrifice offered to these devils, and they returned no more.

* * *

Note. – Men have been killed by goblins. This is not so much due to the fact that goblins are wicked as to the fact that men are afraid of them. Many died in North Ham-kyong, but those again who were brave, and clove them with a knife, or struck them down, lived. If they had been afraid, they too would have died.

HAUNTED HOUSES

There once lived a man in Seoul called Yi Chang, who frequently told as an experience of his own the following story: He was poor and had no home of his own, so he lived much in quarters loaned him by others. When hard pressed he even went into haunted houses and lived there. Once, after failing to find a place, he heard of one such house in Ink Town (one of the wards of Seoul), at the foot of South Mountain, which had been haunted for generations and was now left vacant. Chang investigated the matter, and finally decided to take possession.

First, to find whether it was really haunted or not, he called his elder brothers, Hugh and Haw, and five or six of his relatives, and had them help clean it out and sleep there. The house had one upper room that was fast locked. Looking through a chink, there was seen to be in the room a tablet chair and a stand for it; also there was an old harp without any strings, a pair of worn shoes, and some sticks and bits of wood. Nothing else was in the room. Dust lay thick, as though it had gathered through long years of time.

The company, after drinking wine, sat round the table and played at games, watching the night through. When it was late, towards midnight, they suddenly heard the sound of harps and a great multitude of voices, though the words were mixed and unintelligible. It was as though many people were gathered and carousing at a feast. The company then consulted as to what they should do. One drew a sword and struck a hole through the partition that looked into the tower. Instantly there appeared from the other side a sharp blade thrust out towards them. It was blue in colour. In fear and consternation they desisted from further interference with the place. But the sound of the harp and the revelry kept up till the morning. The company broke up at daylight, withdrew from the place, and never again dared to enter.

In the South Ward there was another haunted house, of which Chang desired possession, so he called his friends and brothers once more to make the experiment and see whether it was really haunted or not. On entering, they found two dogs within the enclosure, one black and one tan, lying upon the open verandah, one at each end. Their eyes were fiery red, and though the company shouted at them they did not move. They neither barked nor bit. But when midnight came these two animals got up and went down into the court, and began baying at the inky sky in a way most ominous. They went jumping back and forth. At that time, too, there came some one round the corner of the house dressed in ceremonial robes. The two dogs met him with great delight, jumping up before and behind in their joy at his coming. He ascended to the verandah, and sat down. Immediately five or six multi-coloured demons appeared and bowed before him, in front of the open space. The man then led the demons and the dogs two or three times round the house. They rushed up into the verandah and jumped down again into the court; backwards and forwards they came and went, till at last all of them mysteriously disappeared. The devils went into a hole underneath the floor, while the dogs went up to their quarters and lay down.

The company from the inner room had seen this. When daylight came they examined the place, looked through the chinks of the floor, but saw only an old, worn-out sieve and a few discarded brooms. They went behind the house and found another old broom poked into the chimney. They ordered a servant to gather them up and have them burned. The dogs lay as they were all day long, and neither ate nor moved. Some of the party wished to kill the brutes, but were afraid, so fearsome was their appearance.

This night again they remained, desiring to see if the same phenomena would appear. Again at midnight the two dogs got down into the court and began barking up at the sky. The man in ceremonial robes again came, and the devils, just as the day before.

The company, in fear and disgust, left the following morning, and did not try it again.

A friend, hearing this of Chang, went and asked about it from Hugh and Haw, and they confirmed the story.

There is still another tale of a graduate who was out of house and home and went into a haunted dwelling in Ink Town, which was said to have had the tower where the mysterious sounds were heard. They opened the door, broke out the window, took out the old harp, the spirit chair, the shoes and sticks, and had them burned. Before the fire had finished its work, one of the servants fell down and died. The graduate, seeing this, in fear and dismay put out the fire, restored the things and left the house.

Again there was another homeless man who tried it. In the night a woman in a blue skirt came down from the loft, and acted in a peculiar and uncanny way. The man, seeing this, picked up his belongings and left.

Again, in South Kettle Town, there were a number of woodmen who in the early morning were passing behind the haunted house, when they found an old woman sitting weeping under a tree. They thinking her an evil bogey, one man came up behind and gave her a thrust with his sickle. The witch rushed off into the house, her height appearing to be only about one cubit and a span.

THE MAGIC INVASION OF SEOUL

A **gentleman of Seoul** was one day crossing the Han River in a boat. In the crossing, he nodded for a moment, fell asleep and dreamed a dream. In his dream he met a man who had Gothic eyebrows and almond eyes, whose face was red as ripened dates, and whose height was eight cubits and a span. He was dressed in green and had a long beard that came down to his belt-string. A man of majestic appearance he was, with a great sword at his side and he rode on a red horse.

He asked the gentleman to open his hand, which he did, and then the august stranger dashed a pen-mark on it as the sign of the God of War. Said he, "When you cross the river, do not go direct to Seoul, but wait at the landing. Seven horses will shortly appear, loaded with network hampers, all proceeding on their journey to the capital. You are to call the horsemen, open your hand, and show them the sign. When they see it they will all commit suicide in your very presence. After that, you are to take the loads and pile them up, but don't look into them. Then you are to go at once and report the matter to the Palace and have them all burned. The matter is of immense importance, so do not fail in the slightest particular."

The gentleman gave a great start of terror and awoke. He looked at his hand and there, indeed, was the strange mark. Not only so, but the ink had not yet dried upon it. He was astonished beyond measure, but did as the dream had indicated, and waited on the river's bank. In a little there came, as he was advised, the seven loads on seven horses, coming from the far-distant South. There were attendants in charge, and one man wearing an official coat came along behind. When they had crossed the river the gentleman called them to him and said, "I have something to say to you; come close to me." These men, unsuspecting, though with somewhat of a frightened look, closed up. He then showed them his hand with the mark, and asked them if they knew what it was. When they saw it, first of all, the man in the official coat turned and with one bound jumped over the cliff into the river. The eight or nine who accompanied the loads likewise all rushed after him and dashed into the water.

The scholar then called the boatmen, and explained to them that the things in the hampers were dangerous, that he would have to make it known to the Palace, and that in the meantime they were to keep close guard, but that they were not to touch them or look at them.

He hurried as fast as possible, and reported the matter to the Board of War. The Board sent an official, and had the loads brought into Seoul, and then, as had been directed, they were piled high with wood and set on fire. When the fire developed, the baskets broke open, and little figures of men and horses, each an inch or so long, in countless numbers, came tumbling out.

When the officials saw this they were frozen with fear; their hearts ceased beating and their tongues lolled out. In a little, however, the hampers were all burned up.

These were the creation of a magician, and were intended for a monster invasion of Seoul, until warned by Kwan.

From that time on the people of Seoul began faithful offerings to the God of War, for had he not saved the city?

THE MYSTERIOUS HOI TREE

Prince Pa-song's house was situated just inside of the great East Gate, and before it was a large Hoi tree. On a certain night the Prince's son-in-law was passing by the roadway that led in front of the archers' pavilion. There he saw a great company of bowmen, more than he could number, all shooting together at the target. A moment later he saw them practising riding, some throwing spears, some hurling bowls, some shooting from horseback, so that the road in front of the pavilion was blocked against all comers.

Some shouted as he came by, "Look at that impudent rascal! He attempts to ride by without dismounting."

They caught him and beat him, paying no attention to his cries for mercy, and having no pity for the pain he suffered, till one tall fellow came out of their serried ranks and said in an angry voice to the crowd, "He is my master; why do you treat him so?" He undid his bonds, took him by the arm and led him home.

When the son-in-law reached the gate he looked back and saw the man walk under the Hoi tree and disappear. He then learned, too, that all the crowd of archers were spirits and not men, and that the tall one who had befriended him was a spirit too, and that he had come forth from their particular Hoi tree.

HONG KIL TONG; OR, THE ADVENTURES OF AN ABUSED BOY

During the reign of the third king in Korea there lived a noble of high rank and noted family, by name Hong. His title was Ye Cho Pansa. He had two sons by his wife and one by one of his concubines. The latter son was very remarkable from his birth to his death, and he it is who forms the subject of this history.

When Hong Pansa was the father of but two sons, he dreamed by night on one occasion that he heard the noise of thunder, and looking up he saw a huge dragon entering his apartment, which seemed too small to contain the whole of his enormous body. The dream was so startling as to awaken the sleeper, who at once saw that it was a good omen, and a token to him of a blessing about to be conferred. He hoped the blessing might prove to be another son, and went to impart the good news to his wife. She would not see him, however, as she was offended by his taking a concubine from the class of "dancing girls." The great man was sad, and went away. Within the year, however, a son of marvellous beauty was born to one concubine, much to the annoyance of his wife and to himself, for he would have been glad to have the beautiful boy a full son, and eligible to office. The child was named Kil Tong, or Hong Kil Tong. He grew fast, and became more and more beautiful. He learned rapidly, and surprised every one by his remarkable ability. As he grew up he rebelled at being placed with the slaves, and at not being allowed to call his parent, father. The other children laughed and jeered at him, and made life very miserable. He refused longer to study of the duties of children to their parents. He upset his table in school, and declared he was going to be a soldier. One bright moonlight night Hong Pansa saw his son in the court-yard practising the arts of the soldier, and he asked him what it meant. Kil Tong answered that he was fitting himself to become a man that people should respect and fear. He said he knew that heaven had made all things for the use of men, if they found themselves capable of using them, and that the laws of men were only made to assist a few that could not otherwise do as they would; but that he was not inclined to submit to any such tyranny, but would become a great man in spite of his evil surroundings. "This is a most remarkable boy," mused Hong Pansa. "What a pity that he is not my proper and legitimate son, that he might be an honor to my name. As it is, I fear he will cause me serious trouble." He urged the boy to go to bed and sleep, but Kil Tong said it was useless, that if he went to bed he would think of his troubles till the tears washed sleep away from his eyes, and caused him to get up.

The wife of Hong Pansa and his other concubine (the dancing girl), seeing how much their lord and master thought of Kil Tong, grew to hate the latter intensely, and began to lay plans for ridding themselves of him. They called some *mootang*, or sorceresses, and explained to them that their happiness was disturbed by this son of a rival, and that peace could only be restored to their hearts by the death of this youth. The witches laughed and said: "Never mind. There is an old woman who lives by the east gate, tell her to come and prejudice the father. She can do it, and he will then look after his son."

The old hag came as requested. Hong Pansa was then in the women's apartments, telling them of the wonderful boy, much to their annoyance. A visitor was announced, and the old woman made a low bow outside. Hong Pansa asked her what her business was, and she stated that she had heard of his wonderful son, and came to see him, to foretell what his future was to be.

Kil Tong came as called, and on seeing him the hag bowed and said: "Send out all of the people." She then stated: "This will be a very great man; if not a king, he will be greater than the king, and will avenge his early wrongs by killing all his family." At this the father called to her to stop, and enjoined strict secrecy upon her. He sent Kil Tong at once to a strong room, and had him locked in for safe keeping.

The boy was very sad at this new state of affairs, but as his father let him have books, he got down to hard study, and learned the Chinese works on astronomy. He could not see his mother, and his unnatural father was too afraid to come near him. He made up his mind, however, that as soon as he could get out he would go to some far off country, where he was not known, and make his true power felt.

Meanwhile, the unnatural father was kept in a state of continual excitement by his wicked concubine, who was bent on the destruction of the son of her rival, and kept constantly before her master the great dangers that would come to him from being the parent of such a man as Kil Tong was destined to be, if allowed to live. She showed him that such power as the boy was destined to possess, would eventually result in his overthrowal, and with him his father's house would be in disgrace, and, doubtless, would be abolished. While if this did not happen, the son was sure to kill his family, so that, in either case, it was the father's clear duty to prevent any further trouble by putting the boy out of the way. Hong Pansa was finally persuaded that his concubine was right, and sent for the assassins to come and kill his son. But a spirit filled the father with disease, and he told the men to stay their work. Medicines failed to cure the disease, and the *mootang* women were called in by the concubine. They beat their drums and danced about the room, conjuring the spirit to leave, but it would not obey. At last they said, at the suggestion of the concubine, that Kil Tong was the cause of the disorder, and that with his death the spirit would cease troubling the father.

Again the assassins were sent for, and came with their swords, accompanied by the old hag from the east gate. While they were meditating on the death of Kil Tong, he was musing on the unjust laws of men who allowed sons to be born of concubines, but denied them rights that were enjoyed by other men.

While thus musing in the darkness of the night, he heard a crow caw three times and fly away. "This means something ill to me," thought he; and just then his window was thrown open, and in stepped the assassins. They made at the boy, but he was not there. In their rage they wounded each other, and killed the old woman who was their guide. To their amazement the room had disappeared, and they were surrounded by high mountains. A mighty storm arose, and rocks flew through the air. They could not escape, and, in their terror, were about to give up, when music was heard, and a boy came riding by on a donkey, playing a flute. He took away their weapons, and showed himself to be Kil Tong. He promised not to kill them, as they begged for their lives, but only on condition that they should never try to kill another man. He told them that he would know if the promise was broken, and, in that event, he would instantly kill them.

Kil Tong went by night to see his father, who thought him a spirit, and was very much afraid. He gave his father medicine, which instantly cured him; and sending for his mother, bade her good-by, and started for an unknown country.

His father was very glad that the boy had escaped, and lost his affection for his wicked concubine. But the latter, with her mistress, was very angry, and tried in vain to devise some means to accomplish their evil purposes.

Kil Tong, free at last, journeyed to the south, and began to ascend the lonely mountains. Tigers were abundant, but he feared them not, and they seemed to avoid molesting him. After many days, he found himself high up on a barren peak enveloped by the clouds, and enjoyed the remoteness of the place, and the absence of men and obnoxious laws. He now felt himself a free man, and the equal of any, while he knew that heaven was smiling upon him and giving him powers not accorded to other men.

Through the clouds at some distance he thought he espied a huge stone door in the bare wall of rock. Going up to it, he found it to be indeed a movable door, and, opening it, he stepped inside, when, to his amazement, he found himself in an open plain, surrounded by high and inaccessible mountains. He saw before him over two hundred good houses, and many men, who, when they had somewhat recovered from their own surprise, came rushing upon him, apparently with evil intent. Laying hold upon him they asked him who he was, and why he came trespassing upon their ground. He said: "I am surprised to find myself in the presence of men. I am but the son of a concubine, and men, with their laws, are obnoxious to me. Therefore, I thought to get away from man entirely, and, for that reason, I wandered alone into these wild regions. But who are you, and why do you live in this lone spot? Perhaps we may have a kindred feeling."

"We are called thieves," was answered; "but we only despoil the hated official class of some of their ill-gotten gains. We are willing to help the poor unbeknown, but no man can enter our stronghold and depart alive, unless he has become one of us. To do so, however, he must prove himself to be strong in body and mind. If you can pass the examination and wish to join our party, well and good; otherwise you die."

This suited Kil Tong immensely, and he consented to the conditions. They gave him various trials of strength, but he chose his own. Going up to a huge rock on which several men were seated, he laid hold of it and hurled it to some distance, to the dismay of the men, who fell from their seat, and to the surprised delight of all. He was at once installed a member, and a feast was ordered. The contract was sealed by mingling blood from the lips of all the members with blood similarly supplied by Kil Tong. He was then given a prominent seat and served to wine and food.

Kil Tong soon became desirous of giving to his comrades some manifestation of his courage. An opportunity presently offered. He heard the men bemoaning their inability to despoil a large and strong Buddhist temple not far distant. As was the rule, this temple in the mountains was well patronized by officials, who made it a place of retirement for pleasure and debauch, and in return the lazy, licentious priests were allowed to collect tribute from the poor people about, till they had become rich and powerful. The several attempts made by the robber band had proved unsuccessful, by virtue of the number and vigilance of the priests, together with the strength of their enclosure. Kil Tong agreed to assist them to accomplish their design or perish in the attempt, and such was their faith in him that they readily agreed to his plans.

On a given day Kil Tong, dressed in the red gown of a youth, just betrothed, covered himself with the dust of travel, and mounted on a donkey, with one robber disguised as a servant, made his way to the temple. He asked on arrival to be shown to the head priest, to whom he stated that he was the son of Hong Pansa, that his noble father having heard of the greatness of this temple, and the wisdom of its many priests, had decided to send him with a letter, which he produced, to be educated among their numbers. He also stated that a train of one hundred ponies loaded with rice had been sent as a present from his father to the priest, and he expected they would arrive before dark, as they did not wish to stop alone in the mountains, even though every pony was attended by a groom, who was armed for defense. The priests were delighted, and having read the letter, they never for a moment suspected that all was not right. A great feast was ordered in honor of their noble scholar, and all sat down before the tables, which were filled so high that one could hardly see his neighbor on the opposite side. They had scarcely seated themselves and indulged in the generous wine, when it was announced that the train of ponies laden with rice had arrived. Servants were sent to look after the tribute, and the eating and drinking went on. Suddenly Kil Tong clapped his hand, over his cheek with a cry of pain, which drew the attention of all. When, to the great mortification of the priests, he produced from his mouth a pebble, previously introduced on the sly, and exclaimed: "Is it to feed on stones that my father sent me to this place? What do you mean by setting such rice before a gentleman?"

The priests were filled with mortification and dismay, and bowed their shaven heads to the floor in humiliation. When at a sign from Kil Tong, a portion of the robbers, who had entered the court as grooms to the ponies, seized the bending priests and bound them as they were. The latter shouted for help, but the other robbers, who had been concealed in the bags, which were supposed to contain rice, seized the servants, while others were loading the ponies with jewels, rice, cash and whatever of value they could lay hands upon.

An old priest who was attending to the fires, seeing the uproar, made off quietly to the yamen near by and called for soldiers. The soldiers were sent after some delay, and Kil Tong, disguised as a priest, called to them to follow him down a by-path after the robbers. While he conveyed the soldiers over this rough path, the robbers made good their escape by the main road, and were soon joined in their stronghold by their youthful leader, who had left the soldiers groping helplessly in the dark among the rocks and trees in a direction opposite that taken by the robbers.

The priests soon found out that they had lost almost all their riches, and were at no loss in determining how the skilful affair had been planned and carried out. Kil Tong's name was noised abroad, and it was soon known that he was heading a band of robbers, who, through his assistance, were able to do many marvellous things. The robber band were delighted at the success of his first undertaking, and made him their chief, with the consent of all. After sufficient time had elapsed for the full enjoyment of their last and greatest success, Kil Tong planned a new raid.

The Governor of a neighboring province was noted for his overbearing ways and the heavy burdens that he laid upon his subjects. He was very rich, but universally hated, and Kil Tong decided to avenge the people and humiliate the Governor, knowing that his work would be appreciated by the people, as were indeed his acts at the temple. He instructed his band to proceed singly to the Governor's city – the local capital – at the time of a fair, when their coming would not cause comment. At a given time a portion of them were to set fire to a lot of straw-thatched huts outside the city gates, while the others repaired in a body to the Governor's yamen. They did so. The Governor was borne in his chair to a place where he could witness the conflagration, which also drew away the most of the inhabitants. The robbers bound the remaining servants, and while some were securing money, jewels, and weapons, Kil Tong wrote on the walls: "The wicked Governor that robs the people is relieved of his ill-gotten gains by Kil Tong – the people's avenger."

Again the thieves made good their escape, and Kil Tong's name became known everywhere. The Governor offered a great reward for his capture, but no one seemed desirous of encountering a robber

THE MAGICAL & THE SUPERNATURAL

of such boldness. At last the King offered a reward after consulting with his officers. When one of them said he would capture the thief alone, the King was astonished at his boldness and courage, and bade him be off and make the attempt. The officer was called the Pochang; he had charge of the prisons, and was a man of great courage.

The Pochang started on his search, disguised as a traveller. He took a donkey and servant, and after travelling many days he put up at a little inn, at the same time that another man on a donkey rode up. The latter was Kil Tong in disguise, and he soon entered into conversation with the man, whose mission was known to him.

"*I goo*," said Kil Tong, as he sat down to eat, "this is a dangerous country. I have just been chased by the robber Kil Tong till the life is about gone out of me."

"Kil Tong, did you say?" remarked Pochang. "I wish he would chase me. I am anxious to see the man of whom we hear so much."

"Well, if you see him once you will be satisfied," replied Kil Tong.

"Why?" asked the Pochang. "Is he such a fearful-looking man as to frighten one by his aspect alone?"

"No; on the contrary he looks much as do ordinary mortals. But we *know* he is different, you see."

"Exactly," said the Pochang. "That is just the trouble. You are afraid of him before you see him. Just let me get a glimpse of him, and matters will be different, I think."

"Well," said Kil Tong, "you can be easily pleased, if that is all, for I dare say if you go back into the mountains here you will see him, and get acquainted with him too."

"That is good. Will you show me the place?"

"Not I. I have seen enough of him to please me. I can tell you where to go, however, if you persist in your curiosity," said the robber.

"Agreed!" exclaimed the officer. "Let us be off at once lest he escapes. And if you succeed in showing him to me, I will reward you for your work and protect you from the thief."

After some objection by Kil Tong, who appeared to be reluctant to go, and insisted on at least finishing his dinner, they started off, with their servants, into the mountains. Night overtook them, much to the apparent dismay of the guide, who pretended to be very anxious to give up the quest. At length, however, they came to the stone door, which was open. Having entered the robber's stronghold, the door closed behind them, and the guide disappeared, leaving the dismayed officer surrounded by the thieves. His courage had now left him, and he regretted his rashness. The robbers bound him securely and led him past their miniature city into an enclosure surrounded by houses which, by their bright colors, seemed to be the abode of royalty. He was conveyed into a large audience-chamber occupying the most extensive building of the collection, and there, on a sort of throne, in royal style, sat his guide. The Pochang saw his mistake, and fell on his face, begging for mercy. Kil Tong upbraided him for his impudence and arrogance and promised to let him off this time. Wine was brought, and all partook of it. That given to the officer was drugged, and he fell into a stupor soon after drinking it. While in this condition he was put into a bag and conveyed in a marvellous manner to a high mountain overlooking the capital. Here he found himself upon recovering from the effects of his potion; and not daring to face his sovereign with such a fabulous tale, he cast himself down from the high mountain, and was picked up dead, by passers-by, in the morning. Almost at the same time that His Majesty received word of the death of his officer, and was marvelling at the audacity of the murderer in bringing the body almost to the palace doors, came simultaneous reports of great depredations in each of the eight provinces. The trouble was in each case attributed to Kil Tong, and the fact that he was reported as being in eight far removed places at the same time caused great consternation.

Official orders were issued to each of the eight governors to catch and bring to the city, at once, the robber Kil Tong. These orders were so well obeyed that upon a certain day soon after, a guard came from each province bringing Kil Tong, and there in a line stood eight men alike in every respect.

The King on inquiry found that Kil Tong was the son of Hong Pansa, and the father was ordered into the royal presence. He came with his legitimate son, and bowed his head in shame to the ground. When asked what he meant by having a son who would cause such general misery and distress, he swooned away, and would have died had not one of the Kil Tongs produced some medicine which cured him. The son, however, acted as spokesman, and informed the King that Kil Tong was but the son of his father's slave, that he was utterly incorrigible, and had fled from home when a mere boy. When asked to decide as to which was his true son, the father stated that his son had a scar on the left thigh. Instantly each of the eight men pulled up the baggy trousers and displayed a scar. The guard was commanded to remove the men and kill all of them; but when they attempted to do so the life had disappeared, and the men were found to be only figures in straw and wax.

Soon after this a letter was seen posted on the Palace gate, announcing that if the government would confer upon Kil Tong the rank of Pansa, as held by his father, and thus remove from him the stigma attaching to him as the son of a slave, he would stop his depredations. This proposition could not be entertained at first, but one of the counsel suggested that it might offer a solution of the vexed question, and they could yet be spared the disgrace of having an officer with such a record. For, as he proposed, men could be so stationed that when the newly-appointed officer came to make his bow before His Majesty, they could fall upon him and kill him before he arose. This plan was greeted with applause, and a decree was issued conferring the desired rank; proclamations to that effect being posted in public places, so that the news would reach Kil Tong. It did reach him, and he soon appeared at the city gate. A great crowd attended him as he rode to the Palace gates; but knowing the plans laid for him, as he passed through the gates and came near enough to be seen of the King, he was caught up in a cloud and borne away amid strange music; wholly discomfiting his enemies.

Some time after this occurrence the King was walking with a few eunuchs and attendants in the royal gardens. It was evening time, but the full moon furnished ample light. The atmosphere was tempered just to suit; it was neither cold nor warm, while it lacked nothing of the bracing character of a Korean autumn. The leaves were blood-red on the maples; the heavy cloak of climbing vines that enshrouded the great wall near by was also beautifully colored. These effects could even be seen by the bright moonlight, and seated on a hill-side the royal party were enjoying the tranquillity of the scene, when all were astonished by the sound of a flute played by some one up above them.

Looking up among the tree-tops a man was seen descending toward them, seated upon the back of a gracefully moving stork. The King imagined it must be some heavenly being, and ordered the chief eunuch to make some proper salutation. But before this could be done, a voice was heard saying: "Fear not, O King. I am simply Hong Pansa [Kil Tong's new title]. I have come to make my obeisance before your august presence and be confirmed in my rank."

This he did, and no one attempted to molest him; seeing which, the King, feeling that it was useless longer to attempt to destroy a man who could read the unspoken thoughts of men, said:

"Why do you persist in troubling the country? I have removed from you now the stigma attached to your birth. What more will you have?"

"I wish," said Kil Tong, with due humility, "to go to a distant land, and settle down to the pursuit of peace and happiness. If I may be granted three thousand bags of rice I will gladly go and trouble you no longer."

"But how will you transport such an enormous quantity of rice?" asked the King.

"That can be arranged," said Kil Tong. "If I may be but granted the order, I will remove the rice at daybreak."

The order was given. Kil Tong went away as he came, and in the early morning a fleet of junks appeared off the royal granaries, took on the rice, and made away before the people were well aware of their presence.

Kil Tong now sailed for an island off the west coast. He found one uninhabited, and with his few followers he stored his riches, and brought many articles of value from his former hiding-places.

His people he taught to till the soil, and all went well on the little island till the master made a trip to a neighboring island, which was famous for its deadly mineral poison, – a thing much prized for tipping the arrows with. Kil Tong wanted to get some of this poison, and made a visit to the island. While passing through the settled districts he casually noticed that many copies of a proclamation were posted up, offering a large reward to any one who would succeed in restoring to her father a young lady who had been stolen by a band of savage people who lived in the mountains.

Kil Tong journeyed on all day, and at night he found himself high up in the wild mountain regions, where the poison was abundant. Gazing about in making some preparations for passing the night in this place, he saw a light, and following it, he came to a house built below him on a ledge of rocks, and in an almost inaccessible position. He could see the interior of a large hall, where were gathered many hairy, shaggy-looking men, eating, drinking, and smoking. One old fellow, who seemed to be chief, was tormenting a young lady by trying to tear away her veil and expose her to the gaze of the barbarians assembled. Kil Tong could not stand this sight, and, taking a poisoned arrow, he sent it direct for the heart of the villain, but the distance was so great that he missed his mark sufficiently to only wound the arm. All were amazed, and in the confusion the girl escaped, and Kil Tong concealed himself for the night. He was seen next day by some of the savage band, who caught him, and demanded who he was and why he was found in the mountains. He answered that he was a physician, and had come up there to collect a certain rare medicine only known to exist in those mountains.

The robbers seemed rejoiced, and explained that their chief had been wounded by an arrow from the clouds, and asked him if he could cure him. Kil Tong was taken in and allowed to examine the chief, when he agreed to cure him within three days. Hastily mixing up some of the fresh poison, he put it into the wound, and the chief died almost at once. Great was the uproar when the death became known. All rushed at the doctor, and would have killed him, but Kil Tong, finding his own powers inadequate, summoned to his aid his old friends the spirits (*quay sin*), and swords flashed in the air, striking off heads at every blow, and not ceasing till the whole band lay weltering in their own blood.

Bursting open a door, Kil Tong saw two women sitting with covered faces, and supposing them to be of the same strange people, he was about to dispatch them on the spot, when one of them threw aside her veil and implored for mercy. Then it was that Kil Tong recognized the maiden whom he had rescued the previous evening. She was marvellously beautiful, and already he was deeply smitten with her maidenly charms. Her voice seemed like that of an angel of peace sent to quiet the hearts of rough men. As she modestly begged for her life, she told the story of her capture by the robbers, and how she had been dragged away to their den, and was only saved from insult by the interposition of some heavenly being, who had in pity smote the arm of her tormentor.

Great was Kil Tong's joy at being able to explain his own part in the matter, and the maiden heart, already won by the manly beauty of her rescuer, now overflowed with gratitude and love. Remembering herself, however, she quickly veiled her face, but the mischief had been done; each had seen the other, and they could henceforth know no peace, except in each other's presence.

The proclamations had made but little impression upon Kil Tong, and it was not till the lady had told her story that he remembered reading them. He at once took steps to remove the beautiful girl and her companion in distress, and not knowing but that other of the savages might return, he did not dare to make search for a chair and bearers, but mounting donkeys the little party set out for the home of the distressed parents, which they reached safely in due time. The father's delight knew no bounds. He was a subject of Korea's King, yet he possessed this island and ruled its people in his own right. And calling his subjects, he explained to them publicly the wonderful works of the stranger, to whom he betrothed his daughter, and to whom he gave his official position.

The people indulged in all manner of gay festivities in honor of the return of the lost daughter of their chief; in respect to the bravery of Kil Tong; and to celebrate his advent as their ruler.

In due season the marriage ceremonies were celebrated, and the impatient lovers were given to each other's embrace. Their lives were full of happiness and prosperity. Other outlying islands were united under Kil Tong's rule, and no desire or ambition remained ungratified. Yet there came a time when the husband grew sad, and tears swelled the heart of the young wife as she tried in vain to comfort him. He explained at last that he had a presentiment that his father was either dead or dying, and that it was his duty to go and mourn at the grave. With anguish at the thought of parting, the wife urged him to go. Taking a junk laden with handsome marble slabs for the grave and statuary to surround it, and followed by junks bearing three thousand bags of rice, he set out for the capital. Arriving, he cut off his hair, and repaired to his old home, where a servant admitted him on the supposition that he was a priest. He found his father was no more; but the body yet remained, because a suitable place could not be found for the burial. Thinking him to be a priest, Kil Tong was allowed to select the spot, and the burial took place with due ceremony. Then it was that the son revealed himself, and took his place with the mourners. The stone images and monuments were erected upon the nicely sodded grounds. Kil Tong sent the rice he had brought, to the government granaries in return for the King's loan to him, and regretted that mourning would prevent his paying his respects to his King; he set out for his home with his true mother and his father's legal wife. The latter did not survive long after the death of her husband, but the poor slave-mother of the bright boy was spared many years to enjoy the peace and quiet of her son's bright home, and to be ministered to by her dutiful, loving children and their numerous offspring.

EAST LIGHT AND THE BRIDGE OF FISHES

Long, long ago, in the region beyond the Everlasting White Mountains of Northern Korea, there lived a king who was waited on by a handsome young woman servant. Every day she gladdened her eyes by looking southward, where the lofty mountain peak which holds the Dragon's Pool in its bosom lifts its white head to the sky. When tired out with daily toil she thought of the river that flows from the Dragon's Pool down out of the mountain. She hoped that some time she would have a son that would rule over the country which the river watered so richly.

One day while watching the mountain top she saw coming from the east a tiny bit of shining vapor. Floating like a white cloud in the blue sky it seemed no bigger than an egg. It came nearer and nearer until it seemed to go into the bosom of her dress. Very soon she became the mother of a boy. It was indeed a most beautiful child.

But the jealous king was angry. He did not like the little stranger. So he took the baby and threw it down among the pigs in the pen, thinking that this would be the last of the boy. But no! the sows breathed into the baby's nostrils and their warm breath made it live.

When the king's servants heard the little fellow crowing, they went out to see what made the noise, and there they beheld a happy baby not seeming to mind its odd cradle at all. They wanted to give him food at once but the angry king ordered the child to be thrown away, and this time into the stable. So the servants took the boy by the legs and laid him among the horses, expecting that the animals would tread on him and he would be thus put out of the way.

But no, the mares were gentle, and with their warm breath they not only kept the little fellow from getting cold, but they nourished him with their milk so that he grew fat and hearty.

When the king heard of this wonderful behavior of pigs and horses, he bowed his head toward Heaven. It seemed the will of the Great One in the Sky that the boy baby should live and grow up to be a man. So he listened to its mother's prayers and allowed her to bring her child into the palace. There he grew up and was trained like one of the king's sons. As a sturdy youth, he practiced shooting with bow and arrows and became skilful in riding horses. He was always kind to animals. In the king's dominions any man who was cruel to a horse was punished. Whoever struck a mare so that the animal died, was himself put to death. The young man was always merciful to his beasts.

So the king named the youthful archer and horseman East Light, or Radiance of the Morning and made him Master of the Royal Stables. East Light, as the people liked to say his name, became very popular. They also called him Child of the Sun and Grandson of the Yellow River.

One day while out on the mountains hunting deer, bears, and tigers, the king called upon the young archer to show his prowess in shooting arrows. East Light drew his bow and showed skill such as no one else could equal. He sent shaft after shaft whistling into the target and brought down both running deer and flying birds. Then all applauded the handsome youth. But instead of the king's commending East Light, the king became very jealous of him, fearing that he might want to seize the throne. Nothing that the young man could do seemed now to please his royal master.

Fearing he might lose his life if he remained near the king, East Light with three trusty followers fled southward until he came to a great, deep river, wide and impassable. How to get across he knew not, for no boat was at hand and the time was too short to make a raft, for behind him were his enemies swiftly pursuing.

In a great strait, he cried out:

"Alas, shall I, the Child of the Sun and the Grandson of the Yellow River, be stopped here powerless by this stream?"

Then as if his father, the Sun, had whispered to him what to do, he drew his bow and shot many arrows here and there into the water, nearly emptying his quiver.

For a few moments nothing happened. To his companions it seemed a waste of good weapons. What would their leader have left to fight his pursuers when they appeared, if his quiver were empty?

But in a moment more the waters appeared to be strangely agitated. Soon they were flecked and foaming. From up and down the stream, and in front of them, the fish were swimming toward East Light, poking their noses out of the water as if they would say:

"Get on our backs and we'll save you." They crowded together in so dense a mass that on their spines a bridge was soon formed, on which men could stand.

"Quick!" shouted East Light to his companions, "let us flee! Behold the king's horsemen coming down the hill after us."

So over the bridge of fish backs, scaly and full of spiny fins, the four young men fled. As soon as they gained the opposite shore, the bridge of fishes dissolved. Yet scarcely had they swum away, when those who were in pursuit had gained the water's edge, on the other side. In vain the king's soldiers shot their arrows to kill East Light and his three companions. The shafts fell short and the river was too deep and wide to swim their horses over. So the four young men escaped safely.

Marching on farther a few miles, East Light met three strange persons who seemed to be awaiting his coming. They welcomed him warmly and invited him to be their king and rule over their city. The first was dressed in seaweed, the second in hempen garments, and the third in embroidered robes. These men represented the three classes of society; first fishermen and hunters; second farmers and artisans; and lastly rulers of the tribes.

So in this land named Fuyu, rich in the five grains, wheat, rice, and millet, bean and sugarcane, the new king was joyfully welcomed by his new subjects. The men were tall, brave and courteous. Besides being good archers, they rode horses skilfully. They ate out of bowls with chop-sticks and used round dishes at their feasts. They wore ornaments of large pearls and jewels of red jade cut and polished.

The Fuyu people gave the fairest virgin in their realm to be the bride of King East Light and she became a gracious queen, greatly beloved of her subjects and many children were born to them.

East Light ruled long and happily. Under his reign the people of Fuyu became civilized and highly prosperous. He taught the proper relations of ruler and ruled and the laws of marriage, besides better methods of cooking and house-building. He also showed them how to dress their hair. He introduced the wearing of the topknot. For thousands of years topknots were the fashion in Fuyu and in Korea.

Hundreds of years after East Light died, and all the tribes and states in the peninsula south of the Everlasting White Mountains wanted to become one nation and one kingdom, they called their country after East Light, but in a more poetical form, – Cho-sen, which means Morning Radiance, or the Land of the Morning Calm.

THE SNEEZING COLOSSUS

Mr. Kim, who lived at the foot of the mountains, was a lazy lout. He had a family to support, but he did not like steady work. He preferred to smoke his pipe – as long as a yardstick – and to wait for something to turn up.

One day, his wife, tired of trying to feed hungry children from empty dishes, gave her husband a good scolding and bade him begone and get something for the household. This consisted of father, mother, and four little folks, whose faces were not often washed, besides a little dog. This puppy, when danger was near, always ran into the house through a little square hole cut in the door, and when safely within barked lustily.

So Mr. Kim went out to the mountains to find something – a root of ginseng, a nugget of gold, or some precious stone, perhaps, if he were lucky. If not, some berries, wild grapes or pears might do. Meanwhile at home, his wife pounded the grain that was left in the larder for the children's dinner.

Mr. Kim rambled over the rocks a long time without seeing anything worth carrying away. When it was about noon he came to one of the mighty mir-yeks, or colossal stone Buddhas, cut out of the solid mountain. It rose in the air many yards high. Ages ago in the days of Buddhism, when monasteries covered the land and Buddhist friars and nuns chanted Sanscrit hymns to the praise of Lord Buddha, devout men, laboring many months, chiseled this towering colossus into human form. Its nose stood out three feet, its mouth was four feet wide. On its flat head was a cap, made of a slab of granite and shaped like a student's mortar-board, on which ten men could stand without crowding one another.

Long gone and forgotten were the monks, and the monastery had fallen to ruins. The forest had grown up around the great stone image until it was nearly hidden by the tall trees surrounding it. In front, from the ground up, the wild grape-vines had gripped the stone with their tendrils and spread their matted branches and greenery until they nearly covered the image up to its neck.

But out of a crevice in the head of the figure grew a pear tree, sprung from a seed dropped long ago by the great-grandfather of one of the birds singing and chirping near by. And, oh joy! at the end of the outer branch was growing a ripe, luscious pear nearly as big as a man's head. What a prize! It would, when cut up, make a dessert for the whole family. Happy Kim! He blessed his lucky star.

Seizing hold of the bushes and wild grape-vines, by dint of great effort Mr. Kim climbed upward and got as far as the chin of the great stone face. Above him protruded the big nose, the nostrils of which gaped like caverns. Yet although he was standing with his foot on the stone lips and holding on to the nose, despite all his exertions, he could get no further up the granite face. He was at his wit's end. Far above hung the delicious looking pear as if to tantalize him. A gentle breeze was swaying the fruit to and fro, and it seemed to say, "Take me if you can."

But the nose, being polished, was slippery and the ears were too smooth to climb. What could he take hold of? Surely to shin up any further was impossible. Must he give up the pear?

A bright thought entered his head. He would crawl up into the right nostril and hope for an exit to the top. So, thinking he might find his way he began like an insect to enter the hole and soon the man Kim disappeared from sight, as with hands and feet he climbed into the darkness.

Wasn't it dangerous to tickle the nostrils of the great stone man in this way?

But whatever Kim may have thought he kept on, determined to get that pear, come what might.

Suddenly a blast loud enough to rend the mountain was heard. *Hash-ho!* Had an earthquake or tempest taken place? Was this rolling thunder?

No, the colossus had sneezed. Thus the stone man got rid of the intruder. The first thing Mr. Kim knew, he was flying through the air, and he tumbled upon the bushes. His wits were gone. He knew nothing. This was about one o'clock in the afternoon.

Mr. Kim lay asleep or unconscious till near sun-down. Then he woke up and realized what had happened. There was the stone nose beetling over him far up toward the sky.

But in sneezing so hard, the colossus had shaken its head also and the big pear had dropped off. Kim found it lying by his side, and picking it up went on his way rejoicing.

At home the little dog looking through the square hole saw him, barked welcome, and a right merry supper they had over the big pear cut into slices, as Mr. Kim told the story of his adventures.

FABLES, FOLKLORE & ANCIENT STORIES

TALES OF ANIMALS & MYTHICAL CREATURES

Mythical creatures include goblins, dragons, magical horses and talking animals. In addition to inspiring awe and holding the attention of the storytelling audience, mythical creatures reflect the cosmology of ancient Koreans. The dragon was associated with power and royalty, and people believed that a Dragon King lived under the ocean's surface (in 'Rabbit's Eyes'). These animal themes occasionally help to express critiques of political authority that would conventionally have led to a commoner's torture or execution. The Dragon King (alternately 'King of the Fishes' in Katharine Pyle's version) is an absolute monarch whose mysterious ailment renders him whiny and gullible. The tiger, another symbol of strength, has a multifaceted characterization. In 'Prince Sandalwood, Father of Korea', Tiger has gone along with Bear in asking Hananim, the Great One of Heaven and Earth, to turn him into a human.

Yet he cannot pass the endurance test of staying sequestered in a cave for 100 days and eating only mugwort and garlic (the imagined origin of kimchee pickled cabbage, a Korean staple). Tiger is impatient and impulsive, and thus vulnerable to trickery. Rabbit (in 'Rabbit's Eyes') is a small creature who relies on wit to escape difficult situations. These animal characters convey

THE WILD-CAT WOMAN

Kim Su-ik was a native of Seoul who matriculated in 1624 and graduated in 1630. In 1636, when the King made his escape to Nam-han from the invading Manchu army, Kim Su-ik accompanied him. He opposed any yielding to China or any treaty with them, but because his counsel was not received he withdrew from public life.

* * *

Tong Chung-so was a Chinaman of great note. He once desired to give himself up to study, and did not go out of his room for three years. During this time a young man one day called on him, and while he stood waiting said to himself, "It will rain to-day." Tong replied at once, "If you are not a fox you are a wild cat – out of this," and the man at once ran away. How he came to know this was from the words, "Birds that live in the trees know when the wind will blow; beasts that live in the ground know when it is going to rain." The wild cat unconsciously told on himself.

The Story

The former magistrate of Quelpart, Kim Su-ik, lived inside of the South Gate of Seoul. When he was young it was his habit to study Chinese daily until late at night. Once, when feeling hungry, he called for his wife to bring him something to eat.

The wife replied, "We have nothing in the house except seven or eight chestnuts. Shall I roast these and bring them to you?"

Kim replied, "Good; bring them."

The servants were asleep, and there was no one on hand to answer a call, so the wife went to the kitchen, made a fire and cooked them herself. Kim waited, meanwhile, for her to come.

After a little while she brought them in a handbasket, cooked and ready served for him. Kim ate and enjoyed them much. Meanwhile she sat before his desk and waited. Suddenly the door opened, and another person entered. Kim raised his eyes to see, and there was the exact duplicate of his wife, with a basket in her hand and roasted chestnuts. As he looked at both of them beneath the light the two women were perfect facsimiles of each other. The two also looked back and forth in alarm, saying, "What's this that's happened? Who are you?"

Kim once again received the roasted nuts, laid them down, and then took firm hold of each woman, the first one by the right hand and the second by the left, holding fast till the break of day.

At last the cocks crew, and the east began to lighten. The one whose right hand he held, said, "Why do you hold me so? It hurts; let me go." She shook and tugged, but Kim held all the tighter. In a little, after struggling, she fell to the floor and suddenly changed into a wild cat. Kim, in fear and surprise, let her go, and she made her escape through the door. What a pity that he did not make the beast fast for good and all!

* * *

Note by the writer. – Foxes turning into women and deceiving people is told of in *Kwang-keui* and other Chinese novels, but the wild cat's transformation is more wonderful still, and something that I have never heard of. By what law do creatures like foxes and wild cats so change? I am unable to find any law that governs it. Some say that the fox carries a magic charm by which it does these magic things, but can this account for the wild cat?

THE OLD WOMAN WHO BECAME A GOBLIN

There was a **Confucian** scholar once who lived in the southern part of Seoul. It is said that he went out for a walk one day while his wife remained alone at home. When he was absent there came by begging an old woman who looked like a Buddhist priestess, for while very old her face was not wrinkled. The scholar's wife asked her if she knew how to sew. She said she did, and so the wife made this proposition, "If you will stay and work for me I'll give you your breakfast and your supper, and you'll not have to beg anywhere; will you agree?"

She replied, "Oh, thank you so much, I'll be delighted."

The scholar's wife, well satisfied with her bargain, took her in and set her to picking cotton, and making and spinning thread. In one day she did more than eight ordinary women, and yet had, seemingly, plenty of time to spare. The wife, delighted above measure, treated her to a great feast.

After five or six days, however, the feeling of delight and the desire to treat her liberally and well wore off somewhat, so that the old woman grew angry and said, "I am tired of living alone, and so I want your husband for my partner." This being refused, she went off in a rage, but came back in a little accompanied by a decrepit old man who looked like a Buddhist beggar.

These two came boldly into the room and took possession, cleared out the things that were in the ancient tablet-box on the wall-shelf, and both disappeared into it, so that they were not seen at all, but only their voices heard. According to the whim that took them they now ordered eatables and other things.

When the scholar's wife failed in the least particular to please them, they sent plague and sickness after her, so that her children fell sick and died. Relatives on hearing of this came to see, but they also caught the plague, fell ill and died. Little by little no one dared come near the place, and it became known at last that the wife was held as a prisoner by these two goblin creatures.

For a time smoke was seen by the town-folk coming out of the chimney daily, and they knew that the wife still lived, but after five or six days the smoke ceased, and they knew then that the woman's end had come. No one dared even to make inquiry.

THE MAN WHO LOST HIS LEGS

There was a merchant in Chong-ju who used to go to Quelpart to buy seaweed. One time when he drew up on the shore he saw a man shuffling along on the ground toward the boat. He crept nearer, and at last took hold of the side with both his hands and jumped in.

"When I looked at him," said the merchant, "I found he was an old man without any legs. Astonished, I asked, saying,

'How is it, old man, that you have lost your legs?'

"He said in reply, 'I lost my legs on a trip once when I was shipwrecked, and a great fish bit them off.'"

"However did that happen?" inquired the merchant. And the old man said, "We were caught in a gale and driven till we touched on some island or other. Before us on the shore stood a high castle with a great gateway. The twenty or so of us who were together in the storm-tossed boat were all exhausted from cold and hunger, and lying exposed. We landed and managed to go together to the house. There was in it one man only, whose height was terrible to behold, and whose chest was many spans round. His face was black and his eyes large and rolling. His voice was like the braying of a monster donkey. Our people made motions showing that they wanted something to eat. The man made no reply, but securely fastened the front gate. After this he brought an armful of wood, put it in the middle of the courtyard, and there made a fire. When the fire blazed up he rushed after us and caught a young lad, one of our company, cooked him before our eyes, pulled him to pieces and ate him. We were all reduced to a state of horror, not knowing what to do. We gazed at each other in dismay and stupefaction.

"When he had eaten his fill, he went up into a verandah and opened a jar, from which he drank some kind of spirit. After drinking it he uttered the most gruesome and awful noises; his face grew very red and he lay down and slept. His snorings were like the roarings of the thunder. We planned then to make our escape, and so tried to open the large gate, but one leaf was about twenty-four feet across, and so thick and heavy that with all our strength we could not move it.

The walls, too, were a hundred and fifty feet high, and so we could do nothing with them. We were like fish in a pot – beyond all possible way of escape. We held each other's hands, and cried.

"Among us, one man thought of this plan: We had a knife and he took it, and while the monster was drunk and asleep, decided to stab his eyes out, and cut his throat. We said in reply, 'We are all doomed to death, anyway; let's try,' and we made our way up on to the verandah and stabbed his eyes. He gave an awful roar, and struck out on all sides to catch us. We rushed here and there, making our escape out of the court back into the rear garden. There were in this enclosure pigs and sheep, about sixty of them in all. There we rushed, in among the pigs and sheep. He floundered about, waving his two arms after us, but not one of us did he get hold of; we were all mixed up – sheep, pigs and people. When he did catch anything it was a sheep; and when it was not a sheep it was a pig. So he opened the front gate to send all the animals out.

"We then each of us took a pig or sheep on the back and made straight for the gate. The monster felt each, and finding it a pig or a sheep let it go. Thus we all got out and rushed for the boat. A little later he came and sat on the bank and roared his threatenings at us. A lot of other giants came at his call. They took steps of thirty feet or so, came racing after us, caught the boat, and made it fast; but we took axes and struck at the hands that held it, and so got free at last and out to the open sea.

"Again a great wind arose, and we ran on to the rocks and were all destroyed. Every one was engulfed in the sea and drowned; I alone got hold of a piece of boat-timber and lived. Then there was a horrible fish from the sea that came swimming after me and bit off my legs. At last I drifted back home and here I am.

"When I think of it still, my teeth are cold and my bones shiver. My Eight Lucky Stars are very bad, that's why it happened to me."

THE BRAVE MAGISTRATE

In olden times in one of the counties of North Ham-kyong Province, there was an evil-smelling goblin that caused great destruction to life. Successive magistrates appeared, but in ten days or so after arrival, in each case they died in great agony, so that no man wished to have the billet or anything to do with the place. A hundred or more were asked to take the post, but they all refused. At last one brave soldier, who was without any influence socially or politically, accepted. He was a courageous man, strong and fearless. He thought, "Even though there is a devil there, all men will not die, surely. I shall make a trial of him." So he said his farewell, and entered on his office. He found himself alone in the yamen, as all others had taken flight. He constantly carried a long knife at his belt, and went thus armed, for he noticed from the first day a fishy, stinking odour, that grew gradually more and more marked.

After five or six days he took note, too, that what looked like a mist would frequently make its entry by the outer gate, and from this mist came this stinking smell. Daily it grew more and more annoying, so that he could not stand it longer. In ten days or so, when the time arrived for him to die, the *yamen*-runners and servants, who had returned, again ran away. The magistrate kept a jar of whisky by his side, from which he drank frequently to fortify his soul. On this day he grew very drunk, and thus waited. At last he saw something coming through the main gateway that seemed wrapped in fog, three or four embraces in waist size, and fifteen feet or so high. There was no head to it, nor were body or arms visible. Only on the top were two dreadful eyes rolling wildly. The magistrate jumped up at once, rushed toward it, gave a great shout and struck it with his sword. When he gave it the blow there was the sound of thunder, and the whole thing dissipated. Also the foul smell that accompanied it disappeared at once.

The magistrate then, in a fit of intoxication, fell prone. The retainers, all thinking him dead, gathered in the courtyard to prepare for his burial. They saw him fallen to the earth, but they remarked that the bodies of others who had died from this evil had all been left on the verandah, but his was in the lower court. They raised him up in order to prepare him for burial, when suddenly he came to life, looked at them in anger, and asked what they meant. Fear and amazement possessed them. From that time on there was no more smell.

THE AWFUL LITTLE GOBLIN

There **was an occasion** for a celebration in the home of a nobleman of Seoul, whereupon a feast, to which were invited all the family friends, was prepared. There was a great crowd of men and women. In front of the women's quarters there suddenly

TALES OF ANIMALS & MYTHICAL CREATURES

appeared an uncombed, ugly-looking boy about fifteen years of age. The host and guests, thinking him a coolie who had come in the train of some visitor, did not ask specially concerning him, but one of the women guests, seeing him in the inner quarters, sent a servant to reprimand him and put him out. The boy, however, did not move, so the servant said to him, "Who are you, anyway, and with whom did you come, that you enter the women's quarters, and even when told to go out do not go?"

The boy, however, stood stock-still, just as he had been, with no word of reply.

The company looked at him in doubt, and began to ask one another whose he was and with whom he had come. Again they had the servant make inquiry, but still there was no reply. The women then grew very angry, and ordered him to be put out. Several took hold of him and tried to pull him, but he was like a fixed rock, fast in the earth, absolutely immovable. In helpless rage they informed the men.

The men, hearing this, sent several strong servants, who took hold all at once, but he did not budge a hair. They asked, "Who are you, anyway?" but he gave no reply. The crowd, then enraged, sent ten strong men with ropes to bind him, but like a giant mountain he remained fast, so that they recognized that he could not be moved by man's power.

One guest remarked, "But he, too, is human; why cannot he be moved?" They then sent five or six giant fellows with clubs to smash him to pieces, and they laid on with all their might. It looked as though he would be crushed like an egg-shell, while the sound of their pounding was like reverberating thunder. But just as before, not a hair did he turn, not a wink did he give.

Then the crowd began to fear, saying, "This is not a man, but a god," so they entered the courtyard, one and all, and began to bow before him, joining their hands and supplicating earnestly. They kept this up for a long time.

At last the boy gave a sarcastic smile, turned round, went out of the gate and disappeared.

The company, frightened out of their wits, called off the feast. From that day on, the people of that house were taken ill, including host and guests. Those who scolded him, those who tied him with ropes, those who pounded him, all died in a few days. Other members of the company, too, contracted typhus and the like, and died also.

It was commonly held that the boy was the Too-uk Spirit, but we cannot definitely say. Strange, indeed!

* * *

Note. – When the time comes for a clan to disappear from the earth, calamity befalls it. Even though a great spirit should come in at the door at such a feast time, if the guests had done as Confucius suggests, "Be reverent and distant," instead of insulting him and making him more malignant than ever, they would have escaped. Still, devils and men were never intended to dwell together.

RABBIT'S EYES: A KOREAN FAIRY TALE

ONCE upon a time the king of the fishes fell ill, and no one knew what was the matter with him. All the doctors in the sea were called in, one after another, and not one of them could cure him.

Once when the fishes were talking about it, a turtle stuck its head out of a crack in a rock. "It is a pity," said the turtle, "that no one has ever thought of asking my advice. I could cure the king in a twinkling. All he has to do is to swallow the eye of a live rabbit, and he will become perfectly well again."

This the turtle said, not because he knew anything at all about the matter, but because he wished to appear wise before the fishes.

Now it so chanced that one of the fishes that heard him was the son of the king's councillor, and he swam straight home and told his father what he had heard the turtle say. The councillor told the king, and the king, who was feeling very ill that day, bade them bring the turtle to him immediately.

When the messengers told the turtle that the king wished to speak to him, the turtle was very much frightened. He drew his head and his tail into his shell and pretended that he was asleep, but in the end he was obliged to go with the messengers.

They soon reached the palace, and the turtle was taken immediately to where the king was. He was lying on a bed of seaweed and looking very ill indeed, and all his doctors were gathered round him.

The king turned his eyes toward the turtle, and spoke in a weak voice. "Tell me, friend, is it true that you said you could cure me?"

Yes, it was true.

"And that all I have to do is to swallow the eye of a live rabbit, and I will be well again?"

Yes, that was true too.

"Then go get a live rabbit and bring it here immediately, that I may be well."

When the turtle heard these words he was in despair. It did not seem at all likely that he could catch a rabbit and bring it down into the sea, but he was so much afraid of the king that he did not dare to explain this to him. He said nothing, but crawled away as soon as he could, wishing he could find some crack where he could hide himself and never be found again.

Suddenly he remembered he had once seen a rabbit frisking about on a hill not far from the seashore, and he determined to set out to find it.

* * *

He crawled out of the sea and started up the hill. He climbed and he climbed, and after a while he came to the top, and there he sat down to rest.

Presently along came the rabbit, and it stopped to speak to him.

"Good day," said the rabbit.

"Good day," said the turtle.

"And what are you doing so far away from the sea?" asked the rabbit.

"Oh, I only came up here to look about and see what the green world was like," answered the turtle.

"And what do you think of it, now you are here?"

"Oh, it's not so bad; but you ought to see the beautiful palaces and gardens we have down under the sea." The turtle began telling the rabbit about them, and he talked so long and said so many fine things about them, that the rabbit began to wish to see them for himself.

"Would it be very hard for me to live down under the water?" he asked.

"Oh, no," said the turtle. "It might be a little inconvenient at first, but that would not last long. If you like, I will take you on my back and carry you down to the bottom of the sea, and then you can see whether it is not all just as grand and beautiful as I have been telling you."

* * *

Well, the rabbit could not resist his curiosity, and he agreed to go with the turtle.

They went to the edge of the sea, and then the rabbit got on the turtle's back, and down they went through the water to the very bottom of the sea. The rabbit did not like it at first, but he soon grew used to it, and when he saw all the fine palaces and gardens that were there, he was filled with wonder.

The turtle took him directly to the palace of the king. There he bade the rabbit get down and wait awhile, and he promised that presently he would show him the king of all this magnificence.

The rabbit was delighted and willingly agreed to wait there while the turtle went to announce him.

But while the turtle was away the rabbit heard two fishes talking in the room next to where he was. He was very inquisitive, so he cocked his ears forward and listened to what they were saying. What was his horror to find that they were talking about taking out his eyes and giving them to the king. The rabbit did not know what to do, nor how he was to escape from the dangerous position he was in.

Presently the turtle came back, and the chief councillor came with him, and immediately the rabbit began to talk. "Well," said he, "it all seems very fine here, and I am glad I came, but I wish now I had brought my own eyes with me so that I could see it better. You see, the eyes I have in my head now are only glass eyes. I am so afraid of getting my own eyes hurt or dusty that I generally keep them in a safe place, and wear these glass eyes instead. But if I had only known how much there would be to look at, I would certainly have brought my own eyes."

When the turtle and the councillor heard this, they were very much disappointed, for they believed the rabbit was speaking the truth, and that the eyes he had in his head at the time were only glass eyes.

"I will take you back to the shore," said the turtle, "and then you can go and get your real eyes and come back again, for there are many more things for you to see here – things more wonderful and beautiful than anything I have yet shown you."

Well, the rabbit was willing to do that, so he got upon the turtle's back, and the turtle swam up and up with him through the sea.

As soon as they reached the shore the rabbit leaped from the turtle's back, and away he went up the hill as fast as he could scamper, and he was glad enough to be out of that scrape, I can tell you. But the turtle waited, and he waited, and he waited, but the rabbit never did come back, and at last the turtle was obliged to go home without him.

As for the king of the fishes, if he ever got well, it was not the eye of a live rabbit that cured him; of that you may be sure.

THE MAGIC RICE KETTLE

There was once an old man who was so poor he was scarcely able to buy food enough to keep him alive.

He had never married, and so he had no children, but he had a little dog and cat that lived with him, and these two he loved as though they were his own son and daughter. What little he had was shared with them, and if they were sometimes hungry, it was because he had nothing in the house to eat.

One day the old man found that all he had was one scant handful of rice.

"Alas, my little dog and cat, what will become of us now?" he cried. "This handful of rice is all that is left to keep us alive. After it is gone, you must seek another master who can feed you better than I. Even if I must starve, that is no reason why you should too."

The little cat mewed, and the dog looked up into his master's face, as though they had understood all he said to them.

The old man put the rice over the fire to cook, and just as it was done, and he was about to feed the animals, the light in the hut was darkened; looking round, he saw a tall stranger standing in the open doorway.

"Good day," said the stranger.

"Good day," answered the old man.

"I have come a long way," said the stranger, "and I am footsore and weary. May I come in and rest?"

Yes, he might do that and welcome.

The stranger came in and sat down in the most comfortable place. "I am hungry as well as weary."

"Alas," cried the old man, "this is a poor house in which to seek for food."

The stranger looked all about him. "Is not that rice that I see?" he asked, pointing to the kettle.

"Yes, it is rice, but my little dog and cat are hungry also, and not another morsel have we in the house beside that."

"Nevertheless, it is right that a man should be fed before dumb brutes," said the stranger. "Give me at least a taste of the rice before you feed them."

The old man did not know how to refuse him.

"Take some of it, then," he said, "but leave a little for them, I beg of you."

At once the stranger dipped into the kettle and began to eat, and he ate so fast that before the old man could stop him, all the rice was gone from the kettle, to the very last grain.

* * *

The old man was cut to the heart to think that his guest could have done this. Now his little dog and cat would have to go to bed hungry. All the same, he said nothing. He took up the empty kettle and was about to put it back on the shelf when the stranger said to him, "Fill the kettle with water and hang it over the fire again."

"Why should I do that?" asked the old man. "Water will not fill our stomachs or satisfy our hunger."

"Nevertheless, do as I bid you," said the stranger.

He spoke in such a way that the old man did not dare to disobey him. Muttering to himself, he filled the kettle with water and hung it over the fire.

The stranger drew out a piece of something that looked like amber and threw it in the pot. At once the water began to boil, and as it did so it became filled with rice. And such rice! The grains were twice as big as usual, and from them arose a smell more delicious than anything the old man had ever smelled before in all his life.

Filled with wonder and fear, he turned toward where the stranger had been sitting, but the guest was gone. He had disappeared, and only the little cat and dog were left in the room, waiting hungrily for their dinner.

The old man lifted the kettle from the fire and began to serve out the rice. And now a still more wonderful thing happened. No matter how much was dipped out from the kettle, still it was always full. He could hardly believe his eyes. He dipped and dipped. Soon all the pots and kettles and bowls in the house were full of rice, and still the more he took out the more there was.

"It is magic," cried the old man. "It must be that the amber the stranger threw in the pot was a charm. If so, puss and my dog and I need never suffer hunger again."

And so it turned out to be. As long as the amber was in the kettle, it was always full of rice to the brim. The rice was always fresh, and delicious too, so that not only the neighbours but the people from the village across the river came to buy it; and they paid well for it.

The little cat and dog grew fat and sleek. As for the man, he not only had enough to eat, but he was able to buy for himself all the clothes he needed and to make presents to those who were poorer than himself.

One evening the old man felt very tired. So many people had come through the day to buy rice that his arm quite ached with serving it out.

He took a bowl and filled it for the cat and dog, and was about to set it on the floor when he noticed to his surprise that the kettle was not as full as it had been. He took another bowl and dipped out some more of the rice. The kettle failed to fill itself.

Again he dipped, and the more he took out, the emptier the kettle grew. The old man was very much frightened. He plunged his hands into the rice that was left in the kettle and began to feel about for the charm, but it was not there. Somehow, that day, while he was dipping out the rice for his customers, he must have dipped out the charm, and some one had carried it off home with his bowl of rice.

The old man was ready to tear his hair with despair. At once he ran out and began to go about the neighbourhood, knocking at all the doors and begging to know whether a piece of amber had been found in the rice the people there had bought that day. But every one told him no. They had found nothing in their bowls but rice.

Worn out with sorrow, he went back to his hut at last and threw himself on the floor to sleep. It was a long time, however, before he could close his eyes. Soon all the money that had been paid him for the rice would be spent, and he was too old to work. Then there would be nothing for him but the same poverty and hunger he had endured for so many years. And his little dog and cat would have to suffer with him unless they were wise enough to run away and seek another master. At last, toward morning, the old man fell asleep, and then the dog and cat began to talk together in low tones.

"This is a bad business," said the dog.

"Bad enough," answered puss. "Our master has been very careless. He deserves to suffer. As for me, I have no notion of being half-starved again the way I used to be. I shall go away and try to find another home where there will be more to eat than here."

"You are very ungrateful," answered the dog. "Instead of planning to run away, you ought to set your wits to work to think how we can help our master."

"But how could we do that? I know of no way."

"Let us go out and hunt for the charm. Perhaps we can find it. Our sense of smell is so keen that if we came anywhere near where it is I am sure we could find it, however well it was hidden. We will go from house to house – all through the village, if need be. I will nose about in the gardens and out-buildings, and you must manage to creep into the houses and hunt about through the rooms."

"Very well," answered the cat. "I am sure I would be glad enough to help our master, and to stay with him too, if only he could give us enough to eat."

So, early the next day, before the old man was awake, the dog and the cat started out together on their search. The people of the village were still asleep, but the cat managed to find a way to creep into several of the houses, and the dog searched about outside, as he had promised to do.

But with all their searchings, they found nothing except some scraps of food here and there. These they ate, and so satisfied their hunger somewhat. Then, when night came, they returned home, footsore and weary.

The old man was very glad to see them. All day he had missed them and had wondered where they were. He had saved some supper for them and was surprised that they did not seem more hungry for it. He was still very sad. All day people had been coming to the hut to buy rice from him, and when they found he had none to sell, they had been very much disappointed. Some of them had even been angry and had scolded him.

The following day the dog and cat continued their search, but night found them still unsuccessful. So it went on, day after day and week after week. At last they had visited every house in the village, but they had seen and heard nothing of the charm.

"Now you see how it is. We are only wasting our time," said the cat. "I knew we could not find it, and I, for one, shall begin to look for another home."

"Nay, but wait a bit," answered the dog. "Have you forgotten that many of our master's customers came from the village across the river? We have not searched there yet."

"No, nor will we as far as I am concerned," answered the cat. "I am no swimmer. I have no idea of getting drowned. If you want to search there, you will have to go by yourself."

The dog began to beg and plead with her. "Very soon," said he, "the river will be frozen, and then we can cross on the ice without your wetting even the smallest toe of your paw. Only come!"

"Very well," said the cat at last. "I will do it; but mind you, we must wait until the river is well frozen, and there is no chance of our breaking through."

The dog agreed to this, and so, one cold day, when the river was as hard as stone, the two friends crossed to the farther side, and at once began to search the houses there.

At the first house they found nothing. At the second it was the same thing; but no sooner had the cat entered the third house than she smelled something that reminded her of the rice that had bubbled up in the magic kettle. She made her way from one room to the other, and at last she came to a small upper chamber that seemed to be unused. And now she could smell the charm more strongly than ever, and the smell seemed to come from the top of a high chest of drawers.

* * *

With a bound puss leaped to the top of it and looked about her. There, pushed well back against the wall, was a heavy wooden box, and the moment the cat put her nose to the keyhole she knew that the charm was inside of it.

She had found the charm, and that was one thing, but how to get it out of the box was quite a different matter. The box was locked, and puss soon found it was impossible to raise the lid. She tried to push it off the chest of drawers, hoping that if it fell on the floor it might burst open, but the box was so heavy that she could not budge it a hair's breadth. It seemed a hopeless matter. If the dog were only there, no doubt he could have pushed the box off; but then he had no way of getting into the house; and even if he did, he could not climb to the top of the chest of drawers.

But when puss went down to tell him about it, he did not seem to think it was such a hopeless matter after all. He was overjoyed that she had found the charm, and was sure that they could get it out of the box some way or other.

"What we need," said he, "is to get a good big rat to come and gnaw a hole in the box for us."

"Yes, but that is not so easy to do," said the cat. "The rats have no love for me, as you very well know. I have caught and eaten too many of them. I believe they would be glad to starve me to death if they only could."

"You might make a bargain with them," said the dog. "They would be glad enough to help you, if you, in return, would promise not to catch any of them for ten years to come."

Well, the cat did not want to make that bargain at all. She was too fond of catching the rats whenever she could. She and the dog argued about it for a long time, but at last she agreed to do as he wished.

The next thing was to get a message to the king of the rats, and puss knew of a way to manage that. She had seen a mousehole near one of the out-buildings, and now she set herself very patiently to wait beside it until the mouse should come out. She had to wait for a long time too. Perhaps the mouse had heard the two friends prowling about. At any rate, it lay so still in its hole that no one would have guessed it was there at all except a cat. At length, toward evening, the mouse thought it might be safe to venture out. But scarcely had it poked its nose out of its hole when the cat pounced upon it and held it in her claws.

The mouse began to beg and plead for mercy. "Oh, good Mrs Cat – oh, dear Mrs Cat, spare me, I pray of you! I have a wife and five little mouselings at home, and they would surely die of grief if any harm came to me."

* * *

"I am not going to hurt you," answered the cat, though her mouth watered to eat it. "Instead, I am going to let you go, if you will promise to carry a message for me to the king of the rats."

When the mouse heard that the cat would let it go, it could hardly believe in its good fortune. It promised that it would do anything the cat wished it to, and at once the cat took her paws off it and set it free. Then she told it what the message was that she wished it to carry for her: she wished the king to send a rat to gnaw a hole in a box so that she could get a charm that was locked away in it; if the king would do this, she, in return, would promise not to hurt or harm any mouse or rat for ten long years.

The mouse listened attentively, and as soon as he was sure he quite understood the message he hurried away to carry it to the king of the rats. He was only gone for a short time, and when he came back he brought a stout, strong young rat with him. This rat had been sent by the king, who was ready to agree to the bargain the cat had proposed, and had sent the strongest, sharpest-toothed rat he had to gnaw the hole in the box.

As soon as the cat heard this, she made her way back into the house, while the rat and the mouse followed close after her, leaving the dog to wait for them outside. The cat led the way to the upper room and showed the rat the box on the chest of drawers. At once he set to work on it. He gnawed and gnawed and gnawed, but the wood was as hard as stone, as well as very thick.

At last he gnawed through it, but the hole was too small for him to crawl through, and he was too exhausted to make it any larger. The cat, indeed, could reach her paw through, and could even feel the charm, but she could not hook it out, though she tried again and again. But here the mouse made itself of use. It slipped through the hole into the box and quickly brought the charm out in its mouth.

When the cat saw the charm she purred with joy. Once again she promised the rat and mouse that she would not even try to catch them or any of their kind for ten years. Then she took the charm in her mouth and ran down to where the dog was.

The dog was even more delighted than she when he saw the charm.

"Oh, my dear master!" he cried. "How happy he will be."

"Yes," said the cat; "but now make haste. If the people in the house discover the charm is gone, they might suspect us, and follow us, and try to get it back."

"Come, then," said the dog. "But, oh, my dear master! I can hardly wait to show him the charm."

* * *

The cat and dog hurried on down to the river, but when they reached the bank they met with a new difficulty. The weather had suddenly turned very warm and the ice had begun to melt. In many places it was gone altogether, and where it was left it was too thin even to bear such small animals as themselves.

"And now what are we to do?" cried the cat. "We will never be able to get back to our village."

"Oh, yes, we can," replied the dog. "Do you mount upon my back. Dig your claws deep into my long hair and hold on tight, and I will carry you across."

The cat was terribly frightened at the thought of such a thing, but still she saw no other way to cross the river. She climbed upon the dog's back, fastened her claws well in his hair, and then he plunged into the water and began to swim across.

All went well until they neared the other bank. A crowd of children had gathered there to see the ice break up. When they saw the dog swimming across with the cat on his back, it seemed to them the funniest thing they had ever seen in all their lives.

The dog was so busy swimming that he did not even notice them, but the cat, upon his back, saw everything that was going on. She herself suddenly began to think what a funny thing it was that she should be riding at ease on the dog's back, while he was swimming so hard.

She tried not to laugh, but she was so amused that at last she could refrain no longer. She burst into a loud cat-laugh, and at once the charm slipped from her mouth plump into the river, and sank to the bottom.

"The charm! The charm!" the cat cried. "I have dropped it in the river, and it has sunk to the bottom."

As soon as the dog heard that, he dived down into the river to regain it. He was in such a hurry that he never thought of telling the cat of what he meant to do.

The cat's claws were fastened so firmly in his hair that she could not have let go if she had wished. Also her mouth was open, so that when they went down into the river she swallowed a great deal of water. By the time the dog came to the top again, panting and snorting, the cat was almost drowned.

But the dog was too angry to think anything of that. "Wait till we get to the shore," he growled. "Just wait until we get to the shore, and see what I will do to you for dropping the charm."

But the cat had no idea of waiting for this. As they came near the shore, she bounded from the dog's back to the dry land, and then she raced away and up a tall tree.

* * *

The dog chased after her, but he could not catch her. For some time he stood at the foot of the tree, barking and growling, but at last he trotted on home with drooping head and ears and a sad heart.

The old man was very glad to welcome the dog home again. He had feared it was lost. He looked out from the door in all directions, hoping to see the cat also, but the cat, which had now climbed down from the tree, had gone to look for another home. It feared the dog's anger too much to venture back to the hut. Moreover, it had no liking for poverty and hunger, and it hoped to find some place where it would be better fed than with the old man.

And now indeed there were hard times in the hut. The old man grew poorer and poorer, and thinner and thinner, and it was just as bad with the faithful dog. The dog spent much of his time down at the river looking sadly at the place where the charm had been lost and wishing there were some way for him to find it.

Now there was a great deal of fishing done in that river, and sometimes one of the fishermen, more kind-hearted than the rest, would throw a fish to the hungry dog. This the dog always carried home to his master, and the two faithful friends would share it together. It was always a feast day when this happened.

* * *

One day one of the fishermen, who had been very lucky, called to the dog and threw him a particularly large fish.

The dog caught it in his mouth and started home with it. Suddenly he smelled something: it was like the magic rice that had bubbled up in the pot; it must be the charm; it could be nothing but that; and the smell came from the fish he was carrying in his mouth.

As soon as the dog was sure of this, he began to run. He could not get home fast enough. He reached the hut and bounded in and laid the fish upon the table.

"Good dog! Good dog!" cried his master. "Have you brought us a fine dinner to-day?"

He took his knife and began to prepare the fish, but scarcely had he cut into it before the blade struck against something hard. The old man looked to see what it was, and what was his joy and amazement to find that it was the charm, which the fish must have swallowed.

The old man was so delighted that he hardly knew how to contain himself.

"Oh, my precious charm!" he cried. "Oh, what good fortune! Oh, how happy I am! Wait until I fill the kettle, my dear little dog, and then what a feast we will have."

He took out the pot and filled it with water, and hung it over the fire. Then he threw the charm into it. At once the rice began to boil and bubble up. The whole house was filled with the delicious smell of it.

It did not take long for the neighbours to find out that the old man had his wonderful rice again. They hastened to buy of him, and soon he had made even more money than before.

One day the cat, which had grown very lean and thin, came sneaking into the house with one of the customers. As soon as the dog saw her he gave a snarl and was about to fly at her, but the old man caught the cat up in his arms. "Oh, my dear little cat," he cried, "how glad I am to see you. But how thin you have grown! Never mind; there is plenty in the house now, and soon you will grow fat again."

So the cat came back to her master again, but for as long as she lived the dog never forgave her, and they never became friends again. The old man did not know that however. He loved them both; he was quite happy to have them as companions, and lived very prosperous and contented until the end of his days.

HYUNG BO AND NAHL BO; OR, THE SWALLOW-KING'S REWARDS

I

In the province of Chullado, in Southern Korea, lived two brothers. One was very rich, the other very poor. For in dividing the inheritance, the elder brother, instead of taking the father's place, and providing for the younger children, kept the whole property to himself, allowing his younger brother nothing at all, and reducing him to a condition of abject misery. Both men were married. Nahl Bo, the elder, had many concubines, in addition to his wife, but had no children; while Hyung Bo had but one wife and several children. The former's wives were continually quarrelling; the latter lived in contentment and peace with his wife, each endeavoring to help the other bear the heavy burdens circumstances had placed upon them. The elder brother lived in a fine, large compound, with warm, comfortable houses; the younger had built himself a hut of broom straw, the thatch of which was so poor that when it rained they were deluged inside, upon the earthern floor. The room was so small, too, that when Hyung Bo stretched out his legs in his sleep his feet were apt to be thrust through the wall. They had no *kang*, and had to sleep upon the cold dirt floor, where insects were so abundant as to often succeed in driving the sleepers out of doors.

They had no money for the comforts of life, and were glad when a stroke of good fortune enabled them to obtain the necessities. Hyung Bo worked whenever he could get work, but rainy days and dull seasons were a heavy strain upon them. The wife did plain sewing, and together they made straw sandals for the peasants and vendors. At fair time the sandal business was good, but then came a time when no more food was left in the house, the string for making the sandals was all used up, and they had no money for a new supply. Then the children cried to their mother for food, till her heart ached for them, and the father wandered off in a last attempt to get something to keep the breath of life in his family.

Not a kernel of rice was left. A poor rat which had cast in his lot with this kind family, became desperate when, night after night, he chased around the little house without being able to find the semblance of a meal. Becoming desperate, he vented his despair in such loud squealing that he wakened the neighbors, who declared that the mouse said his legs were worn off running about in a vain search for a grain of rice with which to appease his hunger. The famine became so serious in the little home, that at last the mother commanded her son to go to his uncle and tell him plainly how distressed they were, and ask him to loan them enough rice to subsist on till they could get work, when they would surely return the loan.

The boy did not want to go. His uncle would never recognize him on the street, and he was afraid to go inside his house lest he should whip him. But the mother commanded him to go, and he obeyed. Outside his uncle's house were many cows, well fed and valuable. In pens he saw great fat pigs in abundance, and fowls were everywhere in great numbers. Many dogs also were there, and they ran barking at him, tearing his clothes with their teeth and frightening him so much that he was tempted to run; but speaking kindly to them, they quieted down, and one dog came and licked his hand as if ashamed of the conduct of the others. A female servant ordered him away, but he told her he was her master's nephew, and wanted to see him; whereupon she smiled but let him pass into an inner court, where he found his uncle sitting on the little veranda under the broad, overhanging eaves.

The man gruffly demanded, "who are you?" "I am your brother's son," he said. "We are starving at our house, and have had no food for three days. My father is away now trying to find work, but we are very hungry, and only ask you to loan us a little rice till we can get some to return you."

The uncle's eyes drew down to a point, his brows contracted, and he seemed very angry, so that the nephew began looking for an easy way of escape in case he should come at him. At last he looked up and said: "My rice is locked up, and I have ordered the granaries not to be opened. The flour is sealed and cannot be broken into. If I give you some cold victuals, the dogs will bark at you and try to take it from you. If I give you the leavings of the wine-press, the pigs will be jealous and squeal at you. If I give you bran, the cows and fowls will take after you. Get out, and let me never see you here again." So saying, he caught the poor boy by the collar and threw him into the outer court, hurting him, and causing him to cry bitterly with pain of body and distress of mind.

At home the poor mother sat jogging her babe in her weak arms, and appeasing the other children by saying that brother had gone to their uncle for food, and soon the pot would be boiling and they would all be satisfied. When, hearing a foot-fall, all scrambled eagerly to the door, only to see the empty-handed, red-eyed boy coming along, trying manfully to look cheerful.

"Did your uncle whip you?" asked the mother, more eager for the safety of her son, than to have her own crying want allayed.

"No," stammered the brave boy. "He had gone to the capital on business," said he, hoping to thus prevent further questioning, on so troublesome a subject.

"What shall I do"? queried the poor woman, amidst the crying and moaning of her children. There was nothing to do but starve, it seemed. However, she thought of her own straw shoes, which were scarcely used, and these she sent to the market, where they brought three *cash* (3/15 of a cent). This pittance was invested equally in rice, beans, and vegetables; eating which they were relieved for the present, and with full stomachs the little ones fell to playing happily once more, but the poor mother was full of anxiety for the morrow.

Their fortune had turned, however, with their new lease of life, for the father returned with a bale of faggots he had gathered on the mountains, and with the proceeds of these the shoes were redeemed and more food was purchased. Bright and early then next morning both parents went forth in search of work. The wife secured employment winnowing rice. The husband overtook a boy bearing a pack, but his back was so blistered, he could with difficulty carry his burden. Hyung Bo adjusted the saddle of the pack frame to his own back, and carried it for the boy, who, at their arrival at his destination in the evening, gave his helper some cash, in addition to his lodging and meals. During the night, however, a gentleman wished to send a letter by rapid dispatch to a distant place, and Hyung Bo was paid well for carrying it.

Returning from this profitable errand, he heard of a very rich man, who had been seized by the corrupt local magistrate, on a false accusation, and was to be beaten publicly, unless he consented to pay a heavy sum as hush money. Hearing of this, Hyung went to see the rich prisoner, and arranged with him that he would act as his substitute for three thousand cash (two dollars). The man was very glad to get off so easily, and Hyung took the beating. He limped to his house, where his poor wife greeted him with tears and lamentations, for he was a sore and sorry sight indeed. He was cheerful, however, for he explained to them that this had been a rich day's work; he had simply submitted to a little whipping, and was to get three thousand cash for it.

The money did not come, however, for the fraud was detected, and the original prisoner was also punished. Being of rather a close disposition, the man seemed to think it unnecessary to pay for what did him no good. Then the wife cried indeed over her husband's wrongs and their own more unfortunate condition. But the husband cheered her, saying: "If we do right we will surely succeed." He was right. Spring was coming on, and he soon got work at plowing and sowing seed. They gave their little house the usual spring cleaning, and decorated the door with appropriate legends, calling upon the fates to bless with prosperity the little home.

With the spring came the birds from the south country, and they seemed to have a preference for the home of this poor family – as indeed did the rats and insects. The birds built their nests under the eaves. They were swallows, and as they made their little mud air-castles, Hyung Bo said to his wife: "I am afraid to have these birds build their nests there. Our house is so weak it may fall down, and then what will the poor birds do?" But the little visitors seemed not alarmed, and remained with the kind people, apparently feeling safe under the friendly roof.

By and by the little nests were full of commotion and bluster; the eggs had opened, and circles of wide opened mouths could be seen in every nest. Hyung and his children were greatly interested in this new addition to their family circle, and often gave them bits of their own scanty allowance of food, so that the birds became quite tame and hopped in and out of the hut at will.

One day, when the little birds were taking their first lesson in flying, Hyung was lying on his back on the ground, and saw a huge roof-snake crawl along and devour several little birds before he could arise and help them. One bird struggled from the reptile and fell, but, catching both legs in the fine meshes of a reed-blind, they were broken, and the little fellow hung helplessly within the snake's reach. Hyung hastily snatched it down, and with the help of his wife he bound up the broken limbs, using dried fish-skin for splints. He laid the little patient in a warm place, and the bones speedily united, so that the bird soon began to hop around the room, and pick up bits of food laid out for him. Soon the splints were removed, however, and he flew away, happily, to join his fellows.

The autumn came; and one evening – it was the ninth day of the ninth moon – as the little family were sitting about the door, they noticed the bird with the crooked legs sitting on the clothes-line and singing to them.

"I believe he is thanking us and saying good-by," said Hyung, "for the birds are all going south now."

That seemed to be the truth, for they saw their little friend no longer, and they felt lonely without the occupants of the now deserted nests. The birds, however, were paying homage to the king of birds in the bird-land beyond the frosts. And as the king saw the little crooked-legged bird come along, he demanded an explanation of the strange sight. Thereupon the little fellow related his narrow escape from a snake that had already devoured many of his brothers and cousins, the accident in the blind, and his rescue and subsequent treatment by a very poor but very kind man.

His bird majesty was very much entertained and pleased. He thereupon gave the little cripple a seed engraved with fine characters in gold, denoting that the seed belonged to the gourd family. This seed the bird was to give to his benefactor in the spring.

The winter wore away, and the spring found the little family almost as destitute as when first we described them. One day they heard a familiar bird song, and, running out, they saw their little crooked-legged friend with something in its mouth, that looked like a seed. Dropping its burden to the ground, the little bird sang to them of the king's gratitude, and of the present he had sent, and then flew away.

Hyung picked up the seed with curiosity, and on one side he saw the name of its kind, on the other, in fine gold characters, was a message saying: "Bury me in soft earth, and give me plenty of water." They did so, and in four days the little shoot appeared in the fine earth. They watched its remarkable growth with eager interest as the stem shot up, and climbed all over the house, covering it up as a bower, and threatening to break down the frail structure with the added weight. It blossomed, and soon four small gourds began to form. They grew to an enormous size, and Hyung could scarcely keep from cutting them. His wife prevailed on him to wait till the frost had made them ripe, however, as then they could cut them, eat the inside, and make water-vessels of the shells, which they could then sell, and thus make a double profit. He waited, though with a poor grace, till the ninth moon, when the gourds were left alone, high upon the roof, with only a trace of the shrivelled stems which had planted them there.

Hyung got a saw and sawed open the first huge gourd. He worked so long, that when his task was finished he feared he must be in a swoon, for out of the opened gourd stepped two beautiful boys, with fine bottles of wine and a table of jade set with dainty cups. Hyung staggered back and sought assurance of his wife, who was fully as dazed as was her husband. The surprise was somewhat relieved by one of the handsome youths stepping forth, placing the table before them, and announcing that the bird king had sent them with these presents to the benefactor of one of his subjects – the bird with broken legs. Ere they could answer, the other youth placed a silver bottle on the table, saying: "This wine will restore life to the dead." Another, which he placed on the table, would, he said, restore sight to the blind. Then going to the gourd, he brought two gold bottles, one contained a tobacco, which, being smoked, would give speech to the dumb, while the other gold bottle contained wine, which would prevent the approach of age and ward off death.

Having made these announcements, the pair disappeared, leaving Hyung and his wife almost dumb with amazement. They looked at the gourd, then at the little table and its contents, and each looked at the other to be sure it was not a dream. At length Hyung broke the silence, remarking that, as he was very hungry, he would venture to open another gourd, in the hope that it would be found full of something good to eat, since it was not so important for him to have something with which to restore life just now as it was to have something to sustain life with.

The next gourd was opened as was the first, when by some means out flowed all manner of household furniture, and clothing, with rolls upon rolls of fine silk and satin cloth, linen goods, and the finest cotton. The satin alone was far greater in bulk than the gourd had been, yet, in addition, the premises were literally strewn with costly furniture and the finest fabrics. They barely examined the goods now, their amazement having become so great that they could scarcely wait until all had been opened, and the whole seemed so unreal, that they feared delay might be dangerous. Both sawed away on the next gourd, when out came a body of carpenters, all equipped with tools and lumber, and, to their utter and complete amazement, began putting up a house as quickly and quietly as thought, so that before they could arise from the ground they saw a fine house standing before them, with courts and servants' quarters, stables, and granaries. Simultaneously a great train of bulls and ponies appeared, loaded down with rice and other products as tributes from the district in which the place was located. Others came bringing money tribute, servants, male and female, and clothing.

They felt sure they were in dreamland now, and that they might enjoy the exercise of power while it lasted, they began commanding the servants to put the goods away, the money in the *sahrang*, or reception-room, the clothing in the *tarack*, or garret over the fireplace, the rice in the granaries, and animals in their stables. Others were sent to prepare a bath, that they might don the fine clothing before it should be too late. The servants obeyed, increasing the astonishment of the pair, and causing them to literally forget the fourth gourd in their amazed contemplation of the wondrous miracles being performed, and the dreamy air of satisfaction and contentment with which it surrounded them.

Their attention was called to the gourd by the servants, who were then commanded to carefully saw it open. They did so, and out stepped a maiden, as beautiful as were the gifts that had preceded her. Never before had Hyung looked on any one who could at all compare with the matchless beauty and grace of the lovely creature who now stood so modestly and confidingly before him. He could find no words to express his boundless admiration, and could only stand in mute wonder and feast himself upon her beauty. Not so with his wife, however. She saw only a rival in the beautiful girl, and straightway demanded who she was, whence she came, and what she wanted. The maid replied: "I am sent by the bird king to be this man's concubine." Whereupon the wife grew dark in the face, and ordered her to go whence she came and not see her husband again. She upbraided him for not being content with a house and estate, numbers of retainers and quantities of money, and declared this last trouble was all due to his greed in opening the fourth gourd.

Her husband had by this time found his speech, however, and severely reprimanding her for conducting herself in such a manner upon the receipt of such heavenly gifts, while yesterday she had been little more than a beggar; he commanded her to go at once to the women's quarters, where she should reign supreme, and never make such a display of her ill-temper again, under penalty of being consigned to a house by herself. The maiden he gladly welcomed, and conducted her to apartments set aside for her.

II

When Nahl Bo heard of the wonderful change taking place at his brother's establishment, he went himself to look into the matter. He found the report not exaggerated, and began to upbraid his brother with dishonest methods, which accusation the brother stoutly denied, and further demanded where, and of whom, he could steal a house, such rich garments, fine furniture, and have it removed in a day to the site of his former hovel. Nahl Bo demanded an explanation, and Hyung Bo frankly told him how he had saved the bird from the snake and had bound up its broken limbs, so that it recovered; how the bird in return brought him a seed engraved with gold characters, instructing him how to plant and rear it; and how, having done so, the four gourds were born on the stalk, and from them, on ripening, had appeared these rich gifts. The ill-favored brother even then persisted in his charges, and in a gruff, ugly manner accused Hyung Bo of being worse than a thief in keeping all these fine goods, instead of dutifully sharing them with his elder brother. This insinuation of undutiful conduct really annoyed Hyung Bo, who, in his kindness of heart, forgave this unbrotherly senior, his former ill conduct, and thinking only of his own present good fortune, he kindly bestowed considerable gifts upon the undeserving brother, and doubtless would have done more but that the covetous man espyed the fair maiden, and at once insisted on having her. This was too much even for the patient

Hyung Bo, who refused with a determination remarkable for him. A quarrel ensued, during which the elder brother took his departure in a rage, fully determined to use the secret of his brother's success for all it was worth in securing rich gifts for himself.

Going home he struck at all the birds he could see, and ordered his servants to do the same. After killing many, he succeeded in catching one, and, breaking its legs, he took fish-skin and bound them up in splints, laying the little sufferer in a warm place, till it recovered and flew away, bandages and all. The result was as expected. The bird being questioned by the bird king concerning its crooked legs, related its story, dwelling, however, on the man's cruelty in killing so many birds and then breaking its own legs. The king understood thoroughly, and gave the little cripple a seed to present to the wicked man on its return in the spring.

Springtime came, and one day, as Nahl Bo was sitting cross-legged in the little room opening on the veranda off his court, he heard a familiar bird-song. Dropping his long pipe, he threw open the paper windows, and there, sure enough, sat a crooked-legged bird on the clothes line, bearing a seed in its mouth. Nahl Bo would let no one touch it, but as the bird dropped the seed and flew away, he jumped out so eagerly that he forgot to slip his shoes on, and got his clean white stockings all befouled. He secured the seed, however, and felt that his fortune was made. He planted it carefully, as directed, and gave it his personal attention.

The vines were most luxurious. They grew with great rapidity, till they had well nigh covered the whole of his large house and out-buildings. Instead of one gourd, or even four, as in the brother's case, the new vines bore twelve gourds, which grew and grew till the great beams of his house fairly groaned under their weight, and he had to block them in place to keep them from rolling off the roofs. He had to hire men to guard them carefully, for now that the source of Hyung Bo's riches was understood, every one was anxious for a gourd. They did not know the secret, however, which Nahl Bo concealed through selfishness, and Hyung through fear that every one would take to killing and maiming birds as his wicked brother had done.

Maintaining a guard was expensive, and the plant so loosened the roof tiles, by the tendrils searching for earth and moisture in the great layer of clay under the tiles, that the rainy season made great havoc with his house. Large portions of plaster from the inside fell upon the paper ceilings, which in turn gave way, letting the dirty water drip into the rooms, and making the house almost uninhabitable. At last, however, the plants could do no more harm; the frost had come, the vines had shrivelled away, and the enormous ripe gourds were carefully lowered, amid the yelling of a score of coolies, as each seemed to get in the others' way trying to manipulate the ropes and poles with which the gourds were let down to the ground. Once inside the court, and the great doors locked, Nahl Bo felt relieved, and shutting out every one but a carpenter and his assistant, he prepared for the great surprise which he knew must await him, in spite of his most vivid dreams.

The carpenter insisted upon the enormous sum of 1,000 cash for opening each gourd, and as he was too impatient to await the arrival of another, and as he expected to be of princely wealth in a few moments, Nahl Bo agreed to the exorbitant price. Whereupon, carefully bracing a gourd, the men began sawing it through. It seemed a long time before the gourd fell in halves. When it did, out came a party of rope-dancers, such as perform at fairs and public places. Nahl Bo was unprepared for any such surprise as this, and fancied it must be some great mistake. They sang and danced about as well as the crowded condition of the court would allow, and the family looked on complacently, supposing that the band had been sent to celebrate their coming good fortune. But Nahl Bo soon had enough of this. He wanted to get at his riches, and seeing that the actors were about to stretch their ropes for a more extensive performance, he ordered them to cease and take their departure. To his amazement, however, they refused to do this, until he had paid them 5,000 cash for their trouble. "You sent for us and we came," said the leader. "Now pay us, or we will live with you till you do." There was no help for it, and with great reluctance and some foreboding, he gave them the money and dismissed them. Then Nahl Bo turned to the carpenter, who chanced to be a man with an ugly visage, made uglier by a great hare-lip. "You," he said, "are the cause of all this. Before you entered this court these gourds were filled with gold, and your ugly face has changed it to beggars."

Number two was opened with no better results, for out came a body of Buddhist priests, begging for their temple, and promising many sons in return for offerings of suitable merit. Although disgusted beyond measure, Nahl Bo still had faith in the gourds, and to get rid of the priests, lest they should see his riches, he gave them also 5,000 cash.

As soon as the priests were gone, gourd number three was opened, with still poorer results, for out came a procession of paid mourners followed by a corpse borne by bearers. The mourners wept as loudly as possible, and all was in a perfect uproar. When ordered to go, the mourners declared they must have money for mourning, and to pay for burying the body. Seeing no possible help for it, 5,000 cash was finally given them, and they went out with the bier. Then Nahl Bo's wife came into the court, and began to abuse the hare-lipped man for bringing upon them all this trouble. Whereupon the latter became angry and demanded his money that he might leave. They had no intention of giving up the search as yet, however, and, as it was too late to change carpenters, the ugly fellow was paid for the work already done, and given an advance on that yet remaining. He therefore set to work upon the fourth gourd, which Nahl Bo watched with feverish anxiety.

From this one there came a band of *gee sang*, or dancing girls. There was one woman from each province, and each had her song and dance. One sang of the *yang wang*, or wind god; another of the *wang jay*, or pan deity; one sang of the *sung jee*, or money that is placed as a christening on the roof tree of every house. There was the cuckoo song. The song of the ancient tree that has lived so long that its heart is dead and gone, leaving but a hollow space, yet the leaves spring forth every spring-tide. The song of laughter and mourning, with an injunction to see to it that the rice offering be made to the departed spirits. To the king of the sun and stars a song was sung. And last of all, one votary sang of the twelve months that make the year, the twelve hours that make the day, the thirty days that make the month, and of the new year's birth, as the old year dies, taking with it their ills to be buried in the past, and reminding all people to celebrate the New Year holidays by donning clean clothes and feasting on good food, that the following year may be to them one of plenty and prosperity. Having finished their songs and their graceful posturing and waving of their gay silk banners, the *gee sang* demanded their pay, which had to be given them, reducing the family wealth 5,000 cash more.

The wife now tried to persuade Nahl Bo to stop and not open more, but the hare-lip man offered to open the next for 500 cash, as he was secretly enjoying the sport. So the fifth was opened a little, when a yellow-looking substance was seen inside, which was taken to be gold, and they hurriedly opened it completely. But instead of gold, out came an acrobatic pair, – being a strong man with a youth dressed to represent a girl. The man danced about, holding his young companion balanced upon his shoulders, singing meanwhile a song of an ancient king, whose riotous living was so distasteful to his subjects that he built him a cavernous palace, the floor of which was covered with quicksilver, the walls were decorated with jewels, and myriad lamps turned the darkness into day. Here were to be found the choicest viands and wines, with bands of music to entertain the feasters: most beautiful women; and he enjoyed himself most luxuriously until his enemy, learning the secret, threw open the cavern to the light of day, when all of the beautiful women immediately disappeared in the sun's rays.

Before he could get these people to discontinue their performance, Nahl Bo had to give them also 5,000 cash. Yet in spite of all his ill luck, he decided to open another. Which being done, a jester came forth, demanding the expense money for his long journey. This was finally given him, for Nahl Bo had hit upon what he deemed a clever expedient. He took the wise fool aside, and asked him to use his wisdom in pointing out to him which of these gourds contained gold. Whereupon the jester looked wise, tapped several gourds, and motioned to each one as being filled with gold.

The seventh was therefore opened, and a lot of yamen runners came forth, followed by an official. Nahl Bo tried to run from what he knew must mean an exorbitant "squeeze," but he was caught and beaten for his indiscretion. The official called for his valise, and took from it a paper, which his secretary read, announcing that Nahl Bo was the serf of this lord and must hereafter pay to him a heavy tribute. At this they groaned in their hearts, and the wife declared that even now the money was all gone, even to the last cash, while the rabble which had collected had stolen nearly every thing worth removing. Yet the officer's servants demanded pay for their services, and they had to be given a note secured on the property before they would leave. Matters were now so serious that they could not be made much worse, and it was decided to open each remaining gourd, that if there were any gold they might have it.

When the next one was opened a bevy of *moo tang* women (soothsayers) came forth, offering to drive away the spirit of disease and restore the sick to health. They arranged their banners for their usual dancing ceremony, brought forth their drums, with which to exorcise the demons, and called for rice to offer to the spirits and clothes to burn for the spirits' apparel.

"Get out!" roared Nahl Bo. "I am not sick except for the visitation of such as yourselves, who are forever burdening the poor, and demanding pay for your supposed services. Away with you, and befool some other *pah sak ye* (eight month's man – fool) if you can. I want none of your services."

They were no easier to drive away, however, than were the other annoying visitors that had come with his supposed good fortune. He had finally to pay them as he had the others; and dejectedly he sat, scarcely noticing the opening of the ninth gourd.

The latter proved to contain a juggler, and the exasperated Nahl Bo, seeing but one small man, determined to make short work of him. Seizing him by his topknot of hair, he was about to drag him to the door, when the dexterous fellow, catching his tormentor by the thighs, threw him headlong over his own back, nearly breaking his neck, and causing him to lie stunned for a time, while the expert bound him hand and foot, and stood him on his head, so that the wife was glad to pay the fellow and dismiss him ere the life should be departed from her lord.

On opening the tenth a party of blind men came out, picking their way with their long sticks, while their sightless orbs were raised towards the unseen heavens. They offered to tell the fortunes of the family. But, while their services might have been demanded earlier, the case was now too desperate for any such help. The old men tinkled their little bells, and chanted some poetry addressed to the four good spirits stationed at the four corners of the earth, where they patiently stand bearing the world upon their shoulders; and to the distant heavens that arch over and fold the earth in their embrace, where the two meet at the far horizon (as pictured in the Korean flag). The blind men threw their dice, and, fearing lest they should prophesy death, Nahl Bo quickly paid and dismissed them.

The next gourd was opened but a trifle, that they might first determine as to the wisdom of letting out its contents. Before they could determine, however, a voice like thunder was heard from within, and the huge form of a giant arose, splitting open the gourd as he came forth. In his anger he seized poor Nahl Bo and tossed him upon his shoulders as though he would carry him away. Whereupon the wife plead with tears for his release, and gladly gave an order for the amount of the ransom. After which the monster allowed the frightened man to fall to the ground, nearly breaking his aching bones in the fall.

The carpenter did not relish the sport any longer; it seemed to be getting entirely too dangerous. He thereupon demanded the balance of his pay, which they finally agreed to give him, providing he would open the last remaining gourd. For the desperate people hoped to find this at least in sufficient condition that they might cook or make soup of it, since they had no food left at all and no money, while the other gourds were so spoiled by the tramping of the feet of their unbidden guests, as to be totally unfit for food.

The man did as requested, but had only sawed a very little when the gourd split open as though it were rotten, while a most awful stench arose, driving every one from the premises. This was followed by a gale of wind, so severe as to destroy the buildings, which, in falling, took fire from the *kang*, and while the once prosperous man looked on in helpless misery, the last of his remaining property was swept forever from him.

The seed that had brought prosperity to his honest, deserving brother had turned prosperity into ruin to the cruel, covetous Nahl Bo, who now had to subsist upon the charity of his kind brother, whom he had formerly treated so cruelly.

THE UNMANNERLY TIGER

"**Mountain Uncle**" was the name given by the villagers to a splendid striped tiger that lived among the highlands of Kang Wen, the long province which from its cliffs overlooks the Sea of Japan. Hunters rarely saw him, and among his fellow-tigers the Mountain Uncle boasted that, though often fired at, he had never been wounded; while as for traps – he knew all about them and laughed at the devices used by man to catch him and to strip him of his coveted skin. In summer he kept among the high hills and lived on fat deer. In winter, when heavy snow, biting winds, and terrible cold kept human beings within doors, old Mountain Uncle would sally forth to the villages. There he would prowl around the stables, the cattle enclosures, or the pig pens, in hopes of clawing and dragging out a young donkey, a fat calf, or a suckling pig. Too often he succeeded, so that he was the terror of the country for leagues around.

One day in autumn, Mountain Uncle was rambling among the lower hills. Though far from any village, he kept a sharp lookout for traps and hunters, but none seemed to be near. He was very hungry and hoped for game.

But on coming round a great rock, Mountain Uncle suddenly saw in his path some feet ahead, as he thought, a big tiger like himself.

He stopped, twitched his tail most ferociously as a challenge, showed fight by growling, and got ready to spring. What was his surprise to see the other tiger doing exactly the same things. Mountain Uncle was sure there would be a terrible struggle, but this was just what he wanted, for he expected to win.

But after a tremendous leap in the air he landed in a pit and all of a heap, bruised and disappointed. There was no tiger to be seen, but instead a heavy lid of logs had closed over his head with a crash and he lay in darkness. Old Mountain Uncle was caught at last. Yes, the hunter had concealed the pit with sticks and leaves, and on the upright timbers, covered with vines and brushwood, had hung a looking-glass. Mountain Uncle had often beheld his own face and body in the water, when he stooped to drink, but this time not seeing any water he was deceived into thinking a real tiger wanted to fight him.

By and by, a Buddhist priest came along, who believed in being kind to all living creatures. Hearing an animal moaning, he opened the trap and lifting the lid saw old Mountain Uncle at the bottom licking his bruised paw.

"Oh, please, Mr. Man, let me get out. I'm hurt badly," said the tiger.

Thereupon the priest lifted up one of the logs and slid it down, until it rested on the bottom of the pit. Then the tiger climbed up and out. Old Mountain Uncle expressed his thanks volubly, saying to the shaven head:

"I am deeply grateful to you, sir, for helping me out of my trouble. Nevertheless, as I am very hungry, I must eat you up."

The priest, very much surprised and indignant, protested against such vile ingratitude. To say the least, it was very bad manners and entirely against the law of the mountains, and he appealed to a big tree to decide between them.

The spirit in the tree spoke through the rustling leaves and declared that the man should go free and that the tiger was both ungrateful and unmannerly.

Old Mountain Uncle was not satisfied yet, especially as the priest was unusually fat and would make a very good dinner. However, he allowed the man to appeal once more and this time to a big rock.

"The man is certainly right venerable Mountain Uncle, and you are wholly wrong," said the spirit in the rock. "Your master, the Mountain Spirit, who rides on the green bull and the piebald horse to punish his enemies, will certainly chastise you if you devour this priest. You will be no fit messenger of the Mountain Lord if you are so ungrateful as to eat the man who saved you from starvation or death in the trap. It is shockingly bad manners even to think of such a thing."

The tiger felt ashamed, but his eyes still glared with hunger; so, to be sure of saving his own skin, the priest proposed to make the toad a judge. The tiger agreed.

But the toad, with his gold-rimmed eyes, looked very wise, and instead of answering quickly, as the tree and rock did, deliberated a long time. The priest's heart sank while the tiger moved his jaws as if anticipating his feast. He felt sure that Old Speckled Back would decide in his favor.

"I must go and see the trap before I can make up my mind," said the toad, who looked as solemn as a magistrate. So all three leaped, hopped, or walked to the trap. The tiger, moving fast, was there first, which was just what the toad, who was a friend of the priest, wanted. Besides, Old Speckled Back was diligently looking for a crack in the rocks near by.

So while the toad and the tiger were studying the matter, the priest ran off and saved himself within the monastery gates. When at last Old Speckled Back decided against Mountain Uncle and in favor of the man, he had no sooner finished his judgment than he hopped into the rock crevice, and, crawling far inside defied the tiger, calling him an unmannerly brute and an ungrateful beast, and daring him to do his worst.

Old Mountain Uncle was so mad with rage and hunger that his craftiness seemed turned into stupidity. He clawed at the rock to get at the toad, but Speckled Back, safe within, only laughed. Unable to do any harm, the tiger flew into a passion of rage. The hotter his temper grew, the more he lost his wit. Poking his nose inside the crack he rubbed it so hard on the rough rock that he soon bled to death.

When the hunter came along he marveled at what he saw, but he was glad to get rich by selling the tiger's fur, bones, and claws; for in Korea nothing sells so well as a tiger. As for the toad, he told to several generations of his descendants the story of how he outwitted the old Mountain Uncle.

TOKGABI AND HIS PRANKS

Tokgabi is the most mischievous sprite in all Korean fairyland. He does not like the sunshine or outdoors, and no one ever saw him on the streets.

He lives in the sooty flues that run under the floors along the whole length of the house, from the kitchen at one end of it to the chimney hole in the ground at the other end. He delights in the smoke and smut, and does not mind fire or flame, for he likes to be where it is warm. He has no lungs, and his skin and eyes are both fire-proof. He is as black as night and loves nothing that has white in it. He is always afraid of a bit of silver, even if it be only a hairpin.

Tokgabi likes most to play at night in the little loft over the fireplace. To run along the rafters and knock down the dust and cobwebs is his delight. His favorite game is to make the iron rice-pot lid dance up and down, so that it tumbles inside the rice kettle and cannot easily be got out again. Oh, how many times the cook burns, scalds, or steams her fingers in attempting to fish out that pot lid when Tokgabi has pushed it in! How she does bless the sooty imp!

But Tokgabi is not always mischievous, and most of his capers hurt nobody. He is such a merry fellow that he keeps continually busy, whether people cry or laugh. He does not mean to give any one trouble, but he must have fun every minute, especially at night.

When the fire is out, how he does chase the mice up and down the flues under the floor, and up in the garret over the rafters! When the mousies lie dead on their backs, with their toes turned upward, the street boys take them outdoors and throw them up in the air. Before the mice fall to the ground, the hawks swoop down and eat them up. Many a bird of prey gets his breakfast in this way.

Although Tokgabi plays so many pranks, he is kind to the kitchen maids. When after a hard day's work one is so tired out that she falls asleep, he helps her to do her hard tasks.

Tokgabi washes their dishes and cleans their tables for good servants; so when they wake up the girls find their work done for them. Many a fairy tale is told about this jolly sprite's doings – how he gives good things to the really nice people and makes the bad ones mad by spitefully using them. They do say that the king of all the Tokgabis has a museum of curiosities and a storehouse full of gold and gems and fine clothes, and everything sweet to eat for good boys and girls and for old people that are kind to the birds and dumb animals. For bad folks he has all sorts of things that are ugly and troublesome. He punishes stingy people by making them poor and miserable.

The Tokgabi king has also a menagerie of animals. These he sends to do his errands rewarding the good and punishing naughty folks. Every year the little almanac with red and green covers tells in what quarter of the skies the Tokgabi king lives for that year, so that the farmers and country people will keep out of his way and not provoke him. In his menagerie the kind creatures that help human beings are the dragon, bear, tortoise, frog, dog and rabbit. These are all man's friends. The cruel and treacherous creatures in Tokgabi's menagerie are the tiger, wild boar, leopard, serpent, toad and cat. These are the messengers of the Tokgabi king to do his bidding, when he punishes naughty folks.

The common, every-day Tokgabi plays fewer tricks on the men and boys and enjoys himself more in bothering the girls and women. This, I suppose, is because they spend more time in the house than their fathers or brothers. In the Land of Rat-tat-tat, where the sound of beating the washed clothes never ceases, Tokgabi loves to get hold of the women's laundry sticks which are used for pounding and polishing the starched clothes. He hides them so that they cannot be found. Then Daddy makes a fuss because his long white coat has to go without its usual gloss, but it is all Tokgabi's fault.

Tokgabi does not like starch because it is white. He loves to dance on Daddy's big black hat case that hangs on the wall. Sometimes he wiggles the fetich, or household idol, that is suspended from the rafters. But, most of all, he enjoys dancing a jig among the dishes in the closet over the fireplace, making them rattle and often tumble down with a crash.

Tokgabi likes to bother men sometimes too. If Daddy should get his topknot caught in a rat hole, or his head should slip off his wooden pillow at night and he bump his nose, it is all Tokgabi's fault. When anything happens to a boy's long braid of hair, that hangs down his back and makes him look so much like a girl, Tokgabi is blamed for it. It is even said that naughty men make compacts with Tokgabi to do bad things, but the imp only helps the man for the fun of it. Tokgabi cares nothing about what mortal men call right or wrong. He is only after fun and is up to mischief all the time, so one must watch out for him.

The kitchen maids and the men think they know how to circumvent Tokgabi and spoil his tricks. Knowing that the imp does not like red, a young man when betrothed wears clothes of this bright color. Tokgabi is afraid of shining silver, too, so the men fasten their topknots together, and the girls keep their chignons in shape, with silver hairpins. The magistrates and government officers have little storks made of solid silver in their hats, or else these birds are embroidered with silver thread on their dresses. Every one who can afford them uses white metal dishes and dresses in snowy garments. Tokgabi likes nothing white and that is the reason why every Korean likes to put on clothes that are as dazzling as hoar frost. Tons and mountains of starch are consumed in blanching and stiffening coats and skirts, sleeves and stockings. On festival days the people look as if they were dipped in starch and their garments encrusted in rock candy. In this manner they protect themselves from the pranks of Tokgabi.

PRINCE SANDALWOOD, THE FATHER OF KOREA

Four little folks lived in the home of Mr. Kim, two girls and two boys. Their names were Peach Blossom and Pearl, Eight-fold Strength and Dragon. Dragon was the oldest, a boy. Grandma Kim was very fond of telling them stories about the heroes and fairies of their beautiful country.

One evening when Papa Kim came home from his office in the Government buildings, he carried two little books in his hand, which he handed over to Grandma. One was a little almanac looking in its bright cover of red, green and blue as gay as the piles of cakes and confectionery made when people get married; for every one knows how rich in colors are pastry and sweets for the bride's friends at a Korean wedding party.

The second little book contained the direction sent out by the Royal Minister of Ceremonies for the celebration of the festival in honor of the Ancestor-Prince, Old Sandalwood, the Father of Korea. Twice a year in Ping Yang City they made offerings of meat and other food in his honor, but always uncooked.

"Who was old Sandalwood?" asked Peach Blossom, the older of the little girls.

"What did he do?" asked Yongi (Dragon), the older boy.

"Let me tell you," said Grandma, as they cuddled together round her on the oiled-paper carpet over the main flue at the end of the room where it was warmest; for it was early in December and the wind was roaring outside.

"Now I shall tell you, also, why the bear is good and the tiger bad," said Grandma. "Well, to begin—

"Long, long ago, before there were any refined people in the Land of Dawn, and no men but rude savages, a bear and a tiger met together. It was on the southern slope of Old Whitehead Mountain in the forest. These wild animals were not satisfied with the kind of human beings already on the earth, and they wanted better ones. They thought that if they could become human they would be able to improve upon the quality. So these patriotic beasts, the bear and the tiger, agreed to go before Hananim, the Great One of Heaven and Earth, and ask him to change at once their form and nature; or, at least, tell them how it could be done.

"But where to find Him – that was the question. So they put their heads down in token of politeness, stretched out their paws and waited a long while, hoping to get light on the subject.

"Then a Voice spoke out saying, 'Eat a bunch of garlic and stay in a cave for twenty-one days. If you do, you will become human.'

"So into the dark cave they crawled, chewed their garlic and went to sleep.

"It was cold and gloomy in the cave and with nothing to hunt or eat, the tiger got tired. Day after day he moped, snarled, growled and behaved rudely to his companion. But the bear bore the tiger's insults.

"Finally on the eleventh day, the tiger, seeing no signs of losing his stripes or of shedding his hair, claws or tail, and with no prospect of fingers or toes in view, concluded to give up trying to become a man. He bounded out of the cave and at once went hunting in the woods, going back to his old life.

"But the bear, patiently sucking her paw, waited till the twenty-one days had passed. Then her hairy hide and claws dropped off, like an overcoat. Her nose and ears suddenly shortened and she stood upright – a perfect woman.

"Walking out of the cave the new creature sat beside a brook, and in the pure water beheld how lovely she was. There she waited to see what would take place next.

"About this time while these things were going on down in the world matters of interest were happening in the skies. Whanung, the Son of the Great One in the Heavens, asked his father to give him an earthly kingdom to rule over. Pleased with his request, the Lord of Heaven decided to present his son with the Land of the Dragon's Back, which men called Korea.

"Now as everybody knows, this country of ours, the Everlasting Great Land of the Dayspring, rose up on the first morning of creation out of the sea, in the form of a dragon. His spine, loins and tail form the great range of mountains that makes the backbone of our beautiful country, while his head rises skyward in the eternal White Mountain in the North. On its summit amid the snow and ice lies the blue lake of pure water, from which flow out our boundary rivers."

"What is the name of this lake?" asked Yongi the boy.

"The Dragon's Pool," said Grandma Kim, "and during one whole night, ever so long ago, the dragon breathed hard and long until its breath filled the heavens with clouds. This was the way that the Great One in the Skies prepared the way for his son's coming to earth.

"People thought there was an earthquake, but when they woke up in the morning and looked up to the grand mountain, so gloriously white, they saw the cloud rising far up in the sky. As the bright sun shone upon it, the cloud turned into pink, red, yellow and the whole eastern sky looked so lovely that our country then received its name – the Land of Morning Radiance.

"Down out of his cloud of many colors, and borne on the wind, Whanung, the Heavenly Prince, descended first to the mountain top, and then to the lower earth. When he entered the great forest he found a beautiful woman sitting by the brookside. It was the bear that had been transformed into lovely human shape and nature.

"The Heavenly Prince was delighted. He chose her as his bride and, by and by, a little baby boy was born.

"The mother made for her son a cradle of soft moss and reared her child in the forest.

"Now the people who dwelt at the foot of the mountain were in those days very rude and simple. They wore no hats, had no white clothes, lived in huts, and did not know how to warm their houses with flues running under the floors, nor had they any books or writings. Their sacred place was under a sandalwood tree, on a small mountain named Tabak, in Ping Yang province.

"They had seen the cloud rising from the Dragon's Pool so rich in colors, and as they looked they saw it move southward and nearer to them, until it stood over the sacred sandalwood tree; when out stepped a white-robed being, and descending through the air alighted in the forest and on the tree.

"Oh, how beautiful this spirit looked against the blue sky! Yet the tree was far away and long was the journey to it.

"'Let us all go to the sacred tree,' said the leader of the people. So together they hied over hill and valley until they reached the holy ground and ranged themselves in circles about it.

"A lovely sight greeted their eyes. There sat under the tree a youth of grand appearance, arrayed in princely dress. Though young looking and rosy in face, his countenance was august and majestic. Despite his youth, he was wise and venerable.

"'I have come from my ancestors in Heaven to rule over you, my children,' he said, looking at them most kindly.

"At once the people fell on their knees and all bent reverently, shouting:

"'Thou art our king, we acknowledge thee, and will loyally obey only thee.'

"Seeing that they wanted to know what he could tell them, he began to instruct them, even before he gave them laws and rules and taught them how to improve their houses. He told them stories. The first one explained to them why it was that the bear is good and the tiger bad.

"The people wondered at his wisdom, and henceforth the tiger was hated, while people began to like the bear more and more.

"'What name shall we give our King, so that we may properly address him?' asked the people of their elders. 'It is right that we should call him after the place in which we saw him, under our holy tree. Let his title, therefore, be the August and Venerable Sandalwood.' So they saluted him thus and he accepted the honor.

"Seeing that the people were rough and unkempt, Prince Sandalwood showed them how to tie up and dress their hair. He ordained that men should wear their long locks in the form of a topknot. Boys must braid their hair and let it hang down over their backs. No boy could be called a man, until he married a wife. Then he could twist his hair into a knot, put on a hat, have a head-dress like an adult and wear a long white coat.

"As for the women, they must plait their tresses and wear them plainly at their neck, except at marriage, or on great occasions of ceremony. Then they might pile up their hair like a pagoda and use long hairpins, jewels, silk and flowers.

"Thus our Korean civilization was begun, and to this day the law of the hat and hair distinguishes us above all people," said Grandma. "We still honor the August and Venerable Prince Sandalwood. Now, good-night, my darlings."

A BRIDEGROOM FOR MISS MOLE

By the river Kingin stands the great stone image, or Miryek, that was cut out of the solid rock ages ago. Its base lies far beneath the ground and around its granite cap many feet square the storm-clouds gather and play as they roll down the mountain.

Down under the earth near this mighty colossus lived a soft-furred mole and his wife. One day a daughter was born to them. It was the most wonderful mole baby that ever was known. The father was so proud of his lovely offspring that he determined to marry her only to the grandest thing in the whole universe. Nothing else would satisfy his pride in the beautiful creature he called his own.

Father Mole sought long and hard to find out where and what, in all nature, was considered the most wonderful. He called in his neighbors and talked over the matter with them. Then he visited the king of the moles and asked the wise ones in his court to decide for him. One and all agreed that the Great Blue Sky was above everything else in glory and greatness.

So up to the Sky the Mole Father went and offered his daughter to be the bride of the Great Blue, telling how with his vast azure robe the Sky had the reputation, both on the earth and under it, of being the greatest thing in the universe.

But much to the Mole Father's surprise, the Sky declined.

"No, I am not the greatest. I must refer you to the Sun. He controls me, for he can make it day or night as he pleases. Only when he rises can I wear my bright colors. When he goes down darkness covers the world and men do not see me at all, but the stars instead. Better take your charming daughter to him."

So to the Sun went Mr. Mole and though afraid to look directly into his face, he made his plea. He would have the Sun marry his attractive daughter.

But the mighty luminary, that usually seemed so fierce, dazzling men's eyesight and able to burn up the grass of the field, seemed suddenly very modest. Instead of accepting at once the offer, the Sun said to the father:

"Alas! I am not master. The Cloud is greater than I, for he is able to cover me up and make me invisible for days and weeks. I am not as powerful as you think me to be. Let me advise you to offer your daughter to the Cloud."

Surprised at this, the Mole Father looked quite disappointed. Now he was in doubt as to what time he had best propose to the Cloud, – when it was silvery white and glistening in a summer afternoon, or when it was black and threatening a tempest. However, his ambition to get for his daughter the mightiest possible bridegroom prompted him to wait until the lightnings flashed and the thunder rolled. Then appearing before the terrible dark Cloud that shot out fire, he told of the charms of his wonderful daughter and offered her as bride.

"But why do you come to me?" asked the Cloud, its face inky black with the wrath of a storm and its eyes red with the fires of lightning.

"Because you are not only the greatest thing in the universe, but you have proved it by your terrible power," replied the Father Mole.

At this the Cloud ceased its rolling, stopped its fire and thunder and almost laughed.

"So far from being the greatest thing in the world, I am not even my own master. See already how the wind is driving me. Soon I shall be invisible, dissolved in air. Let me commend you to the Wind. The Master of the Cloud will make a grand son-in-law."

Thereupon Papa Mole waited until the Wind calmed down, after blowing away the clouds. Then telling of his daughter's accomplishments and loveliness, he made proffer of his only child as bride to the Wind.

But the Wind was not half so proud as the Mole Father had expected to find him. Very modest, almost bashful seemed the Wind, as he confessed that before Miryek, the colossal stone image, his power was naught.

"Why, I smite that Great Stone Face and its eyes do not even blink. I roar in his ears, but he minds it not. I try to make him sneeze, but he will not. Smite him as I may, he still stands unmoved and smiling. Alas, no. I am not the grandest thing in the universe, while Miryek stands. Go to him. He alone is worthy to marry your daughter."

By this time the Mole Father was not only footsore and weary, but much discouraged also. Evidently all appreciated his shining daughter; but would he be able, after all, to get her a worthy husband?

He rested himself a while and then proceeded to Miryek, the colossus of granite as large as a lighthouse, its head far up in the air, but with ears ready to hear.

The Mole Father squeaked out compliments to the image as being by common confession the greatest thing on earth. He presented his request for a son-in-law and then in detail mentioned the accomplishments of his daughter, sounding her praise at great length. Indeed, he almost ruined his case by talking so long.

With stony patience Miryek listened to the proud father with a twinkle in his white granite eyes. When his lips moved, he was heard to say:

"Fond Parent, what you say is true. I am great. I care not for the sky day or night, for I remain the same in daylight and darkness. I fear not the sun, that cannot melt me, nor the frost that is not able to make me crumble. Cold or hot, in summer or in winter time, I remain unchanged. The clouds come and go, but they cannot move me. Their fire and noise, lightning and thunder, I fear not. Yes, I am great." Then the stone lips closed again.

"You will make, then, a good bridegroom for my daughter? You will marry her, I understand?" asked the proud father as his hopes began to rise, though he was still doubtful.

"I would gladly do so, if I were greatest. But I am not," said Miryek. "Down under my feet is the Mole. He digs with his shovellike hands and makes burrows day and night. His might I cannot resist. Soon he shall undermine my base and I shall topple down and lie like common stone along the earth. Yes! by universal confession, the Mole is the greatest thing in the universe and to him I yield. Better marry your daughter to him."

So after all his journeying, the father sought no further. Advised on all sides, and opinion being unanimous, he found out that the Mole was the greatest thing in the universe. His daughter's bridegroom was found at home and of the same family of creatures. He married her to a young and handsome Mole, and great was the joy and rejoicing at the wedding. The pair were well-mated and lived happily ever afterward.

OLD WHITE WHISKERS AND MR BUNNY

White Whiskers was the name of a huge, tawny tiger that lived in the mountains of Kang Wen. He was the proudest tiger in the whole peninsula of Korea. He had the most fiery eyes, the longest tail, the sharpest claws, and the widest stripes of any animal in the mountains. He could pull down a cow, fight all the dogs in any village, eat up a man, and was not afraid of a hunter, unless the man carried a gun. As for calves and pigs, he considered them mere tidbits. He could claw off the roof or break the bars of stables where cattle were kept, devour one pig on the spot, and then, slinging another on his back, could trot off to his lair miles away, to give his cubs their dinner of fresh pork.

White Whiskers was especially proud, because he was the retainer of the great genii of the mountains, that men feared and worshiped and in whose honor they built shrines. One of these Mountain Spirits, when he wanted to, could call together all the tigers in his domain, and then, sitting astride the back of the biggest, he would ride off on the clouds or to victory over Korea's enemies. Both tigers and leopards were his messengers to do his bidding. Only the big and swift and striped tigers were chosen to carry out the Mountain Spirit's orders.

One particular matter of business confided to White Whiskers, the great striped tiger, was to visit daily the shrines in the hill passes to see if offerings were continually made. The people who were in terror of both the Mountain Spirit and his servants the tigers, daily offered sacrifice out of fear. They piled up stone, rags, bits of metal, or laid food on dishes for the Mountain Spirit who was very exacting and tyrannical. The poor folks thought that if they did not thus heap up their offerings the spirit would be angry and send the tigers at night to prowl around the village, scratch at their doors, and eat up donkeys, cows, calves, pigs, and even men, women and children. Then the hunters would go out with matchlocks to slay the man eaters, but by this time, in daylight, the tigers were far up into their lairs in the mountain.

Indeed, it was so hard to get a shot at a tiger that the Chinese, who like to make fun of their neighbors in white coats, declared that during one half of the year the Koreans hunt the tigers, and during the other half the tigers hunt the Koreans. That is, the men go out with their guns in summer; but in winter, when men keep within doors, the hungry wild beasts descend from the mountains for their prey.

Now Old White Whiskers was both proud and crafty. For many years he had eaten up pigs, calves, dogs, donkeys and chickens and had twice feasted on men, besides avoiding all their traps and dodging every one of their bullets. So he began to think he could laugh at all his enemies. Yet, proud as he was, he was destined to be outwitted by a creature without strength or sting, claws or hoofs, as we shall see.

Mr. Rabbit, who burrowed in a hill near the village, had often heard the squealing of unfortunate pigs and the kicking of braying donkeys, as they made dinners for Old White Whiskers.

Thus far, however, by being very cautious, he had kept out of the striped tyrant's way and maw. But one cold winter's day, coming home, tired, weak and hungry, from having no food since yesterday, just as he was crossing a river on the ice, he met Old White Whiskers face to face. From behind a rock by the shore, near Mr. Bunny's burrow, the big tiger leaped out and tried to freeze the rabbit with terror, by staring at him with his great green eyes. Mr. Bunny knew only too well that tigers love to maul and play with their prey before eating it up, and he thought his last hour had come.

Nevertheless Mr. Bunny was perfectly cool. He did not shiver a bit. He had long expected such a meeting and was ready for Old White Whiskers, intending to throw him off his guard.

Fully expecting, in a minute or two, to tear off the little animal's fur and grind his bones for a dinner, the tiger said to the rabbit:

"I'm hungry. I shall eat you up at once."

"Oh, why should you bother with me?" said Mr. Bunny. "I'm so little and skinny as hardly to make a mouthful for Your Majesty. Just listen to me and I'll get you a royal dinner. I'll go up the mountain and drive the game to your very paws. Only you must do exactly what I tell you."

At this prospect of a full dinner, the tiger actually grinned with delight. The way he yawned, showing his red, cavernous mouth, huge white teeth, each as big as a spike, and the manner of his rolling out his long curved tongue, full of rough points like thorns, nearly scared Mr. Bunny out of his wits. The rabbit had never looked down a tiger's mouth before, but he did not let on that he was afraid. It was only the tiger's way of showing how happy he was, when his mouth watered, and he licked his chops in anticipation of a mighty feast.

"I'll do just as you say," said Old White Whiskers to Mr. Bunny, seeing how grateful the rabbit was to have his own life spared.

"It is my ambition to serve the lord of the mountains," said Mr. Bunny. "So, lie down on the ice here, shut your eyes and do not stir. Now mind you keep your peepers closed, or the charm will fail. I'll make a circle of dry grass and then go round and round you, driving the game to you. If you hear a noise and even some crackling, don't open your eyes till I give you the word. 'Twill take some time."

Old White Whiskers, tired of tramping in the forest and prowling around pig-pens all day but getting nothing, was both hungry and tired. So he resolved, while waiting, to take a good nap. As quickly as one can blow out a candle, he was asleep.

Thereupon Mr. Bunny made himself busy in pulling up all the dry grass he could find and piling it around and close up to Old White Whiskers. Delighted to hear the big brute snoring, he kept on until he had a thick ring of combustibles. Then he set it on fire, waiting till it blazed up high. Then he scampered off to see the fun.

Old White Whiskers, awakened by the crackling, yawned and rubbed his eyes with his paws, wondering what the noise could be.

"Hold on!" screamed Mr. Bunny, "keep your promise," and farther he ran away up the hill.

"Rascal!" growled the tiger as the red tongues of flame leaped up all around him. He had to jump high to escape from the flames with his life. Even as it was, one paw was scorched so that he limped, and his fur was singed so badly that all his long hair and fine looks were gone. When he got back home, the other tigers laughed at him.

Henceforth he had to take second place, for the great Mountain Spirit no longer trusted such a stupid servant.

OLD TIMBER TOP

The fairies in the Korean province of Kang Wen, which means River Meadow, were having great fun, when one of their number told how they played a trick on an ox-driver whom they called Old Timber Top. How he got such a strange name this story will tell.

This driver was a rich and stingy fellow who had made a fortune in lumber. He used to buy up all the trees he could. Then he would have them cut down and sawed up into logs and boards. His men would haul them away in their rough carts, drawn by stout bulls, to his lumber yard. In winter time sleds were used, but whether it was the season of snow and ice, or of tree blossoms and flowers, the animal used to draw sleds or carts was always a bull.

For in Korea, horses or donkeys do not know how to pull anything. The ponies and donkeys are too small. Not being used to the work, if harnessed they would kick the wagon all to pieces.

They can carry loads on their backs, but the bulls can do this also, so the creature with horns is considered to be the most valuable of beasts of burden. Besides, he fills the purse and makes good dinners when his owner is through with him.

You can see these patient carriers loaded with brushwood or sticks piled so high they seem to be carrying small mountains of twigs, grass and leaves for kindlings, or with heavy logs of wood for fuel. Yet when the bull is very young, a mere baby, he has a happier time than a colt or little donkey, for he lives in the house and is the children's pet.

Old Timber Top sold his logs and boards at such high prices that the poor suffered. This was because they were cold and could not afford to pay so many strings of cash for fuel. The people used to say that the old fellow would skin a mosquito for his hide and tallow. So sometimes they gave him the nickname of Skin-flay.

Not many of the villagers were able to buy planks of wood thick and heavy and strong enough to keep their pigs from the tigers, which came down from the mountains and prowled about at night in the villages. These long-haired and black-striped beasts got to be so fond of pork, that even in the snow they would, without fearing the cold or the guns of the hunters, claw up the tops of the pens and get down among the squealing prey. They might get a baby pig at once or perhaps drag out and carry off enough of a big pork to feed their cubs for a week. All the stables and cow-houses had to be made very strong, for the tigers, when they had gone a good while without food, seemed to be hungry enough to eat a horse with all his harness on, and even a grown-up cow or ox. Yet as a rule, no tiger cared to taste either beef or horse meat, if he could get young pork or veal.

Old Timber Top was not satisfied to make money at his lumber yard only. It is the custom in Korea to plant the most beautiful trees around tombs or in the cemeteries. When this skin-flint heard of a family which had become so poor that they must needs sell the splendid trees which had been planted around their ancestors' graves he sent his agents to buy the timber.

TALES OF ANIMALS & MYTHICAL CREATURES

These fellows would load up a horse with long ropes, of copper and iron cash, coins that had a square hole in the middle and were strung together with twine made of twisted straw. It was a heavy horse load to carry twenty dollars' worth of coin. Arrived on the spot, after beating the owner down to the lowest price possible, Old Timber Top's men would go out, chop down and saw up the grand trees, leaving only the sawdust on the graves, while the people wept to lose what they loved.

In this way the landscape was spoiled and this made many villagers very angry at such a man, for the Koreans love natural scenery and almost worship fine trees, which had made the country beautiful for centuries.

But what cared Old Timber Top, provided he could pile up his strings of cash and jingle his silver?

In time, this hard old fellow could think of nothing else but how to get richer out of the wants and sufferings of other people. The wealthier he became, the more he wanted. Yet he did not get any happier. Nobody loved him, while many hated him.

At last he thought he would make a trip to Seoul, the great capital city, which every Korean hopes to see sometime. There he expected to receive honor and appointment to rank and office. Timber Top had a relative who was high in the king's service, who, he thought, would assist him; for all Koreans are kind and helpful to each other, especially when they are related.

To be an officer Timber Top knew would permit him, even to wear a gorgeously shining mandarin's hat with wide flaps or wings on it and a long white silk coat with a big square on the breast of velvet or satin, embroidered with storks or dragons, clouds and waves. When he went out on the streets he could strut about, as if he were the lord of the universe; for he would then wear a hat so high and with such a round wide brim, that he would not dare to go out during a high wind, for fear of being blown away, like a ship in a tempest. In such a costume he would be saluted by servants and the common people, who would bow down before him, because they would think him a great man.

But how could he win such a position and gain the glory of it?

He was not a scholar, learned in books, or in law, or a doctor of medicine. Not being a soldier, either, he knew nothing of war. He could not ride on a monocycle, as a general did, drawn or pushed by four men and dressed in a long red coat studded all over with shining metal with a brass helmet on his head, on the top of which was a little dragon. He feared, even if he were appointed, he might fall off the one-wheeled vehicle and show what a fool he was.

Nevertheless this old fellow was so vain and full of conceit that he followed what was once the common custom in Korea. He took his journey to Seoul, leaving his family behind him to live on the cheapest kind of kimchi, with turnips and millet.

Now the Koreans are all famous for giving welcome and showing hospitality to their poor relations, and often they do this even to tramps and lazy people. When a man becomes rich or holds a high office, he usually has around him many hangers on. Some, we should even say, were loafers.

So on arriving in Seoul, Old Timber Top took up his quarters in one part of his relative's big house. There he lived a long time and was treated decently, for he always was saying soft things and making flattering speeches to his host. In fact, he bowed down like a slave when in presence of his august master. Yet, in truth, he was despised even by the servants and work people.

In order not to wear his welcome entirely out he had to make from time to time a handsome present to his patron. This steadily reduced both his income and his fortune, and while these were shrinking his family at home suffered, so that, by and by, he received notice by letter that his business had dried up and soon no more money could be sent to him in Seoul. While he lingered news from home grew worse and worse. His wife was obliged to sell their house to pay debts. The next item was that she and her daughter were living in a wretched shanty at the end of the village and were no longer in society.

All this time those in Seoul who knew that the foolish fellow was as ambitious as ever to wear the fine white clothes of a scholar, or the gay colors of a soldier, declared that Old Timber Top had no brains. They even jested about a pumpkin set on shoulders, or they laughed when they declared that the wood, which he had sold so long, had gone to his head. They debated in the wine shops whether, if his skull were opened, pumpkin seeds or timber would be found inside of it.

So they, also, called him "Old Timber Top," meaning that inside his skull was a wooden head and no better than that of an idol carved out of persimmon wood, such as were so plentiful in the Buddhist temples. Others declared that he had a real head of bone and brains, but "he carried it under his arm pits," as the saying was.

When the fairies heard all this, they unanimously resolved to reform the old fellow, even if they had to make an ox of him.

Timber Top, now poor and bankrupt, knew he must leave Seoul and go home and work for a living. When he made his final call on his rich Seoul relative and told him he must, to his great regret, take his leave and go back to his native village, he was not well received. Being too poor to buy a present to give to his host, on whose bounty he had lived so long, he was answered coldly and told to go and do as he liked.

And this, after years of fawning and gift-making! Not a word of thanks or appreciation! Poor Timber Top was down in the mouth and his heart was cold in his bosom. He knocked on his head with his fists, to find out whether, after all, it had really turned into timber.

On his way back, a big storm came on and when he came to a village inn, cold, wet and hungry, he begged for shelter over night. The woman who kept it was the wife of a butcher, who was then away from home. This was an awful blow to Timber Top's pride, for butchers were held to be the lowest of people, and they were not even allowed to wear hats, like the rest of the men in Korea.

The woman was kind to the traveler. She gave him a hot supper and let him sleep in that room of the house which had the best stone floor, under which the flues from the kitchen fire ran. So he warmed himself and baked his clothes, which were sopping wet, until they were dry. He was so tired that he kept on sleeping till very late next morning, and nearly to the noon hour. He was altogether so comfortable that to him it seemed as if he were a great man in the capital, thus to receive such kind treatment.

Waking up from one of his naps, he heard what he thought was the big butcher, who had come home, asking of his wife in a gruff tone of voice, "Where is that ox? I must sell him this morning, for it is market day," he said.

In less than a minute more, the man and his wife entered the room with four sticks which the fairies had put there, a halter, and a rope, made of twisted rice straw, besides a thick iron ring, such as they put into bulls' noses, to make them obey their masters. Throwing down the iron ring and rope on the floor, in a trice they had thrust the stick under Old Timber Top's back. In a moment more, he felt horns growing out of his head, and his lips becoming thick as sausages. His mouth was as wide as a saucer and had big teeth growing on the upper jaw. A tail sprouted at his other end and the four sticks became four legs.

Before he could quite understand just what was going on, or what the matter could be, Old Timber Top was standing on four legs and the butcher was slipping the ring through his nose. Oh how it did hurt!

It was an awkward job to get the animal out of the room and through the narrow door, and some of the paper on the walls and the furniture suffered. But finally when out in the open air the bull, that was no other than what had been the man Timber Top, went quietly along to the market place. Any attempt to pull his head away, or to stop or run off, or in any way to misbehave, hurt his nose so dreadfully, that he quickly quit. The butcher needed to give only a slight jerk of the rope when the bull changed his gait and was as quiet as a lamb, even though as an animal he was big enough to gore the man and toss him on its horns, or crush him by trampling on him with his hoofs, if once he got angry.

One would have supposed that Timber Top would be a fighting bull, but no! In the market place he stood patiently and quietly for hours, hardly even stamping, when the flies began to bite.

"Oh that I had been as diligent and kept on at my honest occupation in my native village, as that fly!" mused the bull, that still had a man's memory.

At last there came a man with money to buy. He was a drover, who unloaded his pony and paid down many strings, or about twenty pounds, of copper and iron cash. The owner put the halter in the buyer's hand, and the new master then led off Timber Top to be sold to a butcher who lived up in his home town in the north. This fellow intended first to fatten the animal and then turn him into steaks and stewing meat.

But on his way the new owner thought that, because he had made a good bargain, he must stop at a wine shop and have a drink. So he tied Timber Top's nose with the rope to the low wall, which enclosed a turnip field, and went inside the shop.

But while the drover's wine went in his wits went out, and he fell asleep and stayed in the shop a long time. In fact, it was as the old song said:

"First the man takes a dram,
Then the dram takes another dram;
Then the dram takes the man."

Meanwhile Timber Top looked over the low wall, and, yielding to temptation, pulled up with his teeth some of the plants by the roots, first chewing the green leaves and then grinding the turnips and swallowing them.

Presto! The horns drew in and shrivelled up. The ring dropped out of his nose and fell with a crash on the stones of the village path. His two forelegs turned into arms, the hair and hoofs became human legs and Old Timber Top was a man, and himself once again. To make sure of it he felt himself all over; pulled his own nose, felt around his back to see if he had a tail, and rubbed his head for horns. None there! He looked down and found he had only two legs. Then he swung his arms with delight, at being once more a man.

"Well named, Turn-up thou," he mused, "thou green plant with a mustard-like taste. Thou hast turned me inside out. Or, have the fairies been busy?"

He had hardly got these ideas through his half wooden head, that he was on two legs and a man once more and could think like one, than he started on the road home. Just then the drover rushed out of the wine shop and accosted him, saying:

"Have you seen a stray bull anywhere near this place?"

Of course Timber Top using fine language, like a yang ban, said there was no bull in the neighborhood that he could see or knew of, and he had heard none bellowing. Then he gave the drover a look of contempt for being so stupid, and for asking of him, a gentleman, so foolish a question.

Yet after he was out of sight of the drover he slapped his thighs, as Koreans do when they are amused at their own smartness, and went on joyfully. He kept on repeating to himself, "sticks and turnips, turnips and sticks."

Then a big idea struck him, as if it were a tap on a wooden drum, such as one sees in Buddhist temples. It hit his brain so hard and so swelled his head, that his big Korean hat nearly toppled off. Immediately he put this idea into action.

He returned hastily to the inn and into the room in which he had been turned into a bull and stole the butcher's four fairy sticks, which stood in a corner, then he hied at once over the roads towards the capital.

Reaching Seoul, he went to the house of his rich relative, where he had waited ten years for the fortune and the favor which did not come. Going into his host's bedroom, he tapped the high lord of the house with the fairy sticks, not hard, but only lightly.

Forthwith the man's head became horns at the top, with muzzle of thick lips in front. His hands turned into front hoofs and his legs into the hind quarters of a bull. Yet he was not entirely an ox, but only half animal and half man.

Old Timber Top stopped tapping and then went away, to await events, leaving the creature half man and half ox. He knew that soon he would be called in.

When the family of wife, many sons, several daughters, servants, retainers, hangers-on, and what not, saw their master half man and half ox, with horns and hoofs, they were distracted. Each one had his own notion of how to get him back into human form and like his former self. Each one ran all over town and into the adjoining villages to get and call in the mudangs.

These mudangs were the people, mostly women, whose business it was to drive out the imps and bad fairies, such as had, in this case, done the mischief. The kitchen maids stoutly declared that Tokgabi had wrought the change upon their master. They felt quite sure of it; but the men thought that the gods of the mountains were punishing him for his sins. On the other hand, the mudang woman said she would find out and get him back into his human skin, if they paid her enough money.

With drums and dancing and songs, screams, yells, and every sort of noise, the mudangs kept up such a terrible racket that it almost deafened the family. There were several of them called in, and they knew that they would all be well paid.

Meanwhile the doctors also kept on with their awful medicines, besides rubbing, pounding, blowing, and sticking needles into the bull and burning moxa, or little balls of cottony mugwort, on its hide.

Yet not a hoof or horn, not even a hair changed.

The mudangs declared that the imps had got inside the man and they must get them out. One fellow carried a big bottle to trap the imps and cork them in. Another insisted that they would have to use scissors and snip the skin in about a hundred places, thus making small holes to let the evil creatures out. Then they must bottle them up, lest they should get out and overrun the house and infest the whole town.

There seemed not so many chances of getting well as "one hair among nine oxen"; but the wife pleaded that they would put off using the scissors until all other means had failed. She did not want to see her dear husband's skin made into a colander, or sieve, if it could be helped.

At this point, when the din and the despair were worst and had come to a climax, Old Timber Top appeared. As some of the family had collapsed and lay helpless on the floor, and as all were too tired to ask questions, they at once made way for him. After looking at the patient with a face as wise as an owl's, Old Timber Top solemnly announced that only one thing could save him and that was a rare and wonderful drug, of which only he knew the secret, but which he could speedily procure. Of course the wife, sons and daughters instantly promised to give up their all, to see their husband and father himself again.

So while Timber Top went out to get the famous medicine, they all fell asleep, tired out, while the ox-man lay over on his side resting his horns and hoofs on the floor bed; for in Korea they do not have bedsteads, that is, beds raised up from the floor.

As for Old Timber Top, when once out on the street, he immediately began saying to himself, over and over again, "Turnips and sticks, sticks and turnips."

Going to a vegetable shop, he bought a fine large turnip, or turnip-radish, of the kind that grows in Korea, silvery white and about four feet long. He first peeled, then sliced, and finally pounded it into a sauce very fine. Then entering the house in triumph, he woke up the doctors, kicked the servants awake, and announced that the potent drug would soon restore their master. He solemnly bade them all watch and see him do it.

Pulling and hauling all together, five or six fellows were able to get the man-bull on his two hoofs and two feet and then Timber Top put a spoonful of the sauce on the big tongue.

At once a most marvellous change took place!

The horns shortened until they disappeared, the lips thinned, the mouth became smaller. Hoofs, hair, and hide departed into empty air. In the wagging of a dog's tail, the mighty man of the house had become himself again.

All the doctors, jugglers, and mudangs packed up their imp-bottles and medicines, and with their drums, flutes, bags, boxes and wares slunk away, while the family loaded Old Timber Top with grateful thanks and compliments.

As for the master, he declared Timber Top the greatest physician the world ever knew. He invited him to make the house his permanent home and showered upon him many gifts, with plenty to eat, and white clothes starched as white as snow. The hats with which he presented Timber Top were so big around and had a brim so wide, that he used them when covered with oiled paper covers as umbrellas in rainy weather, but he never went out doors when the wind was blowing, for fear he would be whirled down the street. Besides this, he feared there was still much wood in his head, which might turn into a top and spin round, if he were not careful.

Old Timber Top set up a medicine office, practiced among the nobility and became physician to the king. When he visited the palace, he used a red visiting card, a foot long. He had a plastron, or square of velvet embroidery on his breast. He wore a string of amber beads as big as walnuts over his ears. He soon became fat with a double chin and plump fingers, showing that he reeked with prosperity. He lived to a good old age, his family were made comfortable, his sons and daughters married well, and he had seventeen grandchildren before he died.

Yet all the time, the fairies claimed that they did it all. They made the sticks work one way, and the turnips another, and they still play their tricks on the Koreans, especially those with more or less wood in their heads.

A FROG FOR A HUSBAND

Off in a valley among very stony mountains, lived an old farmer named Pak We and his wife. His land was poor and he had to toil from sunrise to sunset and often in the night, when the moon was shining, to get food. No child had ever come to his home and he was in too great straits of poverty to adopt a son. So he took his amusement in fishing in the pond higher up on the hills, that fed the stream which watered his millet and rice fields. Being very skilful he often caught a good string of fish and these he sold in the village near by to get for himself and his wife the few comforts they needed. Thus the old couple kept themselves happy, despite their cheerless life, though they often wondered what would become of them when they got too old to work.

But one summer Pak noticed that there were fewer fish in the pond and that every day they seemed to be less in number. Where he used to catch a stringful in an hour, he could hardly get half that many during a whole day.

What was the matter? Was he getting less skilful? Was the bait poor?

Not at all! His worms were as fat, his hooks and lines in as good order, and his eyesight was as keen as ever.

When Pak noticed also that the water was getting shallower, he was startled. Could it be that the pond was drying up?

Things grew worse day by day until at last there were no fish.

Where once sparkled the wavelets of a pond was now an arid waste of earth and stones, over which trickled hardly more than a narrow rill, which he could jump over. No fish and no pond meant no water for his rice fields. In horror at the idea of starving, or having to move away from his old home and become a pauper, Pak looked down from what had been the banks of the pond to find the cause of all this trouble. There in the mud among the pebbles he saw a bullfrog, nearly as big as an elephant, blinking at him with its huge round eyes.

In a rage the farmer Pak burst out, charging the frog with cruelty in eating up all the fish and drinking up all the water, threatening starvation to man and wife. Then Pak proceeded to curse the whole line of the frog's ancestors and relatives, especially in the female line, for eight generations back, as Koreans usually do.

But instead of being sorry, or showing any anger at such a scolding, the bullfrog only blinked and bowed, saying:

"Don't worry, Farmer Pak. You'll be glad of it, by and by. Besides, I want to go home with you and live in your house.

"What! Occupy my home, you clammy reptile! No you won't," said Pak.

"Oh! but I have news to tell you and you won't be sorry, for you see what I can do. Better take me in."

Old Pak thought it over. How should he face his wife with such a guest? But then, the frog had news to tell and that might please the old lady, who was fond of gossip. Since her husband was not very talkative, she might be willing to harbor so strange a guest.

So they started down the valley. Pak shuffled along as fast as his old shins could move, but the bullfrog covered the distance in a few leaps, for his hind legs were three feet long.

Arrived at his door, Mrs. Pak was horrified at the prospect of boarding such a guest. But when the husband told her that Froggie knew all about everybody and could chat interestingly by the hour, she changed her manner and bade him welcome. Indeed, she so warmed in friendliness that she gave him one of her best rooms. All the leaves, grass and brushwood that had been gathered in the wood-shed to supply the kitchen fire and house flues, was carried into the room. There it was doused with tubs of water to make a nice soft place such as bullfrogs like. After this he was fed all the worms he wanted.

Then after his dinner and a nap, Mrs. Pak and Mr. Pak donned their best clothes and went in to make a formal call on their guest.

Mr. Bullfrog was so affable and charming in conversation, besides telling so many good stories and serving up so many dainty bits of gossip, that Mrs. Pak was delighted beyond expression. Indeed, she felt almost like adopting Froggie as her son.

The night passed quietly away, but when the first rays of light appeared, Froggie was out on the porch singing a most melodious tune to the rising sun. When Mr. and Mrs. Pak rose up to greet their guest and to hear his song, they were amazed to find that the music was bringing them blessings. Everything they had wished for, during their whole lives, seemed now at hand, with more undreamed of coming in troops. In the yard stood oxen, donkeys and horses loaded with every kind of box, bale and bundle waiting to be unloaded and more were coming; stout men porters appeared and began to unpack, while troops of lovely girls in shining white took from the men's hands beautiful things made of jade, gold and silver. There were fine clothes and hats for Mr. Pak, jade-tipped hairpins, tortoise-shell and ivory combs, silk gowns, embroidered and jeweled girdles and every sort of frocks and woman's garments for Mrs. Pak, besides inlaid cabinets, clothes-racks and wardrobes. Above all, was a polished metal mirror that looked like the full autumn moon, over which Mrs. Pak was now tempted to spend every minute of her time.

Four or five of the prettiest maidens they had ever seen in all their lives danced, sang and played sweetest music. The unpacking of boxes, bales and bundles continued. Tables of jade and finest sandalwood were spread with the richest foods and wines. Soon, under the skilful hands of carpenters and decorators, instead of oiled paper on the floors, covering old bricks and broken flat stones set over the flues, and smoky rafters and mud walls poorly papered, there rose a new house. It had elegant wide halls, and large rooms with partitions made of choicest joiner work. It was furnished with growing flowers, game boards for chess and had everything in it like a palace. As for the riches of the larder and the good things to eat daily laid on the table, no pen but a Korean's can tell of them all. In the new storehouse were piles of dried fish, edible seaweed, bags of rice, bins of millet, tubs of kim-chi made of various sorts of the pepper-hash and Korean hot pickle in which the natives delight, to say nothing of peaches, pears, persimmons, chestnuts, honey, barley, sugar, candy, cake and pastry, all arranged in high piles and in gay colors.

The old couple seemed able to eat and enjoy twice as big dinners as formerly, for all the while the adopted Bullfrog was very entertaining. Mr. and Mrs. Pak laughed continually, declaring they had never heard such good stories as he told. The good wife was, however, quite equal to her guest in retailing gossip. One of her favorite subjects, of which she never tired, was the beauty and charm of Miss Peach. She was the accomplished daughter of the big Yang-ban, or nobleman, Mr. Poom, who lived in a great house, with a host of servants and retainers in the next village, and Mrs. Pak insisted there was no young woman in the world like her. It was noticed that Mr. Bullfrog was particularly interested when Miss Peach Poom was the subject of the old lady's praises.

After a week of such luxury, during which Mr. and Mrs. Pak seemed to dwell in the Nirvana, or Paradise, which the good priests often talked about, Mr. Pak's full cup of joy was dashed to earth when the Bullfrog informed him that he intended to marry, and that Mr. Pak must get him a wife. Still worse than that, Pak was informed by the Frog that he would have no one but Miss Peach, the daughter of Poom, so renowned for her beauty and graces.

At this, old Pak went nearly wild. He begged to be excused from the task, but the Bullfrog was inexorable. So, after inprecating his wife's tongue, for her ever putting it into the frog's head to marry Miss Peach, he donned his fine clothes and set out to see Mr. Poom. He expected to be beaten to death for his brazen effrontery in asking a noble lady to marry a frog.

Now this Mr. Poom had long been the magistrate of a district, who had squeezed much money wrongly from the poor people over whom he ruled, and having won great wealth, had retired and come back to his native place to live. This man had two daughters married, but the third, the youngest and most beautiful, Miss Peach, was now eighteen years old.

Arriving at the Pooms' grand mansion, Mr. Pak told of the suitor's wealth, power and fame, high position and promise, and how he had made the old couple happy.

Old Poom had pricked up his ears from the first mention of riches and power, and became highly interested as Pak went on sounding the praises of his prospective son-in-law.

"And what is his name?" asked Mr. Poom.

Here Pak was in a quandary. He knew that the frog family was the oldest and most numerous in the world and was famous for fine voices. He fell into a brown study for a few minutes. Then, looking up he declared that he had so long thought of the suitor's graces and accomplishments, that he had forgotten his name and could not then recall it.

So Mr. Poom, in order to help Pak out, ran over the list of famous families in Korea, reciting the names of the Kims, Sims, Mins, the Hos, Chos, Kos, Quongs and Hongs, etc., etc., for Mr. Poom was an authority on the Korean peerage.

"It is none of these," said Pak. "I deeply regret that I cannot recall the name."

"Strange," said Mr. Poom. "I have named all the families of any standing in the kingdom. What is his office or rank and where do his relations live?"

Pak was pressed so hard by Mr. Poom's searching questions that at last he had to confess that the suitor for the beautiful maiden was not a man but a frog.

"What! do you want me to marry my daughter to a pond-croaker? You shall suffer for thus insulting me in my own house. Slaves, bring the cross-bench and give this wretch twenty blows."

Forthwith, while four men brought out the whipping bench, three others seized poor Pak, stripped off his coat, and bound him with feet and arms stretched out to the bench. Then a tall, stalwart fellow raised the huge paddle of wood to let fall with all his might on the bare flesh of the old man.

But all this while the sky was darkening, and, before the first blow was given, the lightning flashed, the thunder rolled, and floods of rain fell that threatened to overwhelm house, garden, and all in a deluge. The hail, which began to pelt the cattle, was first the size of an egg and then of stones, like cannon-balls.

"Hold," cried the frightened Mr. Poom. "I'll wait and ask further."

Thereupon the lightning and thunder ceased, the sun burst out in splendor.

Mightily impressed by this, Mr. Poom at last agreed to let his daughter become the bride of the frog, not telling her who her husband was to be. Within an hour, while she was getting ready, a string of fine horses and donkeys with palanquins loaded with presents for the bride and her family appeared. Besides boxes of silk dresses and perfumes, head-gear and articles for a lady's boudoir, there were troops of maidens to wait on the bride. Arraying Miss Peach in the loveliest of robes, they also dressed her hair, until, what with satin puffs and frame, jade-tipped silver hairpins, rosettes and flowers, her head-gear stood over a foot high above her forehead, on which was the bride's red round spot. Then when the happy maiden had sufficiently admired herself in the metal mirror and heard the praises of her attendant virgins, she entered the bridal palanquin – a gorgeous mass of splendor. According to custom, her eyes were sealed shut and covered with wax, for a Korean bride sees nothing of her husband until the end of the feast, when she meets him in the bridal chamber.

So to his house she was carried in great pomp and with gay attendance of brilliantly arrayed maidens. The marriage ceremony and the grand supper were happy affairs for all the guests, even though the bride, according to Korean etiquette, was as if blind, quietly and patiently waiting sightless throughout the whole joyful occasion. The actual ceremony was witnessed only by the foster-parents and the bridegroom.

When in the bridal chamber, the bride having unsealed her eyes, and her vision being clear, she looked up at the one she had married and found not a man, but a frog, she was furiously angry. She burst out into a protest against having such a bridegroom.

Gently and in tenderest tones the bridegroom attempted first to comfort her. Then, handing her a pair of scissors, he begged her to rip open the skin along his back from shoulder to thigh, for it was very tight and he was suffering pain from it.

In her bitter disappointment at being married to a frog, she seized the scissors and almost viciously began to cut from nape to waist. Her surprise was great to find what seemed to be silk underneath the speckled skin. When she had slit down two yards or so, her husband the frog stood upon his hind legs. He twisted himself about as if in a convulsion, pulled his whole speckled hide hard with his front paws, and then jumping out of his skin, stood before his bride a prince. Fair, tall, of superb figure, and gorgeously arrayed, he was the ideal of her dreams. A jeweled baldric bound his waist, embroidery of golden dragons on his shoulders and breast told of his rank, while on his head was the cap of royalty with a sparkling diamond in the center. Yet no clothes, handsome as they were, could compare in beauty with his glorious manhood. Never had she seen so fair a mortal.

Happy was the bride whose feelings were thus changed in a moment from repulsion and horror to warmest affection and strongest veneration. The next morning when, to the amazement of his foster-father and mother, Mr. and Mrs. Pak, the prince presented himself and his bride at breakfast, he told the story of his life. As son of the King of the Stars he had committed some offense, in punishment for which his father condemned him to live upon the earth in the form of a frog. Furthermore he had laid upon his son the duty of performing three tasks. These must be done before he should be allowed to come back and live in Star Land. These were, to drink up all the water in the lake, to eat all the fish, and to win a human bride, the handsomest woman in the world.

All the precious things which he had presented to Pak and his wife to make their old days comfortable, and the gifts sent to the bride's house before her wedding-day, had come by power from the skies. Now, leaving his foster-parents on earth to enjoy their gifts, he must return home to his father, taking his bride with him. Scarcely had he spoken these words than a chariot and horses, silver bright, appeared at the door of the house. Bowing low to his foster-parents, and stepping in with his bride, the pair disappeared beyond the clouds.

From this time forth a new double star was seen in the sky.

THE KING OF THE SPARROWS

The Korean children are awakened every morning by the twittering of the sparrows. These little birds build their nests among the vines on the roof and along the eaves. The people plant melon, gourd, and mock orange seeds along the sunny sides of their houses in spring time. All through the summer, and until late in autumn, the walls and roofs are covered with the thick green leaves. Here, in these sheltered places, the sparrow mother lays her eggs and the father sparrow finds worms and feeds her, until the hungry birdies open their little mouths for something to eat. After this, both parents are kept busy in raising their brood and teaching them to fly.

The greatest dangers to the birdlings come from cruel snakes that live on the roof and eat up the young sparrows. Sometimes, to help them against their enemy, the parent sparrows call in the aid of larger birds that are not afraid of the reptiles. These peck at the snake until they drive him away. There is always a lively chattering over the victory.

One day, a young sparrow that had hardly learned to fly was almost seized, and might have been devoured by the roof-snake, but was saved by a big, brave bird that flew at the reptile. Although escaped from the snake's jaws, the sparrow in falling caught its legs in the curtain made of split bamboo, which hung before the verandah of the house, and its limb was put out of joint. There it lay helpless between the splints.

The owner of the house was a kind man, who loved the birds. Taking pity on the poor sparrow, he carefully lifted it up, smoothed its feathers, and quieted the little creature, while its heart kept beating so fast. Then setting its leg in place, he put some moist clay around the broken part, until it should be all right again. Meanwhile, he kept it warm, feeding the birdie until it was strong again. One day he took it in his hand and out-of-doors letting it fly away. Soon it came back and perched on the edge of the roof, twittering thanks to its kind friend. Then it spread its wings to fly to the King of the Sparrows, who lived in the city of Sparrow Capital, where it at once informed His Majesty about the good man who healed and befriended birds when they were in trouble and who had saved the young sparrow's life.

The King of Sparrow Land and all his wise counselors heard the story with great interest. Then they held a meeting and voted to reward richly so good a friend of all sparrows. So they went into the storehouse where were kept beautiful treasures which human beings love. From the collection they chose what they thought would please most their good friend, such as gold, jade, brocade, cups and saucers, rice, horses to ride on, oxen to bear heavy loads and pretty maids to wait on him, besides silk and cotton clothes of all sorts, with delicious things to eat and drink. By some magic process, they packed these into a seed and then gave it to the sparrow in its bill to carry to the good man. They charged the bird on no account to lose it and be sure to give it to no one but the right person.

So the sparrow flew out of Sparrow Land and down to the house of its kind friend. Carefully laying down the seed, it kept near the paper window-frame and made a great twittering, until the man came out to see what was the matter. Recognizing his old acquaintance, he put out his open hand and the sparrow laid the seed in his palm, meanwhile chattering in a lively way and looking in his face as if to tell him how precious the treasure was.

But the good fellow only took it in to his wife and told her how he got it, laughed over the matter and was going to throw it away, thinking it only sparrow fun.

The wife, who was a wise woman, begged her husband to keep it and on a warm day in spring she planted it. It grew to be a luxuriant vine that clothed all one side of the house with its leaves. When one unusually fine large handsome gourd was nearly ripe, the man thought of plucking it for food; but, taking his wife's advice, he waited until full autumn had come. By this time the gourd, having absorbed the sunshine all summer, was fully ripe.

Then they took a saw to open it properly, and lo! a store of riches came out of that gourd, such as neither the man nor his wife had ever dreamed of.

First issued something which spread itself out before them. It was a table of costly jade, such as an Emperor ever eats from.

Next rolled forth a silver bottle of delicious wine and then the daintiest cups, that set themselves on the jade table. Soon a gold tea-caddy appeared filled with the fragrant leaf. Then rolls of silk, fine muslin, satin brocade, and a store of rich clothes, hats, shoes, girdles, and socks enough to last a lifetime appeared before their eyes. After these were rice and cooked food of all sorts ready for a feast. Looking out into the yard, they saw strong horses and fat oxen waiting to do their master's bidding. Last of all, some lovely young girls, as fair as the moon, stepped out of the gourd and proceeded to serve the good things of the feast, as if they had been used to waiting on ladies and gentlemen all their lives. Following the feast, they danced, made music and gave no end of entertainment and service to the man and his wife, who were now as happy as king and queen.

In their once humble home, now made over new, with all the store of good things and plenty of loyal servants and strong animals to serve them, the old couple lived without care and traveled where they pleased.

But when a wicked man, that hated all sparrows and had often driven them away from his house, because he thought them too troublesome, heard of his neighbor's good fortune, he was envious, and wanted to get riches in the same way. So he watched his opportunity and, when a sparrow came near, he threw a stick at the bird and broke its leg. Then he bound up the limb with clay and a bit of rag. He kept the poor sparrow until its leg was well, but dreadfully crooked, and then let it fly away.

In the capital of Sparrow Land, the poor bird told about the bad man's doings. The Sparrow King at once handed out a seed to be given to the enemy of the sparrows. When the naughty man saw the little bird with the crooked legs, he ran out, got the seed and planted it at once. He could hardly wait for the gourd to ripen. Wonderful to relate, however, the vine was most luxurious, covering the whole side of the house and all the thatched roofs of the three dwellings in one, which made up his home. Finally in the autumn he plucked the fruit. Then, sitting down before the pile, with knife and saw, he began to open them.

But instead of good things, and lovely people, and the treasures that make men rich and happy, such as his kind neighbor had received, there came out, one after another, the twelve curses of Korea.

First leaped forth a party of rope dancers, who put out their hands and demanded money. They threatened to live with him and eat at his table unless they got their pay.

There was no help for it. So the cruel man had to give each dancer a long string of cash before he could get rid of the party.

No sooner had he opened the second gourd than out stepped a line of Buddhist priests, who at once began begging for the temples. He was only too glad to buy off these shaven pates.

The saw had no sooner let the light into another gourd, than forth came a band of hired mourners carrying a corpse. They began weeping, wailing and crying out loud enough to waken the dead. It required another rope of cash to get rid of these pests. By this time the cruel man was beginning to feel very poor.

Almost afraid to touch the other gourds, but still greedily hoping for riches, he sawed them open; but one after the other yielded only what took his money and threatened to make him a beggar. From the fourth gourd issued a bevy of dancing girls, who refused to leave the house until he had paid them five thousand cash. From another gourd a pair of acrobats leaped out and began a performance. But knowing that they would charge the more for their tricks, if they were allowed to finish their program, the man bought them off as he had done the others.

Getting poorer and poorer, with no sign of wealth coming from the gourds, he yet felt he must open more, but the result was the same. The strangest people, men and women, such as loafers from the government offices, fortune-tellers, jugglers, and blind folks appeared. These last had sticks in their hands to find the way, and bells at their belts to collect alms. Finally, of all living things, a giant stood forth, that threatened to eat up both the man and his wife.

By this time there was not a coin or a cash left, and, besides being as poor as a rat, the man was hungry. When the twelfth gourd was opened it seemed to have in it all the smells of Korea. Holding their noses, the man and his wife ran out of their house. Happily for them that they did so, for just then a gale of wind blew down the house, and the thatch and timbers burst into flames from the fire that had heated the flues.

Thus stripped of all their possessions, because of the man's cruelty to the birds, the wicked fellow and his wife would have starved, except for the kindness of the good man who treated the sparrows kindly. For the rest of their days the old couple lived on their neighbor's charity.

THE WOODMAN AND THE MOUNTAIN FAIRIES

Over a half thousand years ago there lived in a northern village, near Ping Yang, a wood-cutter named Keel Wee.

He owned a sturdy bull that carried on its back the fuel which he daily cut on the mountains and sold on the main street of his village, at the fair, which was held every fifth day. The docile brute could carry a load of faggots and brushwood piled many feet high over his head and tied down with ropes, so that at a distance nothing but his legs were visible. This beast, although so huge, was the gentlest creature imaginable. The children were all very fond of the big fellow and were accustomed to play with him as if he were one of them, or at least like a pet dog. The reason of this was that when but a week old the bull-calf had been taken from his cow-mother and brought up in the family with the girls and boys. Only the puppy dog, that also occupied the house with the young folks, was a great favorite.

On a fine summer morning, Keel Wee, leaving his beast behind, went up on the mountain and cut enough wood to load up and bring down on another day.

His wife, as she shouted good-bye, told him to be sure and be home in time for supper, for their eldest son had gone a-fishing and a good string of perch was expected.

Shouldering his axe, he started up the mountain path. He had to go pretty far, for near towns or cities in Korea all the timber had long since been cut away. Every year the woodmen have to search farther afield to find fuel.

Arriving in the woods where there was a clearing, Keel Wee prepared to wield his trusty axe. He was about to take off his big hat and outer coat and lay about him, when he spied, at some distance off, two fairy-like beings. They had long hair, looked very wise and were dressed in costume of the Chow dynasty of two thousand years ago. They sat on stones and played the game of go-ban.

Coming near, the woodman took a respectful attitude, and, looking on, soon became interested in the moves of the players. So far from being at all disconcerted at the presence of a stranger, the two fairies seemed by eye-winks to invite him to look on. Feeling quite proud to be thus honored, Keel Wee, leaning his chin upon the handle of his axe, became absorbed in the game and by and by grew quite excited. Forgetting himself and his manners, he stretched forth his right hand to move one of the pieces. At once the fairy nearest to him gave him a crack on the fingers for his impudence, and jerked Keel Wee's arm away. Then without saying a word, he took out from his wallet something that looked like a persimmon seed and put in the woodman's mouth. After this all three were perfectly quiet.

Hour after hour the game proceeded and the players grew more intensely interested. As for Keel Wee, his eyes never winked, so hard did he look at the yellow board covered with the black and white pieces. Several times, when he thought he saw how the fairy on his right could beat in the game, or the one on his left make a better move, he felt like telling one or the other so. When, however, he tried to move his tongue, he found he could not speak, or utter a cry. Somehow he felt as if he were in a dream.

Yet all the time he became more and more wrapped up in the game, so that he determined to see the end of it and know which player had beaten. He forgot that with mountain spirits there is no night or morning, or passing of the hours, nor do they care anything about clocks or bells, because in fairy-land there is no time.

All the while Keel Wee was leaning with his chin on the stout axe-handle, holding it with both hands under his neck.

He took no note of the sun or stars, daylight or darkness and he felt no hunger.

Suddenly the timber of his axe seemed to turn to dust and his chin fell. The next thing he knew he had lost his support. Down went his head, and forward fell his body as he tumbled over, upsetting the checker-board, breaking up the game and scattering the round pieces hither and yon over the ground.

Awaking as out of a sleep, and thoroughly ashamed of himself for his impoliteness, he tried to pick himself up and humbly apologize for the accident which he had caused by his own rudeness. He expected and was ready for a good scolding. But when he looked up, the fairies were gone. Nothing whatever was seen of them or of the playboard and checkers, nor any signs of their having been there, except that when he put his hand on the flat stones, which they had used as seats, he found them warm to his touch.

But where was his axe-handle and what had happened? When he had left home, he had come straight from the barber shop, with his face smooth and clean shaven. Now he put his hand to his breast and found that he had grown a long white beard. As for the iron axe-head, it was there, but rusty and half buried in the ground. He had worn one of the big farmer's hats, which, when turned upside down, might hold a bushel or two of turnips, and when fastened to his head spread over his shoulders like a roof. Where could it be? He looked about him to find it, but saw only the bits of the slats inside the frame and a few scraps of what remained, for the rest had long ago rotted away. Meanwhile he had discovered that his joints were stiff, and he felt like an old man. His clothes were a mass of rags, his hemp sandals were no more, and, on both fingers and toes, had grown long nails like bird's claws. His hair had burst its topknot string and hung down his back like a woman's, only it was grayish-white.

Wondering what it all meant, Keel Wee hobbled down the mountain and found the road that ran into the main street of his village. Rocks and hills, rivers and rills were there, but what a change! Instead of the two grinning idol posts, of male and female faces, carved out of trunks and trees, with sawed-out teeth painted white, and artificial ear flaps of wood nailed on, such as had stood before every Korean hamlet since the days of Kija, there was a line of high thick poles, with iron wire stretching from one to the other and for miles in the distance. These, he found out afterward, were called "lightning-thread-trees" (telegraph poles). In place of the rambling and sprawling three-sided thatched houses and yards, divided off with mats hung from sticks, there was a well-built but odd-looking office of painted wood, with openings through which he saw Korean young men sitting. They were dressed in strange clothes and were fingering outlandish-looking clicking instruments.

His curiosity prompted him to go up and look more closely, when something bumped against his nose and nearly knocked him over. When he tried again to get closer, his face was flattened, his nose nearly broken, and his lips knocked against his teeth so that they swelled. Feeling with his hands to solve the mystery, he touched something hard, which he could yet see through. Just then he heard a young man inside shout to him in Korean:

"Here, you mountain daddy, let that glass alone."

"Glass? Glass?" thought Keel Wee. "What is that?" Yet he could not speak.

He had hardly drawn a long breath when, looking down along two lines of shining iron in the street, he saw a house on wheels coming right at him. There was no horse, no donkey, no bull, no man pulling or pushing it, but overhead was a long pole, at the end of which, where it touched a string, as he thought, though it was an iron wire, was something that looked like a squirrel. It was going round and round as if turning somersaults and seemed to be pushing the moving house along. Inside, near the same stuff which he had already heard was glass, sat a dozen or so Koreans. The whole thing, wheels and all, nearly ran over him as it thundered by, and his mouth opened in wonder, while a man on the end shouted rudely:

"Hello, old goblin, where did you get your pumpkin mouth? Look out or you'll swallow the moon. Get out of the way of the trolley."

Thus did the man they called conductor, or guard, make fun of the poor old fellow, for indeed he did look like one of the mummers, who on New Year's Eve amuse or scare the children by putting on their shoulders the huge round devil heads and false faces that represent the aborigines of Korea and the goblins that once lived in the mountains. These masks are usually shaped like a melon and are cut with eyes, nose and mouth, like those which American boys have fun with on All Hallow Eve.

This was just the trouble. The woodman in tatters, with no topknot, long hair down his back and a white beard floating over his breast, leaning on a long white stick as he hobbled down the street, looked just like one of the ancient aborigines that had long ago been driven into the mountains. Nurses and old women frightened naughty children by simply mentioning their

TALES OF ANIMALS & MYTHICAL CREATURES

names. When one of these mountain men, odd creatures that were half savage in dress and ways, came into the town, all the children laughed and the big dogs barked, while the little ones ran away, for the sight was so unusual. Even the bulls bellowed, the donkeys balked, and the pigs squeaked, as Keel Wee came near. No wonder he was taken for a mountain granddaddy, or a bumpkin dressed up like one, for few of the city or village folks had really ever seen one of the mountain aborigines, any more than they had seen tigers, that are plentiful farther away, but which only the hunters ever caught sight of.

More and more bewildered, Keel Wee wended his way further into the town. He saw that the men no longer wore topknots, or chignons, nor did the lads have on the long braid down their back, which showed that they were youths, but not married yet. Just then some rough boys, supposing that maybe some rustic gawk had mistaken the time of year, jeered at him and cried:

"Hello, hermit, do you think it's New Year's Eve?"

Keel Wee thought he had better ask some questions. So catching sight of a dignified looking gentleman, in black broad-brimmed hat and flowing white clothes, who was coming down the street and toward him, Keel Wee bowed his head low, almost to the ground. As he did so, the stone put in his mouth by the fairies dropped out, and his tongue was loosed. He inquired as follows:

"Exalted sir, can you tell me where may be the wretched hut of my miserable wife and children? She was the daughter of Gee Kim, and your contemptible slave is Keel Wee."

The gentleman, whose dress showed that he was a scholar and person of rank, looked long and hard at the questioner, to satisfy himself that he was not being mocked, or imposed upon by a jester, rope-dancer, sorcerer, or some such disreputable person, and then cried:

"Heavens! man, are you a beggar-spirit of the mountains? Your speech sounds like the dialect spoken in these parts five hundred years ago. In that time such a family lived here, but the head of it, a wood-cutter and fuel-seller, is reported to have gone up into the mountains and was eaten up by a tiger. Yonder in the graveyard are buried ten or more generations of his descendants."

"Tell me, kind sir, what has happened here since King Wang died. It was under his reign that I was born and lived in this village."

Still eyeing the questioner, as if expecting to see him jump out of his rags and declare himself a mummer and the whole affair a joke, the kindly gentleman proceeded to give in outline the history of Korea during the previous five hundred years. There had been many kings. The Tartars first, and then the Japanese had invaded the land. A great war between the Mikado's men and the Chinese had taken place. It was just over and now people rode in cars, talked hundreds of miles over wires, and traveled over iron rails as fast as a dragon could fly, drawn by a steel horse that drank water and fed on wood and black stones that burned. In a word, Korea was in an "era of civilization."

This was too much for Keel Wee. He now realized that he had lived ten times longer than the average man. So, hobbling over to the graveyard, he stumbled among the mounds until he found that one of his clan where the bones of his wife and children lay. Next morning, all that was seen of Keel Wee was a mass of dust, rags, some bones, and much long white hair. Yet, when they buried him, there sprang up around and on his grave strange flowers that no one had ever seen in city or village, but which bloomed only on the high mountains.

KOREAN FOLK & FAIRY TALES

A GLOSSARY OF MYTH & FOLKLORE

A GLOSSARY OF MYTH & FOLKLORE

Aaru Heavenly paradise where the blessed went after death.

Ab Heart or mind.

Abiku (Yoruba) Person predestined to die. Also known as ogbanje.

Absál Nurse to Salámán, who died after their brief love affair.

Achilles The son of Peleus and the sea-nymph Thetis, who distinguished himself in the Trojan War. He was made almost immortal by his mother, who dipped him in the River Styx, and he was invincible except for a portion of his heel which remained out of the water.

Acropolis Citadel in a Greek city.

Adad-Ea Ferryman to Ut-Napishtim, who carried Gilgamesh to visit his ancestor.

Adapa Son of Ea and a wise sage.

Adar God of the sun, who is worshipped primarily in Nippur.

Aditi Sky goddess and mother of the gods.

Adityas Vishnu, children of Aditi, including Indra, Mitra, Rudra, Tvashtar, Varuna and Vishnu.

Aeneas The son of Anchises and the goddess Aphrodite, reared by a nymph. He led the Dardanian troops in the Trojan War According to legend, he became the founder of Rome.

Aengus Óg Son of Dagda and Boann (a woman said to have given the Boyne river its name), Aengus is the Irish god of love whose stronghold is reputed to have been at New Grange. The famous tale 'Dream of Aengus' tells of how he fell in love with a maiden he had dreamt of. He eventually discovered that she was to be found at the Lake of the Dragon's Mouth in Co. Tipperary, but that she lived every alternate year in the form of a swan. Aengus plunges into the lake transforming himself also into the shape of a swan. Then the two fly back together to his palace on the Boyne where they live out their days as guardians of would-be lovers.

Aesir Northern gods who made their home in Asgard; there are twelve in number.

Afrásiyáb Son of Poshang, king of Túrán, who led an army against the ruling shah Nauder. Afrásiyáb became ruler of Persia on defeating Nauder.

Afterlife Life after death or paradise, reached only by the process of preserving the body from decay through embalming and preparing it for reincarnation.

Agamemnon A famous King of Mycenae. He married Helen of Sparta's sister Clytemnestra. When Paris abducted Helen, beginning the Trojan War, Menelaus called on Agamemnon to raise the Greek troops. He had to sacrifice his daughter Iphigenia in order to get a fair wind to travel to Troy.

Agastya A rishi (sage). Leads hermits to Rama.

Agemo (Yoruba) A chameleon who aided Olorun in outwitting Olokun, who was angry at him for letting Obatala create life on her lands without her permission. Agemo outwitted Olokun by changing colour, letting her think that he and Olorun were better cloth dyers than she was. She admitted defeat and there was peace between the gods once again.

Aghasur A dragon sent by Kans to destroy Krishna.

Aghríras Son of Poshang and brother of Afrásiyáb, who was killed by his brother.

Agni The god of fire.

Agora Greek marketplace.

Ahura-Mazda Supreme god of the Persians, god of the sky. Similar to the Hindu god Varuna.

Ajax Ajax of Locris was another warrior at Troy. When Troy was captured, he committed the ultimate sacrilege by seizing Cassandra from her sanctuary with the Palladium.

Ajax Ajax the Greater was the bravest, after Achilles, of all warriors at Troy, fighting Hector in single combat and distinguishing himself in the Battle of the Ships. He was not chosen as the bravest warrior and eventually went mad.

Aje (Igbo) Goddess of the earth and the underworld.

Aje (Yoruba) Goddess of the River Niger, daughter of Yemoja.

Akhet Season of the year when the River Nile traditionally flooded.

Akkadian Person of the first Mesopotamian empire, centred in Akkad.

Akwán Diw An evil spirit who appeared as a wild ass in the court of Kai-khosráu. Rustem fought and defeated the demon, presenting its head to Kai-khosráu.

Alba Irish word for Scotland.

Alberich King of the dwarfs.

Alcinous King of the Phaeacians.

Alf-heim Home of the elves, ruled by Frey.

All Hallowmass All Saints' Day.

Allfather Another name for Odin; Yggdrasill was created by Allfather.

Alsvider Steed of the moon (Mani) chariot.

Alsvin Steed of the sun (Sol) chariot.

Amado Outer panelling of a dwelling, usually made of wood.

Ama-no-uzume Goddess of the dawn, meditation and the arts, who showed courage when faced with a giant who scared the other deities, including Ninigi. Also known as Uzume.

Amaterasu Goddess of the sun and daughter of Izanagi after Izanami's death; she became ruler of the High Plains of Heaven on her father's withdrawal from the world. Sister of Tsuki-yomi and Susanoo.

Ambalika Daughter of the king of Benares.

Ambika Daughter of the king of Benares.

Ambrosia Food of the gods.

Amemet Eater of the dead, monster who devoured the souls of the unworthy.

Amen Original creator deity.

Amen-Ra A being created from the fusion of Ra and Osiris. He champions the poor and those in trouble. Similar to the Greek god Zeus.

Ananda Disciple of Buddha.

Anansi One of the most popular African animal myths, Anansi the spider is a clever and shrewd character who outwits his fellow animals to get his own way. He is an entertaining but morally dubious character. Many African countries tell Anansi stories.

Ananta Thousand-headed snake that sprang from Balarama's mouth, Vishnu's attendant, serpent of infinite time.

Andhrímnir Cook at Valhalla.

Andvaranaut Ring of Andvari, the King of the dwarfs.

Angada Son of Vali, one of the monkey host.

Anger-Chamber Room designated for an angry queen.

Angurboda Loki's first wife, and the mother of Hel, Fenris and Jormungander.

Aniruddha Son of Pradyumna.

Anjana Mother of Hanuman.

Anunnaki Great spirits or gods of Earth.

Ansar God of the sky and father of Ea and Anu. Brother-husband to Kishar. Also known as Anshar or Asshur.

Anshumat A mighty chariot fighter.

Anu God of the sky and lord of heaven, son of Ansar and Kishar.

Anubis Guider of souls and ruler of the underworld before Osiris;

he was one of the divinities who brought Osiris back to life. He is portrayed as a canid, African wolf or jackal.

Apep Serpent and emblem of chaos.

Apollo One of the twelve Olympian gods, son of Zeus and Leto. He is attributed with being the god of plague, music, song and prophecy.

Apsaras Dancing girls of Indra's court and heavenly nymphs.

Apsu Primeval domain of fresh water, originally part of Tiawath with whom he mated to have Mummu. The term is also used for the abyss from which creation came.

Aquila The divine eagle.

Arachne A Lydian woman with great skill in weaving. She was challenged in a competition by the jealous Athene who destroyed her work and when she killed herself, turned her into a spider destined to weave until eternity.

Aralu Goddess of the underworld, also known as Eres-ki-Gal. Married to Nergal.

Ares God of War, 'gold-changer of corpses', and the son of Zeus and Hera.

Argonauts Heroes who sailed with Jason on the ship Argo to fetch the golden fleece from Colchis.

Ariki A high chief, a leader, a master, a lord.

Arjuna The third of the Pandavas.

Aroha Affection, love.

Artemis The virgin goddess of the chase, attributed with being the moon goddess and the primitive mother-goddess. She was daughter of Zeus and Leto.

Arundhati The Northern Crown.

Asamanja Son of Sagara.

Asclepius God of healing who often took the form of a snake. He is the son of Apollo by Coronis.

Asgard Home of the gods, at one root of Yggdrasill.

Ashvatthaman Son of Drona.

Ashvins Twin horsemen, sons of the sun, benevolent gods and related to the divine.

Ashwapati Uncle of Bharata and Satrughna.

Asipû Wizard.

Asopus The god of the River Asopus.

Assagai Spear, usually made from hardwood tipped with iron and used in battle.

Astrolabe Instrument for making astronomical measurements.

Asuras Titans, demons, and enemies of the gods possessing magical powers.

Atef crown White crown made up of the Hedjet, the white crown of Upper Egypt, and red feathers.

Atem The first creator-deity, he is also thought to be the finisher of the world. Also known as Tem.

Athene Virgin warrior-goddess, born from the forehead of Zeus when he swallowed his wife Metis. Plays a key role in the travels of Odysseus, and Perseus.

Atlatl Spear-thrower.

Atua A supernatural being, a god.

Atua-toko A small carved stick, the symbol of the god whom it represents. It was stuck in the ground whilst holding incantations to its presiding god.

Augeas King of Elis, one of the Argonauts.

Augsburg Tyr's city.

Avalon Legendary island where Excalibur was created and where Arthur went to recover from his wounds. It is said he will return from Avalon one day to reclaim his kingdom.

Ba Dead person or soul. Also known as ka.

Bairn Little child, also called bairnie.

Balarama Brother of Krishna.

Balder Son of Frigga; his murder causes Ragnarok. Also spelled as Baldur.

Bali Brother of Sugriva and one of the five great monkeys in the Ramayana.

Balor The evil, one-eyed King of the Fomorians and also grandfather of Lugh of the Long Arm. It was prophesied that Balor would one day be slain by his own grandson so he locked his daughter away on a remote island where he intended that she would never fall pregnant. But Cian, father of Lugh, managed to reach the island disguised as a woman, and Balor's daughter eventually bore him a child. During the second battle of Mag Tured (or Moytura), Balor was killed by Lugh who slung a stone into his giant eye.

Ban King of Benwick, father of Lancelot and brother of King Bors.

Bannock Flat loaf of bread, typically of oat or barley, usually cooked on a griddle.

Banshee Mythical spirit, usually female, who bears tales of imminent death. They often deliver the news by wailing or keening outside homes. Also known as bean sí.

Bard Traditionally a storyteller, poet or music composer whose work often focused on legends.

Barû Seer.

Basswood Any of several North American linden trees with a soft light-coloured wood.

Bastet Goddess of love, fertility and sex and a solar deity. She is often portrayed with the head of a cat.

Bateta (Yoruba) The first human, created alongside Hanna by the Toad and reshaped into human form by the Moon.

KOREAN FOLK & FAIRY TALES

Bau Goddess of humankind and the sick, and known as the 'divine physician'. Daughter of Anu.

Bawn Fortified enclosure surrounding a castle.

Beaver Largest rodent in the United States of America, held in high esteem by the native American people. Although a land mammal, it spends a great deal of time in water and has a dense waterproof fur coat to protect it from harsh weather conditions.

Behula Daughter of Saha.

Bel Name for the god En-lil, the word Is also used as a title meaning 'lord'.

Belus Deity who helped form the heavens and earth and created animals and celestial beings. Similar to Zeus in Greek mythology.

Benten Goddess of the sea and one of the Seven Divinities of Luck. Also referred to as the goddess of love, beauty and eloquence and as being the personification of wisdom.

Bere Barley.

Berossus Priest of Bel who wrote a history of Babylon.

Berserker Norse warrior who fights with a frenzied rage.

Bestla Giant mother of Aesir's mortal element.

Bhadra A mighty elephant.

Bhagavati Shiva's wife, also known as Parvati.

Bhagiratha Son of Dilipa.

Bharadhwaja Father of Drona and a hermit.

Bharata One of Dasharatha's four sons.

Bhaumasur A demon, slain by Krishna.

Bhima The second of the Pandavas.

Bhimasha King of Rajagriha and disciple of Buddha.

Bier Frame on which a coffin or dead body is placed before being carried to the grave.

Bifrost Rainbow bridge presided over by Heimdall.

A GLOSSARY OF MYTH & FOLKLORE

Big-Belly One of Ravana's monsters.

Bilskirnir Thor's palace.

Bodach The term means 'old man'. The Highlanders believed that the Bodach crept down chimneys in order to steal naughty children. In other territories, he was a spirit who warned of death.

Bodkin Large, blunt needle used for threading strips of cloth or tape through cloth; short pointed dagger or blade.

Boer Person of Dutch origin who settled in southern Africa in the late seventeenth century. The term means 'farmer'. Boer people are often called Afrikaners.

Bogle Ghost or phantom; goblin-like creature.

Boliaun Ragwort, a weed with ragged leaves.

Book of the Dead Book for the dead, thought to be written by Thoth, texts from which were written on papyrus and buried with the dead, or carved on the walls of tombs, pyramids or sarcophagi.

Bors King of Gaul and brother of King Ban.

Bothy Small cottage or hut.

Brahma Creator of the world, mythical origin of colour (caste).

Brahmadatta King of Benares.

Brahman Member of the highest Hindu caste, traditionally a priest.

Bran In Scottish legend, Bran is the great hunting hound of Fionn Mac Chumail. In Irish mythology, he is a great hero.

Branstock Giant oak tree in the Volsung's hall; Odin placed a sword in it and challenged the guests of a wedding to withdraw it.

Brave Young warrior of native American descent, sometimes also referred to as a 'buck'.

Bree Thin broth or soup.

Breidablik Balder's palace.

Brigit Scottish saint or spirit associated with the coming of spring.

Brisingamen Freyia's necklace.

Britomartis A Cretan goddess, also known as Dictynna.

Brocéliande Legendary enchanted forest and the supposed burial place of Merlin.

Brokki Dwarf who makes a deal with Loki, and who makes Miolnir, Draupnir and Gulinbursti.

Brollachan A shapeless spirit of unknown origin. One of the most frightening in Scottish mythology, it spoke only two words, 'Myself' and 'Thyself', taking the shape of whatever it sat upon.

Brownie A household spirit or creature which took the form of a small man (usually hideously ugly) who undertakes household chores, and mill or farm work, in exchange for a bowl of milk.

Brugh Borough or town.

Brunhilde A Valkyrie found by Sigurd.

Buddha Founder of buddhism, Gautama, avatar of Vishnu in Hinduism.

Buddhism Buddhism arrived in China in the first century BC via the silk trading route from India and Central Asia. Its founder was Guatama Siddhartha (the Buddha), a religious teacher in northern India. Buddhist doctrine declared that by destroying the causes of all suffering, mankind could attain perfect enlightenment. The religion encouraged a new respect for all living things and brought with it the idea of reincarnation; i.e. that the soul returns to the earth after death in another form, dictated by the individual's behaviour in his previous life. By the fourth century, Buddhism was the dominant religion in China, retaining its powerful influence over the nation until the mid-ninth century.

Buffalo A type of wild ox, once widely scattered over the Great Plains of North America. Also known as a 'bison', the buffalo was an important food source for the Indian tribes and its hide was also used in the construction of tepees and to make clothing. The buffalo was also sometimes revered as a totem animal, i.e. venerated as a direct ancestor of the tribesmen, and its skull used in ceremonial fashion.

Bull of Apis Sacred bull, thought to be the son of Hathor.

Bulu Sacrificial rite.

Bundles, sacred These bundles contained various venerated objects of the tribe, believed to have supernatural powers. Custody or ownership of the bundle was never lightly entered upon, but involved the learning of endless songs and ritual dances.

Bushel Unit of measurement, usually used for agricultural products or food.

Bushi Warrior.

Byre Barn for keeping cattle.

Byrny Coat of mail.

Cacique King or prince.

Cailleach Bheur A witch with a blue face who represents winter. When she is reborn each autumn, snow falls. She is mother of the god of youth (Angus mac Og).

Calabash Gourd from the calabash tree, commonly used as a bottle.

Calchas The seer of Mycenae who accompanied the Greek fleet to Troy. It was his prophecy which stated that Troy would never be taken without the aid of Achilles.

Calpulli Village house, or group or clan of families.

Calumet Ceremonial pipe used by the north American Indians.

Calypso A nymph who lived on the island of Ogygia.

Camaxtli Tlascalan god of war and the chase, similar to Huitzilopochtli.

Camelot King Arthur's castle and centre of his realm.

Caoineag A banshee.

Caravanserai Traveller's inn, traditionally found in Asia or North Africa.

Carle Term for a man, often old; peasant.

Cat A black cat has great mythological significance, is often the bearer of bad luck, a symbol of black magic, and the familiar of a witch. Cats were also the totem for many tribes.

Cath Sith A fairy cat who was believed to be a witch transformed.

Cazi Magical person or influence.

Ceasg A Scottish mermaid with the body of a maiden and the tail of a salmon.

Ceilidh Party.

Cerberus The three-headed dog who guarded the entrance to the Underworld.

Chalchiuhtlicue Goddess of water and the sick or newborn, and wife of Tlaloc. She is often symbolized as a small frog.

Changeling A fairy substitute-child left by fairies in place of a human child they have stolen.

Channa Guatama's charioteer.

Chaos A state from which the universe was created – caused by fire and ice meeting.

Charon The ferryman of the dead who carries souls across the River Styx to Hades.

Charybdis See Scylla and Charybdis.

Chicomecohuatl Chief goddess of maize and one of a group of deities called Centeotl, who care for all aspects of agriculture.

Chicomoztoc Legendary mountain and place of origin of the Aztecs. The name means 'seven caves'.

Chinawezi Primordial serpent.

A GLOSSARY OF MYTH & FOLKLORE

Chinvat Bridge Bridge of the Gatherer, which the souls of the righteous cross to reach Mount Alborz or the world of the dead. Unworthy beings who try to cross Chinvat Bridge fall or are dragged into a place of eternal punishment.

Chitambaram Sacred city of Shiva's dance.

Chrysaor Son of Poseidon and Medusa, born from the severed neck of Medusa when Perseus beheaded her.

Chryseis Daughter of Chryses who was taken by Agamemnon in the battle of Troy.

Chullasubhadda Wife of Buddha-elect (Sumedha).

Chunda A good smith who entertains Buddha.

Churl Mean or unkind person.

Circe An enchantress and the daughter of Helius. She lived on the island of Aeaea with the power to change men to beasts.

Citlalpol The Mexican name for Venus, or the Great Star, and one of the only stars they worshipped. Also known as Tlauizcalpantecutli, or Lord of the Dawn.

Cleobis and Biton Two men of Argos who dragged the wagon carrying their mother, priestess of Hera, from Argos to the sanctuary.

Clio Muse of history and prophecy.

Clytemnestra Daughter of Tyndareus, sister of Helen, who married Agamemnon but deserted him when he sacrificed Iphigenia, their daughter, at the beginning of the Trojan War.

Coatepetl Mythical mountain, known as the 'serpent mountain'.

Coatl Serpent.

Coatlicue Earth mother and celestial goddess, she gave birth to Huitzilopochtli and his sister, Coyolxauhqui, and the moon and stars.

Codex Ancient book, often a list with pages folded into a zigzag pattern.

Confucius (Kong Fuzi) Regarded as China's greatest sage and ethical teacher, Confucius (551–479 BC) was not especially revered during his lifetime and had a small following of some three thousand people. After the Burning of the Books in 213 BC, interest in his philosophies became widespread. Confucius believed that mankind was essentially good, but argued for a highly structured society, presided over by a strong central government which would set the highest moral standards. The individual's sense of duty and obligation, he argued, would play a vital role in maintaining a well-run state.

Coracle Small, round boat, similar to a canoe. Also known as curragh or currach.

Coyolxauhqui Goddess of the moon and sister to Huitzilopochtli, she was decapitated by her brother after trying to kill their mother.

Creel Large basket made of wicker, usually used for fish.

Crodhmara Fairy cattle.

Cronan Musical humming, thought to resemble a cat purring or the drone of bagpipes.

Crow Usually associated with battle and death, but many mythological figures take this form.

Cu Sith A great fairy dog, usually green and oversized.

Cubit Ancient measurement, equal to the approximate length of a forearm.

Cuculain Irish warrior and hero. Also known as Cuchulainn.

Cutty Girl.

Cyclopes One-eyed giants who were imprisoned in Tartarus by Uranus and Cronus, but released by Zeus, for whom they made thunderbolts. Also a tribe of pastoralists who live without laws, and on, whenever possible, human flesh.

Daedalus Descendant of the Athenian King Erechtheus and son of Eupalamus. He killed his nephew and apprentice. Famed for constructing the labyrinth to house the Minotaur, in which he was later imprisoned. He constructed wings for himself and his son to make their escape.

Dagda One of the principal gods of the Tuatha De Danann, the father and chief, the Celtic equivalent of Zeus. He was the god reputed to have led the People of Dana in their successful conquest of the Fir Bolg.

Dagon God of fish and fertility; he is sometimes described as a sea-monster or chthonic god.

Daikoku God of wealth and one of the gods of luck.

Daimyō Powerful lord or magnate.

Daksha The chief Prajapati.

Dana Also known as Danu, a goddess worshipped from antiquity by the Celts and considered to be the ancestor of the Tuatha De Danann.

Danae Daughter of Acrisius, King of Argos. Acrisius trapped her in a cave when he was warned that his grandson would be the cause of his ultimate death. Zeus came to her and Perseus was born.

Danaids The fifty daughters of Danaus of Argos, by ten mothers.

Daoine Sidhe The people of the Hollow Hills, or Otherworld.

Dardanus Son of Zeus and Electra, daughter of Atlas.

Dasharatha A Manu amongst men, King of Koshala, father of Santa.

Deianeira Daughter of Oeneus, who married Heracles after he won her in a battle with the River Achelous.

Deirdre A beautiful woman doomed to cause the deaths of three Irish heroes and bring war to the whole country. After a soothsayer prophesied her fate, Deidre's father hid her away from the world to prevent it. However, fate finds its way and the events come to pass before Deidre eventually commits suicide to remain with her love.

Demeter Goddess of agriculture and nutrition, whose name means earth mother. She is the mother of Persephone.

Demophoon Son of King Celeus of Eleusis, who was nursed by Demeter and then dropped in the fire when she tried to make him immortal.

Dervish Member of a religious order, often Sufi, known for their wild dancing and whirling.

Desire The god of love.

Deva A god other than the supreme God.

Devadatta Buddha's cousin, plots evil against Buddha.

Dhrishtadyumna Twin brother of Draupadi, slays Drona.

Dibarra God of plague. Also a demonic character or evil spirit.

Dik-dik Dwarf antelope native to eastern and southern Africa.

Dilipa Son of Anshumat, father of Bhagiratha.

Dionysus The god of wine, vegetation and the life force, and of ecstasy. He was considered to be outside the Greek pantheon, and generally thought to have begun life as a mortal.

Dioscuri Castor and Polydeuces, the twin sons of Zeus and Leda, who are important deities.

Distaff Tool used when spinning which holds the wool or flax and keeps the fibres from tangling.

Divan Privy council.

Divots Turfs.

Dog The dog is a symbol of humanity, and usually has a role helping the hero of the myth or legend. Fionn's Bran and Grey Dog are two examples of wild beasts transformed to become invaluable servants.

Dōshin Government official.

Dossal Ornamental altar cloth.

Doughty Persistent and brave person.

Dragon Important animal in Japanese culture, symbolizing power, wealth, luck and success.

Draiglin' Hogney Ogre.

Draupadi Daughter of Drupada.

Draupnir Odin's famous ring, fashioned by Brokki.

Drona A Brahma, son of the great sage Bharadwaja.

Druid An ancient order of Celtic priests held in high esteem who flourished in the pre-Christian era. The word 'druid' is derived from an ancient Celtic one meaning 'very knowledgeable'. These individuals were believed to have mystical powers and in ancient Irish literature possess the ability to conjure up magical charms, to create tempests, to curse and debilitate their enemies and to perform as soothsayers to the royal courts.

Drupada King of the Panchalas.

Dryads Nymphs of the trees.

Dun A stronghold or royal abode surrounded by an earthen wall.

Durga Goddess, wife of Shiva.

Durk Knife. Also spelled as dirk.

Duryodhana One of Drona's pupils.

Dvalin Dwarf visited by Loki; also the name for the stag on Yggdrasill.

Dwarfie Stone Prehistoric tomb or boulder.

Dwarfs Fairies and black elves are called dwarfs.

Dwarkanath The Lord of Dwaraka; Krishna.

Dyumatsena King of the Shalwas and father of Satyavan.

Ea God of water, light and wisdom, and one of the creator deities. He brought arts and civilization to humankind. Also known as Oannes and Nudimmud.

Eabani Hero originally created by Aruru to defeat Gilgamesh, the two became friends and destroyed Khumbaba together. He personifies the natural world.

Each Uisge The mythical water-horse which haunts lochs and appears in various forms.

Ebisu One of the gods of luck. He is also the god of labour and fishermen.

Echo A nymph who was punished by Hera for her endless stories told to distract Hera from Zeus's infidelity.

Ector King Arthur's foster father, who raised Arthur to protect him.

Edda Collection of prose and poetic myths and stories from the Norsemen.

Eight Immortals Three of these are reputed to be historical: Han Chung-li, born in Shaanxi, who rose to become a Marshal of the Empire in 21 BC. Chang Kuo-Lao, who lived in the seventh to eighth century AD, and Lü Tung-pin, who was born in AD 755.

Einheriear Odin's guests at Valhalla.

Eisa Loki' daughter.

Ekake (Ibani) Person of great intelligence, which means 'tortoise'. Also known as Mbai (Igbo).

Ekalavya Son of the king of the Nishadas.

Electra Daughter of Agamemnon and Clytemnestra.

Eleusis A town in which the cult of Demeter is centred.

Elf Sigmund is buried by an elf; there are light and dark elves (the latter called dwarfs).

Elokos (Central African) Imps of dwarf-demons who eat human flesh.

Elpenor The youngest of Odysseus's crew who fell from the roof of Circe's house on Aeaea and visited with Odysseus at Hades.

A GLOSSARY OF MYTH & FOLKLORE

Elysium The home of the blessed dead.

Emain Macha The capital of ancient Ulster.

Emma Dai-o King of hell and judge of the dead.

En-lil God of the lower world, storms and mist, who held sway over the ghostly animistic spirits, which at his bidding might pose as the friends or enemies of men. Also known as Bel.

Eos Goddess of the dawn and sister of the sun and moon.

Erichthonius A child born of the semen spilled when Hephaestus tried to rape Athene on the Acropolis.

Eridu The home of Ea and one of the two major cities of Babylonian civilization.

Erin Term for Ireland, originally spelled Éirinn.

Erirogho Magical mixture made from the ashes of the dead.

Eros God of Love, the son of Aphrodite.

Erpa Hereditary chief.

Erysichthon A Thessalian who cut down a grove sacred to Demeter, who punished him with eternal hunger.

Eshu (Yoruba) God of mischief. He also tests people's characters and controls law enforcement.

Eteocles Son of Oedipus.

Eumaeus Swineherd of Odysseus's family at Ithaca.

Euphemus A son of Poseidon who could walk on water. He sailed with the Argonauts.

Europa Daughter of King Agenor of Tyre, who was taken by Zeus to Crete.

Eurydice A Thracian nymph married to Orpheus.

Excalibur The magical sword given to Arthur by the Lady of the Lake. In some versions of the myths, Excalibur is also the sword that the young Arthur pulls from the stone to become king.

Fabulist Person who composes or tells fables.

Fafnir Shape-changer who kills his father and becomes a dragon to guard the family jewels. Slain by Sigurd.

Fairy The word is derived from 'Fays' which means Fates. They are immortal, with the gift of prophecy and of music, and their role changes according to the origin of the myth. They were often considered to be little people, with enormous propensity for mischief, but they are central to many myths and legends, with important powers.

Faro (Mali, Guinea) God of the sky.

Fates In Greek mythology, daughters of Zeus and Themis, who spin the thread of a mortal's life and cut it when his time is due. Called Norns in Viking mythology.

Fenris A wild wolf, who is the son of Loki. He roams the earth after Ragnarok.

Ferhad Sculptor who fell in love with Shireen, the wife of Khosru, and undertook a seemingly impossible task to clear a passage through the mountain of Beysitoun and join the rivers in return for winning Shireen's hand.

Fialar Red cock of Valhalla.

Fianna/Fenians The word 'fianna' was used in early times to describe young warrior-hunters. These youths evolved under the leadership of Finn Mac Cumaill as a highly skilled band of military men who took up service with various kings throughout Ireland.

Filheim Land of mist, at the end of one of Yggdrasill's roots.

Fingal Another name for Fionn Mac Chumail, used after MacPherson's Ossian in the eighteenth century.

Fionn Mac Chumail Irish and Scottish warrior, with great powers of fairness and wisdom. He is known not for physical strength but for knowledge, sense of justice, generosity and canny instinct. He had two hounds, which were later discovered to be his nephews transformed. He became head of the Fianna, or Féinn, fighting the enemies of Ireland and Scotland. He was the father of Oisin (also called Ossian, or other derivatives), and father or grandfather of Osgar.

Fir Bolg One of the ancient, pre-Gaelic peoples of Ireland who were reputed to have worshipped the god Bulga, meaning god of lighting. They are thought to have colonized Ireland around 1970 BC, after the death of Nemed and to have reigned for a short period of thirty-seven years before their defeat by the Tuatha De Danann.

Fir Chlis Nimble men or merry dancers, who are the souls of fallen angels.

Flitch Side of salted and cured bacon.

Folkvang Freyia's palace.

Fomorians A race of monstrous beings, popularly conceived as sea-pirates with some supernatural characteristics who opposed the earliest settlers in Ireland, including the Nemedians and the Tuatha De Danann.

Frey Comes to Asgard with Freyia as a hostage following the war between the Aesir and the Vanir.

Freyia Comes to Asgard with Frey as a hostage following the war between the Aesir and the Vanir. Goddess of beauty and love.

Frigga Odin's wife and mother of gods; she is goddess of the earth.

Fuath Evil spirits which lived in or near the water.

Fulla Frigga's maidservant.

Furies Creatures born from the blood of Cronus, guarding the greatest sinners of the Underworld. Their power lay in their ability to drive mortals mad. Snakes writhed in their hair and around their waists.

Furoshiki Cloths used to wrap things.

Gae Bolg Cuchulainn alone learned the use of this weapon from the woman-warrior, Scathach and with it he slew his own son Connla and his closest friend, Ferdia. Gae Bolg translates as 'harpoon-like javelin' and the deadly weapon was reported to have been created by Bulga, the god of lighting.

Gaea Goddess of Earth, born from Chaos, and the mother of Uranus and Pontus. Also spelled as Gaia.

Gage Object of value presented to a challenger to symbolize good faith.

Galahad Knight of the Round Table, who took up the search for the Holy Grail. Son of Lancelot, Galahad is considered the purest and most perfect knight.

Galatea Daughter of Nereus and Doris, a sea-nymph loved by Polyphemus, the Cyclops.

Gandhari Mother of Duryodhana.

Gandharvas Demi-gods and musicians.

Gandjharva Musical ministrants of the upper air.

Ganesha Elephant-headed god of scribes and son of Shiva.

Ganges Sacred river personified by the goddess Ganga, wife of Shiva and daughter of the mount Himalaya.

Gareth of Orkney King Arthur's nephew and knight of the Round Table.

Garm Hel's hound.

Garuda King of the birds and mount Vishnu, the divine bird, attendant of Narayana.

Gautama Son of Suddhodana and also known as Siddhartha.

Gawain Nephew of King Arthur and knight of the Round Table, he is best known for his adventure with the Green Knight, who challenges one of Arthur's knights to cut off his head, but only if he agrees to be beheaded in turn in a year and a day, if the Green Knight survives. Gawain beheads the Green Knight, who simply replaces his head. At the appointed time, they meet, and the Green Knight swings his axe but merely nicks Gawain's skin instead of beheading him.

Geisha Performance artist or entertainer, usually female.

Geri Odin's wolf.

Ghommid (Yoruba) Term for mythological creatures such as goblins or ogres.

Giallar Bridge in Filheim.

Giallarhorn Heimdall's trumpet – the final call signifies Ragnarok.

Giants In Greek mythology, a race of beings born from Gaea, grown from the blood that dropped from the castrated Uranus. Usually represent evil in Viking mythology.

Gilgamesh King of Erech known as a half-human, half-god hero similar to the Greek Heracles, and often listed with the gods. He is the personification of the sun and is protected by the god Shamash, who in some texts is described as his father. He is also portrayed as an evil tyrant at times.

Gillie Someone who works for a Scottish chief, usually as an attendant or servant; guide for fishing or hunting parties.

Gladheim Where the twelve deities of Asgard hold their thrones. Also called Gladsheim.

Gled Bird of prey.

Golden Fleece Fleece of the ram sent by Poseidon to substitute for Phrixus when his father was going to sacrifice him. The Argonauts went in search of the fleece.

Goodman Man of the house.

Goodwife Woman of the house.

Gopis Lovers of the young Krishna and milkmaids.

Gorgon One of the three sisters, including Medusa, whose frightening looks could turn mortals to stone.

Graces Daughters of Aphrodite by Zeus.

Gramercy Expression of surprise or strong feeling.

Great Head The Iroquois Indians believed in the existence of a curious being known as Great Head, a creature with an enormous head poised on slender legs.

Great Spirit The name given to the Creator of all life, as well as the term used to describe the omnipotent force of the Creator existing in every living thing.

Great-Flank One of Ravana's monsters.

Green Knight A knight dressed all in green and with green hair and skin who challenged one of Arthur's knights to strike him a blow with an axe and that, if he survived, he would return to behead the knight in a year and a day. He turned out to be Lord Bertilak and was under an enchantment cast by Morgan le Fay to test Arthur's knights.

Gruagach Mythical creature, often a giant or ogre similar to a wild man of the woods. The term can also refer to other mythical creatures such as brownies or fairies. As a brownie, he is usually dressed in red or green as opposed to the traditional brown. He has great power to enchant the hapless, or to help mortals who are worthy (usually heroes). He often appears to challenge a boy-hero, during his period of education.

Gudea High priest of Lagash, known to be a patron of the arts and a writer himself.

Guebre Religion founded by Zoroaster, the Persian prophet.

Gugumatz Creator god who, with Huracan, formed the sky, earth and everything on it.

Guha King of Nishadha.

A GLOSSARY OF MYTH & FOLKLORE

Guidewife Woman.

Guinevere Wife of King Arthur; she is often portrayed as a virtuous lady and wife, but is perhaps best known for having a love affair with Lancelot, one of Arthur's friends and knights of the Round Table. Her name is also spelled Guenever.

Gulistan *Rose Garden*, written by the poet Sa'di

Gungnir Odin's spear, made of Yggdrasill wood, and the tip fashioned by Dvalin.

Gylfi A wandering king to whom the Eddas are narrated.

Haab Mayan solar calendar that consisted of eighteen twenty-day months.

Hades One of the three sons of Cronus; brother of Poseidon and Zeus. Hades is King of the Underworld, which is also known as the House of Hades.

Haere-mai Maori phrase meaning 'come here, welcome.'

Haere-mai-ra, me o tatou mate Maori phrase meaning 'come here, that I may sorrow with you.'

Haere-ra Maori phrase meaning 'goodbye, go, farewell.'

Haji Muslim pilgrim who has been to Mecca.

Hakama Traditional Japanese clothing, worn on the bottom half of the body.

Hanuman General of the monkey people.

Harakiri Suicide, usually by cutting or stabbing the abdomen. Also known as seppuku.

Hari-Hara Shiva and Vishnu as one god.

Harmonia Daughter of Ares and Aphrodite, wife of Cadmus.

Hatamoto High-ranking samurai.

Hathor Great cosmic mother and patroness of lovers. She is portrayed as a cow.

Hati The wolf who pursues the sun and moon.

Hatshepsut Second female pharaoh.

Hauberk Armour to protect the neck and shoulders, sometimes a full-length coat of mail.

Hector Eldest son of King Priam who defended Troy from the Greeks. He was killed by Achilles.

Hecuba The second wife of Priam, King of Troy. She was turned into a dog after Troy was lost.

Heimdall White god who guards the Bifrost bridge.

Hel Goddess of death and Loki's daughter. Also known as Hela.

Helen Daughter of Leda and Tyndareus, King of Sparta, and the most beautiful woman in the world. She was responsible for starting the Trojan War.

Heliopolis City in modern-day Cairo, known as the City of the Sun and the central place of worship of Ra. Also known as Anu.

Helius The sun, son of Hyperion and Theia.

Henwife Witch.

Hephaestus or **Hephaistos** The Smith of Heaven.

Hera A Mycenaean palace goddess, married to Zeus.

Heracles An important Greek hero, the son of Zeus and Alcmena. His name means 'Glory of Hera'. He performed twelve labours for King Eurystheus, and later became a god.

Hermes The conductor of souls of the dead to Hades, and god of trickery and of trade. He acts as messenger to the gods.

Hermod Son of Frigga and Odin who travelled to see Hel in order to reclaim Balder for Asgard.

Hero and Leander Hero was a priestess of Aphrodite, loved by Leander, a young man of Abydos. He drowned trying to see her.

Hestia Goddess of the hearth, daughter of Cronus and Rhea.

Hieroglyphs Type of writing that combines symbols and pictures, usually cut into tombs or rocks, or written on papyrus.

Himalaya Great mountain and range, father of Parvati.

Hiordis Wife of Sigmund and mother of Sigurd.

Hoderi A fisher and son of Okuninushi.

Hodur Balder's blind twin; known as the personification of darkness.

Hoenir Also called Vili; produced the first humans with Odin and Loki, and was one of the triad responsible for the creation of the world.

Hōichi the Earless A biwa hōshi, a blind storyteller who played the biwa or lute. Also a priest.

Holger Danske Legendary Viking warrior who is thought to never die. He sleeps until he is needed by his people and then he will rise to protect them.

Homayi Phoenix.

Hoodie Mythical creature which often appears as a crow.

Hoori A hunter and son of Okuninushi.

Horus God of the sky and kinship, son of Isis and Osiris. He captained the boat that carried Ra across the sky. He is depicted with the head of a falcon.

Hotei One of the gods of luck. He also personifies humour and contentment.

Houlet Owl.

Houri Beautiful virgin from paradise.

Hrim-faxi Steed of the night.

Hubris Presumptuous behaviour which causes the wrath of the gods to be brought on to mortals.

Hueytozoztli Festival dedicated to Tlaloc and, at times, Chicomecohuatl or other deities. Also the fourth month of the Aztec calendar.

Hugin Odin's raven.

Huitzilopochtli God of war and the sun, also connected with the summer and crops; one of the principal Aztec deities. He was born a full-grown adult to save his mother, Coatlicue, from the jealousy of his sister, Coyolxauhqui, who tried to kill Coatlicue. The Mars of the Aztec gods. In some origin stories he is one of four offspring of Ometeotl and Omecihuatl.

Hurley A traditional Irish game played with sticks and balls, quite similar to hockey.

Hurons A tribe of Iroquois stock, originally one people with the Iroquois.

Huveane (Pedi, Venda) Creator of humankind, who made a baby from clay into which he breathed life. He is known as the High God or Great God. He is also known as a trickster god.

Hymir Giant who fishes with Thor and is drowned by him.

Iambe Daughter of Pan and Echo, servant to King Celeus of Eleusis and Metaeira.

Icarus Son of Daedalus, who plunged to his death after escaping from the labyrinth.

Ichneumon Mongoose.

Idunn Guardian of the youth-giving apples.

Ifa (Yoruba) God of wisdom and divination. Also the term for a Yoruban religion.

Ife (Yoruba) The place Obatala first arrived on Earth and took for his home.

Igigi Great spirits or gods of Heaven and the sky.

Igraine Wife of the duke of Tintagel, enemy of Uther Pendragon, who marries Uther when her first husband dies. She is King Arthur's mother.

Ile (Yoruba) Goddess of the earth.

Imhetep High priest and wise sage. He is sometimes thought to be the son of Ptah.

Imam Person who leads prayers in a mosque.

Imana (Banyarwanda) Creator or sky god.

In The male principle who, joined with Yo, the female side, brought about creation and the first gods. In and Yo correspond to the Chinese Yang and Yin.

Inari God of rice, fertility, agriculture and, later, the fox god. Inari has both good and evil attributes but is often presented as an evil trickster.

Indra The King of Heaven.

Indrajit Son of Ravana.

Indrasen Daughter of Nala and Damayanti.

Indrasena Son of Nala and Damayanti.

Inundation Annual flooding of the River Nile.

Iphigenia The eldest daughter of Agamemnon and Clytemnestra who was sacrificed to appease Artemis and obtain a fair wind for Troy.

Iris Messenger of the gods who took the form of a rainbow.

Iseult Princess of Ireland and niece of the Morholt. She falls in love with Tristan after consuming a love potion but is forced to marry King Mark of Cornwall.

Ishtar Goddess of love, beauty, justice and war, especially in Ninevah, and earth mother who symbolizes fertility. Married to Tammuz, she is similar to the Greek goddess Aphrodite. Ishtar is sometimes known as Innana or Irnina.

Isis Goddess of the Nile and the moon, sister-wife of Osiris. She and her son, Horus, are sometimes thought of in a similar way to Mary and Jesus. She was one of the most worshipped female

Egyptian deities and was instrumental in returning Osiris to life after he was killed by his brother, Set.

Istakbál Deputation of warriors.

Izanagi Deity and brother-husband to Izanami, who together created the Japanese islands from the Floating Bridge of Heaven. Their offspring populated Japan.

Izanami Deity and sister-wife of Izanagi, creator of Japan. Their children include Amaterasu, Tsuki-yomi and Susanoo.

Jade It was believed that jade emerged from the mountains as a liquid which then solidified after ten thousand years to become a precious hard stone, green in colour. If the correct herbs were added to it, it could return to its liquid state and when swallowed increase the individual's chances of immortality.

Jambavan A noble monkey.

Jason Son of Aeson, King of Iolcus and leader of the voyage of the Argonauts.

Jatayu King of all the eagle-tribes.

Jesseraunt Flexible coat of armour or mail.

Jimmo Legendary first emperor of Japan. He is thought to be descended from Hoori, while other tales claim him to be descended from Amaterasu through her grandson, Ninigi.

Jizo God of little children and the god who calms the troubled sea.

Jord Daughter of Nott; wife of Odin.

Jormungander The world serpent; son of Loki. Legends tell that when his tail is removed from his mouth, Ragnarok has arrived.

Jorō Geisha who also worked as a prostitute.

Jotunheim Home of the giants.

Ju Ju tree Deciduous tree that produces edible fruit.

Jurasindhu A rakshasa, father-in-law of Kans.

Jyeshtha Goddess of bad luck.

A GLOSSARY OF MYTH & FOLKLORE

Ka Life power or soul. Also known as ba.

Kai-káús Son of Kai-kobád. He led an army to invade Mázinderán, home of the demon-sorcerers, after being persuaded by a demon. Known for his ambitious schemes, he later tried to reach Heaven by trapping eagles to fly him there on his throne.

Kaikeyi Mother of Bharata, one of Dasharatha's three wives.

Kai-khosrau Son of Saiawúsh, who killed Afrásiyáb in revenge for the death of his father.

Kai-kobád Descendant of Feridún, he was selected by Zál to lead an army against Afrásiyáb. Their powerful army, led by Zál and Rustem, drove back Afrásiyáb's army, who then agreed to peace.

Kailyard Kitchen garden or small plot, usually used for growing vegetables.

Kali The Black, wife of Shiva.

Kalindi Daughter of the sun, wife of Krishna.

Kaliya A poisonous hydra that lived in the jamna.

Kalki Incarnation of Vishnu yet to come.

Kalnagini Serpent who kills Lakshmindara.

Kal-Purush The Time-man, Bengali name for Orion.

Kaluda A disciple of Buddha.

Kalunga-ngombe (Mbundu) Death, also depicted as the king of the netherworld.

Kama God of desire.

Kamadeva Desire, the god of love.

Kami Spirits, deities or forces of nature.

Kamund Lasso.

Kans King of Mathura, son of Ugrasena and Pavandrekha.

Kanva Father of Shakuntala.

Kappa River goblin with the body of a tortoise and the head of an ape. Kappa love to challenge human beings to single combat.

Karakia Invocation, ceremony, prayer.

Karna Pupil of Drona.

Kaross Blanket or rug, also worn as a traditional garment. It is often made from the skins of animals which have been sewn together.

Kasbu A period of twenty-four hours.

Kashyapa One of Dasharatha's counsellors.

Kauravas or Kurus Sons of Dhritarashtra, pupils of Drona.

Kaushalya Mother of Rama, one of Dasharatha's three wives.

Kay Son of Ector and adopted brother to King Arthur, he becomes one of Arthur's knights of the Round Table.

Keb God of the earth and father of Osiris and Isis, married to Nut. Keb is identified with Kronos, the Greek god of time.

Kehua Spirit, ghost.

Kelpie Another word for each uisge, the water-horse.

Ken Know.

Keres Black-winged demons or daughters of the night.

Keshini Wife of Sagara.

Khalif Leader.

Khara Younger brother of Ravana.

Khepera God who represents the rising sun. He is portrayed as a scarab. Also known as Nebertcher.

Kher-heb Priest and magician who officiated over rituals and ceremonies.

Khnemu God of the source of the Nile and one of the original Egyptian deities. He is thought to be the creator of children and of other gods. He is portrayed as a ram.

Khosru King and husband to Shireen, daughter of Maurice, the Greek Emperor. He was murdered by his own son, who wanted his kingdom and his wife.

A GLOSSARY OF MYTH & FOLKLORE

Khumbaba Monster and guardian of the goddess Irnina, a form of the goddess Ishtar. Khumbaba is likened to the Greek gorgon.

Kia-ora Welcome, good luck. A greeting.

Kiboko Hippopotamus.

Kikinu Soul.

Kimbanda (Mbundu) Doctor.

Kimono Traditional Japanese clothing, similar to a robe.

King Arthur Legendary king of Britain who plucked the magical sword from the stone, marking him as the heir of Uther Pendragon and 'true king' of Britain. He and his knights of the Round Table defended Britain from the Saxons and had many adventures, including searching for the Holy Grail. Finally wounded in battle, he left Britain for the mythical Avalon, vowing to one day return to reclaim his kingdom.

Kingu Tiawath's husband, a god and warrior who she promised would rule Heaven once he helped her defeat the 'gods of light'. He was killed by Merodach who used his blood to make clay, from which he formed the first humans. In some tales, Kingu is Tiawath's son as well as her consort.

Kinnaras Human birds with musical instruments under their wings.

Kinyamkela (Zaramo) Ghost of a child.

Kirk Church, usually a term for Church of Scotland churches.

Kirtle One-piece garment, similar to a tunic, which was worn by men or women.

Kis Solar deity, usually depicted as an eagle.

Kishar Earth mother and sister-wife to Anshar.

Kist Trunk or large chest.

Kitamba (Mbundu) Chief who made his whole village go into mourning when his head-wife, Queen Muhongo, died. He also pledged that no one should speak or eat until she was returned to him.

Knowe Knoll or hillock.

Kojiki One of two myth-histories of Japan, along with the *Nihon Shoki*.

Ko-no-Hana Goddess of Mount Fuji, princess and wife of Ninigi.

Kore 'Maiden', another name for Persephone.

Kraal Traditional rural African village, usually consisting of huts surrounded by a fence or wall. Also an animal enclosure.

Krishna The Dark one, worshipped as an incarnation of Vishnu.

Kui-see Edible root.

Kumara Son of Shiva and Paravati, slays demon Taraka.

Kumbha-karna Ravana's brother.

Kunti Mother of the Pandavas.

Kura Red. The sacred colour of the Maori.

Kusha or Kusi One of Sita's two sons.

Kvasir Clever warrior and colleague of Odin. He was responsible for finally outwitting Loki.

Kwannon Goddess of mercy.

Labyrinth A prison built at Knossos for the Minotaur by Daedalus.

Lady of the Lake Enchantress who presents Arthur with Excalibur.

Laertes King of Ithaca and father of Odysseus.

Laestrygonians Savage giants encountered by Odysseus on his travels.

Laili In love with Majnun but unable to marry him, she was given to the prince, Ibn Salam, to marry. When he died, she escaped and found Majnun, but they could not be legally married. The couple died of grief and were buried together. Also known as Laila.

Laird Person who owns a significant estate in Scotland.

Lakshmana Brother of Rama and his companion in exile.

Lakshmi Consort of Vishnu and a goddess of beauty and good fortune.

Lakshmindara Son of Chand resurrected by Manasa Devi.

Lancelot Knight of the Round Table. Lancelot was raised by the Lady of the Lake. While he went on many quests, he is perhaps best known for his affair with Guinevere, King Arthur's wife.

Land of Light One of the names for the realm of the fairies. If a piece of metal welded by human hands is put in the doorway to their land, the door cannot close. The door to this realm is only open at night, and usually at a full moon.

Lang syne The days of old.

Lao Tzu (Laozi) The ancient Taoist philosopher thought to have been born in 571 BC a contemporary of Confucius with whom, it is said, he discussed the tenets of Tao. Lao Tzu was an advocate of simple rural existence and looked to the Yellow Emperor and Shun as models of efficient government. His philosophies were recorded in the Tao Te Ching. Legends surrounding his birth suggest that he emerged from the left-hand side of his mother's body, with white hair and a long white beard, after a confinement lasting eighty years.

Laocoon A Trojan wiseman who predicted that the wooden horse contained Greek soldiers.

Laomedon The King of Troy who hired Apollo and Poseidon to build the impregnable walls of Troy.

Lava Son of Sita.

Leda Daughter of the King of Aetolia, who married Tyndareus. Helen and Clytemnestra were her daughters.

Legba (Dahomey) Youngest offspring of Mawu-Lisa. He was given the gift of all languages. It was through him that humans could converse with the gods.

Leman Lover.

Leprechaun Mythical creature from Irish folk tales who often appears as a mischievous and sometimes drunken old man.

Lethe One of the four rivers of the Underworld, also called the River of Forgetfulness.

Lif The female survivor of Ragnarok.

Lifthrasir The male survivor of Ragnarok.

Lil Demon.

Liongo (Swahili) Warrior and hero.

Lofty mountain Home of Ahura-Mazda.

Logi Utgard-loki's cook.

Loki God of fire and mischief-maker of Asgard; he eventually brings about Ragnarok. Also spelled as Loptur.

Lotus-Eaters A race of people who live a dazed, drugged existence, the result of eating the lotus flower.

Ma'at State of order meaning truth, order or justice. Personified by the goddess Ma'at, who was Thoth's consort.

Macha There are thought to be several different Machas who appear in quite a number of ancient Irish stories. For the purposes of this book, however, the Macha referred to is the wife of Crunnchu. The story unfolds that after her husband had boasted of her great athletic ability to the King, she was subsequently forced to run against his horses in spite of the fact that she was heavily pregnant. Macha died giving birth to her twin babies and with her dying breath she cursed Ulster for nine generations, proclaiming that it would suffer the weakness of a woman in childbirth in times of great stress. This curse had its most disastrous effect when Medb of Connacht invaded Ulster with her great army.

Machi-bugyō Senior official or magistrate, usually samurai.

Macuilxochitl God of art, dance and games, and the patron of luck in gaming. His name means 'source of flowers' or 'prince of flowers'. Also known as Xochipilli, meaning 'five-flower'.

Madake Weapon used for whipping, made of bamboo.

Maduma Taro tuber.

Mag Muirthemne Cuchulainn's inheritance. A plain extending from River Boyne to the mountain range of Cualgne, close to Emain Macha in Ulster.

Magni Thor's son.

Mahaparshwa One of Ravana's generals.

Maharaksha Son of Khara, slain at Lanka.

Mahasubhadda Wife of Buddha-select (Sumedha).

Majnun Son of a chief, who fell in love with Laili and followed her tribe through the desert, becoming mad with love until they were briefly reunited before dying.

Makaras Mythical fish-reptiles of the sea.

Makoma (Senna) Folk hero who defeated five mighty giants.

Mana Power, authority, prestige, influence, sanctity, luck.

Manasa Devi Goddess of snakes, daughter of Shiva by a mortal woman.

Manasha Goddess of snakes.

Mandavya Daughter of Kushadhwaja.

Man-Devourer One of Ravana's monsters.

Mandodari Wife of Ravana.

Mandrake Poisonous plant from the nightshade family which has hallucinogenic and hypnotic qualities if ingested. Its roots resemble the human form and it has supposedly magical qualities.

Mani The moon.

Manitto Broad term used to describe the supernatural or a potent spirit among the Algonquins, the Iroquois and the Sioux.

Man-Slayer One of Ravana's counsellors.

Manthara Kaikeyi's evil nurse, who plots Rama's ruin.

Mantle Cloak or shawl.

Manu Lawgiver.

Manu Mythical mountain on which the sun sets.

Mara The evil one, tempts Gautama.

Markandeya One of Dasharatha's counsellors.

Mashu Mountain of the Sunset, which lies between Earth and the underworld. Guarded by scorpion-men.

Matali Sakra's charioteer.

Mawu-Lisa (Dahomey) Twin offspring of Nana Baluka. Mawu (female) and Lisa (male) are often joined to form one being. Their own offspring populated the world.

Mbai (Igbo) Person of great intelligence, also known as Ekake (Ibani), which means 'tortoise'.

Medea Witch and priestess of Hecate, daughter of Aeetes and sister of Circe. She helped Jason in his quest for the Golden Fleece.

Medusa One of the three Gorgons whose head had the power to turn onlookers to stone.

Melpomene One of the muses, and mother of the Sirens.

Menaka One of the most beautiful dancers in Heaven.

Menat Amulet, usually worn for protection.

Mendicant Beggar.

Menelaus King of Sparta, brother of Agamemnon. Married Helen and called war against Troy when she eloped with Paris.

Menthu Lord of Thebes and god of war. He is portrayed as a hawk or falcon.

Mere-pounamu A native weapon made of a rare green stone.

Merlin Wizard and advisor to King Arthur. He is thought to be the son of a human female and an incubus (male demon). He brought about Arthur's birth and ascension to king, then acted as his mentor.

A GLOSSARY OF MYTH & FOLKLORE

Merodach God who battled Tiawath and defeated her by cutting out her heart and dividing her corpse into two pieces. He used these pieces to divide the upper and lower waters once controlled by Tiawath, making a dwelling for the gods of light. He also created humankind. Also known as Marduk.

Merrow Mythical mermaid-like creature, often depicted with an enchanted cap called a cohuleen driuth which allows it to travel between land and the depths of the sea. Also known as murúch.

Metaneira Wife of Celeus, King of Eleusis, who hired Demeter in disguise as her nurse.

Metztli Goddess of the moon, her name means 'lady of the night'. Also known as Yohualtictl.

Michabo Also known as Manobozho, or the Great Hare, the principal deity of the Algonquins, maker and preserver of the earth, sun and moon.

Mictlan God of the dead and ruler of the underworld. He was married to Mictecaciuatl and is often represented as a bat. He is also the Aztec lord of Hades. Also known as Mictlantecutli. Mictlan is also the name for the underworld.

Midgard Dwelling place of humans (Earth).

Midsummer A time when fairies dance and claim human victims.

Mihrab Father of Rúdábeh and descendant of Zohák, the serpent-king.

Milesians A group of iron-age invaders led by the sons of Mil, who arrived in Ireland from Spain around 500 BC and overcame the Tuatha De Danann.

Mimir God of the ocean. His head guards a well; reincarnated after Ragnarok.

Minos King of Crete, son of Zeus and Europa. He was considered to have been the ruler of a sea empire.

Minotaur A creature born of the union between Pasiphae and a Cretan Bull.

Minúchihr King who lives to be one hundred and twenty years old. Father of Nauder.

Miolnir *See* Mjolnir.

Mithra God of the sun and light in Iran, protector of truth and guardian of pastures and cattle. Alo known as Mitra in Hindu mythology and Mithras in Roman mythology.

Mixcoatl God of the chase or the hunt. Sometimes depicted as the god of air and thunder, he introduced fire to humankind. His name means 'cloud serpent'.

Mjolnir Hammer belonging to the Norse god of thunder, which is used as a fearsome weapon which always returns to Thor's hand, and as an instrument of consecration.

Mnoatia Forest spirits.

Moccasins One-piece shoes made of soft leather, especially deerskin.

Modi Thor's son.

Moly A magical plant given to Odysseus by Hermes as protection against Circe's powers.

Montezuma Great emperor who consolidated the Aztec Empire.

Mordred Bastard son of King Arthur and Morgawse, Queen of Orkney, who, unknown to Arthur, was his half-sister. Mordred becomes one of King Arthur's knights of the Round Table before betraying and fatally wounding Arthur, causing him to leave Britain for Avalon.

Morgan le Fay Enchantress and half-sister to King Arthur, Morgan was an apprentice of Merlin's. She is generally depicted as benevolent, yet did pit herself against Arthur and his knights on occasion. She escorts Arthur on his final journey to Avalon. Also known as Morgain le Fay.

A GLOSSARY OF MYTH & FOLKLORE

Morholt The Knight sent to Cornwall to force King Mark to pay tribute to Ireland. He is killed by Tristan.

Morongoe the brave (Lesotho) Man who was turned into a snake by evil spirits because Tau was jealous that he had married the beautiful Mokete, the chief's daughter. Morongoe was returned to human form after his son, Tsietse, returned him to their family.

Mosima (Bapedi) The underworld or abyss.

Mount Fuji Highest mountain in Japan, on the island of Honshū.

Mount Kunlun This mountain features in many Chinese legends as the home of the great emperors on Earth. It is written in the *Shanghaijing* (*The Classic of Mountains and Seas*) that this towering structure measured no less than 3300 miles in circumference and 4000 miles in height. It acted both as a central pillar to support the heavens, and as a gateway between Heaven and Earth.

Moving Finger Expression for taking responsibility for one's life and actions, which cannot be undone.

Moytura Translated as the 'Plain of Weeping', Mag Tured, or Moytura, was where the Tuatha De Danann fought two of their most significant battles.

Mua An old-time Polynesian god.

Muezzin Person who performs the Muslim call to prayer.

Mugalana A disciple of Buddha.

Muilearteach The Cailleach Bheur of the water, who appears as a witch or a sea-serpent. On land she grew larger and stronger by fire.

Mul-lil God of Nippur, who took the form of a gazelle.

Muloyi Sorcerer, also called mulaki, murozi, ndozi or ndoki.

Mummu Son of Tiawath and Apsu. He formed a trinity with them to battle the gods. Also known as Moumis. In some tales, Mummu is also Merodach, who eventually destroyed Tiawath.

Munin Odin's raven.

Murile (Chaga) Man who dug up a taro tuber that resembled his baby brother, which turned into a living boy. His mother killed the baby when she saw Murile was starving himself to feed it.

Murtough Mac Erca King who ruled Ireland when many of its people – including his wife and family – were converting to Christianity. He remained a pagan.

Muses Goddesses of poetry and song, daughters of Zeus and Mnemosyne.

Musha Expression, often of surprise.

Muskrat North American beaver-like, amphibious rodent.

Muspell Home of fire, and the fire-giants.

Mwidzilo Taboo which, if broken, can cause death.

Nabu God of writing and wisdom. Also known as Nebo. Thought to be the son of Merodach.

Nahua Ancient Mexicans.

Nakula Pandava twin skilled in horsemanship.

Nala One of the monkey host, son of Vishvakarma.

Nana Baluka (Dahomey) Mother of all creation. She gave birth to an androgynous being with two faces. The female face was Mawu, who controlled the night and lands to the west. The male face was Lisa and he controlled the day and the east.

Nanahuatl Also known as Nanauatzin. Presided over skin diseases and known as Leprous, which in Nahua meant 'divine'.

Nandi Shiva's bull.

Nanna Balder's wife.

Nannar God of the moon and patron of the city of Ur.

Naram-Sin Son or ancestor of Sargon and king of the Four Zones or Quarters of Babylon.

A GLOSSARY OF MYTH & FOLKLORE

Narcissus Son of the River Cephisus. He fell in love with himself and died as a result.

Narve Son of Loki.

Nataraja Manifestation of Shiva, Lord of the Dance.

Natron Preservative used in embalming, mined from the Natron Valley in Egypt.

Nauder Son of Minúchihr, who became king on his death and was tyrannical and hated until Sám begged him to follow in the footsteps of his ancestors.

Nausicaa Daughter of Alcinous, King of Phaeacia, who fell in love with Odysseus.

Nebuchadnezzar Famous king of Babylon. Also known as Nebuchadrezzar.

Necromancy Communicating with the dead.

Nectar Drink of the gods.

Neith Goddess of hunting, fate and war. Neith is sometimes known as the creator of the universe.

Nemesis Goddess of retribution and daughter of night.

Neoptolemus Son of Achilles and Deidameia, he came to Troy at the end of the war to wear his father's armour. He sacrificed Polyxena at the tomb of Achilles.

Nephthys Goddess of the air, night and the dead. Sister of Isis and sister-wife to Seth, she is also the mother of Anubis.

Nereids Sea-nymphs who are the daughters of Nereus and Doris. Thetis, mother of Achilles, was a Nereid.

Nergal God of death and patron god of Cuthah, which was often known as a burial place. He is also known as the god of fire. Married to Aralu, the goddess of the underworld.

Nestor Wise King of Pylus, who led the ships to Troy with Agamemnon and Menelaus.

Neta Daughter of Shiva, friend of Manasa.

Ngai (Gikuyu) Creator god.

Ngaka (Lesotho) Witch doctor.

Niflheim The underworld In Norse mythology, ruled over by Hel.

Night Daughter of Norvi.

Nikumbha One of Ravana's generals.

Nila One of the monkey host, son of Agni.

Nin-Girsu God of fertility and war, patron god of Girsu. Also known as Shul-gur.

Ninigi Grandson of Amaterasu, Ninigi came to Earth bringing rice and order to found the Imperial family. He is known as the August Grandchild.

Niord God of the sea; marries Skadi.

Nippur The home of En-lil and one of the two major cities of Babylonian civilization.

Nirig God of war and storms, and son of Bel. Also known as Enu-Restu.

Nirvana Transcendent state and the final goal of Buddhism.

Nis Mythological creature, similar to a brownie or goblin, usually harmless or even friendly, but can be easily offended. They are often associated with Christmas or the winter solstice.

Noatun Niord's home.

Noisy-Throat One of Ravana's counsellors.

Noondah (Zanzibar) Cannibalistic cat which attacked and killed animals and humans.

Norns The fates and protectors of Yggdrasill. Many believe them to be the same as the Valkyries.

Norvi Father of the night.

Nott Goddess of night.

Nsasak bird Small bird who became chief of all small birds after winning a competition to go without food for seven days. The

Nsasak bird beat the Odudu bird by sneaking out of his home to feed.

Nü Wa The Goddess Nü Wa, who in some versions of the Creation myths is the sole creator of mankind, and in other tales is associated with the God Fu Xi, also a great benefactor of the human race. Some accounts represent Fu Xi as the brother of Nü Wa, but others describe the pair as lovers who lie together to create the very first human beings. Fu Xi is also considered to be the first of the Chinese emperors of mythical times who reigned from 2953 to 2838 BC.

Nuada The first king of the Tuatha De Danann in Ireland, who lost an arm in the first battle of Moytura against the Fomorians. He became known as 'Nuada of the Silver Hand' when Diancecht, the great physician of the Tuatha De Danann, replaced his hand with a silver one after the battle.

Nunda (Swahili, East Africa) Slayer that took the form of a cat and grew so big that it consumed everyone in the town except the sultan's wife, who locked herself away. Her son, Mohammed, killed Nunda and cut open its leg, setting free everyone Nunda had eaten.

Nut Goddess of the sky, stars and astronomy. Sister-wife of Keb and mother of Osiris, Isis, Set and Nephthys. She often appears in the form of a cow.

Nyame (Ashanti) God of the sky, who sees and knows everything.

Nymphs Minor female deities associated with particular parts of the land and sea.

Obassi Osaw (Ekoi) Creator god with his twin, Obassi Nsi. Originally, Obassi Osaw ruled the skies while Obassi Nsi ruled the Earth.

Obatala (Yoruba) Creator of humankind. He climbed down a golden chain from the sky to the earth, then a watery abyss, and formed land and humankind. When Olorun heard of his success, he created the sun for Obatala and his creations.

Oberon Fairy king.

Odin Allfather and king of all gods, he is known for travelling the nine worlds in disguise and recognized only by his single eye; dies at Ragnarok.

Oduduwa (Yoruba) Divine king of Ile-Ife, the holy city of Yoruba.

Odur Freyia's husband.

Odysseus Greek hero, son of Laertes and Anticleia, who was renowned for his cunning, the master behind the victory at Troy, and known for his long voyage home.

Oedipus Son of Leius, King of Thebes and Jocasta. Became King of Thebes and married his mother.

Ogdoad Group of eight deities who were formed into four male-female couples who joined to create the gods and the world.

Ogham One of the earliest known forms of Irish writing, originally used to inscribe upright pillar stones.

Oiran Courtesan.

Oisin Also called Ossian (particularly by James Macpherson who wrote a set of Gaelic Romances about this character, supposedly garnered from oral tradition). Ossian was the son of Fionn and Sadbh, and had various brothers, according to different legends. He was a man of great wisdom, became immortal for many centuries, but in the end he became mad.

Ojibwe Another name for the Chippewa, a tribe of Algonquin stock.

Okuninushi Deity and descendant of Susanoo, who married Suseri-hime, Susanoo's daughter, without his consent. Susanoo tried to kill him many times but did not succeed and eventually forgave Okuninushi. He is sometimes thought to be the son or grandson of Susanoo.

Olokun (Yoruba) Most powerful goddess who ruled the seas and marshes. When Obatala created Earth in her domain, other gods began to divide it up between them. Angered at their presumption, she caused a great flood to destroy the land.

Olorun (Yoruba) Supreme god and ruler of the sky. He sees and controls everything, but others, such as Obatala, carry out the work for him. Also known as Olodumare.

Olympia Zeus's home in Elis.

Olympus The highest mountain in Greece and the ancient home of the gods.

Omecihuatl Female half of the first being, combined with Ometeotl. Together they are the lords of duality or lords of the two sexes. Also known as Ometecutli and Omeciuatl or Tonacatecutli and Tonacaciuatl. Their offspring were Xipe Totec, Huitzilopochtli, Quetzalcoatl and Tezcatlipoca.

Ometeotl Male half of the first being, combined with Omecihuatl.

Ometochtli Collective name for the pulque-gods or drink-gods. These gods were often associated with rabbits as they were thought to be senseless creatures.

Onygate Anyway.

Opening the Mouth Ceremony in which mummies or statues were prayed over and anointed with incense before their mouths were opened, allowing them to eat and drink in the afterlife.

Oracle The response of a god or priest to a request for advice – also a prophecy; the place where such advice was sought; the person or thing from whom such advice was sought.

Oranyan (Yoruba) Youngest grandson of King Oduduwa, who later became king himself.

Orestes Son of Agamemnon and Clytemnestra who escaped following Agamemnon's murder to King Strophius. He later returned to Argos to murder his mother and avenge the death of his father.

Orpheus Thracian singer and poet, son of Oeagrus and a Muse. Married Eurydice and when she died tried to retrieve her from the Underworld.

Orunmila (Yoruba) Eldest son of Olorun, he helped Obatala create land and humanity, which he then rescued after Olokun flooded the lands. He has the power to see the future.

Osiris God of fertility, the afterlife and death. Thought to be the first of the pharaohs. He was murdered by his brother, Set, after which he was conjured back to life by Isis, Anubis and others before becoming lord of the afterworld. Married to Isis, who was also his sister.

Otherworld The world of deities and spirits, also known as the Land of Promise, or the Land of Eternal Youth, a place of everlasting life where all earthly dreams come to be fulfilled.

Owuo (Krachi, West Africa) Giant who personifies death. He causes a person to die every time he blinks his eye.

Palamedes Hero of Nauplia, believed to have created part of the ancient Greek alphabet. He tricked Odysseus into joining the fleet setting out for Troy by placing the infant Telemachus in the path of his plough.

Palermo Stone Stone carved with hieroglyphs, which came from the Royal Annals of ancient Egypt and contains a list of the kings of Egypt from the first to the early fifth dynasties.

Palfrey Docile and light horse, often used by women.

Palladium Wooden image of Athene, created by her as a monument to her friend Pallas who she accidentally killed. While in Troy it protected the city from invaders.

Pallas Athene's best friend, whom she killed.

A GLOSSARY OF MYTH & FOLKLORE

Pan God of Arcadia, half-goat and half-man. Son of Hermes. He is connected with fertility, masturbation and sexual drive. He is also associated with music, particularly his pipes, and with laughter.

Pan Gu Some ancient writers suggest that this God is the offspring of the opposing forces of nature, the yin and the yang. The yin (female) is associated with the cold and darkness of the earth, while the yang (male) is associated with the sun and the warmth of the heavens. 'Pan' means 'shell of an egg' and 'Gu' means 'to secure' or 'to achieve'. Pan Gu came into existence so that he might create order from chaos.

Pandareus Cretan King killed by the gods for stealing the shrine of Zeus.

Pandavas Alternative name for sons of Pandu, pupils of Drona.

Pandora The first woman, created by the gods, to punish man for Prometheus's theft of fire. Her dowry was a box full of powerful evil.

Papyrus Paper-like material made from the pith of the papyrus plant, first manufactured in Egypt. Used as a type of paper as well as for making mats, rope and sandals.

Paramahamsa The supreme swan.

Parashurama Human incarnation of Vishnu, 'Rama with an axe'.

Paris Handsome son of Priam and Hecuba of Troy, who was left for dead on Mount Ida but raised by shepherds. Was reclaimed by his family, then brought them shame and caused the Trojan War by eloping with Helen.

Parsa Holy man. Also known as a zahid.

Parvati Consort of Shiva and daughter of Himalaya.

Passion Wife of desire.

Pavanarekha Wife of Ugrasena, mother of Kans.

393

Peerie Folk Fairy or little folk.

Pegasus The winged horse born from the severed neck of Medusa.

Peggin Wooden vessel with a handle, often shaped like a tub and used for drinking.

Peleus Father of Achilles. He married Antigone, caused her death, and then became King of Phthia. Saved from death himself by Jason and the Argonauts. Married Thetis, a sea nymph.

Penelope The long-suffering but equally clever wife of Odysseus who managed to keep at bay suitors who longed for Ithaca while Odysseus was at the Trojan War and on his ten-year voyage home.

Pentangle Pentagram or five-pointed star.

Pentecost Christian festival held on the seventh Sunday after Easter. It celebrates the holy spirit descending on the disciples after Jesus's ascension.

Percivale Knight of the Round Table and original seeker of the Holy Grail.

Persephone Daughter of Zeus and Demeter who was raped by Hades and forced to live in the Underworld as his queen for three months of every year.

Perseus Son of Danae, who was made pregnant by Zeus. He fought the Gorgons and brought home the head of Medusa. He eventually founded the city of Mycenae and married Andromeda.

Pesh Kef Spooned blade used in the Opening the Mouth ceremony.

Phaeacia The Kingdom of Alcinous on which Odysseus landed after a shipwreck which claimed the last of his men as he left Calypso's island.

Pharaoh King or ruler of Egypt.

Philoctetes Malian hero, son of Poeas, received Heracles's bow and arrows as a gift when he lit the great hero's pyre on Mount Oeta. He was involved in the last part of the Trojan War, killing Paris.

Philtre Magic potion, usually a love potion.
Pibroch Bagpipe music.
Pintura Native manuscript or painting.
Pipiltin Noble class of the Aztecs.
Pismire Ant.
Piu-piu Short mat made from flax leaves and neatly decorated.
Po Gloom, darkness, the lower world.
Polyphemus A Cyclops, but a son of Poseidon. He fell in love with Galatea, but she spurned him. He was blinded by Odysseus.
Polyxena Daughter of Priam and Hecuba of Troy. She was sacrificed on the grave of Achilles by Neoptolemus.
Pooka Mythical creature with the ability to shapeshift. Often appears as a horse, but also as a bull, dog or in human form, and has the ability to talk. Also known as púca.
Popol Vuh Sacred 'book of counsel' of the Quiché or K'iche' Maya people.
Poseidon God of the sea, and of sweet waters. Also the god of earthquakes. His is brother to Zeus and Hades, who divided the earth between them.
Pradyumna Son of Krishna and Rukmini.
Prahasta (Long-Hand) One of Ravana's generals.
Prajapati Creator of the universe, father of the gods, demons and all creatures, later known as Brahma.
Priam King of Troy, married to Hecuba, who bore him Hector, Paris, Helenus, Cassandra, Polyxena, Deiphobus and Troilus. He was murdered by Neoptolemus.
Pritha Mother of Karna and of the Pandavas.
Prithivi Consort of Dyaus and goddess of the earth.
Proetus King of Argos, son of Abas.

Prometheus A Titan, son of Iapetus and Themus. He was champion of mortal men, which he created from clay. He stole fire from the gods and was universally hated by them.

Prose Edda Collection of Norse myths and poems, thought to have been compiled in the 1200s by Icelandic historian Snorri Sturluson.

Proteus The old man of the sea who watched Poseidon's seals.

Psyche A beautiful nymph who was the secret wife of Eros, against the wishes of his mother Aphrodite, who sent Psyche to perform many tasks in hope of causing her death. She eventually married Eros and was allowed to become partly immortal.

Ptah Creator god and deity of Memphis who was married to Sekhmet. Ptah built the boats to carry the souls of the dead to the afterlife.

Puddock Frog.

Pulque Alcoholic drink made from fermented agave.

Purusha The cosmic man, he was sacrificed and his dismembered body became all the parts of the cosmos, including the four classes of society.

Purvey To provide or supply.

Pushkara Nala's brother.

Pushpaka Rama's chariot.

Putana A rakshasi.

Pygmalion A sculptor who was so lonely he carved a statue of a beautiful woman, and eventually fell in love with it. Aphrodite brought the image to life.

Quauhtli Eagle.

Quern Hand mill used for grinding corn.

Quetzalcoatl Deity and god of wind. He is represented as a feathered or plumed serpent and is usually a wise and benevolent god. Offspring of Ometeotl and Omecihuatl, he is also known as Kukulkan.

Ra God of the sun, ruling male deity of Egypt whose name means 'sole creator'.

Radha The principal mistress of Krishna.

Ragnarok The end of the world.

Rahula Son of Siddhartha and Yashodhara.

Raiden God of thunder. He traditionally has a fierce and demonic appearance.

Rakshasas Demons and devils.

Ram of Mendes Sacred symbol of fatherhood and fertility.

Rama or **Ramachandra** A prince and hero of the Ramayana, worshipped as an incarnation of Vishnu.

Ra-Molo (Lesotho) Father of fire, a chief who ruled by fear. When trying to kill his brother, Tau the lion, he was turned into a monster with the head of a sheep and the body of a snake.

Rangatira Chief, warrior, gentleman.

Regin A blacksmith who educated Sigurd.

Reinga The spirit land, the home of the dead.

Reservations Tracts of land allocated to the native American people by the United States Government with the purpose of bringing the many separate tribes under state control.

Rewati Daughter of Raja, marries Balarama.

Rhadha Wife of Adiratha, a gopi of Brindaban and lover of Krishna.

Rhea Mother of the Olympian gods. Cronus ate each of her children, but she concealed Zeus and gave Cronus a swaddled rock in his place.

Rill Small stream.

Rimu (Chaga) Monster known to feed off human flesh, which sometimes takes the form of a werewolf.

Rishis Sacrificial priests associated with the devas in Swarga.

Rituparna King of Ayodhya.

Rohini The wife of Vasudeva, mother of Balarama and Subhadra, and carer of the young Krishna. Another Rohini is a goddess and consort of Chandra.

Rōnin Samurai whose master had died or fallen out of favour.

Rubáiyát Collection of poems written by Omar Khayyám.

Rúdábeh Wife of Zál and mother of Rustem.

Rudra Lord of Beasts and disease, later evolved into Shiva.

Rukma Rukmini's eldest brother.

Rustem Son of Zál and Rúdábeh, he was a brave and mighty warrior who undertook seven labours to travel to Mázinderán to rescue Kai-káús. Once there, he defeated the White Demon and rescued Kai-káús. He rode the fabled stallion Rakhsh and is also known as Rustam.

Ryō Traditional gold currency.

Sabdh Mother of Ossian, or Oisin.

Sabitu Goddess of the sea.

Sagara King of Ayodhya.

Sahadeva Pandava twin skilled in swordsmanship.

Sahib diwan Lord high treasurer or chief royal executive.

Saiawúsh Son of Kai-káús, who was put through trial by fire when Sudaveh, Kai-káús's wife, told him that Saiawúsh had taken advantage of her. His innocence was proven when the fire did not harm him. He was eventually killed by Afrásiyáb.

Saithe Blessed.

Sajara (Mali) God of rainbows. He takes the form of a multi-coloured serpent.

Sake Japanese rice wine.

Sakuni Cousin of Duryodhana.

Salam Greeting or salutation.

Saláman Son of the Shah of Yunan, who fell in love with Absál, his nurse. She died after they had a brief love affair and he returned to his father.

Salmali tree Cotton tree.

Salmon A symbol of great wisdom, around which many Scottish legends revolve.

Sám Mighty warrior who fought and won many battles. Father of Zál and grandfather to Rustem.

Sambu Son of Krishna.

Sampati Elder brother of Jatayu.

Samurai Noblemen who were part of the military in medieval Japan.

Sanehat Member of the royal bodyguard.

Sango (Yoruba) God of war and thunder.

Sangu (Mozambique) Goddess who protects pregnant women, depicted as a hippopotamus.

Santa Daughter of Dasharatha.

Sarapis Composite deity of Apis and Osiris, sometimes known as Serapis. Thought to be created to unify Greek and Egyptian citizens under the Greek pharaoh Ptolemy.

Sarasvati The tongue of Rama.

Sarcophagus Stone coffin.

Sargon of Akkad Raised by Akki, a husbandman, after being hidden at birth. Sargon became King of Assyria and a great hero. He founded the first library in Babylon. Similar to King Arthur or Perseus.

Sarsar Harsh, whistling wind.

Sasabonsam (Ashanti) Forest ogre.

Sassun Scottish word for England.

Sati Daughter of Daksha and Prasuti, first wife of Shiva.

Satrughna One of Dasharatha's four sons.

Satyavan Truth speaker, husband of Savitri.

Satyavati A fisher-maid, wife of Bhishma's father, Shamtanu.

Satyrs Elemental spirits which took great pleasure in chasing nymphs. They had horns, a hairy body and cloven hooves.

Saumanasa A mighty elephant.

Scamander River running across the Trojan plain, and father of Teucer.

Scarab Dung beetle, often used as a symbol of the immortal human soul and regeneration.

Scylla and Charybdis Scylla was a monster who lived on a rock of the same name in the Straits of Messina, devouring sailors. Charybdis was a whirlpool in the Straits which was supposedly inhabited by the hateful daughter of Poseidon.

Seal Often believed that seals were fallen angels. Many families are descended from seals, some of which had webbed hands or feet. Some seals were the children of sea-kings who had become enchanted (selkies).

Seelie-Court The court of the Fairies, who travelled around their realm. They were usually fair to humans, doling out punishment that was morally sound, but they were quick to avenge insults to fairies.

Segu (Swahili, East Africa) Guide who informs humans where honey can be found.

Sekhmet Solar deity who led the pharaohs in war. She is goddess of healing and was sent by Ra to destroy humanity when people turned against the sun god. She is portrayed with the head of a lion.

Selene Moon-goddess, daughter of Hyperion and Theia. She was seduced by Pan, but loved Endymion.

A GLOSSARY OF MYTH & FOLKLORE

Selkie Mythical creature which is seal-like when in water but can shed its skin to take on human form when on land.

Seneschal Steward of a royal or noble household.

Sensei Teacher.

Seriyut A disciple of Buddha.

Sessrymnir Freyia's home.

Set God of chaos and evil, brother of Osiris, who killed him by tricking him into getting into a chest, which he then threw in the Nile, before cutting Osiris's body into fourteen separate pieces. Also known as Seth.

Sgeulachd Stories.

Shah Nameh *The Book of Kings* written by Ferdowski, one of the world's longest epic poems, which describes the mythology and history of the Persian Empire.

Shaikh Respected religious man.

Shaivas or Shaivites Worshippers of Shiva.

Shakti Power or wife of a god and Shiva's consort as his feminine aspect.

Shaman Also known as the 'Medicine Men' of Indian tribes, it was the shaman's role to cultivate communication with the spirit world. They were endowed with knowledge of all healing herbs, and learned to diagnose and cure disease. They could foretell the future, find lost property and had power over animals, plants and stones.

Shamash God of the sun and protector of Gilgamesh, the great Babylonian hero. Known as the son of Sin, the moon god, he is also portrayed as a judge of good and evil.

Shamtanu Father of Bhishma.

Shankara A great magician, friend of Chand Sadagar.

Shashti The Sixth, goddess who protects children and women in childbirth.

Sheen Beautiful and enchanted woman who casts a spell on Murtough, King of Ireland, causing him to fall in love with her and cast out his family. He dies at her hands, half burned and half drowned, but she then dies of grief as she returns his love. Sheen is known by many names, including Storm, Sigh and Rough Wind.

Shesh A serpent that takes human birth through Devaki.

Shi-en Fairy dwelling.

Shinto Indigenous religion of Japan, from the pre-sixth century to the present day.

Shireen Married to Khosru. Her beauty meant that she was desired by many, including Khosru's own son by his previous marriage. She killed herself rather than give in to her stepson.

Shitala The Cool One and goddess of smallpox.

Shiva One of the two great gods of post-Vedic Hinduism with Vishnu.

Shogun Military ruler or overlord.

Shoji Sliding door, usually a lattice screen of paper.

Shu God of the air and half of the first divine couple created by Atem. Brother and husband to Tefnut, father to Keb and Nut.

Shubistán Household.

Shudra One of the four fundamental colours (caste).

Shuttle Part of a machine used for spinning cloth, used for passing weft threads between warp threads.

Siddhas Musical ministrants of the upper air.

Sif Thor's wife; known for her beautiful hair.

Sigi Son of Odin.

Sigmund Warrior able to pull the sword from Branstock in the Volsung's hall.

Signy Volsung's daughter.

Sigurd Son of Sigmund, and bearer of his sword. Slays Fafnir the dragon.

Sigyn Loki's faithful wife.

Símúrgh Griffin, an animal with the body of a lion and the head and wings of an eagle. Known to hold great wisdom. Also called a symurgh.

Sin God of the moon, worshipped primarily in Ur.

Sindri Dwarf who worked with Brokki to fashion gifts for the gods; commissioned by Loki.

Sirens Sea nymphs who are half-bird, half-woman, whose song lures hapless sailors to their death.

Sisyphus King of Ephrya and a trickster who outwitted Autolycus. He was one of the greatest sinners in Hades.

Sita Daughter of the earth, adopted by Janaka, wife of Rama.

Skadi Goddess of winter and the wife of Niord for a short time.

Skanda Six-headed son of Shiva and a warrior god.

Skraeling Person native to Canada and Greenland. The name was given to them by Viking settlers and can be translated as 'barbarian'.

Skrymir Giant who battled against Thor.

Sleipnir Odin's steed.

Sluagh The host of the dead, seen fighting in the sky and heard by mortals.

Smote Struck with a heavy blow.

Sohráb Son of Rustem and Tahmineh, Sohráb was slain in battle by his own father, who killed him by mistake.

Sol The sun-maiden.

Soma A god and a drug, the elixir of life.

Somerled Lord of the Isles, and legendary ancestor of the Clan MacDonald.

Soothsayer Someone with the ability to predict or see the future, by the use of magic, special knowledge or intuition. Known as seanagal in Scottish myths.

Squaw North American Indian married woman.

Squint-Eye One of Ramana's monsters.

Squire Shield- or armour-bearer of a knight.

Srutakirti Daughter of Kushadhwaja.

Stirabout Porridge made by stirring oatmeal into boiling milk or water.

Stone Giants A malignant race of stone beings whom the Iroquois believed invaded Indian territory, threatening the Confederation of the Five Nations. These fierce and hostile creatures lived off human flesh and were intent on exterminating the human race.

Stoorworm A great water monster which frequented lochs. When it thrust its great body from the sea, it could engulf islands and whole ships. Its appearance prophesied devastation.

Stot Bullock.

Styx River in Arcadia and one of the four rivers in the Underworld. Charon ferried dead souls across it into Hades, and Achilles was dipped into it to make him immortal.

Subrahmanian Son of Shiva, a mountain deity.

Sugriva The chief of the five great monkeys in the Ramayana.

Sukanya The wife of Chyavana.

Suman Son of Asamanja.

Sumantra A noble Brahman.

Sumati Wife of Sagara.

Sumedha A righteous Brahman who dwelt in the city of Amara.

Sumitra One of Dasharatha's three wives, mother of Lakshmana and Satrughna.

Suniti Mother of Dhruva.

Suparshwa One of Ravana's counsellors.

Supranakha A rakshasi, sister of Ravana.

Surabhi The wish-bestowing cow.

Surcoat Loose robe, traditionally worn over armour.

Surtr Fire-giant who eventually destroys the world at Ragnarok.

Surya God of the sun.

Susanoo God of the storm. He is depicted as a contradictory character with both good and bad characteristics. He was banished from Heaven after trying to kill his sister, Amaterasu.

Sushena A monkey chief.

Svasud Father of summer.

Swarga An Olympian paradise, where all wishes and desires are gratified.

Sweating A ritual customarily associated with spiritual purification and prayer practised by most tribes throughout North America prior to sacred ceremonies or vision quests. Steam was produced within a 'sweat lodge', a low, dome-shaped hut, by sprinkling water on heated stones.

Syrinx An Arcadian nymph who was the object of Pan's love.

Tablet of Destinies Cuneiform clay tablet on which the fates were written. Tiawath had given this to Kingu, but it was taken by Merodach when he defeated them. The storm god Zu later stole it for himself.

Taiaha A weapon made of wood.

Tailtiu One of the most famous royal residences of ancient Ireland. Possibly also a goddess linked to this site.

Tall One of Ravana's counsellors.

Tammuz Solar deity of Eridu who, with Gishzida, guards the gates of Heaven. Protector of Anu.

Tamsil Example or guidance.

Tangi Funeral, dirge. Assembly to cry over the dead.

Taniwha Sea monster, water spirit.

Tantalus Son of Zeus who told the secrets of the gods to mortals and stole their nectar and ambrosia. He was condemned to eternal torture in Hades, where he was tempted by food and water but allowed to partake of neither.

Taoism Taoism (or Daoism) came into being at roughly the same time as Confucianism, although its tenets were radically different and were largely founded on the philosophies of Lao Tzu (Laozi). While Confucius argued for a system of state discipline, Taoism strongly favoured self-discipline and looked upon nature as the architect of essential laws. A newer form of Taoism evolved after the Burning of the Books, placing great emphasis on spirit worship and pacification of the gods.

Tapu Sacred, supernatural possession of power. Involves spiritual rules and restrictions.

Tara Also known as Temair, the Hill of Tara was the popular seat of the ancient High-Kings of Ireland from the earliest times to the sixth century. Located in Co. Meath, it was also the place where great noblemen and chieftains congregated during wartime, or for significant events.

Tara Sugriva's wife.

Tartarus Dark region, below Hades.

Tau (Lesotho) Brother to Ra-Molo, depicted as a lion.

Taua War party.

Tefnut Goddess of water and rain. Married to Shu, who was also her brother. She, like Sekhmet, is portrayed with the head of a lion. Also known as Tefenet.

Telegonus Son of Odysseus and Circe. He was allegedly responsible for his father's death.

A GLOSSARY OF MYTH & FOLKLORE

Telemachus Son of Odysseus and Penelope who was aided by Athene in helping his mother to keep away the suitors in Odysseus's absence.

Temu The evening form of Ra, the Sun God.

Tengu Goblin or gnome, often depicted as bird-like. A powerful fighter with weapons.

Tenochtitlán Capital city of the Aztecs, founded around AD 1350 and the site of the 'Great Temple'. Now Mexico City.

Teo-Amoxtli Divine book.

Teocalli Great temple built in Tenochtitlán, now Mexico City.

Teotleco Festival of the Coming of the Gods; also the twelfth month of the Aztec calendar.

Tepee A conical-shaped dwelling constructed of buffalo hide stretched over lodge-poles. Mostly used by native American tribes living on the plains.

Tepeyollotl God of caves, desert places and earthquakes, whose name means 'heart of the mountain'. He is depicted as a jaguar, often leaping at the sun. Also known as Tepeolotlec.

Tepitoton Household gods.

Tereus King of Daulis who married Procne, daughter of Pandion King of Athens. He fell in love with Philomela, raped her and cut out her tongue.

Tezcatlipoca Supreme deity and Lord of the Smoking Mirror. He was also patron of royalty and warriors. Invented human sacrifice to the gods. Offspring of Ometeotl and Omecihuatl, he is known as the Jupiter of the Aztec gods.

Thalia Muse of pastoral poetry and comedy.

Theia Goddess of many names, and mother of the sun.

Theseus Son of King Aegeus of Athens. A cycle of legends has been woven around his travels and life.

Thetis Chief of the Nereids loved by both Zeus and Poseidon. They married her to a mortal, Peleus, and their child was Achilles. She tried to make him immortal by dipping him in the River Styx.

Thialfi Thor's servant, taken when his peasant father unwittingly harms Thor's goat.

Thiassi Giant and father of Skadi, he tricked Loki into bringing Idunn to him. Thrymheim is his kingdom.

Thomas the Rhymer Also called 'True Thomas', he was Thomas of Ercledoune, who lived in the thirteenth century. He met with the Queen of Elfland, and visited her country, was given clothes and a tongue that could tell no lie. He was also given the gift of prophecy, and many of his predictions were proven true.

Thor God of thunder and of war (with Tyr). Known for his huge size, and red hair and beard. Carries the hammer Miolnir. Slays Jormungander at Ragnarok.

Thoth God of the moon. Invented the arts and sciences and regulated the seasons. He is portrayed with the head of an ibis or a baboon.

Three-Heads One of Ravana's monsters.

Thrud Thor's daughter.

Thrudheim Thor's realm. Also called Thrudvang.

Thunder-Tooth Leader of the rakshasas at the siege of Lanka.

Tiawath Primeval dark ocean or abyss, Tiawath is also a monster and evil deity of the deep. She took the form of a dragon or sea serpent and battled the gods of light for supremacy over all living beings. She was eventually defeated by Merodach, who used her body to create Heaven and Earth.

Tiglath-Pileser I King of Assyria, who made it a leading power for centuries.

Tiki First man created, a figure carved of wood, or other representation of man.

Tirawa The name given to the Great Creator (**see** Great Spirit) by the Pawnee tribe who believed that four direct paths led from his house in the sky to the four semi-cardinal points: north-east, north-west, south-east and south-west.

Tiresias A Theban who was given the gift of prophecy by Zeus. He was blinded for seeing Athene bathing. He continued to use his prophetic talents after his death, advising Odysseus.

Tirfing Sword made by dwarves which was cursed to kill every time it was drawn, be the cause of three great atrocities, and kill Suaforlami (Odin's grandson), for whom it was made.

Tisamenus Son of Orestes, who inherited the Kingdom of Argos and Sparta.

Titania Queen of the fairies.

Tlaloc God of rain and fertility, so important to the people, because he ensured a good harvest, that the Aztec heaven or paradise was named Tlalocan in his honour.

Tlazolteotl Goddess of ordure, filth and vice. Also known as the earth-goddess or Tlaelquani, meaning 'filth-eater'. She acted as a confessor of sins or wrongdoings.

Tohu-mate Omen of death.

Tohunga A priest; a possessor of supernatural powers.

Toltec Civilization that preceded the Aztecs.

Tomahawk Hatchet with a stone or iron head used in war or hunting.

Tonalamatl Record of the Aztec calendar, which was recorded in books made from bark paper.

Tonalpohualli Aztec calendar composed of twenty thirteen-day weeks called trecenas.

Totec Solar deity known as Our Great Chief.

Totemism System of belief in which people share a relationship with a spirit animal or natural being with whom they interact. Examples include Ea, who is represented by a fish.

Toxilmolpilia The binding up of the years.

Tristan Nephew of King Mark of Cornwall, who travels to Ireland to bring Iseult back to marry his uncle. On the way, he and Iseult consume a love potion and fall madly in love before their story ends tragically.

Triton A sea-god, and son of Poseidon and Amphitrite. He led the Argonauts to the sea from Lake Tritonis.

Trojan War War waged by the Greeks against Troy, in order to reclaim Menelaus's wife Helen, who had eloped with the Trojan prince Paris. Many important heroes took part, and form the basis of many legends and myths.

Troll Unfriendly mythological creature of varying size and strength. Usually dwells in mountainous areas, among rocks or caves.

Truage Tribute or pledge of peace or truth, usually made on payment of a tax.

Tsuki-yomi God of the moon, brother of Amaterasu and Susanoo.

Tuat The other world or land of the dead.

Tupuna Ancestor.

Tvashtar Craftsman of the gods.

Tyndareus King of Sparta, perhaps the son of Perseus's daughter Grogphone. Expelled from Sparta but restored by Heracles. Married Leda and fathered Helen and Clytemnestra, among others.

Tyr Son of Frigga and the god of war (with Thor). Eventually kills Garm at Ragnarok.

Tzompantli Pyramid of Skulls.

Uayeb The five unlucky days of the Mayan calendar, which were believed to be when demons from the underworld could reach Earth. People would often avoid leaving their houses on uayeb days.

Ubaaner Magician, whose name meant 'splitter of stones', who created a wax crocodile that came to life to swallow up the man who was trying to seduce his wife.

Uile Bheist Mythical creature, usually some form of wild beast.

Uisneach A hill formation between Mullingar and Athlone said to mark the centre of Ireland.

uKqili (Zulu) Creator god.

Uller God of winter, whom Skadi eventually marries.

Ulster Cycle Compilation of folk tales and legends telling of the Ulaids, people from the northeast of Ireland, now named Ulster. Also known as the *Uliad Cycle*, it is one of four Irish cycles of mythology.

Unseelie Court An unholy court comprising a kind of fairies, antagonistic to humans. They took the form of a kind of Sluagh, and shot humans and animals with elf-shots.

Urd One of the Norns.

Urien King of Gore, husband of Morgan le Fey and father to Yvain.

Urmila Second daughter of Janaka.

Usha Wife of Aniruddha, daughter of Vanasur.

Ushas Goddess of the dawn.

Utgard-loki King of the giants. Tricked Thor.

Uther Pendragon King of England in sub-Roman Britain; father of King Arthur.

Utixo (Hottentot) Creator god.

Ut-Napishtim Ancestor of Gilgamesh, whom Gilgamesh sought out to discover how to prevent death. Similar to Noah in that he was sent a vision warning him of a great deluge. He built an ark in seven days, filling it with his family, possessions and all kinds of animals.

Uz Deity symbolized by a goat.

Vach Goddess of speech.

Vajrahanu One of Ravana's generals.

Vala Another name for Norns.

Valfreya Another name for Freyia.

Valhalla Odin's hall for the celebrated dead warriors chosen by the Valkyries.

Vali The cruel brother of Sugriva, dethroned by Rama.

Valkyries Odin's attendants, led by Freyia. Chose dead warriors to live at Valhalla. Also spelled as Valkyrs.

Vamadeva One of Dasharatha's priests.

Vanaheim Home of the Vanir.

Vanir Race of gods in conflict with the Aesir; they are gods of the sea and wind.

Varuna Ancient god of the sky and cosmos, later, god of the waters.

Vasishtha One of Dasharatha's priests.

Vassal Person under the protection of a feudal lord.

Vasudev Descendant of Yadu, husband of Rohini and Devaki, father of Krishna.

Vasudeva A name of Narayana or Vishnu.

Vavasor Vassal or tenant of a baron or lord who himself has vassals.

Vedic Mantras, hymns.

Vernandi One of the Norns.

Vichitravirya Bhishma's half-brother.

Vidar Slays Fenris.

Vidura Friend of the Pandavas.

Vigrid The plain where the final battle is held.

Vijaya Karna's bow.

Vikramaditya A king identified with Chandragupta II.

Vintail Moveable front of a helmet.

Virabhadra A demon that sprang from Shiva's lock of hair.

Viradha A fierce rakshasa, seizes Sita, slain by Rama.

Virupaksha The elephant who bears the whole world.

Vishnu The Preserver, Vedic sun-god and one of the two great gods of post-Vedic Hinduism.

Vision Quest A sacred ceremony undergone by Native Americans to establish communication with the spirit set to direct them in life. The quest lasted up to four days and nights and was preceded by a period of solitary fasting and prayer.

Vivasvat The sun.

Vizier High-ranking official or adviser. Also known as vizir or vazir.

Volsung Family of great warriors about whom a great saga was spun.

Vrishadarbha King of Benares.

Vrishasena Son of Karna, slain by Arjuna.

Vyasa Chief of the royal chaplains.

Wairua Spirit, soul.

Wanjiru (Kikuyu) Maiden who was sacrificed by her village to appease the gods and make it rain after years of drought.

Weighing of the heart Procedure carried out after death to assess whether the deceased was free from sin. If the deceased's heart weighed less than the feather of Ma'at, they would join Osiris in the Fields of Peace.

Whare Hut made of fern stems tied together with flax and vines, and roofed in with raupo (reeds).

White Demon Protector of Mázinderán. He prevented Kai-káús and his army from invading.

Withy Thin twig or branch which is very flexible and strong.

Wolverine Large mammal of the musteline family with dark, very thick, water-resistant fur, inhabiting the forests of North America and Eurasia.

Wroth Angry.

Wyrd One of the Norns.

Xanthus & Balius Horses of Achilles, immortal offspring of Zephyrus the west wind. A gift to Achilles's father Peleus.

Xipe Totec High priest and son of Ometeotl and Omecihuatl. Also known as the god of the seasons.

Xiupohualli Solar year, composed of eighteen twenty-day months. Also spelt Xiuhpōhualli.

Yadu A prince of the Lunar dynasty.

Yakshas Same as rakshasas.

Yakunin Government official.

Yama God of Death, king of the dead and son of the sun.

Yamato Take Legendary warrior and prince. Also known as Yamato Takeru.

Yashiki Residence or estate, usually of a daimyō.

Yasoda Wife of Nand.

Yemaya (Yoruba) Wife of Obatala.

Yemoja (Yoruba) Goddess of water and protector of women.

Yggdrasill The World Ash, holding up the Nine Worlds. Does not fall at Ragnarok.

Ymir Giant created from fire and ice; his body created the world.

Yo The female principle who, joined with In, the male side, brought about creation and the first gods. In and Yo correspond to the Chinese Yang and Yin.

Yomi The underworld.

Yudhishthira The eldest of the Pandavas, a great soldier.

Yuki-Onna The Snow-Bride or Lady of the Snow, who represents death.

Yvain Son of Morgan le Fay and knight of the Round Table, who goes on chivalric quests with a lion he rescued from a dragon.

Zahid Holy man.

Zál Son of Sám, who was born with pure white hair. Sám abandoned Zál, who was raised by the Símúrgh, or griffins. Zal became a great warrior, second only to his son, Rustem. Also known asNím-rúz and Dustán.

Zephyr Gentle breeze.

Zeus King of gods, god of sky, weather, thunder, lightning, home, hearth and hospitality. He plays an important role as the voice of justice, arbitrator between man and gods, and among them. Married to Hera, but lover of dozens of others.

Zohák Serpent-king and figure of evil. Father of Mihrab.

Zu God of the storm, who took the form of a huge bird. Similar to the Persian símúrgh.

Zukin Head covering.

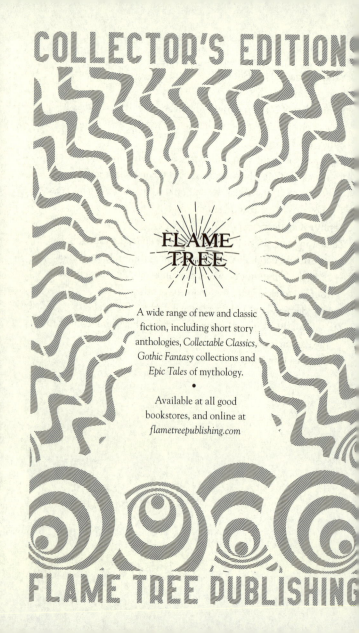